WARPED INTENTIONS

A NOVEL

S.B. REDD

ISBN-10: 1937705129
ISBN-13: 978-1-93770512-1
Also available in E-book
ISBN-13: 978-1-98311527-4
Library of Congress Control Number: 2010940677

Printed in the United States of America
SECOND PRINTING

𝜇

MavLit Publishing, LLC
www.maverick-books.com
P.O. Box 1103
Irmo, S.C. 29063

Cover Design: Maverick Literary
Cover Photo: Dreams Time

WARPED INTENTIONS

A NOVEL

S.B. REDD

Author's Note

Thank you for joining me on this literary journey. I wrote *Warped Intentions* while I was in pursuit of a publisher for my debut novel, *Temptation.com*. I had submitted *Temptation.com* for consideration to a handful of publishiers in the fall of 2007. One publisher responded favorably, and my submission was up for consideration with its acquisition panel.

While waiting for their response, I began toying around with another manuscript. In all my literary works, I always know what I want to write about in terms of plot and issue that I want to address before I begin putting thoughts to paper or computer screen. My challenge is always getting there.

I eventually learned of my fate with *Temptation.com* in early 2008, which was about the same time that I finished *Warped Intentions*. Looking back, it was a relatively short timeframe, but it sure as hell seems to be forever while you're waiting.

Now if you're trying to do the math, yes, *Warped Intentions* had been on my flash drive for more than three years. I will say that I did revise the original manuscript, but much of it is in tact. All along, I always thought a 2011 or 2012 publish date was a realistic goal.

In terms of storyline and genre, I feel that *Warped Intentions* is much closer to the kind of work that I want readers make association of me. There are some extra steamy segments in here, but I'd like to think this book's genre is contemporary fiction and it reminds me of a literary project that I once started but never finished during the mid-1990s.

The book's main character, Garner Davis, could be any young and ambitious man that you know. He has his strengths and weaknesses, although it seems throughout time a woman is often linked inexorably to him. Just think of Adam and Eve. Although it was Adam's decision that sealed mankind's fate as we know, a woman was there with him.

Isn't it a shame that men always seem to do mindless things in the presence—or pursuit—of a woman?

Garner is a survivor. He comes from a less-than-privileged background, yet he takes advantage of an opportunity that was afforded to him—a college education—that opened a door of opportunity for his life to experience things both for the good and bad.

He is outspoken. There were times in his past when he took a stance for what he thought was right, and he didn't back down. Sometimes, those who are willing to do that also pay a price that may or may not make it better for those who come after them.

He is passionate and skillful. Just ask the women and the people who have worked around him. He's a quick learner and he has a knack for becoming good at whatever he sets his mind to doing. But he's also one who takes risks. In short, Garner is the kind of person whom you could love and/or hate depending on your experience with him.

Because he is a young man, at thirty-two, there are still life lessons that he must learn. One of them is realizing who has your best interests at heart. There is an inner voice that lets us know, if we're willing to pay attention to it. You just hope and pray that one day that he will some day because you just never know who's watching you.

Make it happen, everyone!

SBR
s.b.redd@maverick-books.com
www.mavlit.blogspot.com
www.maverick-books.com

WARPED INTENTIONS

A NOVEL

S.B. REDD

Chapter 1

Garner always thought Spencer Watts had a crazy streak in him. At seventy-one years old, he had been around long enough to have been remembered as a mentor to some of the civil rights activists who gained their notoriety during the 1960s and 1970s.

Unlike some who believed in a non-violent approach from that era, Spencer was one of the fiery ones whose disposition advocated for burn, baby, burn.

His deep bass voice boomed. "Say, you light, bright, almost white motherfucker. Whatcha doing for the cause?"

"What cause, Mr. Watts?"

"The cause for your people . . . Or have you forgotten who you were?"

"I've never forgotten who I was."

Watts felt he could talk shit to Garner Davis, thirty-two, any time he wanted because he bragged of being the driving force behind Garner getting his job at WCAE Channel 6 in Columbia, South Carolina as the NBC affiliate's first black sports director.

He wrote letters to the editor in the *Columbia Palmetto, Charleston Chronicle*, and *Greenville Register* newspapers questioning whether the state's capital would ever see a black male's face reporting news rather than it being plastered across the screen for having committed some crime.

Threatening to use some of his civil rights' influence, he went as far as contacting Clay Jones, his U.S. congressional representative, to conjure up community pressure on the Columbia market's No. 1 station for its lack of racial diversity.

Spencer let out a raspy laugh as they went inside the Ruby Tuesday's across the I-77 freeway from the Fort Jackson U.S. Army base. "I hope you haven't, goddamn it.

"You damn near have to watch out for what you pray for. I asked them to bring in a black person. They brought in somebody who just barely passes for black!"

Garner, a former college baseball player, spoke in a soft baritone voice. He had thick, wavy brown hair; light gray eyes; a tall, lean athletic build of six-two and one hundred and ninety-five pounds. He also had an arguably a perfect smile, shaped by wearing braces during his childhood years in Richmond, Virginia.

Although they were a motley couple of sorts whenever they were together, they endeared each other from the first time they met. Spencer approached Garner in the WCAE lobby just as he showed up for work during his second week on the job.

"Listen here, you can talk about my skin color all you want," Garner said. "All I will say is that I am old enough that my birth certificate clearly states 'Negro' on it."

"So fuckin' what? My birth certificate says 'Colored' on it," Spencer reacted. "Shiiit, you better send me a copy of that one. Then again, you might need to show me the original. That's the only way I'll believe your ass!"

Ruby Tuesday's was still quiet. Servers and other personnel were moving about at a more leisurely pace while preparing the place for the imminent lunch rush crowd.

As he had done so many times around Garner, Spencer indulged himself to checking out the hostesses and other women who walked past him. His habit included a deviant glance at the woman's backside accompanied by subtle reactions like his raising of an eyebrow or a slight nodding of his head if she was worthy of a second look.

Garner jabbed at Spencer's bicep with his elbow. "Don't you have anything better to do?"

"It depends," Spencer answered.

A woman in her late-twenties of mocha complexion wearing a long-sleeved burgundy blouse and dark slacks that concealed more of her wide hips approached Garner and Spencer. She paid particular attention to Spencer, who had a distinguished look about him. A retired history professor from the state's largest historically black college located in Orangeburg, he often appeared in public wearing a jacket, tie, slacks and stylish loafers. He sported a well-kept graying beard and moustache that augmented his low-cut afro. He still walked upright for a man in his seventies, standing just a shade over six feet tall.

She greeted him with smile accented by a silver cap on one of her front teeth. "Dr. Watts, it's so nice to see you today. It looks like you're still taking great care of yourself."

"Why thank you, darling, you're looking very stunning as usual," he answered, grinning.

"Is there two in your party today?"

"Yes there is." A generous touch of sophistication often seasoned Spencer's dialogue with women.

"Oh, and this is Garner Davis, a protégé of mine. Garner this is, uh, uh . . ."

"Joleesa."

"Ah, yes, Joleesa. She's one of the brightest restaurant managers that I know."

Garner acknowledged her. "I'm pleased to meet you, Joleesa."

"Would a corner booth be fine with you, Dr. Watts?" Joleesa led Spencer and Garner into the dining area. Spencer made sure to position himself between Garner so he could have an exclusive view of her backside. He made a mental note to himself how her ass cheeks jiggled with each step.

As she placed the menus on the table, Spencer made mention to Joleesa that he had a lot of time on his hands since he retired from teaching a little more than a year ago.

"Miss Joleesa, when are you ever free from the restaurant?"

She waved off Spencer. "Dr. Watts, you know how it is—I'm here when nobody else is here." Then she steered him in another direction. "I haven't seen Mrs. Shirley lately. How has she been?"

"Oh, she's doing quite well, thank you." Depending on his mood, Spencer was dismissive whenever he discussed his wife of forty-four years. "But let me know when you might have some time off, all right?"

"Enjoy your meal. It was very nice meeting you, Garner."

Spencer smirked at Garner with every intention of sending the message to him that he still had what it took as a ladies' man.

Garner rolled his eyes derisively.

Spencer nodded back towards the front of the restaurant. "Did you check her out?" Garner shrugged, wondering whom he meant.

"Joleesa, fool!"

"Not really—"

"Now that's the kind of ass that will keep you young!"

Garner shook his head; he had heard everything.

"I guess that's the highlight of an old man's day like yours being able to spot—if you can even see—something like that. I hope that's not all I'll have to do when I'm your age."

Spencer browsed through the menu. "If your light, bright, almost white ass live that long." He peered over his reading glasses. "Now if I'd asked her outright then I could see you saying that. I was just making a very candid observation."

"Now tell me, Watts, is there ever a time you don't think about a woman's ass?"

Spencer allowed the menu to partially rest on the table. Then he pushed his glasses farther down the bridge of his nose, peering over them again. He maintained his silence for several seconds.

"Yeah, there is."

"And when is that?"

Spencer leaned against his right forearm. "When I'm thinking about some pussy."

Garner chortled. "I guess I left myself open for that one; it's obvious you had your mind on both."

Spencer reared back in the booth. He boasted about how he could still fuck at least three times a week—and without the help of the colored pills being advertised on television commercials.

"I've always lived by the saying that a nice guy never gets paid," he said. "And he damned sho' never gets laid. So it ain't never bothered me one bit when my wife would try holdin' back on the pussy, because I always kept myself a couple of spare pillows to lie on, if you know what I mean—"

"No, I don't know what you mean, ol' man," Garner answered, smirking at Spencer. "First of all, I think your choice of pussy was rather limited back in your day."

Spencer barely kept his voice low.

"The fuck you talkin' 'bout? Man, back in the day, a woman went crazy over a Negro with a college education. Shit, didn't matter if his ass was as light and bright like you or black as your momma's skillet!"

Garner leaned back in his seat, folding his arms. "Just what in the hell did you mean I was a protégé of yours? I don't think I want to be seen as somebody who walks on his damned tongue whenever a woman passes by."

"What's wrong with being my protégé? It just might give your ass some credibility."

Moments later, another woman in her twenties had stopped by the table greeting the two men. Garner already knew what he wanted: the peppercorn steak platter without the cheese and mushrooms, the steamed vegetables and the salad bar. He also ordered ginger ale since he never drank before he went to work.

Spencer looked over at Garner and winked before making eye contact with the server. He made sure that his thin wire-framed glasses were resting again on the bridge of his nose.

"What do you think about the tossed salad? Is that something you would recommend?"

Garner dipped his head sheepishly. The server responded with her preference for the chicken salad on the menu.

"I'll take your recommendation." Spencer also ordered a Bud Light to go with his meal.

Garner instigated Spencer for his off-colored comment after the hostess started for the kitchen. "Tossed salad, humph!"

"You ain't ever had any tossed salad before, young buck?"

"Let's just say I don't go around asking women whom I don't know if they want their assholes licked."

"Now, look, if you want to find out the freak in a woman, just hint at them if they like tossed salad and see how they react." Spencer laughed at his own remark. He bragged of having crossed that issue many years ago with his long-time mistress, Raynee Bickford, a current biology professor at the same college from where he retired.

Garner asked, "Why should I be talking about licking out of a woman's ass with some old man who's just one hump away from the grave?"

"Are you worried that I'll go around talking your business?"

"No, I just don't think that's something two men should be talking about. It doesn't really sound right."

"Then what does sound right?"

Garner shook his head, pondering aloud. "You know what? I don't have any clue why I even hang out with you like I do."

"Want to know why?"

"Yeah, tell me."

"You wish you could be as smooth as I am."

"Shiiiit," Garner reacted, "I think the correct word is wrinkled. And if that's the case, I definitely would not want to be like you!"

The tenor of Garner and Spencer's conversation remained jocular although they had moved on to a different topic. A reading and news buff, Spencer often prodded Garner for inside information on any hot sports topics.

According to a couple of friends at Sho' Fly's barber shop on North Main Street, Spencer said rumors were circulating that some changes might be coming down the pike with the state university's major college football program in Columbia.

"Come on, man, you know I gotta set those assholes straight over at the shop."

"I'll let you in on a secret." Garner then stopped to chew through his peppercorn steak before continuing. "I've got an appointment at four o'clock to talk with the athletic director in his office. I figure it would a good opportunity to put his egotistical ass on the spot whether he's going to seriously consider a black candidate for the Chanticleers, and not just for a token interview."

Spencer's dark brown eyes widened and he managed a wide grin before he took in a long sip from his Bud Light in a bottle.

"You shittin' me!" He let out a small belch. "You mean you gonna do something like that?"

"Why not?" he answered, shrugging his shoulders. "I've seen too many people in this business not have the balls to report on shit like that. They rather patronize by stroking people's backs and basically sucking their dicks just to get a bone or two thrown at them for a scoop.

"They're like a bunch of fuckin' prostitutes and they're being pimped by their so-called sources that could care less about them."

Spencer began laughing at Garner's comment. He stopped and took another long sip from his beer. "You know what?"

"What?"

"I prayed for somebody like you. You really hadn't forgotten about your people."

Garner took the last bite of his steak. Then he finished off his ginger ale and made a reminder gesture with his right index finger towards Spencer.

"I just hope I don't ever forget how to fuck when I'm your age. And with that, I've gotta get back to the station."

Spencer constrained Garner for one last thing before he got up.

"You're still not married, right?"

"Yeah, that's right. But I'm not hurting for any pussy. I've got options out there just like you had back in the day."

"Shiiiit, and still do!" Spencer reacted. "Look here, I know somebody who's a math professor over at the college across the street from mine in Orangeburg. I think you might like her. She just might be your kind of woman."

"What does she look like?"

"She's a nice girl . . ."

"Uh-oh, so she's ugly or she's fat. Or both—"

"Nah, she ain't never been married and she's working towards her doctorate degree. You think I'd try to introduce you to somebody who's stupid, ugly and, well, you know, large?"

Garner sighed in disgust. "Look, the last time you introduced me to a woman, she needed a lot of help: A dermatologist for all that acne; an orthodontist for her upper teeth, lower teeth, and that horse's overbite; hell, I even thought she needed an optometrist because she looked a lil' cross-eyed."

"Man, you wouldn't know a nice girl if she sat on your face . . . Shit, if I—"

"I said as a favor for you," Garner raised his voice to enunciate each word, "call me with her phone number."

"Good. Just for that, I'll even pay for lunch this time, you light, bright, almost white motherfucker!"

Garner was reduced to a chuckle and shaking his head, conceding the best thing he could ever do with Spencer's comments was allowing them to run through one ear and pass out the other.

Chapter 2

There was enough going on in the Columbia market, which afforded Garner opportunities to re-establish his identity as a hardhitting reporter rather than the malcontent that was perceived of him in Houston.

He did not mind reporting on anything involving the city's two historically black colleges, the state's major university, or even the two minor-league professional sports franchises that were all located around the downtown area. The most cumbersome part of his day was answering the phones—especially during the football season—and the most annoying question was always what date the Super Bowl would be played. Those inquiries started coming in the month of October.

Usually, the caller was a housewife whose husband delegated her to plan for the game party. The phone calls continued through the end of January.

Garner would often hiss to himself, *Tell your stupid ass husband to buy himself a goddamned TV guide, lady! And why would it matter anyway? He's gonna be drunk before the kickoff!*

The most amusing phone calls were those from the major university's Chanticleers fans because they were historically some of the most faithful imaginable, supporting a perennially mediocre athletic program.

After more than a century competing, the Chanticleers' football program had an overall record of 515-517-44 entering the 2007 season. Yet even when the program won just one game out of eleven in 1998, and then it went winless in eleven games in 1999, it was described to Garner during his job interview their fans still filled Winnetka-Benson Stadium on Saturdays with more than eighty thousand strong.

"Humph, must be another one of them," Garner was quick to presume. He composed himself to answer the phone in his best profession voice and demeanor.

"WCAE sports, Garner Davis—"

A familiar voice resonated into his ear. "You got a pen ready?"

"You couldn't wait to give me this one?"

"Shut up, light, bright white motherfucker and take down this number! Her name is Tamira Lake. She pronounces her name TA-MEER-A and not TA-MY-RA. She's in the math department. Her office number is four, nine, zero . . . and her home number is three, nine, three . . . She'll be expecting to hear from you today."

Garner adjusted himself in his office chair. "Can you give an accurate description of how she looks?" He stuffed the notepad that he wrote down Ms. Lake's number into the desk drawer to his right. "It's the least you can do since I'm doing this favor for you."

"Sure, she has titties, a pussy, and an ass," Spencer said, laughing at his own comment. "And she wants to meet a nice, professional black man. That's all you should be concerned about."

"Uh, wait a minute. You say what?"

"I said she wants to meet a nice, professional black man. That's all you should concern yourself with."

Garner rolled his eyes while twirling his pen between his fingers. He leaned back into his chair, resting his feet atop the desk.

"You know something, a wise older guy once told me that nice guys don't get paid, and nice guys damned sure don't get laid—"

"Then what's your excuse? You know what I'm about to call your ass again!"

Just as he hinted at Spencer, Garner's evening broadcast report featured sound bytes from his interview with athletic director Bud

Thacker commenting on whether he would fire current football coach Shep Pershington after another mediocre season. He apprised Thacker that these rumors were also being circulated in various social circles that an announcement was imminent.

"You have said that you expect for the Chanticleers program to not only become competitive in the Southeastern Athletic Conference [SEAC], but eventually compete for national championships. Do you feel that Shep Pershington is leading this program in that direction?"

The camera captured a wide shot of Thacker sitting in his leather office chair.

"Our program has six wins and five losses and, uh, we have a final game to play in two weeks at our in-state rival in Clemson.

"We, uh, will evaluate the program at the appointed time and place. We, uh, will not be speculative in any form or fashion. Coach Pershington is the head coach of our football program."

Another sound byte from his interview captured a tight shot of Thacker's facial expression showing just how uncomfortable he was with Garner pressing the issue about racial diversity within his program.

"You are aware that there are only six schools out of one hundred and nineteen among Division I-A football programs that have blacks as head coaches?"

Thacker was reluctant to answer. *"I know the numbers are low."*

The camera also caught him making an awkward move to adjust his sitting position.

"You have gone on record saying that you want to be very proactive when it comes to achieving diversity in your program. Currently, there are no black head coaches here at this university; you have no blacks in any current senior administrative capacity; your athletic program generates more than $42 million a year, of which at least three-fourths of the money can be attributed to football, where roughly two-thirds to three-fourths of the athletes on the team is black—"

Thacker interrupted Garner.

"I have been here less than two years at this university. We have yet to have any head coaching or other high-level administrative vacancies to become available."

Garner pressed with his next question. *"I'm aware of that. If the scenario did exist, are you in a position to comment on how proactive you would be? And do you think the fanbase would be ready to embrace a black head coach to lead a college football program of the size and notoriety as the Chanticleers?"* Thacker attempted to remain resolute during the interview. But Garner's questioning started to take its toll. Thacker's forehead became a reflection of the bright light of the television camera that was aimed at him. He responded even more carefully.

"Yes, I have gone on record stating we want to be very proactive in all things. But, uh, I'd rather not comment on that at this time." Thacker leaned back into his chair. *"All I will say once again is that Coach Pershington is still the head coach of our program.*

"The answer to your second question is if and when I'm faced with the situation of addressing our key personnel, uh, I will be making the best decision possible for this program because, uh, I have a business fiduciary responsibility to the president of this university."

Still basking in his aggressive reporting of the Chanticleers, Garner placed a call to the Orangeburg area.

"Hello, this is Tamira—"

"Good evening, this is Garner Davis. Mr. Spencer Watts said you might be expecting me to call you."

"Oh, yes, Dr. Watts!"

"I called you as soon as I finished up everything after our evening broadcast," Garner said.

"Broadcast?"

"Yeah, broadcast. Didn't Mr. Watts tell you that I'm the sports director at Channel 6 here in Columbia?"

Tamira was careful to enunciate each word. "He mentioned you were in television, but I don't watch Channel 6 for my news and I'm not into any sports." Her phone voice seemed rather formal and haughty.

It was his desire to throttle down the cerebral energy a couple of notches. Rather than defending himself, Garner laughed off Tamira's remark.

"Well, since we share a common interest in Mr. Watts, let me first say that I've known him almost as long as I've been here in Columbia. That's been about a year and a half. Uh, how long have you known Mr. Watts?"

"Oh, Dr. Watts, he's just a dirty, crazy old man who's been forever trying to get me married," she answered.

"That's him! But I won't get into that—"

"Thank you."

Tamira chose not to tell Garner that she and Spencer initially met six years ago at a symposium hosted by their respective schools for aspiring college students in the Orangeburg and surrounding counties. They were paired on the same panel and they have since remained in contact.

She long admired Spencer for his public speaking skills and academic accomplishments. He once told her that he turned down several offers to teach at larger, more prestigious mainstream colleges and universities.

Throughout the years, Tamira was more than aware of Spencer's wandering eye for her, and she kept him at a manageable distance. She turned down every lunch or dinner invitation Spencer offered, reminding him that it was never appropriate for her to be seen in a non-professional setting with a married man.

Tamira did tell Garner that Spencer Watts was the person who encouraged her to pursue her doctorate degree, with an emphasis in applied mathematics, after putting it off for several years.

"I wonder why that doesn't surprise me . . ."

She chortled. "You know, Dr. Watts is like that whenever he likes somebody. He has a way of, shall we say, infiltrating their lives."

"He does that with me all of the time reminding me that he was the person responsible for me coming to Columbia. So, for that reason, he feels like he can remind me of my responsibility to the black community."

"Oh, yes, he's very big on that."

"Too bad you're not into sports and you don't watch Channel 6. I'm sure that Spencer is probably gloating right now."

"Why would he?"

"I told him this afternoon that I would be asking the athletic director some hard questions. On of them had to do with whether he would consider hiring a black head football coach. You should have seen how constipated this guy turned during the interview."

"Hmmm . . . I guess that would be interesting to hear if I were into sports."

"Well, pardon me for asking this, I presume you've sacrificed a good bit of your personal life for this degree?"

"Yes, I'd agree with that analysis. There have been a lot of days when a man is the last thing I've wanted to see."

"Well, from my point of view, I know a man would be the last thing I'd want to see."

"I know that's right!"

Silently, Garner reminisced about some of the women he met in the past who were barely removed from horrific relationships. Those encounters never got beyond the initial conversation. Applying some of his interviewing skills, he figured his best chance to salvage any favorable impression would be inducing Tamira into talking more about herself.

"How long have you been working towards your doctorate?"

"Oh, this is already my third semester. I should complete my work and my dissertation in three more semesters."

"I can tell how proud you are of yourself for pursuing this."

"Words can't express the sentiment! And if I were to apply for a department chair position and a full professorship, a doctorate degree is paramount. The program I've entered is very prestigious. Only sixty people have been awarded their Ph.D. of Math since 1990."

Garner also learned from Tamira that she completed her undergraduate work at the state's largest historically black college where Spencer taught and retired from after thirty-nine years. She went on to complete her master's in Mathematical Science at the state's other major university located in Clemson. She remained on that side of the state and worked at the high school level for ten years in the Greenville area. For the past seven years, she has worked as an associate professor in Orangeburg.

Because she aspired to attain a full professorship and be paid accordingly, she chose the university in Columbia because it would best assist her finding suitable work once she completed her degree.

"I hope I'm not boring you with all this, am I?"

"Oh, no," he said, fighting not to yawn. "I hope I wasn't boring you talking about football. I find this rather intriguing. I have an aunt who earned her doctorate in Education, and I remember helping her write her published work."

"Well, um, Gary—"

"It's Garner."

"I can remember vector analysis, differential equations and numerical analysis, but I'm terrible with names. Please accept my apology." She inhaled through her nose, stretching. "Speaking of apologies, I must plunge into these books of mine. I hope you understand—perhaps we can talk again real soon?"

Garner had every intention on cursing out Spencer Watts after his conversation with Tamira. All he could think about was his senior acquaintance trying to hook him up with Stephen Q. Urkel's sister. He joked to himself she must be the proud owner of some nerd-mobile like a tan colored AMC Pacer, and since it was so outdated, it afforded her the opportunity to formulate her own fuel from Okefenokee Swamp water.

"Next time remind me to wear a fucking dunce cap when I talk to your chick, Tamira."

Spencer giggled. "Man, what are you talking about?"

"You know goddamned well what I'm talking about!" Garner lashed out at Spencer. "I'll probably need to stop off at the store, buy myself some Hush Puppies shoes and a pair of pants four sizes too big so that I can pull them up to my rib cage.

"Oh, and I forgot one other thing: I probably need to stop off at the optometrist—no, fuck that, at the gas station—and empty a couple of Coke bottles and put them up to my face!"

Spencer coaxed Garner into calming down. He got around to asking Garner had he been able to ask Tamira out on a date.

"How?" Garner reacted. "It didn't take a fucking rocket scientist to realize, first of all, that she was caught up on herself. And it was obvious in order to have a conversation with her you needed to let her do all the talking.

"No wonder she ain't never been married! Einstein's been dead a long time."

Spencer reminded Garner of his promise. "Are you gonna fuckin' chicken out on me? You don't know what she even looks like. She could be finer than you could ever imagine."

One of Garner's reasons for hanging out with Spencer was that he admired the man for his ability to charm women. In addition to Raynee Bickford, he was aware of Spencer's philandering with Constance Sumter, a forty-something businesswoman who owned a string of hair salons throughout Columbia, as well as with Laronda Jackson, a thirty-something who worked as an administrator of a nursing home community in the Irmo area where he lived.

"I'm going to tell you in advance, don't try to play matchmaker for me ever again. It's not like I can't find any pussy for myself."

Spencer chuckled at Garner's reminder. "Yeah, all you light, bright, almost white motherfuckers think you've got the market cornered."

"Fuck you, ol' man!"

"Bye, Negro!"

Chapter 3

Garner decided on hanging out at Gallardo's Mexican restaurant across the street from the station rather than making the twenty-five minute trek back to his place in the northeast Columbia area. Usually, he would have left the station around 7:15 p.m., making a mad dash eastbound on Garners Ferry Road to the I-77 northbound on-ramp. Then he would take the freeway over to the Farrow Road exit near the Blythewood community. He'd spend time in his condo until 9:30 p.m. before returning back to the station.

When he went alone to restaurants, Garner preferred sitting in a booth. He was informed there would be a ten-minute wait before one would become available. So, he decided to kill time by contacting a couple of his sources in the business for the latest update on the Chanticleers' football coaching situation.

Neither person—former Division I-A head football coach Andy Jay Dalton back in Texas or a sports agent Marty Simien in Louisiana—was available.

Impulsively, he dialed another number.

"Hello?"

Garner cleared his throat before he addressed Sabryan Fletcher, thirty-four, a registered nurse at Houston's famed medical center. He last visited her three weeks earlier. They met at a hospital fundraiser in 2003 while he was on assignment to interview the keynote speaker, Darius McBailey, an all-star forward for Houston's professional basketball franchise.

"I really appreciate you answering." He tried conveying a tone of contrition.

"Oh, it's you. Humph. Shit, if I'd known I would have hung up on your fucking lying, whorish ass!"

"You're still not going to believe me, are you?"

"Why should I?" she answered. "I gave you my heart, my soul, my love and even my asshole for you, and you used me. When will you ever realize that you can't go through life stepping on a woman's emotions?"

Garner knew this diatribe was inevitable.

Already, Sabryan had mailed him a postcard to WCAE that read, "Son of a Bitch!" That was in reaction to her receiving a cell phone photo of him walking with his right arm draped around the shoulder of Kadrece Kendricks, thirty-five, an acquaintance of his from Tallahassee. The photo was taken by her youngest sister Yurayna, who worked the front desk at the Westheimer Hotel located in Houston's Galleria area, a day after Sabryan and Garner had one of their most spontaneous encounters.

Yurayna considered posting the picture on WCAE's Facebook page, but Sabryan told her it wasn't worth the hassle. When confronted, Garner gave Sabryan the alibi that he and Kadrece were old college classmates. They had not seen each other since before he left Tallahassee back in 2003, a span of more than four years. He also claimed that he happened to run into her at the mall out by Highway 6 and Westheimer; he offered to give Kadrece a ride back to her hotel rather than allowing her to pay cab fare.

"Look, the only contact that happened was when we hugged—I told you I had not seen her in almost five years—and when I put my arm on her after I had cracked a joke with her."

Sabryan shouted, "Do you expect for me to believe that shit? That's just disrespectful. You come to visit me, and you decide that you would offer some bitch a ride back to her hotel room?"

"Well, that's exactly what happened."

"I'm not like some stupid bitch who flunked out of HCC [Houston Community College]. In case you've forgotten, we've had this issue before about you and other women."

Garner withheld from Sabryan that he and Kadrece had been en-gaged in several candid and provocative conversations, and they con-sidered rekindling their casual romance. They agreed to meet while she was in Houston for a lawyer's convention.

Kadrece was always aware of his involvement with Sabryan. He went as far as explaining to her that his relationship with Sabryan had grown stagnant because of her inflexible work schedule and her unwillingness to visit him in South Carolina. He also told Kadrece that he preferred being involved once again with somebody who was as spontaneous and talkative in and out of the bedroom.

When they considered taking matters to bed, Kadrece profusely apologized that she could not go through with it. She tried explain-ing to Garner that if she did have sex with him she just might fall deeply for him; she was not ready to handle those kinds of emotions. Garner was reluctant to keep their friendship on its current terms.

"You know, Garner, I was always nervous about maintaining a long-distance relationship once you moved to South Carolina. I thought I would have a problem with you having women there in Columbia. I just never thought you would be that damned bold to see another bitch while visiting me!" Sabryan screamed.

"Why would I ruin the relationship that we've had for another woman?" he said, making wild hand gestures while walking outside.

She scoffed back at him. "And what makes it so bad I saw the picture of her. She looks like some damned piece of trash you'd find over in Fifth Ward off Jensen. I have no idea what you saw in the bitch."

Garner knew that if he defended Kadrece's appearance it would infer guilt on his part. Kadrece, an unabashed free spirit, was Sa-bryan's antithesis. Since graduating from law school, she preferred wearing her mini-dreadlocks. She was slightly taller, standing five-ten. She was very much proud of her thickness, in all the right places, and she had no intent on changing it for anybody.

"Why would I mess with something from over there on Jensen? Now that would be foolish—"

"Obviously, it didn't mean anything that I went along with you literally fucking me up my ass when we were in the parking lot at my job before you were seen with that bitch?" She shifted the phone her left ear to her right. "Now I'm the one that feels like a damned fool. Don't you know that hospital security could have caught us, called HPD [Houston Police Department] and had us arrested, and I could have lost my job?"

Garner walked in the direction of the stores in the shopping center, opposite of the TV station. "Now wait a minute, you're the one that wanted me to do that." Now he paced in the direction of the television station. "Who was the one that called me at midnight and asked me to come by her job because she was feeling horny and lonely?

"Who was the one that told me she intentionally wore nothing under her RN's skirt?

"Who was it that suggested we do something totally different? And who was it who begged who to fuck who up the ass while who was leaning against my [rental] car?

"You did!

"And, weren't you the one who rubbed some K-Y on my dick, held your ass cheeks apart, and made sure that I didn't miss putting it up in there?"

Sabryan had heard enough. She protested, "Damn it, you just don't get it, Garner! It's always been about you. Always! I can't believe that I even said that I was in love with you because you're . . . one . . . selfish . . . motherfucker!"

Garner loathed for women to become emotional with him. He often thought back to his childhood when his mother, Miriam, sobbed herself to sleep while she languished in an abusive fourteen-year marriage to his father, Aaron.

The worst incidents occurred whenever Aaron was in a drunken rage. He would proclaim how he was the king of his household and everyone in there had better do as he demanded or else.

Although Aaron was never physically abusive to Garner, he spoke derisively to him.

"I don't know why I keep foolin' myself believing that you're my son, 'cause you don't look anything like me. So who's gonna believe that some high yella boy is mine, anyway?"

Garner asked, "Dad why do you say things like that to me?"

"Why don't you ask your goddamned mother?"

Garner bore Miriam's extremely light-skinned features where as his siblings were darker complexioned like Aaron. Miriam had long, thick brown hair, slanted green eyes and she was tall and slender. Eventually, he would go to Miriam with the same question. Usually, she consoled him with a hug, adding, "If God wanted you to look more like your father, He would have allowed that to have happen. Don't be ashamed of who you are, because some people in life are just going to say ignorant things about you, and to you."

Garner still was curious. "Does that mean dad's saying ignorant things about me?"

Miriam would place her hand over young Garner's mouth. "One of these days you'll figure that out for yourself . . ."

His most chilling memory of Aaron's drunkenness occurred late one night when he was eight. In another rage, Aaron made boisterous demands that Miriam prepared dinner for him. Because she took too long, he dragged her in the bedroom, slapped her around, ripped off her gown and mounted her in spite of her crying and protests to get off. Aaron eventually rolled off and went to sleep, snoring loudly. Miriam went off into the bathroom; Garner had listened to the entire episode standing in the hallway.

"I'm not selfish!" he yelled, while walking back towards the restaurant's entrance.

"The hell you're not! What about my having to put up with you keeping contact with that Creole bitch who worked for that station in Shreveport?"

He huffed into the phone. "Idria Dalzell was just a contact for a story that I had been following—"

She interrupted him, rolling her neck and propping her right hand on her hip. "And I suppose it was all right for you to go out with her when you were on assignment in Dallas? You're also going to tell me that you two didn't fuck?"

"Nothing ever happened between us." The truth was that he did maintain a yearlong romance with Idria. "We just went out after the game. We hung out at a southwest bar and grill that I liked, and then we left. I suppose I should have just gone back to the hotel room and locked myself up?"

She retorted, "At least I would know you would not be out there making yourself available for another woman." Then she posed another question to him. "And I suppose there was nothing that should have made me curious about some woman giving you a bathrobe for Christmas?"

"No, I have no idea who gave it to me. All I know there was a package on my desk when I showed up for work," he answered, knowing all along that Idria had sent it to him.

Sabryan rolled her eyes, hissing. "Garner, you'd be surprised the flowers and cards I get at the hospital. [Do] you know what happens with every last one of them?"

"Did you smell the flowers and did you actually read the cards?"

"No, asshole, because I was your lady. I always had someone to throw it away. That's what you're supposed to do when you're committed to somebody. You don't let anything like that come between you and the person you say that you love!"

"Well, personally, I think you're just insecure and jealous," Garner scoffed. "You're not making any sense to me!"

There was a long pause after Garner's response. He took the initiative once more by petitioning Sabryan. "Why is it you've never tried listening to me to find out what really happened?"

Sabryan wiped away the tears that streamed down to her cheeks. She screamed, "Why would anybody give a fucking whore a chance to explain why he walked around in a hotel with some bitch he also probably fucked?"

The phone clicked before he could respond.

Chapter 4

Garner went on air during the eleven o'clock night broadcast reporting Shep Pershington requested for, and was granted by Thacker, a buyout of his $940,000-a-year contract with one year remaining on it. He cited Pershington claimed to have seen the writing on the wall by what he perceived was Thacker's lack of commitment.

"We have joining us on air live by phone the University's head, make that, soon-to-be former head coach Shep Pershington.

"The Chanticleers do not play this weekend. Their big game at their in-state rival, the Bengals, in Clemson is next week . . . Coach, amid all the speculation did you think it would come down to you requesting a buyout?"

Pershington said, *"No, I really didn't think so, because I felt we had been doing a good enough job. We came here five years ago and the program had lost twenty-one of its previous twenty-two games. Quite frankly, the cupboard was bare and we've rather painstakingly managed to replenish it."*

Garner mentioned that Pershington predicted before the 2007 season the Chanticleers would qualify for a bowl game, and it would win at least seven regular-season games. After all, the Chanticleers had improved their won-lost record in each of the four previous seasons under him. The team qualified for bowl game consideration in 2006 winning six out of eleven games; it was the only SEAC program that finished with a winning record and was not invited to a bowl game.

He went on to give further background to the viewers that Pershington was well on his way of fulfilling that prediction when the

Chanticleers won four of their first five games. After the team lost 31-24 to Alabama's Crimson Crusaders, marking its fourth consecutive loss, his job security became the topic of much scrutiny.

Do you think there may have been some impatience by the fanbase, or perhaps by the school's administration?"

Pershington answered, *"I think, uh, the fans have been great. How many places do you know that has fans coming eighty thousand or more strong to every home game during a time the program had lost thirty-eight of forty-four contests over a four-year period?*

"Had that happened at last week's opponent, there may have been serious consequences for the coaching staff after one bad year.

"So do I think there may have been impatience by the administration? You tell me. I know in this business we are hired to be fired; I guess I chose not to be fired."

"Will you be coaching next week's game against the Bengals?"

"As far as I know I will be—"

While Garner was wrapping up his interview with Pershington, Tamira happened to have caught a glimpse of Garner's name as it flashed across the screen while changing channels. She immediately flipped back to Channel 6.

When she recognized just how handsome he was, she nearly dropped her glass of cranberry-apple juice into her lap.

Some of the juice spilled on her thigh. She never got around to checking out the show she intended to watch on the public television channel. She grabbed her cordless phone, searching for the number that Garner called from earlier in the week. She had deleted his entry.

Instinctively, she ran into her bedroom and flipped through her Columbia phone directory searching for a number listed under Garner's name. There was none listed for a Garner Davis, so she searched her address book.

She then phoned Spencer Watts.

My god, he can't be!

She was impatient for Spencer to answer.

"Hello?"

She was quick to poise herself. "Dr. Watts, I'm sorry to bother you at this time of the night. This is Tamira Lake in Orangeburg. I hope

I did not awake you."

Spencer yawned rather lazily. "If you'd called maybe in another twenty minutes, it might as well be tomorrow before you catch me."

"I promise I won't take much of your time. I spoke to a person who said you gave him my phone number. His name is Gary Davis."

"You mean Garner Davis?"

"Yes, that's it," she said, managing a weak laugh. "He said the same thing to me. That's the second time I've referred to him as Gary. Anyway, would you happen to have another number for him other than the one at the television station?"

Tamira's inquiry piqued Spencer's curiosity. He immediately thought about Garner and the animated phone conversation they last had.

He teased Tamira. "Hmmm, could it be that somebody saw a certain person on TV and she realized that he wasn't a bad looking guy?"

"Oh, Dr. Watts, I thought about calling Garner after we talked a couple of days ago. You know I've been extremely busy . . . but for whatever reason I have misplaced his phone number."

"Well, what did you think of him?"

"He seems to be articulate—"

"He's really good people once you get to know him."

"That's nice to know. I said I would not be taking much of your time, Dr. Watts, so—"

"Oh, yeah, his number . . . I'll give you his cell phone number; that's really the only other one that I have."

Tamira thanked Spencer and she gave her regards to Mrs. Shirley. Then she tried contacting Garner. As the phone rang, she reflected on his rather sculpted, angular face—the kind that could have very well appeared in a magazine advertisement.

She breathed a sigh of relief that her call went into his voice mailbox.

"Good evening, Garner, this is Tamira Lake whom you called a few days ago," she said. *"I had been thinking about calling you, but I had misplaced your number. If you get a chance, please give me a call tomorrow at the school. The best time to catch me is during my office hour, which will be from noon to*

one o'clock.

"I hope to hear from you."

Garner played Tamira's message twice to confirm what he actually heard. After pondering it further, he suspected Tamira used the *misplaced-his-number excuse* in her message as a smoke screen for her actually contacting Spencer to find out more about him. He even went as far as musing that perhaps Spencer was an accomplice in helping her out all along, and he was getting the biggest laugh out of it.

Humph.

It was one thing to have shoot-the-shit sessions with a retired college professor who believes he can chase women like he once did half of a century ago. That didn't require a great expanse of intellect in a conversation. All he had to do was talk about sports and a woman's anatomy, and he was speaking in Spencer's native language.

Yet it was another thing venturing into the unknown with a person whom he joked to himself had an intelligence quotient higher than the 803 area code that he lived in.

Taking a deep breath, Garner followed through with what he would not have fathomed doing less than two months ago.

She recognized his voice. "You caught me at a very good time, Mr. Davis. I just got finished with an advisory session with a student of mine who's scheduled to complete his requirements for graduation this semester."

"I remember what that was like," Garner related. "That wasn't long ago when I think about it."

"May I ask how long ago?"

"It was nine years, no, make that eleven years ago."

Tamira, who was approaching her forty-fifth birthday, already calculated that she was at least ten years older than him. She hinted at it by noting that she had been in the teaching profession for seventeen years.

"Have you been teaching in Orangeburg all of that time?"

"Oh, no, I've only been here at this school for six years. You've forgotten that I told you I taught at the high school level for ten years."

"My fault," he said, explaining, "We deal with administrators, instructors, coaches and students at both levels. The one thing that seems to be consistent is that the administrators, instructors and coaches all feel that in some way they're baby sitting the students.

"Do you find that to be true?"

"Well, it really depends. Babysitting to me means when you're watching over somebody that by reason cannot supervise him or herself. I think our job is to help people to reach conclusions and decisions for themselves," she answered.

"If anything, you do have some students that need a little bit of coaxing in order to get the best out of them. It's really gratifying when that light finally clicks on."

He went on to make mention of an assignment he was scheduled for in Orangeburg that weekend. "Hey, I'll be there to cover the big game involving the Buffaloes. So I figured maybe we could hang out afterward for a while."

"And what do you mean by hanging out for a while, Mr. Davis?"

"Hmmm, from what I can tell a lady of your professional caliber sometimes prefers not doing the mundane; is that right?"

She agreed with him.

"That's why I feel it would be my pleasure if we could just meet for a cup of coffee and further conversation at the bookstore down the street from the mall."

"That sounds like a winner."

"Here's what I'll do: I'll call you once I'm in Orangeburg before the game. And then I'll call you afterward."

Chapter 5

The game that Garner covered from Buffaloes Stadium in Orangeburg went as expected. The home team easily crushed its opponent 42-14 and it was in a position to win the conference title with one game remaining on its schedule.

Garner phoned Tamira after he filed his live report for the six o'clock broadcast; they agreed on meeting around seven o'clock.

"How will I know I'm meeting Ms. Tamira Lake?"

She gave a slow description of herself for added effect. "You'll know that you're meeting Ms. Tamira Lake because I'm medium-caramel complexioned . . . I have brown hair . . . I wear it short, but not short-short.

"I'm about five-foot-six . . . I'm sort of medium in build, although some might say I'm slim . . . I'll be wearing dark jeans, a long-sleeved blouse and a light pullover sweater."

Wow.

Medium-caramel complexion; five feet, six inches; at best a medium build. Tamira's self-description did little to excite Garner. It was opposite of what he had envisioned of her. He reasoned a woman would not have openly told him their height and body frame had she been unattractive or ashamed of herself.

He began describing himself as wearing dark blue slacks, a black

Polo shirt with the WCAE logo on it. She interrupted him once he started describing his features.

"Mr. Davis, oh, I'm sorry, Garner. I'll see you there in, what, fifteen minutes."

The abrupt ending to their conversation threw him off slightly; it was not enough to make him overly suspicious since he was not far from the bookstore. When he reached the parking lot, he reflected on his last trip to a bookstore being a touchy-feely experience: He spent more time with his hands pawing and stroking Sabryan's ass rather than helping her find books for her nursing training session.

Inside Regal Books, Garner wandered his way to its center where there were steps leading to the bottom level. Just before the stairwell, he found a table beside the café stand's counter that also gave him visual access to the main entrance.

As he waited for somebody who might fit Tamira's description, he peered off to his right then left and then back to his right. He dropped his head slightly and mused once again to himself how an environment for the well-read and literary connoisseur that offered samplings of cookies, odd pastries, espresso and other variations of coffee was not his preference for unwinding after a Saturday game assignment since he moved to South Carolina.

Usually, he would stop off at a southwestern-style restaurant and order a sizzling plate of steak fajitas, a platter of chips and salsa, washing it all down with a large margarita without the salt. And had he been in Houston, the better complement to a meal and setting like that would have been his being able to gaze into Sabryan's caramel-toned face and brown eyes.

He was interrupted by a female's voice with proper diction.

"Garner?" He reacted with a double take to a woman mature in features and demeanor.

She was dressed modestly, wearing small studded earrings and little makeup, and just as she described herself. Before he could respond, she had already extended her hand towards him.

"I'm Tamira Lake. I'm very pleased to meet you." She flashed a smile; her eyes were admiring of him.

Garner stood up. He sensed her reluctance to let go of his hand.

"So, we finally meet?"

"Yes, we do—"

Garner, moving awkwardly, pulled out a seat for Tamira, causing her to release her grip.

"You must have known that I like visiting bookstores," she said. "I think it's a good, safe place to meet somebody for the first time."

"Like I told you over the phone, I figured a lady of your caliber might appreciate a place like this."

Garner always felt he could charm a woman without actually charming one. He paused to study Tamira's features: a slender face with bangs that stopped just short of her thinly arched eyebrows that shorten her longer facial length; thin but rather succulent, kissable lips; and her eyes were focused on him. If he were a still photographer, he would rate her as plausibly photogenic.

He mentioned, "I'm sure you've probably heard this observation from some men that they're probably intimidated once they meet you? You definitely appear to be the embodiment of beauty and intelligence."

That might have been dismissed had that come from a man of lesser intellect and not as handsome as Garner. She responded, "You know where flattery will get you—"

"I just happen to be in a profession that prides itself on facts and truth," he said.

Tamira knew that Garner had touched upon a long-standing frustration of hers from dating. She never would have imagined being three weeks shy of her forty-fifth birthday that she had yet to marry nor have children.

To his favor, Garner fit the physical description of the type of man she preferred, and perhaps more.

"Uh, Garner, what convinced you to contact me after talking with Dr. Watts?"

"Is this some interview?"

"No, it isn't an interview."

He shifted in his chair. "OK, seriously speaking, I feel sometimes in life a person needs to be open minded about some things. Sometimes, we need to do things we normally would not do."

"Meaning?"

"Listening to some seventy-something-year-old man who thinks he can still do the same things he once did half of a century ago."

Tamira smiled at Garner's comment. "You and Dr. Watts must really get along well?" She also assessed his demeanor exuded an arrogance that reminded her favorably of Spencer Watts.

"It's scary some times. Next to my high school and college baseball coaches, I've never gotten along with a male like that in my life. Not even with my father," Garner said.

"It's good to have a mentor in life," she related. "Perhaps some day I'll be seen as a mentor to some young lady."

Tamira's questions more than confirmed Garner's suspicion that Spencer had collaborated with her. That explained why Spencer was so insistent. It also clarified to him the comment she made while they spoke earlier in the week why Spencer had a way of infiltrating the lives of those people he liked.

"Would you like that coffee that we talked about?" he asked, hoping for an avenue to change topics.

"Please."

"I'm not really a coffee drinker, so would you mind coming with me over to the counter and order what you'd like?"

Garner allowed for Tamira to walk just ahead of him. This was his subtle way of getting a better look at her since he did not notice her when she entered the bookstore.

At the counter, Tamira ordered a mug of espresso roast decaffeinated along with a banana-nut bread muffin. Garner did not order anything; there was nothing on the menu that appealed to him. Nor did he like the strong fragrance from the coffee beans.

She suggested that he should try the banana-nut bread muffins. "I would buy and entire loaf if they actually sold it that way."

As they walked casually back towards the table, Garner, who was more than glad to get away from the café counter, mentioned to Tamira that he shared similar feelings for his mother's fruitcake as she had for the bookstore's banana-nut bread muffins.

He fondly reminisced holidays in Richmond. "Some people have paid my mother as much as twenty-five dollars for just one fruitcake in one of those Bundt cake pans that you use for pound cakes. And all she would do for a fruitcake loaf is pour the batter into one of those aluminum loaf pans.

"When we were younger," he added, "she used to make fruitcake cookies out of the same batter. Mmmm, you're talking about good!"

Tamira pinched off the corner of her muffin. "It does sound rather delicious. But I can't say that I'm as adept as your mother in the kitchen—thank god for restaurants, microwave ovens, and salad bars."

"I'm sure you can be if you really wanted to be." He nodded to emphasize his point to her. "Maybe if you had an incentive you could discover that cooking talent inside you."

"Apparently you weren't listening to me, Garner, that flattery will get you everywhere."

Tamira smiled once again before taking another sip from her brew. She then took another pinch off her muffin, guarding against dropped crumbs with a napkin under it.

"Are you sure you don't want a bite of this muffin?"

"Oh, I'm sure about that."

Garner learned that Tamira was from Bamberg, a smaller rural town roughly twenty-five minutes away from Orangeburg; she was also the oldest of four children, of which she had two brothers and a sister. Her father, Roosevelt, was a retired elementary school principal while her mother, Maxine, started out as a homemaker but later sold Avon. She went back to college, earning her degree in business.

"Hey, I actually looked up your name to find out if it was common, and it isn't. Did your mother ever explain to you why she named you Tamira?"

Tamira folded her arms. Then she adjusted herself in the seat looking directly at him.

"I'll answer it this way. When I was in grade school, everyone used to make the mistake and call me Tamara. Some days, I would come home and ask my mom did she make a mistake, because somebody must be wrong.

"My mom wouldn't get mad at me. She would just tell me, 'I named you the way I named you because I want people to know that I'm not raising my girl to be like the other girls.'

"I guess she was right because none of those girls and boys that asked me those questions about my name ever amounted to anything. I still see them from time to time whenever I visit my parents."

There was a sudden influx of bookstore patrons in the immediate area. Garner noticed it was also crowded in other parts of the store. Tamira suggested they moved over where the chess and backgammon boards were situated. She was coy at alluding to backgammon as one of several games of choice for the mathematically inclined.

"Tell me, Garner. When was the last time you've played backgammon?" she queried.

"Probably since high school; my sister and I would play it."

She could not contain her arrogance. "There's a little bit of probability and theory involved with this game, although some might say it's a matter of luck, you know, the roll of the dice. I prefer to consider the former."

That sounded like a challenge that Garner, a former college athlete, was too proud not to pass up. He won the roll of the dice to go first.

"I guess that meant I had a one-in-six chance of beating you, right?"

"Well, sort of—"

Tamira started out moving her checkers towards her home quadrant at a faster rate than Garner; however, a double five gave him a slight advantage. With two checkers less than four pips away from him bearing off, a roll of five and three limited him to moving just one checker into his home quadrant.

A play earlier, Tamira had managed to complete covering all her pips with at least two checkers inside her home quadrant. On her next move, she rolled a five and three and that forced his last checker to the bar. She went on to finish him off with a single-game score of ten.

She gave him a smug look after the game. "It's a shame that you had a four-percent chance of rolling the wrong combination, Garner."

"Well, the way I see it, there's a fifty-fifty chance that I'll beat you the next game and the one after that," he retorted. "How about going two out of three?"

Tamira could not resist the opportunity to prove her superiority just like in the academic world. The second game opened with her rolling a double six and putting the early pressure on Garner. But he trumped her aggressive play by rolling dice combinations that sent her checkers to the bar. He went on to beat her easily by a score of thirty-three, requiring a mere forty-five moves.

Garner shrugged his shoulders. "All right, are we going to go winner take all, or winner by the biggest combined margin of victory? If you choose combined margin of victory, that means I'm already up by twenty-three points."

Tamira was unimpressed by Garner's needling her. She had not mentioned that she won several backgammon tournaments while she worked towards her master's more than a decade ago.

She declared, "Okay, let's go winner take all. Because when I'm finished beating you, it will be decisive."

Garner smiled mischievously. *Humph. Maybe Spencer's line about tossed salad could be used in this setting*, he thought.

"Was there something wrong that I said?"

"Oh, no, not at all," he answered, smiling.

Tamira leaned back in her chair, crossing her left leg over her right thigh. She smiled back him.

He observed, "I bet you're not a shy or reticent person once people get to know you."

She brought her hand down from her face. "How did you know that?"

He leaned forward in his seat, maintaining eye contact with her. "First of all, I noticed you're a competitive person. You didn't like me winning just now. Secondly, I think you choose to open up to those that can appeal to you intellectually more than physically.

"Thirdly—"

She shifted in her seat, interrupting him. "Were you a Psychology major in school?"

"No, I was just a Communications major."

"Ah, I see, you're one of those kinds of guys . . ."

He returned his attention to Tamira. "What kind of guy is that?"

She said, "The kind of guy that . . . oh, never mind! Are you ready to meet your backgammon fate?"

In the third game, the dice continued to tumble in Garner's favor and he played even more aggressive. He was quick to move twelve of his checkers into his home quadrant, occupying five of six pips with at least two checkers. By the time he got all fifteen checkers into his home quadrant, he bumped two of her checkers to the bar.

His dominating lead did come into question after he rolled a double two. He could only bear off three of his checkers, leaving one exposed on the fourth pip in his home quadrant. A roll of a four and one enabled her to put his exposed checker on the bar. Three turns later, a roll of six and four helped him move out from her home quadrant. He escaped danger for good when she rolled a six and five, and he followed with a roll of five and two. She barely got all her checkers inside her home quadrant by the time he bore off all his checkers.

He beamed at her, savoring a single-game winning margin of sixty-eight points. "What you just experienced was a man overcoming odds and obstacles—a great story in my line of work."

She was rue with contempt. "I think that's why I do not watch sports. But you won fair and square." She extended her hand in concession, to which Garner gently grasped it. Her hand felt surprisingly soft. His eyes moved upward to study her face again. But before she could comment, Garner also announced it was time for him to head back to Columbia.

This came as a bit of surprise to her. She was intrigued by his exhibition of quick thinking while employing strategy around a backgammon board. Few men had ever earned the distinction of defeating her in one of her best games.

"Garner, I really enjoyed myself playing backgammon."

"I'm glad that you did."

They stood and started walking towards one of the store's exits. Tamira did not hide her interest as she walked casually next to him. Had Garner even been with Kadrece he may have made some kind of physical contact.

Despite Tamira turning out to be a pleasant woman both aesthetically and socially, Garner still felt no attraction for her or sense of chemistry. He further expressed it by the time they reached her car, a black 2008 Toyota Camry Solara hardtop model.

As they exchanged additional pleasantries and goodbyes, he extended his right hand towards her.

"It was very nice meeting you."

She reacted, "No hug?" The limpness in her hand may have suggested that he bruised her ego.

Garner withdrew his hand. "I thought you would appreciate a gentleman. Perhaps we can talk again during the week?"

She managed a faint smile. "Sure, please do that. It was a pleasure meeting you."

He watched her ease into her car similar to the way she first sat down inside the bookstore. She waved wistfully in his direction before driving away.

As Garner headed over towards his vehicle, a pewter 2007 Infiniti G35 Coupe, the image of Tamira's disappointment was just as self-gratifying as watching somebody squirm during an interview.

On his drive back to Columbia along I-26 westbound, Garner found it tempting to call Spencer and inform him how he thwarted his matchmaking effort by setting up Tamira for a big fall at the end of their meeting.

Yeah, he smirked to himself, *nice guys never get laid!*

Chapter 6

About two weeks later

Garner reported the night before that current Tennessee professional football franchise assistant coach Larry Fritzer emerged as the leading candidate for the Chanticleers' job, and Thacker had discussed offering him a five-year contract worth more than $1.2 million annually. With incentives, the package could pay as much as $1.75 million annually.

He also reported Tallahassee State University's assistant coach Carlos Whitehall, one of a dozen black offensive coordinators currently at the Division I-A level, emerged as the only other candidate that Thacker had considered all along. No contract was discussed with Whitehall, but Garner was told by his coaching contact in Texas that Thacker would only conduct negotiations with him if a deal fell through with Fritzer.

When Garner arrived at his desk the following afternoon, his phone had been ringing as if it was stuck in some programming loop. He promised himself that he would not spend all of his office time answering questions from anxious and frenetic Chanticleers fans wondering when Thacker would hire a new coach.

"Good afternoon, WCAE, Garner Davis—"

"Hey, Garner, uh, you reckon we'll be in good hands if Thacker hires Fritzer? Uh, I don't know about the guy down in Tallahassee." The man had a distinct drawl reminiscent of a Billy Bob character. "I mean, he's black; and not trying to take sides, it just seems every black coach that I know of hadn't done too well. I don't think we need somebody that's going to be learning on the job."

Garner removed the phone from his ear, glancing at it perturbed. He then shook his head in disgust before he responded. It was tempting for him to remind the caller how there were proportionately more white coaches with lesser qualifications that have proven to be just as futile with their head coaching opportunities. But the man had a point, to a lesser extent. Garner was aware as of the 2007 season only four of the seventeen blacks that had ever held big-time coaching jobs in the history of college football lasted beyond their original contract. Only two ever found another Division I-A head coaching job after they were forced to resign or fired.

He replied, "All I can say is that it appears Thacker is going after one with previous head coaching experience and one that has no head coaching experience. Both work on the offensive side of the ball, so I think Thacker wants to hire somebody that would generate a lot of excitement around here. One thing I've seen about Thacker is that he's all about money. Offense equals money."

"You reckon that Tennessee assistant coach would leave the Oilers to come here to Columbia?"

"I don't think money's going to be the issue. I think it's a question of whether Fritzer believes he has a chance to win here."

"You reckon so, huh? Hey, buddy, thanks for talking with me. Go Chanticleers!"

Garner was incredulous by the caller's fanaticism. Yet he understood that was the kind of zeal that filled Winnetka-Benson Stadium—located less than two miles away from WCAE—with more than eighty thousand strong for every home football game.

He exhaled loudly and positioned himself in front of his computer screen, scanning the various news sites. His train of thought was interrupted again just as he clicked on a wire story about the Chanticleers men's basketball program.

"WCAE, Garner Davis—"

"Uh, hi, is this really Garner Davis?" The female's voice was cautious.

"Yes, it really is."

"I'm sure you're a busy man, so I won't take long." She spoke in a soft, pleasant tone; her diction led him to believe she was a woman of color. "Ummm, I really don't call men out of the clear blue but I've wanted to let you know that I have been checking you out on TV for a while."

"Well, thank you for the comment. It's nice to know there are female viewers out there."

"Can I ask you something?"

"What's that? It can't be worse than answering questions about the Chanticleers' program."

The woman giggled. Garner was not sure to presume whether she was a mentally unstable person. That had already happened to him on a couple of occasions with a caller from Gilbert, a rural community west of Columbia.

"I'm actually a Chanticleers fan."

"You wouldn't hold that against me?"

"You're forgiven—this time." She then apprised him of her intent for calling him. "A couple of lady friends of mine have all wondered whether you were black or white. Most of them think you're white. I mean, you do have that straight hair, those sexy eyes and you're so articulate."

First, Garner erupted into hearty laughter. But then he went silent, pondering the female caller's question a little further. It struck a chord within him, evoking childhood memories.

Back in Richmond, Garner attended predominantly black schools within the city limits because his mother was unable to move from their neighborhood south of the James River after forcing out Aaron. It was not until he had gone off to college and graduated before his mother was in a position to move into a new development farther south in Chesterfield County.

Classmates' taunts of "high yella," "white boy," "half breed" and "cat eyes" were all too common descriptors used in place of his given name. Periodically, some would derisively swear in his face that one of his parents was white because of his fairer features.

"Did I offend you?"

He was doubled over in laughter. "Oh, no. Not at all. I've been hearing stuff like that a very long time. I can promise you that it says 'Negro' plainly on my birth certificate."

"I knew you were black. That's all I'll say about that right now."

"You know that kind of an answer can lead you down a path you might not want to take."

"I think I'm old enough to make that choice. Let me decide that for myself."

Garner recalled to himself some of the stereotypes that many women that he encountered held about lighter skinned men: There was the one that men of his complexion were rabid about oral sex just like their white counterparts. They lacked the skill and masculine presence of their darker skinned counterparts in the bedroom. Another clichéd perception was that lighter skinned men, well, simply were not as well endowed.

Once again, he went silent.

"You must be one of those deep thinkers . . . I bet you can be a real patient guy."

"A deep thinker to me is somebody that likes to talk philosophical. I'm far from that."

"I really doubt that you are."

"You just never know—"

"Hey, I told you that I would not take much of your time. Just to let you know that I'm not some anonymous kook, my name is Vernise Aikens," she volunteered to him. "And I work in law enforcement here in Columbia. My office is on the northwest side of town just off I-26 near the Columbiana Mall . . . Maybe we could meet there one day for lunch?"

Whoa.

Garner had never encountered a woman who was as direct as this Vernise. She struck him as one who knew exactly what she wanted. It had always been his theory that those types of women made for great sex partners.

Although there was no still, small voice imploring him not to pursue his curiosity, he reasoned that what had already transpired with Vernise might still make a good conversation piece with Spencer.

"Uh, what makes you think I'm somebody you'd want to meet?" he queried.

She retorted, "Maybe I'm somebody you'd want to meet. You'll never know until you find out."

"I'll tell what, I can't take you up on that offer today. Tomorrow might work better for me. Can I get back with you on that?"

"I'll help you out. Seven . . . one . . . nine . . . ten . . . fourteen . . . that's my cell."

Garner did not immediately write down Vernise's number. The station's daily production meeting was more of a priority; it was scheduled to start in less than five minutes.

When he emerged from the meeting, he wrote Vernise's number on the same notepad that he wrote down Tamira's. No sooner than he exhaled, wondering if he had done the right thing, he noticed his cell phone buzzing.

The familiar bass resonated into his ear slot. "Man, if it weren't for the fact I see you on TV, I would have assumed you had gone into exile. Where in the hell have you been?"

"I've been going to and fro, doing what I'm paid to do. Obviously, you still ain't got anything else to do but bother me."

"You know what? I'm in a good mood, motherfucker. So don't start any shit with me and there won't be any—"

Garner hoped that Spencer would not bring up any reference to Tamira, whom he had not contacted since their meeting at the bookstore.

"Hey, ol' man, I've got a sneaking suspicion that Thacker wants to move really fast on this coaching search now that people like me are hot on his trail. So you know I want to stay ahead of all the competition."

Spencer was calling from his cell phone. The static was significant.

"Hey, man, do what you have to do. 'Cause, shiiit, heh-heh-heh, the old man's going to do what he's gotta do here in Orangeburg."

"From Orangeburg?"

"Yeah, that's right. Orangeburg, motherfucker!"

"I don't want to know about it. But, hey, will you be back through here around 7:30?"

"I just might."

"If you are, leave me a message on my cell phone and meet me over at Gallardo's, the Mexican restaurant across the street from the station. You know where it is?"

"Let me see . . ."

"You know where the Target store and that shopping center is across the street from the station?"

"Yeah, over there—"

"Gallardo's is in front of all that."

"Sounds good to me; I'll call you if I'm in the area."

Before Garner left the station for Gallardo's, he placed a call to Whitehall, who informed him the night before that he would be on a recruiting visit in Thomasville, Georgia.

"Garner, the way I see it right now, I might have a few more irons out there are starting to warm up in the next few days," Whitehall said. "The Chanticleers are just coals for that fire."

"It's obvious that you've done about all you could do as an assistant."

"That's what it's always been about—opportunity."

"I might as well ask you this. When you spoke with Thacker a couple of days ago did he ever give you the feeling that he took you as a serious, well-qualified candidate? Or were you, well, just there as a token interview?"

Garner heard the door chime going off in Whitehall's car. He presumed he was close to his destination.

"I'll tell you like this . . . I'm in a profession where sometimes for the sake of getting your name out there you have to do things you might not agree with. For me, it was just that. Think about it. The man who interviews you is sitting next to two other white people at an airport restaurant bar over in Jacksonville.

"Not once did he ask me about my plan for taking that place to a championship-level program like we have here in Tallahassee. And not once did he mention anything about contract. So I knew where I stood with him."

"Hmmm, I think that sounds like he's had Fritzer between the crosshairs all along."

"You got it!

Whitehall apprised Garner that Fritzer is likely to accept a five-year contract that was worth more like $1.5 million a year, with incentives that could reach $2 million, and he might be in Columbia to sign it as early as the next day. He then told Garner that he withdrew his name from consideration less than a half-hour before he called.

"Hey, Garner, I appreciate the information you gave me about Columbia. Let me know if I could help you in any way in the future."

Whitehall then hung up.

Garner shook his head, realizing certain people only talked if it afforded them the opportunity to advance their own agenda—that was the nature of his business. Whitehall was the one who initiated contact with him when it was rumored that he was on Thacker's wish list of candidates before Pershington resigned under pressure.

At first, Garner's visage beamed with excitement knowing that Whitehall pointed him in the right direction on the coaching search. Then it turned somber because he cringed at the thought of having promised Spencer that he would meet him at Gallardo's.

Grudgingly, he left the station and walked with urgency across the street to his now favorite Mexican-Southwestern grill restaurant. He noticed Spencer's metallic gold Mercedes C230 Kompressor with glossy tires in the parking lot. Once inside, he spotted Spencer wearing his usual tie, slacks and loafers. He also wore a full-length leather coat.

The two men shook hands and bumped their right shoulders in the process.

Garner asked, "You don't mind we go over to the bar area? I'll probably just have some chips and salsa."

"That's fine with me; Ms. Raynee hooked me up with little bit of something-something before I left her place, anyway."

"I knew your old, crazy ass had been doing something you probably shouldn't be doing!"

"Fuck you mean old and crazy? Shit, as long as I can still fuck, I'm not old, you young light, bright, almost white motherfucker!"

"Say, can't you call me anything other than that?"

"Well, what should I call you—Casper?"

"How about *Gar-ner?*" he said, mouthing his name.

"All right, damn it, Garner. Now, you satisfied?"

"You better hope whoever you were with feels that way. I'm sure she's talking about your old ass even as we speak."

A hostess approached Garner and Spencer asking them for their seating preference. Garner informed her they would take seats over in the dimly-lit bar area that had televisions in three of the corners.

Spencer took off his leather jacket and draped it across the back of the seat. He sat with his back to one of the television sets. He mentioned to Garner this was his first time visiting the place.

"Young buck, I've lived in Columbia now twenty-five years, and I never even bothered to come to a place on this side of town." The east side of town had been one of Columbia's rapidly developing sectors. He pointed out it was ironic they were down the road from Heathwood School, which was regarded as the city's premier private school attended mostly by the well-to-do.

"You know what never ceases to amaze me? I'm seventy-one years old, right? When I was a teenager, I was never allowed to walk in the front door of a place like this. If there was a place that did serve black folks, I had to go around to the goddamned back. All of this has happened in my lifetime."

"I'm pretty sure it was like that for my mother and my grandparents up in Richmond."

"You never told me you were from Richmond?"

"I thought I told you that. Maybe you forgot because you've been too busy talking shit to me."

"See, I call myself being nice to your ass. Don't fuck it up!"

Garner acknowledged to Spencer that progress like that had been made in seemingly a short period.

"You know, that's why I always seem to be hard on young bucks like you. There's going to come a day when you're going to have to tell those that will be coming after you the stories about what really happened. They will only otherwise know about it from their history books and whatever they might see on TV."

"So that's why you've always been on me about doing something for the cause?"

"Something like that. So, what's been going on with that coaching search?"

Garner looked around. Then he leaned over towards Spencer, lowering his voice. "Funny you'd ask that. Your man Whitehall's removed his name from consideration. He's saying the job is going to go to Fritzer. It's just a matter of them agreeing on the money, which I understand they're not too far away."

"Damn, wouldn't that been something if a brother'd been coming to Columbia? I guess that still might happen in my lifetime."

"You never know, but not right now."

A server had come by the table to take the two men's order. Spencer ordered his usual Bud Light and Garner requested for an appetizer along with a water and lemon. Unlike at Ruby Tuesday's, Spencer didn't bother to observe the server's backside.

"Whatever happened with you and my girl, Tamira?"

Garner stared at the television set off to his right before he answered. "We met at a bookstore, we played some backgammon—which I beat her—and that's it."

"That's not what I heard."

"What did you hear?"

"I heard that you acted like you didn't want to be bothered with her."

"Who told you that?"

Spencer leaned forward on his right elbow on the bar table, pointing in Garner's direction. "You know she tells me almost everything."

"Humph, I'm not surprised by that."

The server had returned with Spencer's beer and Garner's salsa and chips and water with lemon. Spencer looked to his left and studied the server' backside. He shook his head in disapproval. "Not much to talk about there . . ."

Then he returned his attention to Garner. He went on to give Garner a quick history lesson on the way it was while he attended the larger of Columbia's two private black colleges located across from each other on Harden Street.

"Hey, back in my day it was not unusual for black families or people in general taking an interest in a young person to try and point him or her in the right direction with somebody they thought would be suitable for them."

Garner raised his eyebrow, offering a slightly arrogant look. "I don't understand what you mean?"

Spencer paused to take a long sip from his bottle. "I know you don't. If you listen to me, you might learn something."

Garner motioned with his hand that he was yielding the conversation back to Spencer. He leaned forward against his elbow. "This better be good."

"Just listen, motherfucker!"

"Go ahead, damn it!" Garner sat back in his seat.

"As I was saying, what that usually meant was the educated black folk made sure that their children only went around other educated black folk. They weren't going to let their kids get involved with just anybody."

"So you called yourself trying to match me up with somebody that's educated?"

Spencer spoke slowly to emphasize his point while peering over his glasses. "I was more like trying to introduce you to a nice young lady that was looking for a nice, professional black man like I had already told your ass once before."

Garner reacted with a smirk; his arms were now folded. "You know there's a saying about nice guys not getting laid—"

"That should not have mattered." Spencer also leaned back in his bar chair. "Sometimes a little kindness can get you all the pussy you could ever want."

"Listen to who's talking!" Garner smirked once again. "Either you must be one of the kindest people around. Or you must be one of the kindest and dirtiest old men around!"

Spencer repositioned himself at the table, leaning on his left elbow.

He pulled his glasses down to the tip of his nose. "If my memory serves me correct, didn't I tell you earlier today don't start any shit and there wouldn't be any shit?"

Humph.

Garner mimicked Spencer's gesture. "Uh, ol' man, can I ask a favor of you once again?"

"What might that be?"

"I don't tell you who you should be fucking around on Mrs. Shirley, so please don't try to recommend whom I should consider meeting."

Spencer hunched his shoulders in partial concession. "Hey, it's your world. I was just trying to make it a little better for you!" His experience led him to recognize that he was getting nowhere with Garner.

The usual jocular tenor to their conversation was dampened. Seconds later, Garner checked his cellular phone. It was nearly 8:15 p.m. Rather than getting into an argument with Spencer, he told him that he needed to place some late phone calls pertaining to the coaching search. The two men arose, shook hands and bumped right shoulders; Garner left a ten dollar bill to cover both of their orders.

As he headed back to the station, Garner determined nothing that Spencer lectured to him on matchmaking had meant anything to him. After all, this was the twenty-first century. Times were different. Expectations were different. And to some extent, he concluded, the people were much different.

Chapter 7

The phone rang next to Garner's king-size bed around 8:30 the following morning. Tommy Ellworthy, the Chanticleers' sports information director, called to confirm that Larry Fritzer would be in Columbia around one o'clock at the football stadium's luxury lounge to be introduced as the next head coach.

"Sorry I couldn't be of much help to you during the coaching search. But I'm sure you understand why."

Still groggy and half-awake Garner made light of Tommy's apology. "You should have been in on a couple of the conversations that Bud Thacker and I had during this search."

"I was probably there during one of them."

"You think so?"

"Oh, yes, Bud had my eyes watering from laughter the afternoon you called telling him how you had figured out he was after Larry and Carlos Whitehall and he told you, 'I'm not saying anything!'"

"You should have seen how mad he was to know that one of you guys in the media was hot on his trail."

"I bet I'll get a Mother's Day card from him for that." Garner went on to thank Tommy for the reminder. "See you later—"

With a deep sigh, Garner resigned to himself to recognizing in greater scheme of things, the Chanticleers' coaching search would not have been as big of a news item had he been working at ESPN, his dream destination. All he might have gained as one of ESPN's reporters was another notch added to his credibility.

He reminded himself that his career was revived after a one-year hiatus when WCAE offered him the job. At KIAH, the independent in Houston, his entire time there was marred by controversy.

Garner accepted the job in Houston with the understanding that he would be given raises at intervals after six months, twelve months and then twenty-four months. His starting salary at KIAH paid him nearly twice as much as what he earned in Tallahassee, where he was hired upon graduating from the city's historically black college.

Despite all of his stellar work—Garner was voted the state's top sports anchor in his first year—the station hedged on its promise when it offered him only a five percent cost-of-living raise after a year. He was doubly infuriated when he found out through a fellow reporter colleague that Kerry Starr, the station's No. 2 sports anchor, earned $97,000 a year—about $20,000 more than he earned.

Garner reacted so angrily that he filed a grievance with the corporate office. He waited six months for a response; he never received one. So, he took his grievance publicly, making it known in Houston's major newspaper, the *Post-Courier,* that KIAH, for all its moves in the right direction with diversity in the newsroom, presumably did not equate opportunity and pay for its black reporters. He wrote,

> *Historically, blacks in television journalism have made disproportionately less income than their white counterparts. Those before me would not complain because their keeping quiet kept the door of opportunity open for my generation of black professionals that succeeded them. And while I am most appreciative for what they've done, somebody has to watch out for the next generation of black professionals.*

The station responded by issuing Garner a five-day suspension. He refused to sign the formal reprimand; the station elected to dismiss him, acting within its spectrum of authority according to Quill Broadcasting's corporate policy.

Chapter 8

Garner spent about forty-five minutes gathering material from the online sites of newspapers in Tennessee and across South Carolina that could be used throughout the day on Fritzer. He called back to the station requesting for B-roll material from the database of any affiliate station in Tennessee that might be used for visuals before getting dressed.

After he left his place around 10 a.m., he made another phone call while he was headed towards the I-77 on-ramp from Killian Road.

"Vernise Aikens—"

"Good morning, this is Garner Davis. Did I catch you at a bad time?"

In Vernise's background, an office phone had gone off; a colleague had picked it up.

"Actually, yes, you did."

There was a brief pause while Garner accelerated through third, fourth and finally into fifth gear. "Well that makes two of us. But I'm calling you because, first of all, I wanted to tell you that you really had me thinking a lot about you after calling me yesterday.

"The other reason why I called is that I'll be doing a lot of on-air work today. In fact, I'm on my way to this assignment and I don't think I'll have much time to get away to possibly meet you like you suggested."

"Well, that's nice of you to call me. That's really impressive. So where are you going?

"To the University."

"I see . . . Well, I saw you again on TV yesterday evening. After talking to you, I think you look even cuter than I first thought. You know, I didn't tell any of my friends that I called you."

Garner felt his ego inflating. "So you're keeping that nugget of information to yourself, hmmm?"

"Maybe," she reacted. "I guess if any of them had really wanted to know any one of them would have called you themselves, don't you agree?"

Unlike the pace of the initial conversation that he had with Tamira, Garner felt more at ease with Vernise. It helped that she was not as guarded and distant. It actually evoked memories why he and Sabryan had hit it off.

"I bet you're very confident in who you are," he said. "I can sense that in your voice."

"I have to be in what I'm doing."

"What might that be?"

"I'm a special investigator. I'm the only female in our unit and I'm a supervisor to go along with it."

"Law enforcement?"

"Yes, uh-huh—"

"Do you work for Richland or Lexington County?"

"How about Federal."

Now this was another first for Garner; it was almost akin to engaging in conversation with Tamira and her pursuit of the highest level of academia.

"Hold on." She clicked over to another call.

"Sure."

The delay lasted for several seconds. "Sorry about that, Garner." She alerted him to another interruption. "I'd really like to continue with our conversation. But I've just been reminded of this meeting I need to walk into. I really appreciate you calling me—is this your cell number that you're calling from?"

"Uh-huh—"

"Well, maybe I'll return the favor and call *you* next time. When do you think you might be done with work today?"

"The Chanticleers will be announcing Larry Fritzer as the new head football coach this afternoon around one, but my day won't end until after the eleven o'clock broadcast tonight."

"I think you mention that last night. Well, I'm sure that I'll see you at least once today on TV . . . I guess we'll talk again soon."

Garner was so caught up with Vernise that he missed his intended exit on Key Road, which would have been a more direct path to the university's athletic complex; he would have gone by the *Columbia Palmetto* newspaper building and production plant along the backside of the stadium, coming out on Andrews Road.

The next exit on I-77 was Bluff Road. While waiting at the light, as absurd as it sounded to him, Garner tried to making sense why was he so intrigued by someone anonymous to him. He reasoned it was just as risky to meet somebody online, although there were no pictures and personality profiles to go by.

Hell, even with Tamira, he had Spencer's meddlesome old ass for some point of reference, though aided by his flippant clues. And he still was wrong.

All he had was a voice. She professed to be a Chanticleers fan and presumably the profession she worked in.

Could I have called a woman out of the blue?

Humph.

It just wouldn't sound right. He shook his head at the thought.

HONK! HONK! HONK!

Someone in a maroon Buick Lacrosse reminded him the light had turned green. He reacted to the driver without a menacing hand gesture.

The Bluff Road route took him directly by Winnetka-Benson Stadium. There was already a sizeable crowd of Chanticleers fans assembled in the parking area at the Reeves Boulevard intersection.

Garner shook his head rather sympathetically for the people braving the seasonably mid-forties temperatures in early December. He joked, "It's a shame I'll have to be out there with those damned fools."

The route along Reeves Boulevard eventually winded left and it became Andrews Road, which took him back over to the intersection at Chanticleer Drive. There, he turned right, crossing the railroad tracks, and he turned left into the first driveway in the university's athletic complex.

"Yo, Garner!" yelled his cameraman Pete DiCarlo, a burly man in his mid-thirties from Philadelphia, as he passed by. He was already armed with his camera, battery packs adorned along his belt, and a microphone for his colleague. The tripod was back in the truck.

Garner honked his horn and parked just beyond the buildings.

"I feel sorry for you today," Pete told Garner. "The last time the Chanticleers had a coaching change the guy before you lost his voice by the end of the six o'clock broadcast. It was real bad. Hope that won't happen to you—"

"I just want to get it over with. You should have seen what it's already like over at the stadium. There's probably five hundred or so people already over there."

"That's the Chanticleers for you. I've been here twelve years and now my fourth coach."

He apprised Pete about taking some shots over by the stadium. Then he smirked.

"The worst part for me already was watching all those silly fans whoop it up thinking this guy Fritzer is going to be their savior. I'm not even from here, and I can see this program isn't going anywhere . . . Oh, well, they don't pay me to make fun of their fans on air."

Chapter 9

The next morning, Garner barely woke up in time to keep his appointment at The Right Cut. By his standards, the haircut was overdue. He made it a habit to visit the barbershop every two to three weeks—which used to coincide with his visits to Houston—but with the coaching search that extended this last interval to six weeks.

Emboldened by his new appearance, Garner was barely inside his car when he fidgeted for his cell phone.

"Why this is a pleasant surprise," Vernise responded to him calling her.

"You really think so?"

"Of course, I didn't really expect that you would call me today. I told you that I would be calling you. In fact, I had planned on doing that in a while."

"Is there something wrong with that?"

"Oh, no. Not at all."

"Will your schedule allow for us to meet for lunch today?"

"Sure, at 12:30. Meet me in front of the Belk's before you reach the food court entrance at the Columbiana Mall. Are you familiar where that is?"

Garner noticed he had set himself up for a case of *déjà vu*.

"I've been here in Columbia almost two years. Since I don't live on that side of town, I've probably just passed by the place maybe once or twice." Actually, he had gone to the Columbiana Mall on several occasions.

She gave him precise directions. "In fact, to make it easy, look for me standing at that corner on the far end." Then she volunteered, "I'm about five feet, eight inches tall. I weigh about one hundred and fifty pounds. I'm brown skinned—I like to say with enough crème to change my coffee. I'll have brownish red hair that will be braided in the back."

Vernise's description was alluring to him. He tempered what he heard by reminding himself to remain cautious, a virtue of his profession he tried to abide by: always questions everything; never overreact to rumors; never be satisfied until the facts are verified.

This time, Garner decided that he would control the outcome of their conversation. He informed Vernise that he had just stopped in front of a Verizon cellular phone store to pay his bill, although he was not within three miles of one.

"You don't do your bills online?"

"Yeah, there are things that I do pay online; I figured since I was near a branch that I would just take care of it—it's all going to come out of the same account. I'm sure you've probably have some things you want to get done. So I'll see you at 12:30?"

"That sounds good to me."

Garner and Vernise arrived simultaneously in the parking lots adjacent to the Belk's. Vernise parked her unmarked charcoal gray Crown Victoria cruiser closer to the mall's food court side of Belk's whereas Garner parked on the Sears side of the store.

From his view in the parking lot, Garner noticed a woman emerging out of a metallic blue Toyota Avalon XLE. He also noticed another woman getting out of a silver Ford Explorer XLT model. Neither fit the description that Vernise gave him. He was slow to walk over to their meeting place. Then he rounded the corner. A woman whose height and hairstyle was reasonably close to what had been described to him was crossing the driveway. She wore dark slacks and a gray polo shirt that was partially concealed by her dark windbreaker; she looked very much the part of a law enforcement officer.

A car had stopped just shy of the pedestrian crosswalk, yielding to her. His heart rate increased. She had a slender, yet full face; a narrow, pointed nose; and moderately full lips. The brownish red hair that she had described as being braided in the back was thick, as was her shaped eyebrows.

The only thing misleading about her was her actual skin shade. Her complexion was like his, although reddened by some sun exposure. As she neared him, she flashed a bright and broad smile.

"Garner?"

He was wearing olive colored slacks and a light brown business shirt along with a fashionable black leather jacket and brown loafers. He looked more like a salesperson on his lunch break than the Columbia market's most aggressive and competent sports anchor.

"You look even better in person; I'm Vernise Aikens."

He struggled not to stammer. "And I'm impressed."

They paired up and began walking towards the mall's food court. They appeared so natural together—as if the meeting was a part of their lunch date routine.

"Did you think some ugly lady would call you out of the blue?"

Garner continued looking straight ahead. He eventually replied, "I was hoping I would not be disappointed. I'll just say that I was cautiously optimistic."

"You were?" She looked to her right.

"Until a few moments ago, you had the advantage. You saw me on TV who knows how many times. So you at least had an idea what I looked like."

They walked at a brisk pace. Perhaps some of it had to do with the fact it was unseasonably balmy, in the mid-sixties, and overcast with a threat of rain. As they reached the entrance, he stepped ahead and opened the door for her. He looked over his shoulder at her. Their eyes locked in on each other; they froze for an instant. He flashed a smile, attempting to break up the awkward moment. She walked past him inside. His eyes were trained upon her backside; he also made a subtle nod of approval.

Vernise pointed to her left and angled over towards the second merchant space whose specialty was Cajun chicken. "I've been hooked on this place ever since one of my partners turned me on to it. I prefer the Bourbon over the blackened chicken."

Garner never stopped by there during any of his previous visits to Columbiana Mall. The fast-food place next to it was his preference. He gazed at the food on display beneath the protective glass. There was jambalaya, green beans, wedged potatoes, cabbage and broccoli, corn, red beans and rice, blackened chicken, Bourbon chicken, and sweet and sour chicken.

A diminutive woman behind the counter recognized Vernise. She spoke in a distinctive non-Cajun dialect. He was not sure whether she was Mexican or Filipino.

"I miss you. You busy lately?" the woman inquired.

"Well, yes I have been," Vernise answered. "I'll have the chicken-and-two platter, Bourbon plus jambalaya and the wedged potatoes."

"You together?"

Garner answered, "Yeah, we're together. I'll have the chicken-and-two platter like her with blackened chicken, green beans and wedged potatoes."

"What you want to drink?"

He glanced at Vernise before he spoke for both of them. "Two large Cokes."

She smiled. "I like a man who takes charge."

Garner carried the tray with their orders over to the seating area. She chose a bench about mid-depth, sitting with her back to the merchant stands. He rounded the bench and sat across from her; a large potted plant was behind him.

"I can tell you're not from the South."

"You're right." She started into her chicken. "My father was military. He married a white French woman who was born on the island of Martinique in the Caribbean. I was actually born in Germany on an army base. We moved around a lot until I reached high school. We lived in California."

"Do you consider yourself a California girl?"

"I guess. I lived there until I finished college."

Vernise divulged to him that she attended one of the state's colleges at its Dominguez Hills campus on a tennis scholarship. She told him she majored in Sociology. She also joined the school's Army ROTC program after she suffered a major a shoulder injury after her junior season. She went on to serve out her mandatory commission by achieving the rank of first lieutenant. She was last stationed at Fort Gordon, Georgia, where she specialized in Intelligence Operations. She applied for a federal law enforcement job shortly before leaving the military in November 1994. She was hired eighteen months later.

"I also have two children—a son [Pierre] who's seventeen and a daughter [Jenora] who's fourteen—that do not live with me."

"Was that your choice?"

She bristled at the question. "I'd rather not talk about that. What I'd rather talk about is how impressed I was in the way you handled yourself in front of a camera on Wednesday."

"Oh, you saw one of the live reports that I filed?"

"Uh, how about I was there watching you," she answered. "I decided to sneak away and check out the new coach. Did you forget that I'm a big Chanticleers fan?"

Garner gave her a perplexed expression. He conceded there was a crowded scene outside of the stadium's luxury lounge. "I just don't recall seeing anybody like you there—"

"You were standing in back among the cameras, right?"

He acknowledged her observation, nodding. "Yeah, I was back there."

"Is it always crowded like that at news conferences?"

"It can be a shark pit at times. The funny thing about the media, especially the television media, you know like in the movies how you see reporters and cameramen making fools of themselves pushing and shoving and running after people like headless chickens? It's all true."

"I didn't see you carrying yourself like that."

"And you won't." He shook his head for added effect.

She chuckled. "Well, if you talked to my friends, they would say that you might be one of those people."

"Your friends are, umm, I'd rather not talk about it."

Vernise cracked another smile, prodding him to continue with his thought. "So you'd rather just leave it out there, huh? Suit your-self—"

"About what?" he reacted.

"What you really think about my friends."

"For all I know, your friends don't exist, and you could be using *your friends* to find out what you want about me."

"Good observation." She took a long sip of her Coke through the straw. "But you should at least give me the benefit of doubt."

Garner felt the last thing he needed to do was create a bad first impression appearing so dogmatic and inflexible. Especially with someone whose beauty exceeded even Sabryan's.

It was nearing 1:30 p.m.; they had finished their plates.

She asked, "What do you think of the blackened chicken?"

"I think I'll be coming back here again." He gestured to her that he had just remembered something. "You know what? I still want to know why you decided to contact me so unexpectedly. I've thought about that, and I still reached the conclusion that it would not make any sense had I been the one calling you."

Vernise straightened herself, staring at Garner. Then she began placing her black Coach handbag across her right shoulder. She que-ried, "What if I told you that I get real wet when I'm watching you, and I decided that I wanted do something about it?"

She stood up, going through the motions of brushing off her slacks and straightening her jacket. She announced, "It's about time for me to get back to the office."

She reached into her jacket pocket and pulled out a notepad and pen. Writing left-handed, she scribbled something rather swiftly be-fore handing him a yellow tear-off. She pointed to the slip of paper. "If you want to do something about it, here's how you can contact me other than on my cell phone."

Garner coolly folded the sheet with his left index and middle fin-gers, pushing it in his shirt pocket. He reached into his jacket pocket, retrieving his wallet. He pulled out one of his business cards and he likewise scribbled something on it before he handed it to her.

She was coy to place the card in one of her handbag pouches; she started walking towards the exit. Just as he had done as they entered the mall's food court, he extended the same courtesy as they exited it. He even took note of her backside once again, making another similar subtle nod of approval.

They took the walk path over to the sidewalk that went along side of Belk's. They stopped near where they initially greeted each other. She flashed another broad and bright smile and he nodded. Then he extended his hand towards her, to which she grasped softly.

For another instant, their eyes were locked on each other. Their body language hinted at something more desirous. She allowed her lips to part as she gazed upward at him. He felt inclined to make a corresponding move but resisted the thought.

She released his hand. "I better get going."

Shit!

He was reluctant to walk away. "Hey, by the way, did you really get wet while you're watching me on air?"

She stopped in mid-stride. She looked over her right shoulder smiling again at him. She also ran her tongue back and forth across the inner half of her top lip before answering.

"If I told you, then I'd have to kill you."

Chapter 10

While he remained in the mall's parking lot, Garner took a moment to pause and reflect. What provoked him to this was how no woman had ever divulged to him that she might be aroused while watching him on television.

And why not? he thought to himself, because as outrageous as it sounded, the more believable her parting line became to him.

That brought a smile to his face. He reveled in her non-verbal communication, prompting him to savor a moment of personal exaltation. Then he closed his eyes and visualized once again the kind of woman whom he met: Beyond her blush gray eyes, and a broad and bright smile that lit up her slender but full face, she was bold and portrayed herself as having been there a few times in her life and having done it all. He also deduced that may have also explained for her ease while interacting with him.

Humph.

For that reason, Garner resolved there was no way that he would allow Vernise to have that last word. He pulled out the slip of paper, holding it at steering wheel level.

Unfolding it, the message read,

Your place or mine? 316 Late Hollow Lane, Lexington 515.6837

He placed the slip of paper in the center console holder; he punched in a number on his cell phone.

Vernise recognized that he called. "You caught me at a good time."

"Hmmm, why would I not be surprised?"

"I had a very nice lunch date with you. So, ummm, do you think you have what it takes to do something about what we discussed?"

"I'll let you be the judge of that."

"And you just might get a fair and impartial shot."

"How about tonight?"

There was an unexpected pause in their dialogue. Garner heard conversation between Vernise and another male in the background. Words like "case," "investigation," "suspects," and "The Bureau" were used freely and frequently.

She returned to him. "Sorry about that, dear . . . Now, uh, what were we talking about?"

"Tonight—"

"Oh, yessss . . . tonight. Your place or mine?"

Damn!

With clenched jaw, Garner apologized to Vernise for the interruption on his cell phone.

"Hello, this is Garner."

"Good afternoon, Garner, did I catch you at a bad time?" The female spoke with proper diction. Then he heard a click from the other line.

Fuck, he mouthed, *you're goddamned right it is!*

"Hello?"

Garner inhaled deeply and was slow to exhale, shaking his head with much regret. He finally composed himself to say, "I'm sorry. There must have been some static. I experience it some times while driving along certain spots on the freeway."

"Well, this is Tamira Lake. I can tell by the few times I've seen you on television that you've been quite busy lately . . . How have you been?"

Mischievous and disparaging thoughts of Professor Double Zeros for no chemistry and no personality came to mind. Tamira's voice was the least likely one that Garner expected to hear. He thought he tactfully disposed of her a few weeks ago when he refused to hug or kiss her after their date, offer an invitation to call him, or even suggest that he would contact her.

"It's been just that—busy. You actually caught me at a good time because I was on my way to the station."

"Well, I won't take up much of your time since you were on your way to work. I was thinking that maybe if you were available this weekend we could discuss that rematch at the backgammon board, or perhaps something else."

Garner suspected that Spencer had instigated her into calling him again. A worst-case scenario, he thought, was maybe she was a lover of cruel and unusual punishment. "So you've determined that my superior performance was purely luck, and now you seek redemption?"

"Actually, Garner, I thought you were quite the gentleman whom Dr. Watts had described of you. And for that reason, I felt comfortable calling you this time to find out if you'd like to meet again.

"The backgammon proposition was just a starting point; it does not have to be the end-all."

He queried, "May I ask this of you?"

"Yes—" There was a hint of anticipation in Tamira's voice.

Garner sneered at the thought that maybe she realized that she had a personality. But given his preference for conversation, he remained tactful. "Before I forget about it, how have your courses gone for you this semester?"

"Oh, they went quite well for me. I think I made significant inroads at impressing my curriculum advisor. And I'll start on work towards my dissertation next semester. That's the hard part."

"I can imagine," he related. "My aunt told me there is always this exclusive body of egos that comprises a dissertation committee, and they feel they have the right to suppress or deny you from joining their so-called community."

She chucked at his assessment. "I won't go as far as saying that, but there are many that have an exorbitant opinion of themselves."

Garner cleared his throat and rolled his eyes. "I would feel honored that you would give me an audience, Ms. Tamira Lake. But on one condition—"

"Okay . . ."

"I'll have a better idea whether this would be logistically conducive after the production meeting that I'm required to participate in, uh, less than twenty minutes. So may I call you later this afternoon?"

"Sure, I'm about to leave the school now. And I expect to be home later this evening."

"Oh, by the way, have you tuned in to any of our broadcasts lately?"

"Yes, I have. And I think you have a very strong presence in front of a camera."

"Why, thank you for the compliment. I'll call you in before I go on air today."

"I'll look for your call, bye now."

Whew!

It had been a while since Garner had successfully employed some slight of conversation with a woman. He actually felt good about himself. He wondered how often had Spencer Watts executed similar maneuvers over the years.

Nonetheless, the allure of Vernise was more appealing. He re-dialed her number three times because he continued punching in the wrong number. Finally, he dialed it correctly.

"Hi, you've reached Vernise. I'm unable to answer your call. Please leave a message at the sound of the tone."

Garner slammed his open palm against the armrest to his console. He cursed, "That damned bitch with an IQ higher than the 803 area code!" She would be the spoiler of his move with Vernise. He nearly missed the I-26 to I-77 northbound ramp. A man in a blue Ford F-350 honked several times at Garner because he cut off the driver while changing into the farthest left lane. He raised his hand in an apologetic gesture to the irate driver.

With the immediate traffic drama abated, he tried Vernise again; it was the same response. He left a message with her.

"Hi, Vernise, I hope we could settle the question later on whether it might be your place or mine. I'll try again later this afternoon, probably before I go on air tonight."

Garner went to his computer terminal after the afternoon budget meeting. He plotted on Mapquest.com the Lexington address that Vernise gave him. It detailed that she lived roughly three miles away from the I-20/Augusta Highway exit.

He poised himself to contact Vernise after writing down the information. But his No. 2 guy, Alan Hudson, derailed his attempt, requesting help with editing his package on the state high school football championship preview.

Twenty minutes later, Garner resumed work on his own package, as well as the entire sports segment for the six o'clock show. All along, he also glanced intermittently at the clock on his computer screen. He figured Vernise would be home from work by 5:30.

"Hi, you've reached Vernise. I'm unable to answer your call. Please leave a message at the sound of the tone."

He pounded his fist on his office desk in reaction to Vernise's cell phone greeting. He felt embarrassed that he already made three futile attempts. He barely managed his most professional voice when he left his last message.

"Vernise, this is Garner again . . . I'm about to go on air. Call me when you're available."

Thoughts of Vernise evading him produced greater anxiety. He wondered whether she was merely a tease, and nothing more. Sure, the moment might have been very friendly at the mall. It just seemed illogical to him that a person would all of a sudden not make herself available.

Fuck!

This was not supposed to happen to him. Maybe his nice guys don't get laid caveat had come back to haunt him. He berated himself for not making a better choice having clicked off to another call while something hot was in the making.

With his hormones raging after the six o'clock broadcast, Garner was determined not to spend a weekend without any female company. He mulled contacting Kadrece, but that would require some work. Unable to catch up with Vernise, he felt he was down to a final option.

"Hello?"

"I apologize for calling later than I had promised. Things got a little wild before we went on the air tonight."

"Is that right?"

"Yes that's right. Alan Husdson, my No. 2 guy, approached me about repackaging his piece on the high school playoffs, and there were some things that came up on the news wire service that I decided to work into our briefs. And before I knew it, it was 5:30 and it was time to go over our script."

"Hmmm . . . I'm sure you have a packaged response for every situation that involves a woman."

"That's not true."

"Oh, can't you take a joke?"

"That was a joke?"

"Yes, it was."

Humph.

Now, Tamira was the one taking potshots at him.

"I guess I missed it," he said. "I'm just ready to unwind. It's been a long day and a long week."

"I feel the same way. But for me, it's also been a long semester. That's one of the reasons why I had called you."

Tamira was well into her unwinding mode. She felt she deserved it. Usually, she would wear her favorite sweat suit having already arranged her four course books and three notebooks on her study table. She would have turned on her computer and printer, and she'd have a mug of cranberry apple juice sitting on a coaster. And depending on the week, she would have a stack of papers to mull through from the six classes she taught at the college.

On this particular night, she was free from the workload. The semester was over. She came home, took a shower, and slipped directly into a black silk robe. She popped in CDs from Earth, Wind & Fire, Stevie Wonder, and Rachelle Ferrell.

"Do you have anything planned for the weekend?" Stevie Wonder's "Ribbon in the Sky" made for a soothing ambience in her living room while she stretched out on the sofa with one leg bent and with her free hand stroking her pubic hair.

"Honestly, no."

"You know when we met at the bookstore that had been the first time I'd gone out to meet a guy all year."

"I find that hard to believe."

"Really, like I had told you, a lot of days after I'd come home from the school or had completed my research a man is the last thing I'm thinking about."

"Ummm, I take it a man is not the last thing you're thinking about right now?"

Tamira chortled at Garner's inference. She complimented him on his sense of humor. She divulged that she was actually connoisseur of comedy. Garner shook his head in disagreement, but went along with it.

"Comedy is a great way of keeping one's sanity," she said. "It offers you a chance to make satire of the things of the day and things you might not particularly agree with."

"Well, I hope you would agree with this. Would you be willing to come to Columbia later tonight? I know of a couple of places—they're not comedy clubs—that still should be rather lively even between 11:30 and midnight."

She was eager to respond, "I usually do not go on dates at that time of the night. But I could make this an exception."

Chapter 11

Tamira began preparing for her date with Garner around 9 p.m. There was a sense of anticipation she had not felt since she dated Orlando Cope, an optometrist in the Charleston area.

Garner was a favorable reminder of Orlando with his ability to engage in highly erudite conversations. Their light-skinned features were also common traits that she admired; it was also a weakness of hers.

Orlando and Tamira met for the first time while attending an Atlantic Coast Athletic Association (ACAA) basketball tournament party hosted in Charlotte back in 1995. They dated for nearly five years, providing some of the happiest years of her life.

She loved the fact Orlando had aspirations of creating his own optical center chains *à la* Pearle Vision's model for success. A native of New York, he came down south to attend the historically black college in Greensboro, North Carolina, where he earned his bachelor's in Biology. He later attended a school of optometry at the mainstream state university located in Birmingham, Alabama, where he earned his Optometry degree.

In less than ten years after obtaining his license to practice, he had opened offices in South Carolina's coastal towns of Beaufort,

Charleston, Hilton Head, and Myrtle Beach, catering to an affluent clientele. He also had offices in towns of Rock Hill, Florence and Aiken. He predicted by 2011 he would have thriving offices in all of the state's prominent cities, and that would give him the advantage to embark on his corporate dream to franchise his operations in other states.

"A degreed and professional man with goals is defined as ambitious. Whereas a man without a degree that has goals is nothing more than a hustler," she once confided in a female friend of hers.

"Give me the former, and you can have the latter."

After Tamira moved to Orangeburg in 2000, their relationship soured when marriage and children was discussed. She was opposed to the idea of giving up her career to become solely a housewife and mother of a family that he was emphatic to start. Orlando unceremoniously broke up with her, citing that he simply wanted to go his separate way. He never relented to any efforts at reconciling.

It was in the aftermath of her break up, the same Spencer Watts who had a wandering eye for her was also there to help collect the chips that were smashed and grounded into dust. That was when she finally considered his matchmaking offers—but according her own terms.

Garner was the first man whom she felt remotely matched up to the lofty precedent that Orlando set. For that reason, the thought of going out on a late-night date was exciting. It also reminded her of a few spontaneous encounters she had with Orlando.

Her most memorable one was a surprise trip down to Savannah's Tybee Island, where he already arranged for a suite, a fruit basket with cheese squares and a bottle of Dom Pérignon chilling on the table upon their arrival. When she excused herself to the bathroom to freshen up, he had a set of hanging diamond earrings in the box waiting for her on the nightstand adjacent to the bed. She responded to his charisma and the way he romanced her by accommodating him sexually in ways that she once reserved for the man she would marry.

For Garner, Tamira felt in the mood to don a black skirt with a deep-cut, leopard print blouse along with a matching leopard print jacket and three-inch black pumps. She altered her short, tapered hairstyle by layering the entire top and feathering her bangs. She also chose a plum-colored lipstick to bring out her medium complexion.

She left her Orangeburg home around 10:30 p.m., ensuring she would arrive at the WCAE parking lot before 11:30 p.m. She arrived there in forty minutes; there were eight cars out there along with four satellite-equipped station trucks behind a gated area. She sat nervous in anticipation of Garner's emergence from the building. Just as strongly as her heart was beating through her blouse, she felt a similar throbbing between her thighs.

Around 11:40 p.m., Tamira spotted employees walking one by one out to their vehicles. She realized she had parked much farther away, but not too far that she could not recognize Garner when he left the building. He was rather obvious by the way he walked slowly while looking in the distance. She noticed that he stopped and leaned against his G35 Coupe. He wore just a suit jacket and seemed unfazed by the upper-thirties temperatures.

Instead of drawing unwanted attention by honking, she drove her car beside his. Garner approached the driver's side of her Solara, smiling. She let down her window and smiled back at him.

"What's wrong? You've never seen a lady dressed for the occasion?"

He was slow to answer, stunned in fact. "Ummm, of course I have. Are you ready to go?"

Tamira let her window back up and turned off her engine. She made a graceful exit from her car and walked past the front of both vehicles, making sure that Garner got a view of her. His eyes followed her all the way inside his car.

"Good evening, Mr. Davis." She adjusted herself in the passenger seat. Then she gave a quick inspection of her immediate surroundings. "You are a man of distinct taste."

She did not let Garner on that Orlando drove a Porsche 911 Carrera whenever they went on late-night dates similar to this.

"You look absolutely stunning, Ms. Lake. But let's get past the formal greetings, okay?"

"Very well, can I at least say that you look quite handsome tonight?"

"Why, thank you."

If Garner had felt he was in the company of a winner earlier in the day with Vernise, he conceded that he exercised poorer judgment on Tamira.

That damned Spencer Watts wasn't shitting me after all. She was, umm . . . damm! She is that nice woman whom he described to me.

He made mental notes that every move she made was carefully considered and then executed with an equal amount of grace. Behind it was an aura of confidence that exceeded the tenor of any conversation they previously shared. He was also drawn to her fragrance—Calvin Klein's Realities—that wafted amidst them.

She inquired, "I presume that you like what you are viewing?"

He offered a slight nod. Then he started the car and easily let off the clutch, cruising out of the parking lot.

"You should consider yourself privileged because I am rarely seen this way," she said.

Initially, he considered taking her to one of those dives along North Main that Spencer once mentioned to him. He figured that might have suited the woman previously rated with the double zeroes. But with what was in his immediate presence, he realized that a place like Club Epicenter located on Gervais Street was more appropriate.

They started their trek westbound on Garners Ferry Road. "I used to go out like this at times while I lived in Houston."

"I hear that Houston is a very large city."

"It is. You can travel from Columbia to where you live in Orangeburg and still be inside Houston's city limits."

"That is a very large city."

He mentioned to her his favorite hangouts were the jazz gigs that were hosted at various places around town.

"Is that right? Did you know that I had some Joe Sample in my CD player when you called?"

"Hmmm, I like his work with The Crusaders."

"I bet you can't guess the guest singer to one of their greatest hits, 'Street Life'."

He retorted, "I bet you that I can. And if I guess it right, what's in it for me?"

"You will be entitled to my most sincere congratulations."

"Well, for entitlement to your most sincere congratulations, the answer is Randy Crawford."

Tamira nodded, offering a kind of smile that he had never seen before, one that slowly drew him into her lair. Her allure was far more refined than what he had ever encountered in a woman.

She took the liberty to recline her seat, making sure that she crossed her right leg over her left thigh. Inhaling deeply, she placed her head against the headrest as if she had done it several times before in his company.

She asked, "Did you go alone to those jazz gigs?"

Garner paused before replying. He tried camouflaging his reaction by peering off into his driver's side mirror and then the rear-view mirror while he changed lanes.

"Sometimes I did."

"And sometimes you—"

"Yes, I went with somebody."

With some resignation, he divulged to her that he would make the circuit with Sabryan, although he did not mention her by name. "A pretty good friend," he said. He did not speak again until he veered left onto Devine Street. That route took them into the Five Points district, which featured several nightspots and gathering places for the major university's student population and its peripheral clientele.

"Was she your ex?"

"A former girlfriend."

"I see . . . where do you plan on taking us?"

"Club Epicenter. Are you familiar with it? I hear it's a nice place that doesn't attract any of that hip-hop/rap crowd."

"You've ever gone there before?"

"Never."

"I've had a few acquaintances to go there on Friday nights. They feel it's a nice place to hang out especially after you've gone to a concert or a party. It's much better than going to a Waffle House."

Garner was determined not to let things be stuck in neutral. In his opinion, there were only so many general topics that could be discussed before an individual loses interest. Besides, this woman simply looked too damned good to be talking about his past dates with Sabryan. Nor did he care to listen to her refer to her acquaintances that might have stopped off at Club Epicenter for reasons that had nothing to do with neither of them.

He came upon the Devine and Harden Street intersection. While waiting for the right-turn green light he stole another glance at Tamira, who happened to have brushed part of her feathered bang to the side. He noticed the set of hanging diamond earrings. She grazed her hand against his while it was still on the gearshift knob.

He said, "You know I actually thought about the Blue Dolphin restaurant earlier today when you called me. So it's interesting that we will be going to a place just down the street from there."

"Did you think of going there with me?"

"I can't say that I was at the time. I thought about a conversation that a couple of people in the newsroom, uh, never mind—"

"Never mind what?"

"I don't like talking about other people that I work with." The light turned green. He darted through the traffic to make the two lights in the Five Points area. He slowed down again for the left-turn light at Gervais.

Tamira was amused by his impatience in traffic.

"Well, that can be a problem," she said. "Of course, you have those that only talk about self and self only. Remember when I mentioned to you about exorbitant egos?"

Garner chortled at Tamira's description. It reminded him of some coaches and athletes that he had encountered in his profession. "Exorbitant egos," he said, nodding. "I'll need to use that some day very soon."

"Will you tell everyone on television where you got that from?"

"I don't know. But I'm certain it might bring a smile to my face because I know it have will come from you."

The traffic on Gervais was thick. He reduced to creeping in second gear. The pedestrian flow actually allowed him time to sneak another glance at Tamira, whose smile sparkled by the reflection of headlights.

"So you like that, huh?"

She glanced at him. "Why of course. Do you like it?"

Garner allowed his mind to wander in lust. He recalled to himself that Kadrece was the last person to use those same words; it happened the first time they had sex at his apartment in Tallahassee. She had reclined on her side in anticipation of him joining her. Her body type, although much fuller than what he was accustomed to experiencing at the time, reminded him of an artist's rendition of women from the Renaissance era. She was all woman and more; he found her to be far more sensual than he ever fathomed.

"Do you like it?" he remembered her whispering into his ear. *"Do you like this dark, chocolate wet pussy grabbing your sweet red dick?"* He shook his head, as if he had a nervous twitch to rid himself of those recollections, and cleared his throat.

"How do you deal with men that may voice any attraction to you?"

Tamira uncrossed her leg but kept her seat reclined. "If the attraction is mutual, I'll let him know in non-verbal terms. You hope that he is adept at identifying those forms of communication.

"If the attraction is not mutual, well, it depends." Then she positioned herself to study his reaction. "Are you saying that you're attracted to me, and on what premise?"

"To be succinct, the answer would be yes." He kept his eyes on the traffic ahead of him. "Is the attraction mutual?"

She sighed. "You've not done anything to preclude my inclination."

He pointed out to her that they were approaching Club Epicenter. "You know what? I think we make a pretty nice couple going inside this place tonight."

"I agree."

He executed a parallel parking maneuver without hitch. He bragged about having a sports car with nimble handling in traffic. Tamira giggled while Garner found a parking spot along the main drag. He reacted with a surprised look.

"What was so funny?"

"Relax, Garner, I'm not going to bite you—at least not publicly."

"Relax, Garner, I'm not going to bite you—at least not publicly."

After turning off the engine, he rested the side of his face in his palm.

She said, "I could tell by your bodily movements that you were rather tense, and you've been searching for some icebreaker with me."

"I've been fine with you since I beat you two out of three at that backgammon board."

"Is that right?" she huffed. "Well, we just might have to address that matter."

Garner reacted to Tamira the only way that he knew. He remained silent, keeping his eyes trained upon her for several seconds. The cars passing by and the periodic honking of horns were the only sounds produced around them. Meanwhile, she brought her seat up from the reclining position.

"So, are we going to just admire each other, or are we going to Club Epicenter?" she queried him.

"Only after—"

"And what that might be?"

Garner leaned forward and placed his left hand below her chin. He pressed his lips into hers while he inhaled her fragrance through his nostrils. Tamira felt a rush of excitement immediately flow between her thighs. She felt her heart pounding through her blouse.

He withdrew from the kiss and her lips remained parted. Her eyes appeared to glaze. Without commenting, he leaned forward again and kissed her. She reciprocated his effort, cradling his head. This time, she felt the sensation in her nipples.

He whispered, "Now who's tense? I told you I've been relaxed all along."

"Whew! I suppose that you have," she commented, fanning herself. "It is getting a little warm in here."

Chapter 12

Garner offered Tamira his hand as she emerged from his car. He noticed her legs were not as thin as he presumed when she wore slacks. He pulled her closer to him no sooner than she straightened herself. This time, he kissed her on the cheek. She offered no resistance.

He motioned that they head over to Club Epicenter. The traffic allowed them to jay walk hand-in-hand across Gervais. Not a single car honked at them to hurry.

Once they reached the curb, he queried, "Are you the spontaneous kind, or do you have to plan every single detail?"

"Mmmm, I think I'm a little bit of both. If I plan for certain things, then I can allow for the spontaneity to occur."

That brought a mischievous thought to Tamira. She recalled the days when she was involved with Sampson Nettles, a college administrator from northern Georgia, while she worked in Greenville.

They would meticulously plan their trysts so that his wife, Barbara, would not interrogate him when he returned home. Once on a whim, and at Tamira's suggestion, they agreed to stop off at an adult bookstore along I-85 in Georgia. She wore a skirt and blouse with nothing underneath. They agreed to sit in a booth that offered pay-per-view movies of the arcade kind.

While in there, she proceeded to masturbate in his presence and then masturbate him. Then she sucked him back to an erection and sat atop him, doing all the work that led to another tingling climax for both of them. She always suspected they had a small audience by the way the store attendant winked and nodded at them when they left.

"What's so funny now?" Garner asked.

"Oh, nothing."

As they waited for their turn to enter Club Epicenter, a man approached Garner. He stood about five-ten. He was dark skinned and stocky, and it reminded him of his father, Aaron.

"Aren't you the guy that's on TV?" He looked Garner up and down.

"I might be—"

"I'm just a bit surprised that you're into sistas. I thought you might hang out with your own kind."

Garner didn't react to the man's comment; he looked over at Tamira who looked back at him.

"Not trying to offend you, man, but I see a lot of brotha's hanging out with white chicks these days. I just didn't know that there were more white guys diggin' on the sistas."

"Well, not trying to offend you, *brotha*, but it clearly states 'Negro' on my birth certificate."

The man reacted with a smug expression. "Day-um, you could have fooled me!"

Tamira grabbed Garner by the hand; she easily discerned his disgust. Garner remained cool, kept his mouth shut, and they walked away.

Once inside the place, Garner noticed it was not filled to capacity. He was quick to surmise that Columbia's nightlife around midnight was not like Houston's. The popular places in his previous place of residence would still be jamming until 2 a.m.

Thus, they easily found a table off to the corner near the back of the establishment. Tamira recognized the local band attempted a cover of Dave Koz's "After Dark". Although she was not musically inclined, she could discern the band's sax player was like a hackneyed phrase with his play. She mused silently to herself how the band needed to take a break and ditch him.

She positioned her seat next to Garner. "You know you might have had to secure the services of an attorney had you reacted to that guy."

"I should be used to that, but it still annoys the hell out of me." He offered a half-hearted smirk. "You know what's funny? Spencer Watts has a line he likes to bull shit me with at times, but it doesn't bother me. I know he's not being malicious."

Garner sighed deeply and shook his head. "Then there are those that say something to you, and you can sense their hateful intent."

He alluded to his school age experiences. He mentioned how he used to get into many fights because he was reviled as the "white boy" among his classmates. Ironically, he noted, his brother Norris never helped him in any of those fights. Tamira, who offered a sympathetic look, placed her hand atop his and softly grasped it.

"It's not like I need any consolation."

"Well, I'm giving you my unsolicited comment, anyway." She adjusted herself in her seat. "A man I once dated for several years who had fair features like you. We once ran into somebody at a gas station near Conway—which is before you get to Myrtle Beach—that said something similar to what you heard.

"Orlando, which was his name, punched the guy in the mouth. He was a hot head from New York City. I take it you're not from there."

"No, I'm not. I'm from Richmond."

"Richmond, Virginia? Isn't that where the first black governor since reconstruction was elected?"

"Yeah, that's where Douglas Wilder ran the state of Virginia. He's now serving as mayor of Richmond."

"Well, Orlando's parents were black Dominicans of the Afro-Caribbean kind."

He interrupted her. "Funny you would mention that. My mother is extremely light complexioned. My father's really dark skinned like that asshole."

"Wow, your mother's genes must be very strong—"

"I guess. I think that's what pissed me off because he reminded me of the attitude my father often had towards me. My mother used to tell me not to worry about what he'd say to me."

Tamira elected not to take the conversation down that path. She noticed the server approaching their table. They were informed about a two-drink cover per individual. Garner successfully negotiated with the server—thanks to a five dollar tip—allowing for his drink and Tamira's to satisfy the club's requisite. She ordered a glass of white wine while he ordered a Smirnoff cooler. The server returned with their beverages sooner than he expected.

"So, Garner, what do you plan to be doing, and where do you plan to be in the next three or four years?"

"Hopefully I'll be working in a larger market or at a network like ESPN."

"Interesting."

Garner remained intent on not allowing their conversation to drift into oblivion. "I was kind of surprised that you allowed me to kiss you the way I did out in my car. Did that imply the attraction is mutual?"

"I'll let you be the judge of that."

"All right . . . Well, what if I told you I was feeling spontaneous right now. What would your reaction be?"

She took a small sip from her wineglass, noting that it was exceptionally cold the way she liked it. "Hmmm, my reaction would be the way I had kissed you back."

That brought a smile to Garner; he liked the way she went for his tongue during his second attempt. It didn't seem she was going through any motions. He took a long sip from his cooler, closing his eyes to reflect.

He wondered how Vernise would have reacted. He fantasized after what happened inside his car maybe they would have scrapped going inside Club Epicenter. He would have sought a quick decision whether it was her place or his for where the clothes would be strewn on the carpet.

Hmmm, has Vernise's loss become my gain with Tamira?

"I've got to at least make this admission to you: I mentioned at the bookstore you appeared to be the embodiment of beauty and intelligence, but it lacked the conviction compared to the way I feel like conveying to you tonight."

"Does that mean the way you kissed me just a while ago had some conviction?"

He took another sip of his cooler. He gave her a quick stare. Then he smiled once again. "Matter of fact, there was some."

"You know, in everyone's life you go through just trying to learn what one times one is—one times one equals one." She paused for emphasis. "Then at some point you try to figure out why does one times one actually equal one."

Garner appeared bemused by her statement. Before he could comment, she leaned forward drawing near to Garner's face, smiling. She complimented him on being such a handsome man. He could feel warmth from her breath against his face.

"You have some of the dreamiest eyes I've ever seen. I'm sure you've been told many times about their effect on a woman."

Then she rolled her tongue along her top lip gazing at him enticingly. She also placed her right hand under the table and ran it along his thigh. "Are you as spontaneous as you've tried to figure out how I might be?"

"I'll let you be the judge of that, Ms. Tamira Lake."

"Are we getting formal again?"

"No, just a formal invitation of us going to my place, if that's all right with you."

They interacted as though they were oblivious to the rest of the patrons. Tamira responded by inching her hand farther along Garner's thigh until it reached his crotch. She immediately recognized the other thickness from his body. Her brown eyes gleamed with approval; Garner kept his eyes affixed upon her lips.

"Well, Mr. Garner Davis, I think I will accept that offer."

They left Club Epicenter walking even closer, and in unison. There was a glow on her face.

Inside his car, he leaned over and kissed her. He felt so engrossed in the moment that he ran his hand along her blouse, slipping inside it to fondle her right breast and nipple. She didn't pull away; she sensed another wave of throbbing and wetness that she could no longer suppress or ignore. Her soft moans were accompanied by a noticeable change in her breathing pattern.

"Your hands feel so good right now." She spoke in a barely audible whisper. "My body aches to feel you . . ."

Garner closed his eyes, visualizing just what she might attempt to indulge. An inordinate amount of pre-cum flowed inside his briefs; his dick's throbbing made him feel like he was a teenager embarking on his maiden experience. He inhaled her fragrance once more, long and deep through his nose..

"The word 'sophomoric' is coming to mind," he finally said. "I think we're a bit more sophisticated to be fogging up the windows."

"I agree."

Chapter 13

There was a part of Garner—his dick and balls—that wanted to drive from Gervais Street to his condo in ten minutes. The other part of him—his intellect—reasoned that he needed drive to his place in Blythewood without rushing. A sound mind prevailed over a sexually charged body.

Once he reached the I-26 freeway extension that began where Huger Street ended, he placed his hand on Tamira's thigh, giving it light strokes. She responded by guiding his hand under her skirt.

"I thought this might warm your hand. Do you like it?"

He glanced over at Tamira, smiling. "It feels nice."

"Your hands feel very nice. I can sense the strength in them."

"It's interesting that a man can only do what a woman allows him to do."

"That's correct. You know they say a woman is a very mysterious creature."

"Mmmm, there may be some truth to that."

"I feel in part because we're such emotional beings. And when a man delves to experience a woman, he doesn't realize that he's often times opening Pandora's Box."

"If I'm not mistaken, Pandora's Box was trouble?"

"Oh, I've always aspired to lead a very simple life. But I do have desires. I have sexual needs. Many that often go unfulfilled perhaps by my own volition."

"So, if going out on a late date with me was considered an exception that you made, are you making an exception even for that?"

She corrected him. "Exceptions go contrary to volition because they are exemptions to a set standard; volitions are choices made." She studied his reaction. Perhaps it was the teacher in her to do just that. A woman of her sophistication appeared so out of character; he still couldn't fathom this sexual side of her.

So, he concerned himself with how he might perform in bed with her. Two months had passed since the silky walls of a woman's aroused pussy enveloped his dick.

"Then what is the value of tonight for you?"

Tamira exhaled, appearing hardly amused by his searching to understand her. She offered another example that he might grasp. Leaning towards him, she ran her hand across his crotch as she had done in Club Epicenter. His body temperature rose with each circular motion she made. Then she gave him a soft kiss on his earlobe. He didn't flinch from the warmth he felt by her nostrils, or by the light flickering of her tongue against his skin. She returned to her reclined position in his seat, offering another seductive smile.

He began letting up on the accelerator. "We're almost at my place."

"It doesn't seem like we've been on the road that long," she observed.

Garner lived in a ground-level condo at one of Columbia's newest properties. Many of the current residents worked at Provident Palmetto Hospital located just two miles away. The entrance to his condo was enclosed by a privacy fence, which made for a cozy hangout on a warm night. He guided her by the hand to the porch; they indulged in a long embrace. She whispered, "Garner, you're such a handsome man . . ."

He silenced her with a deep kiss. He pushed his tongue between her lips, to which she accommodated. He felt her breasts press into his chest. He reached under her skirt, grasping her ass cheeks; he was surprised by their firmness. He rubbed his erection against her body. She responded by clutching his body tighter.

"You're definitely that embodiment of beauty and intelligence that so many of us men never seem to experience or appreciate." He kissed her again; this time she went for his tongue, sucking it hard. They came up for air at the same time.

With one sweeping motion, Garner lifted Tamira off her feet and opened his door, carrying her into his place. It took her by surprise, but she reacted coolly to his move. She wondered how that would have felt on what's regarded as the happiest day of a woman's life.

"I must say that I'm impressed. It's not every day that a man carries a woman beneath his threshold."

Garner let Tamira down gently once he reached mid-depth in his living room area. She collected herself and walked towards the king sofa in front of her. But he stopped her just shy of it, placing his hand on her shoulder. He tweaked her to turn around, drawing her to him again. She gazed into his light-colored eyes, smiling and admiring his features.

"Remember my reference to Pandora's Box?"

He nodded to her comment.

"It is of my volition to unveil the mysteries within it."

"No exceptions?" he retorted.

Tamira smiled and arched her neck, kissing him fully on his lips. She also guided his right hand to her left breast, allowing him to knead it softly through the cut of her blouse. She sensed her wetness gathering at the crotch lining of her stockings.

Instinctively, he ventured to grab her ass cheeks, but she stepped back and slid down her skirt. She kicked off her pumps and shed her stockings. He guided her to recline on his king sofa while he knelt before her.

"Keep them apart," he said.

Tamira accommodated Garner with outstretched legs. With careful flicks by his tongue, the living room was soon filed with her most sensual utterances. She arched her back while his tongue made flutters over her moist slit and swollen clit; he was emboldened by her squirming. He relished in her arousal and faint musk. He also found it very much a turn-on that she maintained a hairy pussy. He reasoned that her thick, curly tuft was symbolic of the sacrifices she'd made by her own volition.

Her breathing became rushed. "Oh, I need you tonight, Garner!" Then she composed herself once more, looking down at Garner's head bobbing up and down. "Oooooh, your tongue is hitting all the right spots, baby!"

Those were comments that he wished were coming from Vernise, but Tamira had helped him forget about the missed opportunity. He noticed amid his living room's relative darkness that she brought a soft pillow up to her mouth to muzzle her shrieks.

"Oh, Garner, you're going to make me cum before I know it. Oh, I need it soooo badly!"

Her plain appearance at the bookstore once suggested she needed a good dose of dick, but her stunning appearance that night suggested that she wanted a good dose of dick. After a couple of deep tongue plunges inside her pussy, her breathing quickened, accompanied by her arching her back. She dug her nails into his shoulders, pushing her pussy hard into his face. He noticed this time that her engorged bud was fast deflating as she made loud grunts.

She tried gathering herself. "Whew! You definitely know how to work that tongue of yours!" She motioned for him to come up to her. She then she kissed and licked all the nectar that glistened from his face. They entered into another tongue kiss. Without a word uttered, she helped remove his clothing.

No sooner than his slacks and briefs hit the carpet, she stroked his manhood and offered it her affections with her lips and tongue. That was followed by subtle slurping and gurgling.

For a woman whom he once perceived as having no chemistry and personality, she surprised him once again. He arched his neck and stared at the ceiling, running his hands through her short hairstyle. Then he looked down at the action: her head bobbed back and forth; no other woman he'd ever been involved with sucked his dick like that.

She suggested, "Why don't you lie down for me?" She proceeded to cradle his balls with her left hand and stroke his dick with her right hand. Her tongue trailed up and down his shaft.

"Does that feel good to you?"

He managed a faint smile. "Better than you can imagine. I've been in need of a woman's touch probably just as much as you needed that orgasm."

Tamira beamed and kissed his dick. Then she returned to sucking and licking his balls while stroking his dick harder. He managed to synchronize thrusting his pelvis to the activity. His countenance became one of anxiety.

"You know what's going to happen—"

She paused, making eye contact with him. "What might that be?"

"I don't know if I can take any more."

"Mmmm, yes you can . . . I'll show you why."

Garner studied the silhouette of her body. Her thirty-six C breasts were like perfect crescents; her body was curvaceous despite her narrow hips. He joined her standing up. They engaged in an embrace sensuous enough to be captured in a portrait.

With her body pressed against his, he admired Tamira's features. She then kissed his chest. "I do have something I've wanted to tell you."

He smiled back at her. She said, "I thought you would have noticed that I'm much older than you."

"I did," he answered. "But since you never made it an issue, I decided not to make it one as well."

"I'm glad you didn't." She kissed him again. "However, that was not what I wanted to tell you."

"What was it?"

"My birthday was a couple of days ago. I turned forty-five, and being with you right now is probably the best birthday present I could have imagined for myself."

The smile that he managed in response concealed his mischief. He thought that maybe he was right by avoiding her after their meeting at the bookstore. He was more than convinced that nice guys never got laid in those situations.

Tamira motioned for him to lie down on his back on the carpet. She showed no problem guiding his thick member inside her. Besides, she was too aroused not for it to have happened. Immediately, she worked her hips back and forth atop him while she balanced herself with her hands positioned flat on his stomach.

With each gyration of her hips, she created a rhythm between them that made it all worth his while. She did much of the work just as she did with Sampson Nettles, but without a suspect audience. Garner concentrated on not busting his nut too soon; he noticed she kept her eyes closed, although she shifted her head from side to side.

"I bet you didn't think I had this in me?" she said, biting her bottom lip. "I bet you didn't realize a woman in her mid-forties is still at her sexual peak —"

She hunched forward on him and increased her rate riding his shaft. He reached around her hips and clutched her ass. He marveled at the softness of her skin and the firmness of her body.

Hell, it was just as firm as Sabryan's and she worked out religiously and was ten years younger. He almost made the mistake of divulging that thought.

"I can honestly say that I never—"

She interrupted him. "Had a woman as mature as me?"

She rode his shaft harder; he refused to acknowledge her. She knew exactly what he wanted to say, anyway.

"And as sensual?"

Then she slowed down to grind her pussy into his dick, balancing herself again with her hands on his stomach. She arched her back, affixing her eyes on his ceiling, whispering, "Right there, baby . . . Right there!" Her eyes were shut and her mouth was agape.

Garner ceased his thrusts, allowing her to enjoy her moment. She flinched and shuddered to each wave of orgasm that overcame her.

"You look so sexy, Tamira."

"I feel sexy!"

Tamira got on all fours, looking over her right shoulder. "Is this what you had in mind?"

"It's a start."

With the pressure to delay his ejaculation no longer an issue, he positioned himself behind her, delivering long and smooth strokes while she accommodated him with rhythmic movements from her hips. He motioned her to dip her head down toward the carpet, giving him a better angle inside her.

"Keep it right there."

"Do you like it that way?"

"Uh-huh."

"How about this way?"

Tamira had motioned him to stop while she turned onto her back; however, Garner suggested that they take the action to his bedroom. He carried her down the hallway to the second room on the right. The bedroom was dark, but he knew exactly how many steps it would take before he reached the bed.

There, he placed her gently on the mattress and they resumed their activity. Once they achieved a rhythm, she accommodated his vigorous thrusts by holding her legs outstretched for him. Then she coiled her legs around his waist.

"Give it to me, baby," she coaxed him. "I want all of you."

Two months of infrequent jacking off was about to be forgotten. As he felt his ejaculation nearing, he slowed down his pace to savor the contours of her pussy enveloping his dick. Tamira also sensed his dick stiffening—she clutched his ass, guiding him to the threshold of ecstasy.

His arched his back on his final stroke. "Oh, your pussy's been so sweet to me tonight!" He felt his dick pulsate against her walls; the semen left his body with great intensity.

She cradled his head against her shoulder as his body relaxed. "You might not know it, but that was the one exception that I made tonight with you—"

Then she kissed him and wiped the beads of sweat from his brow. She got up and strode off to his bathroom. When she returned, she had a bath towel wrapped around her and she was headed for the living room.

She queried, "Aren't you going to get ready, too?" The light was left on in his bathroom. She now stood at the doorway to his bedroom. Garner, who was naked and outstretched on his bed, sat up, resting against the palm of his hands.

"You want me to take you back now?"

"You didn't think I would spend the night with you?"

"Not exactly, but since things developed the way they did I thought you wouldn't mind."

Her inference that he took her back to the station seemed so cold. Maybe it was her way of making sense of the moment, he thought. But he was in no mood to be driving back to the station at two in the morning.

Although he got out of his bed, he walked toward Tamira, who still awaited his response. This was really her first opportunity to actually get a good glimpse of his body—a reasonably broad chest and moderately large thighs and average sized calves, yet there was no doubt that he appeared athletic in build. She noticed his dick had not shriveled up but instead dangled rather noticeably.

"Do you really want to drive back to Orangeburg at this time of night?"

"Garner, I'm not a little girl. I can take pretty good care of myself."

He placed his hands on Tamira's waist. He dipped his head to solicit a kiss from her. She accommodated him with a moist, searching effort, causing a familiar response between his legs. He reached under the towel and grasped her ass. He felt a mixture of their bodily fluids seeping down to his fingertips.

He replied, "I'm sure you can. I think you're just concerned whether your car will still be there once you return."

"That's only part of it. This would be considered very spontaneous. I would have rather planned for this. Then I could bring what I needed. I don't have a tooth brush or any of my other stuff."

Garner grasped Tamira's hand; she clutched on to the towel. He led her back over to the bed where he sat down and positioned her before him. "Don't worry about a tooth brush. You've already helped yourself to my soap and towels."

He patted her ass. "So what's wrong? Are you concerned that I might see the real Tamira Lake when the morning sun hits your face?"

That provoked Tamira to a mild dose of hearty laughter. "No, I won't transform into some zombie." She regained her composure. "It's just that a woman likes to be prepared in certain situations. We like to plan things."

"Well, it's not like I planned on sitting naked in front of a lady at two in the morning with thoughts of being inside her once again, either—"

"My, aren't we greedy?"

"No, how about pleasantly satisfied and wanting more of you."

Garner pried the towel from around Tamira's body. He drew her closer and proceeded to suck and nibble on her breasts, alternating from the right to the left and back. Tamira reacted by clutching his head into her bosom; the sensation was too great to resist.

Chapter 14

When the morning sun did pierce its way into Garner's bedroom, he was already awake staring at his white-textured sheetrock ceiling and contemplating his next move. To his right, Tamira appeared to be sleeping rather content. And, no, the sun didn't really tell her age. He ran his hand across his dick and balls. They still felt thick and full, yearning for more.

Garner decided he had nothing to lose. Since Tamira had her back to him, he ventured to enter her from behind. Pussy from that position was just as good as any other, he thought, and he found her slit still silky wet from five hours ago. He made slow, careful thrusts; the sensation of pressing his entire groin area into her ass cheeks made it even more arousing. He reached around and clutched her equally supple breasts.

She reached back and stroked his hip while he pushed his dick deeper. She also responded by pushing her ass against him, moaning. Then she looked over her left shoulder at him. "Is this your idea of saying good morning to me?"

"Not a bad idea, would you agree?"

"Not really—"

Now, she had eased away and sat up. Then she blurted, "I meant that I didn't agree with you."

He found it incredible that she would react that way after what they started.

"What do you mean you're not agreeing with me?"

She was terse with him. "I have other things on my mind right now, and I would appreciate if you would stop."

Garner stared agape. Surely, this must have been her way of joking back into her former zero personality, zero chemistry persona once again.

Shit, he cursed to himself. As soon as he thought about being a nice guy, this is what happened.

They just don't get laid!

"I'm not going to question you why you don't want to do this; you could have at least let me finish what I started," he ranted, shaking his head.

"You never asked me; therefore, I don't see why I'm obligated to accommodate you."

Tamira had now stood up, searching for the towel that she had covered herself when Garner had talked her out of going back to Orangeburg. But that was over near the bedroom door, a good eight feet away. It seemed almost contradictory that Garner, who just minutes ago was admiring her beauty and intelligence, was now cursing at her resisting him.

She left the bathroom door partially open. Instead of following her in there maybe to grope and fondle her as two consenting adults might do, he found himself telling her from a distance that there was a brand new toothbrush in his medicine cabinet and it was still in the wrapper.

"Thank you."

Humph.

Thank you for what? he huffed. He heard the shower water running. He knew there was finality with her statement. He felt she had just taken him on a joy ride. Now he was being kicked to the curb at his own expense. It seemed not fair, but he tried reasoning to himself that at any time a man can get some pussy out of it he was already ahead of the game; it was a bonus if he could get more.

Grudgingly, he got out of the bed still naked. He ventured off into the living room where he gathered her clothing and brought them back into the bedroom. When she emerged from the bathroom, she was covered in another bath towel. Her hair was still relatively intact from the previous night's activity.

"I thought you might appreciate me bringing your clothes in here."

"I do."

Garner took his turn in the bathroom, and he emerged from it minutes later in some dark denim jeans and wearing a plain black and teal t-shirt.

"Would you like to stop for some breakfast on the way back into Columbia?"

Tamira, who entertained herself by watching C-Span, clicked off the television. He offered her his hand. She rebuffed his offer. When she stood up, he attempted to draw her closer to him for a kiss, but she looked away, placing her hand against his chest.

Damn, what did I do?

He opened the door for her. He did not even bother sneaking a glance at her behind. Once inside his car, Tamira looked straight ahead without mincing words. He felt as though he had been reduced to driving back to the station like a cab driver and she was his fare.

They were two exits away from Garners Ferry Road along I-77 southbound after they passed the Forest Drive exit. Garner, attempting to break the tension, noticed that Tamira appeared bored with him.

"May I ask why I'm getting the silent treatment?" He heard her exhale loudly through her nose. She continued looking straight ahead, but had now leaned her head against the headrest.

"I would rather not talk about it right now. I've got some things I need to do today, and I know it's going to consume a lot of my mental energy."

"Is that what this is all about?"

"Not really."

"I'm not a mind reader."

"Garner, I, uh—"

He noticed she was uncomfortable with what she wanted to tell him. He ran his hand through his hair. Then he down shifted into third and then into second before he turned right onto Garners Ferry.

"Never mind," she said.

"Would it be too much to ask you if you had a nice time at all with me?"

"No."

"Well, we're close to the station."

"I noticed. Did you forget that I drove the same route last night?"

Sheesh!

"Look, I apologize if I offended you for this morning."

"You don't need to apologize."

They remained silent the rest of the way. Tamira's car was parked about three-fourths of the way to the rear where most of the employees were from the night before.

He parked his car next to her driver's door. She left without any parting comment or glances. He kept his head tilted downward, gazing at the instrument buttons on his console and punching "1" on his preset station buttons for the sports talk radio.

Then he heard the muffled closing of her door. He waited for her to start her engine before he took off with a slight screech of his tires, which was contrary to the way he left the parking lot just the night before.

Chapter 15

Tamira's sudden one-eighty left Garner befuddled. More than three weeks passed since she went silent on him. He searched within, and he came up with perhaps it was payback for all his negative comments leading up to their date. He supposed things had a way of coming back around and, for all he knew, she could be talking as derisively behind his back.

He suspected Spencer Watts' old ass had double-crossed him. After all, he knew Spencer and Tamira went back a few years, so there was that possibility.

Even if he did talk negatively about Tamira, he tried convincing himself it could not have had any bearing on the night they spent at his place. After all, she was the one who called him unexpectedly wanting to know what he would be doing that weekend.

And his last attempt at more pussy? Humph. He figured that was no big deal since women could be fickle whenever sex was involved. What really did not make any sense to him was why she would be as consenting in the first place?

The way he saw it, what woman would allow a man to ejaculate inside her, in this day and age, unless she had some extremely positive thoughts for him?

Shit, he lamented. *She wouldn't be so crazy to have done that to me?"*

He did not want to entertain the unthinkable, for he had made it to thirty-two without having helped populate the South in spite of his aversion for wearing a condom. Then he tried reasoning maybe she tripped out because she was now forty-five and she couldn't justify telling her lady friends about a man that looked young enough to be mistaken for one of her undergraduates.

Humph. Now that would be a stroke for his ego.

Enough of the bullshit!

All he wanted was some kind of explanation from Tamira and the issue would be settled. If she didn't like him after they fucked, so be it. But she had not afforded him that courtesy.

Some goddamned embodiment of beauty and intelligence, he hissed. The more he thought about Tamira, the more he felt that he could no longer remain quiet.

"Hi, sorry I'm not available. Please leave a message . . ."

"Tamira, this is Garner. If this is your idea of telling me that I was terrible in bed, it's not a problem. But you could at least be woman enough to tell me."

He folded his cell phone and placed on his belt holster. Yeah, at least she knew how he felt about her bitching out on him. Now he could move on.

Work was always a safe haven for Garner whenever women issues got the best of him. The biggest news of the day was disgraced professional football star Michael Vick's sentencing to twenty-three months in federal prison for his involvement in a dog fighting operation that he bankrolled and his participation in the sordid treatment of them.

Between answering phone calls from viewers that wanted to vent their opinions, Garner tried roaming the news wire to dissect and extract bits of information he needed to compose a script for the evening broadcast. He preferred writing his own than regurgitating parts of wire stories before a Teleprompter, as what some lazy anchors do in the business. He also considered using voice messages and e-mails that streamed in during the day as a source for the local reaction to Vick's sentencing. At least he would answer the proximity question of Journalism; it would used during the final forty-five seconds to a minute of the sports segment.

Just as he rubbed his eyes and stretched, the buzzing on his hip holster startled him.

"This is Garner . . ." He hoped maybe Tamira would have had the nerve to call him.

"What's going on?" The familiar deep bass voice resonated into his ear. "I know you've got something to say about my man Vick being locked up for two years!"

"You know I do. So you're not mad at me any more?"

"Why should I be mad at you?"

"Never mind." Garner felt it was good that Spencer showed a short memory, or perhaps he managed to shoot one over the old man's head.

"Look, man, you know those white people had it in for my man!"

"What is your reason for that?"

"They had to make a statement that appeased those damned dog lovers. All of 'em were white, you know. And you know white people look out for each other."

"I don't know about that—"

Spencer was on a roll with his sentiment. "How many times do you see a young black man's face posted on a TV screen for shit they say he did?"

Garner attempted to reason with him. "That's the key word. They say that he did it, and he said he did it."

Spencer huffed with annoyance. "Man, you sound just like all those white people that I ran into today at a board meeting. Every last one of them motherfuckers said Michael Vick got what he deserved. Shit reminded me of back in the day. And I'm like, do you think that judge would have sentenced some white boy for the same length? And do you think those white people would have gone after Michael Vick the same way had he been Michael Vick with blond hair and blue eyes?

"Shiiiit, I should say not!"

Garner, inhaling deeply, tried to remain focused on the conversation. "I've got two questions to ask you about your guy: Why would he even put himself in that situation in the first place? He should have known his ass would be in trouble once his stupid cousin ran off to his house trying to evade police. All he did was direct them to all that evidence."

"See, that's what I'm talkin' about. Okay, so they arrest his dumb ass for some drug charges. But you know white people are going to snoop around looking for shit when they see a nigga in a million dollar home. You know they're going to say why in the fuck is he there in the first place? So they looked around and found all that on my man."

Garner rolled his eyes. "That might be true. But my problem with your man is that nobody around him ever meant him any good. They were all leeches. Classic niggers, if you want my opinion."

"You got some nerve calling somebody a nigger—"

"We don't need to go there; I have every right to call them that."

"All I got to say is that those white people found a way to pull down another black man. That's the kind of shit that bothers me the most. I risked my life back in the day to make life better, and it's the same shit that happened back then. Nobody wanted to see a black man make anything out of himself. Nobody!

"And what make it bad is light, bright, almost white motherfuckers like you helped do it."

Garner closed his eyes in an effort to remain calm. Very deliberately, he said, "Do you think somebody like Jim Brown in his prime would have financed a dog fighting operation like Michael Vick? Sure, we know what Jim Brown has done after his playing days, but he never put himself in that position while he played."

Spencer argued, "Don't bring Jim Brown into this conversation!"

"You don't understand where I'm going. In your day, when you were my age, it was still an era where mainstream America saw the best that blacks had to offer. People like you were among the best we had to offer, and you were fighting for the best for those of us that would come after you.

"Are you with me so far?"

"All right—"

"Are you going to say that Michael Vick—forget about him being an average quarterback and in most cases the fastest player on the football field—is the best that blacks have to offer? Is that what you fought for?" Garner queried.

That moved Spencer to silence. Garner waited for his response. Spencer hissed, "Times are different. These days, you're seen as the best that we have to offer by how much money you have, and how much money that you can make. And a white man still hates to see a black man make more than him!"

Garner adjusted himself in his chair, shaking his head. "I can tell you a thing or two about that. In my case, it wasn't about how much I made. It was the fact I was his goddamned boss and they didn't want to pay me for being his boss!"

"Let's stick to the subject, young buck."

So Garner went on to say, "All right, I've got one more point to make: Michael Vick tried to do wrong the right way, and he had the wrong people around him. It's that simple. He bought a house outside of the city limits. He paid his taxes and he tried keeping a low profile.

"Do you think some white person would have run off to his cousin's place trying to elude the police?

"Do you think that if that were a white athlete would a relative and two of his so-called homies turn on him once the Feds started leaning on them?"

Spencer interrupted Garner. "What in the hell do you know about homies?"

"I told you that I was from Richmond. Check it out. Most years, it's been one of the ten most dangerous cities in America."

"I've heard enough." Spencer dismissed any further discussion on the topic. "That's not the reason why I called you, anyway.

"What are you doing this weekend?"

Garner was glad that Spencer called. At least somebody was thinking of him. Vernise remained a mystery after he left messages on her cell phone and at her home number.

"What do you have going on?"

"Look here . . . I know I didn't ask you this last year because I was still getting to know your almost white ass, but I figure this year I would invite you to a holiday get-together at my place here in Irmo."

Humph, what the fuck, Garner thought. He lowered his voice. "Is there going to be a bunch of old, crazy bastards like you there?"

"Can't have too many of them. Place would be like a goddamned mortuary. Besides, you forget who you're talking to, young buck!"

Garner rolled his eyes. "I haven't forgotten. Somebody that thinks he can still fuck at the scent of pussy from a mile away."

"Shiiiit, don't go tellin' everyone that . . . you know it's still true!"

"Whatever."

Spencer coughed and then cleared his throat. "Say, why don't you call Tamira. See if she might want to come over, too. You know I could call her. But I figure it might help your fuckin' image if you had a woman with you."

Garner laughed with sarcasm, which provoked Spencer to teasing him.

"You know she told me that y'all went out again. She thanked me for introducing her to you."

"Is that right? Let's just say she is a very dynamic lady. I'm sure that some man might find her to be a woman who might 'addeth not any sorrow' to him."

"Didn't I tell you that she was a good woman?"

"Uh, ol' man, I think you missed it."

"Ah, man, I was just fuckin' with you," Spencer said, chuckling. "Hey, shit happens. It doesn't work out some times. I told you she tells me almost everything."

Perviously, Garner mulled whether it would be difficult to show his face around Spencer even if Tamira told him almost everything. But then he decided that he had nothing to be ashamed of especially since the night was not a disaster—at least in his opinion. It all came down to her having a change of attitude.

"Sounds like both of you have a rather close relationship."

"She's like a daughter to me."

"I thought you have a daughter."

"Yeah, and she's married."

Garner nodded. *Yeah, right, the bitch told you everything.* "Well, I don't think I'll be calling your girl any time soon. But I wouldn't mind coming."

"Good, because we're going to have card tables, dominoes tables and whatever else all set up."

Garner entertained a mischievous thought that was perhaps fitting with Spencer. "Aren't you too old to be hosting orgies?"

"Say, young buck, I said whatever else, as in a drink bar." Spencer went on to enunciate each word. "Don't you know that niggas don't do orgies? That's white folks shit. But then I forgot who I'm talking to—"

"Fuck you, ol' man!"

"Fuck you, too!"

"You know something? I'm going to have to teach your old ass a lesson on the dominoes table."

"Bring your almost white ass on! I got something for you."

"Bye, ol' man."

"Later, Negro."

When Garner returned to his condo after the night broadcast, he turned on ESPN for its late-night programming. College basketball was on that channel, and a west coast professional basketball game was on the ESPN2 channel. He flipped through the other channels, but nothing really caught his attention. He checked e-mails from WCAE.

Finally, he checked his voice mail. There were four messages.

"Say, young buck, forgot to tell you that you can stop by the place any time after seven. The address is listed in the phone book under Dr. Spencer F. Watts on Kennerly Thorne Drive."

The second message came from a telemarketer informing him that he could call an 800 number and claim his free trip to Hawaii.

Yeah, right!

The next message brought a smile to his face.

"Garner, darling, this is your mother in Richmond, Virginia. You remember her, don't you? Everyone here is doing fine. Your brother Norris has a new job at Southern Chesapeake Railroad, and your sister Carla is doing fine.

"You remember your nephew Corliss? Carla told me that he had the lead part in his school's Christmas play.

"Let me know if you're coming up here for the holiday. I'll make you a couple of fruitcakes in a long muffin pan just for you . . . call me now!"

He was on his way to the bathroom when the final message played.

"Uh, hi, Garner. This is Vernise Aikens. I'm very sorry for not getting back with you. I've gotten all your messages, but I've not been able to return them because I've been on a case outside the state, and we were not allowed to have contact with anybody that's not family. That's just our policy for security reasons.

"I didn't have a chance to explain anything to you. Call me at your convenience. I'm at home; it's about 10:30 in the evening. Bye!"

Chapter 16

It would have been convenient for Garner to blame Vernise for his inability to sleep after listening to her message. But it didn't help that his dick and balls were sensitive to touch and movement.

Wearing loose clothing like boxer shorts didn't appear to be the answer for overcoming his rush of testosterone. If it were left to him, he would be more than glad to blow a load within five minutes of entering a woman's hot, wet pussy than having to rely on taking matters into his own hand.

Humph.

The mind was supposed to be more powerful than one's hormones. Shit, somebody lied. He tried closing his eyes, thinking about things that would calm him. But what was so calming in his life?

Work?

Hah!

That would only disgust him and he'd never go to sleep. He felt he shouldn't be working his way back up the ladder via some mid-major market like Columbia, which was ranked eighty-first among the top-one hundred television markets.

Spirituality?

That drew a sigh. He'd grown disillusioned with church—a clique of modern-day Pharisees and Sadducees and an unsavory bunch of sanctified schemers and hustlers.

Humph.

For $58.95, according to Dr., Bishop, Apostle and Prophet I. M. Slackfoot, you can unlock the blessings of heaven unto your life. And for a $1,500 offering, you'll receive Bishop Slackfoot's personally autographed book on "How to Owe No Man Anything" and an individual prophesy on CD for your life . . .

On a more personal encounter, he once sought counseling by a pastor at one of the churches he attended in Tallahassee. The first thing the pastor did was refer to a printout that detailed how long he'd been a member and how much he had tithed. It was as if the man was Santa Claus of the Sanctified checking whether or not Garner dutifully contributed to the title-free ownership of the pastor's 6,500 square foot, ten-bedroom home and his sparkling silver Mercedes CL600 Coupe in the parking lot.

So many pastors and ministers had distorted the good news for their personal gain. He was aware how it had been described by one of the writers in the Bible that people needed to be vigilant of "peddlers" of the gospel.

Another place he attended in Houston turned him off even more. Just as he considered in Tallahassee, he approached the pastor about some of his moral struggles in his many female relationships. The pastor broke out with vile of his anointed oil, spoke in tongues, and prophesied to Garner that he had a lust spirit and he needed to cast out the demons that tormented him. When the pastor phoned for one of his assistant pastors and a staff evangelist for assistance, Garner told the man that he appreciated his help and walked out of the office.

"Brother, God is not a man who he be mocked!" the pastor threatened.

The following Sunday, Garner went against his better thinking by attending that same church. The pastor started on one message, speaking on the power of agreement. But when he made eye contact with Garner he changed it, claiming he had to obey God by preaching what God wanted him to preach. The message was a thinly veiled attack on him, serving as a reminder to the church's parishioners why it was so important for them to live holy lives. He warned them that fornicators, adulterers and the like had no part in heaven. "And they had crucified their flesh along with their passions and lust."

Garner never returned to that place.

So, these days, any comfort Garner's derived by spiritual means has been between him and his Maker, and not from any time spent under another man's so-called mentoring.

Family?

That drew a longer sigh.

Garner sat up in his bed Indian style, resting his face between his open palms. He closed his eyes and pondered some of the issues that he's had to make sense of. He felt he had a duty to represent his family as best as he could; he had no feeling either way. For each good thought that he had, there was also one that negated it.

There was, for example, the favored status he had among Miriam's relatives. Specifically among his maternal grandmother's lineage, Garner recalled his grandmother, Ruth Brazelle Wicks, and her kin would boast so much about him looking just like Miriam. They also made such a big deal out of any of his accomplishments.

As a teenager in high school, his great-aunt Doris Brazelle Edmonds, a former schoolteacher, told him before she died that her mother, Eliza Brazelle, and her grandmother, Hattie, were mistresses of white men. That explained why they had such fair-skinned features. She went on to tell him although the family's history traced back to coastal North Carolina, it was akin to the quadroons of Louisiana.

"We didn't like that [Miriam] married that Aaron person," he remembered Doris telling him. His aunt's implication became clearer to him in college when he took a history course from a black perspective.

There, he was introduced to the term mulatto. He learned about some families prided themselves for maintaining their lighter skinned features by marrying those of similar hue not so much for conceit but for socioeconomic benefits. He also recalled that might explain why some of those same relatives never said anything positive about Norris or Carla; his siblings often showed resentment towards him.

That same course enlightened him about resentment and rifts that have existed and have been perpetuated throughout the generations between blacks of lighter and darker hues. That helped him to understand why his father may have spoken so scornfully towards him. It also explained why his some of his classmates ostracized or picked on him so many times.

He reached over and replayed Miriam's message. *"Garner, darling, this is your mother in Richmond, Virginia."* That brought another smile to him. *"You remember me, don't you?"*

How could he not forget her?

She was the one that worked an eight-to-five job at a court reporting firm on Grace Street, three blocks west of the *Richmond Wave* newspaper, and a part-time job at the Ukrop's family grocery store for most of their childhood. To her credit, as he would tell anyone, she was the one who ensured that he and his siblings made it through high school and participate in their respective activities. She also said they would be on their own if they did anything beyond the twelfth grade.

Garner's opportunity to leave Richmond came in the form of a baseball scholarship that was made possible by a friendship between his high school coach, Demario Sutton, and his would-be college coach, Cooper Rawlings. Sutton and Rawlings were teammates in the Atlanta minor-league farm system. Although he had first and second cousins among the Brazelles that went off to college and graduated, he was the only one among his siblings who had accomplished it.

He reflected on Miriam being the one who interceded on his behalf whenever Aaron entered into one of his drunken rages. She was the one who dared Aaron to kill her whenever he decided he wanted to whip Garner unmercifully with one of his leather belts. He came to realize most parents loved their children, even having a favorite. Garner was the apple of Miriam's eye.

While ironing her clothes for the week on Sunday nights, Miriam told him how she often prayed for him. "Your brother and sister, they'll be all right. But you . . ."

"Why do you say that mom?" a young Garner would ask her.

He recalled Miriam would become quiet. Sometimes she would excuse herself and go to the bathroom, wiping away the tears. She never told him about her giving birth to him was both a joyous and sad moment for her.

Other times, Miriam would smile and look lovingly towards Garner. There would be a gleam in her green eyes. Those were the times that she referred to him as her "little boy."

She would say, "Every parent wants to have at least one of their children to make it. And you're going to be that one. I don't expect anything less from you. That's why I stay on you the way I do, little boy."

Garner then asked, "Why do you keep calling me little boy when I'm not a little boy any more?"

"Because no matter how old you get, you'll always be my little boy!"

Relationships?

There was something about a woman's voice and her touch that made for a soothing effect for him. That's because the opposite sex comprised the only friends he knew during his early adult years. He didn't learn until he attended college in Tallahassee that women found him attractive. Paige Leonard, a buxom girl of pecan tan hue from Pensacola, Florida was the first to call him cute and introduced him to what pussy really felt like.

He let out a deep sigh reminiscing about Paige. He often went to class wearing passion marks that lined his neck from her succulent brown lips and bright teeth, making him also the ridicule of his baseball teammates.

Ah, but that pussy of hers. That shapely ass. Those titties and the first time she encouraged him to fuck between them . . .

Fuck it!

Garner slipped his dick through the fly of his black boxers and admired it. Contrary to the mockery he withstood during his time in Richmond, he knew it had been a source of pleasure for several women, including Tamira's. He reminisced about her being in the same bed with him, having no problem taking his length and thickness, while riding it as if it was her favorite attraction at an amusement park.

He stroked his dick to three-quarter thickness. He recalled that she looked so damned sensual. As he slid his boxers farther down his thighs, he savored the memory of her walls caressing his dick. With her eyes closed and head shifting from right to left and back again, she looked so stately and confident. He felt he should have discovered older women sooner.

There was some baby oil in the nightstand drawer off to his right. He squirted some on his dick; it was still nothing like the wetness that flow when a woman's fully aroused.

"Ah, shit!" Garner whispered loudly. He now reminisced about a memorable occasion he had with Kadrece. They were so damned spontaneous. He recalled the afternoon he took her to the airport for a job interview in Atlanta. They parked on the second level of the tri-level parking garage. As he helped her out the car, she strategically allowed her skirt to hike upward, exposing her black thong between her flowing slit.

Garner stroked himself with urgency, remembering vividly how she gave him a tug on his crotch and he immediately sprung to attention.

She was so damned seductive whenever she spoke to him in those moments. "I'm going to be gone for a couple of days and I won't have anything to put into my oven."

Kadrece walked to the back of his old burgundy Monte Carlo. She bent over against the rear spoiler and trunk, inviting him to fuck her in broad daylight. Garner remembered how his dick slipped between her luscious chocolate cheeks and dark mocha lips like a hot knife through butter.

As her ass jiggled to his thrusts, Kadrece simultaneously teased her clit until it throbbed. Sensing her bud had swollen to the brink of explosion, she braced herself against his tight, athletic body for the pending torrent of bliss that would soon hit ashore.

She exhorted, "Oh, baby, give me all that sweet red dick of yours! I want to taste you all the way to Atlanta, goddamn it!"

Garner felt his dick expand inside her. Prolonging the moment, she turned around and knelt before him, applying her warm lips and tongue to his flesh to lick and suck off their mixture of her nectar and his pre-cum. Then she arose, leaned against his car, and guided him back inside her. She bent her knees and pushed her ass harder against him demanding that he slapped her ass cheeks.

Just as he held on to that mental image of her turning around to engulf his dick, he also released heavy spurts on his hand, thigh, and stomach. He remembered Kadrece relaxed her throat and made deep gulping and gurgling sounds to accommodate him. She was a receptacle to every drop that easily met her expectation.

While looking up at him, he remembered her sucking his flaccid shaft clean and licking and kissing his balls before she stood up and straightened her clothing.

Whew, I really need that one . . .

Chapter 17

It bothered Garner why Tamira still had not called him. *Oh, well. Maybe Spencer was right about one thing: Shit happens.*

He leaned back in his office chair and pondered, but was interrupted by the phone ringing.

"WCAE, this is Garner—"

"Hi, Garner, this is Vernise Aikens. I hope this will be the last time I have to mention my last name when I call you."

"That's entirely up to you."

"Why are you tripping?"

"I'm not. You said you hope it would be the last time that you needed to mention your last name when identifying yourself on the phone."

"Anyway—"

"Yeah, isn't this how we met?"

"Not exactly, but yes," she answered. "I called you again today because I really felt bad not being able to explain to you what had happened."

Having already rolled his eyes up towards the ceiling, Garner reared further back in his office chair and placed his heels on his desk. He figured he could use a light moment in the midst of a busy day.

"Hello?"

"I'm still here," he assured her. "I just happened to be finishing up part of my script for this evening's broadcast. This Mitchell investigation should get a lot of play over the next several days. Like I usually do, I try to bring a story like this home to the viewers, although this has very little impact here in South Carolina."

"I can tell you that are people in some very influential places that would like to enhance their reputations by using that report," she said.

"Is that something you'd be willing to go on record to tell me?"

"I wouldn't risk my career for that."

"This could be off the record . . ."

"Don't kid yourself."

"I'm not going to make this a debate, but I don't see much to this Mitchell investigation. He went on a lot of hearsay and questionable sources to name some players. And with some players, sure, some of the stuff had been corroborated by cancelled checks, invoices and paid receipts. But come on!

"I know for a fact that a lot of the guys that probably used stuff like HGH used it only because they believed they would recover faster from injuries. I know from my playing days that there are some injuries that only time can heal, and drugs of any kind just won't help. The sad thing about it is that for many of these guys they're already seen as guilty without a chance yet to clear their name."

"I'll say it again," she interrupted him. "Watch out. You might see this information being recycled somewhere down the road. Remember, I'm an investigator."

Humph.

Despite not hearing her voice in more than a month, Garner recognized how easily they interacted. It was as though they resumed a conversation they started from earlier in the day. That rapport was one of the reasons why he found it difficult to depart from her presence at the mall.

He volunteered, "I noticed you had left a message last night, but I returned at a late hour, like after 12:30 in the morning."

"You should have called because I was still up."

"Are you a night owl?"

"Sort of. Only when I have a lot on my mind."

"Oh, I can only imagine."

Vernise refused to allow her mind to slip into that trap. She had only her friend, an eight-inch battery operated plastic black dick that hummed sweet melodies to her dripping pussy and pulsating clit during her many times of need.

"Well, since I was the one that pretty much ruined things last time, I'd like to make it up to you by inviting you over for dinner," she said. "Would seven o'clock work for you?"

Garner inhaled deeply through his mouth, allowing his chest to expand. He exhaled slowly for added drama to the conversation. He explained that he never left the station following the six o'clock broadcast until 6:45 p.m.

She proposed, "How about 7:30? Are you afraid that I can't cook and I'll just order pizza?"

"Not really. I was just thinking whether the logistics would work. Usually, I'll just go across the street, get something, and then come back to the station until the night broadcast. Some times I'll go back to my place, but then I'll return to the station between 10 and 10:15 p.m."

Vernise smacked her lips into the phone. "You're making it tough on yourself; I don't give up so easy."

Garner knew using his work schedule was an easy excuse for being inflexible; it never stopped him when he was in Houston or Talla-hassee if he really wanted to spend time with a woman between the evening broadcasts.

"So, what is your idea of not ordering pizza?"

"What would you like?" she queried.

"You know, I've been very slack lately cooking for myself . . . I'll tell what," he said. "Just make sure whatever you fix does not have mushrooms, zucchini, eggplant, spinach, or squash in it."

He paused and pondered his other preferences. "Also, make sure if you're preparing any red meat that it's well done. And, um, I don't eat sushi, squid, shark, deer, rabbit, and 'possum . . . the usual nasty stuff."

Vernise rolled her eyes and shook her head. She then playfully replied, *"Ya-t-il autre chose vous voudriez inclure sur votre liste, monsieur?"*

"Huh?"

"Is there anything else you'd like to include on your list, sir?"

"Uh, no—""So I can expect you over here around 7:30?"

"Mmmm, yeah."

"Great. I'll be wearing bells! *A bientôt!*"

Chapter 18

It was 2:45 p.m. when Vernise called Garner. She left work two hours later to get a jump on the rush-hour madness along Fernandina Road back out to Piney Grove Road. She sped past cars using the left lane on Piney Grove, jockeying her metallic silver Volvo S80 into position to make the right-turn signal at Bower Parkway.

On Bower Parkway, she stopped off at Publix, where she successfully navigated her way past the senior citizens shuffling at a snail's pace in the aisles. She also endured and tolerated Soccer Mom Jenny and her unruly bunch at the checkout counter. Then it was a mad dash on Bower Parkway back to the freeway where she bobbed and weaved through traffic on I-26 eastbound and subsequently I-20 westbound until she exited on Augusta Highway.

Heading northbound on Augusta Highway, she drove well above the posted fifty-mile-per-hour speed limit for the next two miles until she reached Kittywake Road. She turned right and took the winding road into her neighborhood. She turned into her driveway just before 5:45, enabling her to sneak in a fifteen-minute power nap.

Beyond the work required for preparing dinner, emptying a small wastebasket in her bathroom was the most energy Vernise expended. She kept an immaculate house and she was meticulous about where she placed everything.

In each bedroom, the beds were decorated with large turquoise colored comforters and pillows that were neatly arranged against the headboards. Beneath them, the black bed sheets were tucked so uniformly that they could pass the military test of bouncing a nickel on them. And in the master bedroom where she slept, there was not a single item of clothing that could be found on the floor or any piece of furniture.

All her dresses, slacks, blouses, and pantsuits were on hangers in the walk-through closet. She had a shoe rack for the shoes she wore the most. All her evening shoes were kept in the box that she purchased them, and they were arranged on a shelf where the box's side with the shoe size and color were facing her.

In her kitchen area, all the dishes, cooking pots, pans and skillets were arranged in the cabinets according to its usage, pattern, and size. Her storage closet had items like paper towels, plastic wraps, and canned goods neatly arranged and grouped. Her spices were stored on three spice racks.

The same order could be said about her refrigerator. There were no unwrapped food items. They were either stored in a plastic container or neatly wrapped in aluminum foil. The fruit was stored in the fruit bin. Vegetables were stored in the vegetables bin. Sandwich meats were stored in its proper place. Eggs were placed in the egg rack. The margarine and butter were stored in its proper bin. The freezer was not overstuffed with many miscellaneous items.

About ten minutes past six, Vernise removed her light beige business suit and slacks, bra and panties. She slipped into a white and light blue runner's jersey and matching trunks. As she began working in the kitchen, she clicked on her twenty-seven-inch television set to WCAE so she could catch a glimpse of Garner while gauging how much time she had before his arrival.

While sautéing the chicken in canola oil, Vernise reflected on how she would have never become aware of Garner had it not been for her over-hearing a white colleague of hers, Fred Braxton, an ardent Bengals fan, going through one of his usual diatribes of antagonizing and mocking several office colleagues that were Chanticleers fans like her.

"Looks like y'all will be singing 'I'll Be Home for Christmas' yet another year." She remembered Braxton erupting into a belly-grabbing laugh. "Yeah, this will be our, what, thirty-second bowl game appearance. And how many have you guys gone to and won? I think I can count them on one hand, heh-heh-heh—"

Vernise interrupted Braxton. "You know what? It must be true about you Bengals guys. Somebody told me that if you ask a Bengals' fan what two and two is, they'll tell you it's third-and-six. Humph! Not too bright, my friend."

"Well, this much I can count: we've won, what, nine out of the last ten games we've played against you losers—that's nine against one." Braxton held up his left index finger for emphasis. "And you're coming to our place? Humph! Can you spell *dom-in-ation*?"

Braxton smirked again at Vernise. He then sought out Britt Hopkins, his lone Bengals ally in the office, where he attempted to talk under his breath about the Chanticleers. The conversation was not soft enough. Vernise overheard Braxton ranting to Hopkins.

"A friend of mine told me a while back that WCAE had hired some nigger as its sports director, more power to him. But now this nigger is attempting to smear a credible institution of higher learning by accusing it of being no more than a bunch of good ol' boys, and now it needs to hire a black football coach," he said.

"*Jeeesus* fucking Christ! Nobody owes these niggers anything!"

Vernise remained silent. But his comment piqued her curiosity to watch WCAE at least once to find out for herself why Braxton became so annoyed. She liked what she viewed of Garner. Taking advantage of the many databases at her disposal, she felt compelled to conduct more research on Garner, which yielded evidence that he was most importantly single.

As she warmed up the barbecue sauce glaze on the stove, she reminisced how nervous she was the day she decided to contact him at the station. Her heart had not beat that fast and strong since she took part in a 2004 assignment involving an unpublicized shootout between colleagues in her unit and a group of drug dealers that barricaded themselves at an Edisto Beach timeshare, resulting in a one death and eight arrests.

For all her matter-of-fact exterior and demeanor that commanded intense loyalty and respect among her colleagues at work, Vernise privately longed for a man in her life to provide her a sense of completeness. At age forty-two, she felt she could take certain calculated risks like the way she had approached Garner.

The sports segment came on at 6:23; she had already completed the pasta side dish. She substituted the zucchini and squash with thinly sliced cucumber and finely chopped green peppers, adding among other things oregano, Italian dressing and sliced cherry tomatoes. She took a seat at her kitchen table and viewed him with great adulation.

"... *The Mitchell Report was supposed to shed light on one of baseball's sore spots with its slow response to action addressing performance enhancing drug culture that pervaded the sport during the entire decade of the 1990s through 2006,*" he said. "*The reaction to it has been mixed, albeit several big names were mentioned ...*"

Garner's on-air presence and his voice actually aroused Vernise. Her erect nipples and pulsating clit reminded her how long it had been since she had a man's tongue providing stimulation to her body along with his throbbing dick making sweet conversation and melody between her pussy lips.

With eyes closed and fantasizing that Garner indulged in some pillow talk with her in French, the native language of her mother, Thèrese, Vernise ran her hand across her right breast and gave her nipple a slight tweak before slowly trailing her hand down across her stomach, then resting it between her thighs. She rubbed her clit through the thin fabric while she started rotating her hips. She visualized him kneeling before her parted thighs, which rested on his shoulders.

Right there, baby. Lick me right there!

Vernise had a large, sweet and sticky collection of her nectar bleeding through her runner's trunks. She grimaced that she didn't bring her friend into the kitchen area. So she licked her fingers clean, resolving that she would address that matter. She still had the dessert to prepare.

For the sweet potato soufflé, she mixed in her nutmeg, cinnamon, butter, brown sugar, an egg and milk and placed it into a Pyrex dish. She also sprinkled on a crushed pecan topping before placing it into the oven at three hundred and twenty-five degrees for about thirty-five minutes. Then, referring to a family croissant recipe made from scratch, she also placed the dozen or so pastries onto a cookie sheet for the same amount of baking time. She also prepared a lemon-strawberry glaze topping for the croissants.

She glanced at the clock situated above her kitchen door from the dining. Realizing it was 6:55 p.m., she sprinted off to the bathroom to freshen up. She also brought her oven alarm clock as a reminder.

Lathering her hands with a bar of scented cucumber-aloe vera that came directly from France, she massaged it into her thirty-eight C breasts in a circular motion. She stopped to pinch and roll her nipples. Her knees buckled at the sensation. Satisfied that her nipples were at attention, she turned her back to the water allowing its intensity to massage into her back muscles.

After rinsing off her upper body, she supported herself with her right hand against her standalone shower tile and massaged lather onto her pubic mound. She then addressed her pulsating clit's cry for relief with quick circular motions with her left hand until her inner walls finally relaxed from its contractions.

She gasped, *"Oh, merde! Cela se sent bien ainsi!"* She repeated it in English. "Oh, shit! That feels so good!"

As she collected herself, she applied soap directly to her left hand and braced herself against the shower tile with her right hand. Having saved her favorite for last, she inserted her middle finger into her asshole. She closed her eyes and fantasized that she stood over Garner's his face. Then squatting down on it, while his tongue roamed her puckered region, she also imagined imploring him to tongue fuck her asshole.

Finally, after sensing another build up of wetness between her thighs, she faced the shower head. She then massaged her clit with the steady stream of water until she squealed and shuddered additional obscenities.

The oven alarm clock went off just as she composed herself. She toweled off and pranced via a walk-in closet that led directly into her master bedroom. She sprayed some Obsession fragrance onto her neck, breasts, and stomach and slipped into a light blue flower print blouse and matching Capris.

She sprinted back into the kitchen, saving her soufflé and croissants from an unwanted fate.

Chapter 19

The doorbell rang shortly after 7:30 p.m. Vernise, a stickler for punctuality, allowed for Garner's transgression because it was his first time visiting her. But it did not stop her from pacing the kitchen area during what she felt was anxious moments. Her penchant for order, detail and execution of strategy had been ingrained into her since childhood. Her father, Vernon Dancy, allowed few excuses when something had not reached an acceptable, logical conclusion.

Garner said, "I would have been here a few minutes earlier, but I stopped off at the store to bring this with me."

Vernise thought Garner looked even better than she already fantasized about him. She opened the door wider, allowing him to walk past her. "I'll take your jacket."

Shifting the wine bottle from one hand to the other as he removed his brown Perry Ellis jacket, Garner inhaled the aroma coming from her kitchen. "Whatever you have smells good!"

She looked him over. "I thought you were talking about my new fragrance."

Garner tilted his head to his left. "I was talking about back there."

Vernise motioned for the wine bottle while leading Garner to the kitchen area. She offered him a seat in one of the designer metal-framed chairs at the glass table.

Although he hailed from Richmond, Garner felt he'd been adequately exposed to multicultural settings during his stints in Florida and Texas. He mentioned that he had a college teammate who was of Cuban descent, and he played dominoes with students from Jamaica. He also noted to Vernise that he took two semesters of Spanish in both high school and college, although he used very little of it.

Vernise was quick to recognize where Garner was headed. She volunteered about her heritage. And when she joined him at the table, sitting to his right, she added, "When I was growing up my mother taught us how to cook and made all of us talk to her in French."

"I tried that with my children, but they didn't care to learn neither. I think a lot of that has to do with them living with their father."

Garner had already had made a mental note from the last time he asked Vernise about her children. He changed subjects before she did it.

"I want to thank you for inviting me over to your place. I guess you've answered the question of your place or mine—you do remember that?"

"Oh, I was wondering if you had forgotten."

Garner scanned the kitchen area. He gazed up at her cathedral ceiling and the three window panes that were at least fifteen feet above where they sat.

Meanwhile, Vernise reared back in her chair crossing her left leg over her right thigh. She ran her left hand through her hair, making sure that it trailed to the back. She had not taken it out of the bun that she wore for work. "This is a little out of character for me cooking like this on a weeknight. I usually wait until the weekend when I'm off."

"I'm flattered that you would go through such an effort for me."

Vernise waved off Garner. She was not one for taking too many compliments. She detested professional ass kissers on her job—a product of Maj. Dancy's influence that taught her to be wary of people who were quick to offer too many compliments too soon.

She announced, "For dinner, I prepared sautéed chicken breast with peach barbecue glaze, a pasta dish, sweet potato soufflé; and for dessert a family favorite of mine, croissants with a lemon-strawberry glaze, shaved almonds and powdered sugar on top. It's really simple stuff to make. It didn't take long."

Garner still was impressed. First, he never heard of sautéed chicken breast and peach barbecue glaze. And while he understood pasta what was, he never had fancy croissants.

"All of that sounds good to me. One day you've got to give me your recipe." He cleared his throat, nodding at her. "I have you to know that I can cook a little bit."

"Is that right?"

"Actually, growing up, we had no choice. Our mom worked a full-time job and a part-time job. On weekends, she would show us how to fix certain meals for during the week," he said. "It was my sister's job to cook for us. I'd still like to think I was the one who probably learned the most from my mom."

"Interesting . . . Well, there were four of us, two boys and two girls. My mom was definitely the cook. I guess you would expect that given that she was French. My dad was great at barbecuing. He's from Kansas City."

Garner barely nodded his head. He related to Vernise about his experience with some great barbecue while he was in Houston. Meanwhile, she arose from the table and went over to the stove to prepare his plate.

"Yes, they say Texas barbecue is good. But if you ever watch the Food Channel, I saw a show that sampled barbecue from Texas, Memphis, Kansas City and Virginia, slash, North Carolina. Fourth place was Virginia and North Carolina; third place went to Memphis; second was Texas; in first place was Kansas City."

This was his first opportunity to check out Vernise from a great vantage point. Her light-colored Capris made for a delectable sight just as she had described the croissant pastry to him. He noticed there was no excessive jiggling and rumpling by her ass cheeks. He also paid special attention to her toned calves. She also walked with a bit of an athlete's swagger coupled with a diva's sophistication.

When she turned around with his plate, he recognized for the first time her cleavage along with some subtle jiggling of her breasts beneath her blouse. Garner was not sure whether it was the food that had caused his mouth to salivate or her body.

The phone rang, provoking her to react with some annoyance. She excused herself, clicking on a cordless phone next to the refrigerator. He recognized she held a rushed conversation in French, pacing the kitchen floor.

"Maman, j'ai quelqu'un ici avec moi. Oui, c'est un gars. Puis-je me vous téléphonez plus tard?"

There was a lengthy pause. Then she spoke again.

"Où est papa? Devrait avoir su. Au revoir."

Garner picked up that Vernise's mother called her, and she might have inquired about her father. He also figured out that she might have told her mother good-bye before hanging up. The rest, well, he hoped that maybe she would volunteer giving him the gist of the conversation.

Vernise went back towards the stove and prepared herself a plate. She walked slowly back to the table appearing sheepish.

"Désolé de cela. Oops!" She caught herself, smiling. "I forgot. That happens to me sometimes after I talk to my mother."

"That you're still thinking in French?"

"Oui. Just like that."

"So, how does your father deal with the multi-lingual stuff?"

"He doesn't. He just ignores my mom whenever she gets mad at him and she's cursing at him in French. They're actually a great couple."

Vernise began cutting into her chicken with her fork. But just as she brought a chunk smothered with the peach glaze up to her mouth, she cracked a smile reminiscent of when he first met her in front of Belk's. In fact, she had to put down her fork so that she could get out the deep laughter she could not contain.

"You know how funny my parents are? Once, when my mom was upset about something my brother, Robaire, had done. She went to my dad in a tizzy and ranting to him in French. He figured out that she wasn't cursing at him, but she was pointing at my brother. I was in the room when all this happened.

"Do you remember the episode from *Sanford and Son* when the white cop tried asking Fred and Lamont some questions about a robbery they reported?"

"I think I do—"

"Well, Fred and Lamont looked at themselves. Then they looked at the black cop, Smitty, who translated to them in jive asking had they been ripped off. Then they responded." Garner had now recalled the episode, joining her in the laughter.

She continued, "My dad looked at my mom. Then looked at me and I had to translate to him what she was yelling to him in French. Then he answered her . . . I told you they were great!"

Garner did his best not to show any melancholy for his family, for there was no way he could ever consider his parents being great. There were too many fights and drunken binges to remember that left his mother bitterly sobbing or his siblings nursing injuries that Aaron had inflicted on them.

The only great thing worth remembering was his mother's resolve to make life better for herself and her children.

"You said you lived in California. Did you have any problems with other kids because of your parents?"

"Not really. I think that maybe some of it had to do where I lived. I went to high school in Chatsworth, in the San Fernando Valley, in fact. Lots of rich kids live there. We were probably on the poor end compared to many of the ones I got to know. We actually live in Northridge, which is right next to it."

"How did you end up living there?"

"My dad got a sweet Defense Department job after retiring from the Army. Oh, I forgot to tell you, I'm the youngest in my family. I'm also a daddy's girl."

Rich kids? Humph. The only ones Garner recalled that ever had any money were the ones that stole money from the other kids. And as he reached his teen-age years, those that had the largest bankrolls were into selling drugs and other criminal enterprises.

Nonetheless, Garner felt even more drawn to Vernise. He also recognized Vernise's body movements and language hinted the same thing. He mused to himself that at any time if Vernise wanted to strip naked before him he would not offer any objections.

His sudden silence piqued her curiosity. "What's on your mind?"

"I've not had this much fun with somebody in a long time."

"I'm having a lot of fun, too. Would you like dessert now?" Garner smiled, looking rather devious in her direction.

"Croissants, that is."

"Oh yeah, croissants; I'll try a couple."

"*D'accord.*"

Vernise did not divulge to Garner the other reasons why she spoke in French: When she's attracted to a man and she's thinking of fucking him. Also, a favorite explanation of hers is that French is the universal language of love and sex.

Although Nilam Armstead had been the last man in her life, she had already spoken about as much French around Garner as she had done the entire time she and Nilam were an item. When she returned, she presented him two warm pastries on a saucer and another dinner fork wrapped in a napkin.

Meanwhile, her pussy had made telepathy to her the only thing that could taste as sweet as the dessert was either her pussy or a man's cum flowing down her throat.

Garner took a bite and with eyes closed, he slowly shook his head, expressing obvious pleasure. He could barely ignore the erection that strained for freedom inside his slacks.

"Do you like it?"

"That's an understatement. I bet you've had a few men to propose to you after cooking just one meal to them."

"Not exactly, but I've had a few to propose to me."

"I'm sure you've had more than a just few propositions in your time, and it wasn't for marriage."

She rephrased the question. "You mean, umm, for sex? Like in *voulez-vous couchez avec moi?* Please sleep with me tonight?"

He nodded his head, still chewing. Vernise chortled at the question. "Do you want to know what the latest one guy asked me? Pardon my French, *Je veux faire quelque chose de bizarre pour vous.*"

Garner told Vernise he recognized the word bizarre, but that was it. She translated it to him meaning a man recently told her that he wanted to do something freaky to her, explaining the word bizarre had the same connotation as freaky.

"Quite honestly, I could see why he would want to ask something like that with you." He always figured the topic of sex eventually would surface in a conversation with a woman, if there was any mutual interest or attraction.

Vernise reacted with some surprise. "Is that right? Is that only way you see me right now?"

"Uh, well, no. That's not what I meant." He cleared his throat.

"Then what is it you meant?"

"Look, you're very, very, very attractive. It's not like I really need to remind you of that. All I meant to say was . . . oh, forget it . . ."

Vernise made a self-satisfied gesture with her head. Then she leaned back into her chair, she folded her arms conveying a message of being in control while Garner, sensing there may be some tension between them, searched for an avenue to save face.

Drawing once again on his reporter instincts, Garner lured Vernise into talking about herself. "Didn't you tell me at the mall that you played tennis in college?"

She waved him off. "That was another life."

"Well, baseball was another life for me. But I can't escape that I did play baseball."

Tennis was Vernise's first love. She started playing at age nine when her family had settled in Chatsworth, practicing against boys. She played in her first tournament at age eleven. By the time she was twelve she became as competitive with kids who played twice as long as she.

She was an All-Valley performer when she reached high school. But she made her biggest gains between her tenth and eleventh grade years. She dominated her competition, advancing to the state tournament. She lost in a third-set tiebreaker in the championship match to a girl who went on to become a collegiate All-America and a regular on the professional tour. As a high school senior, she returned to the state championship match, winning in straight sets.

"Hold on, I'll show you how much I played tennis." After several minutes, Vernise returned from her bedroom with a large scrapbook that was full of medals, ribbons, newspaper clippings, awards certificates and her national letter of intent to the California State University campus in Carson, a suburb of Los Angeles.

As she flipped through the pages for him, Garner noticed a *Los Angeles Press-Examiner* headline DANCY CRUISES TO STATE 4-A TITLE that was dated in 1982. Being the knowledgeable sports person that he was, he asked Vernise if she competed against the likes of Lori McNeil and Zina Garrison. They were the standard for black female tennis players during the 1980s, and prior to the emergence of Venus and Serena Williams and Chanda Rubin in the late 1990s.

"I wasn't as good as Lori and Zina, but I wasn't that far away."

"I hope you don't take this the wrong way, but what kept you from getting there?"

Vernise became crestfallen. "Remember I told you that I had a shoulder injury? She slammed shut her scrapbook.

"I never understood why something that I loved so much was taken away from me. I never thought that was fair." She made wild hand gestures. "I practiced hard. I played hard. I made third team All-America after my junior year and then, *poof!*

"Gone!"

"What happened?"

"One day I woke up and my shoulder felt like somebody had stuck a butcher's knife through it. Doctors told me that I had a torn labrum and a torn rotator cuff, which was almost unheard of for a tennis player. Usually, it's an elbow, knee, or back. But I blew out my shoulder. I missed my entire senior year of college, and I was red shirted. I tried coming back; it just wasn't there. I lost confidence in my game."

Garner noticed Vernise's upper lip quivered and her eyes welled with tears. "You know what? You're the first man who ever asked me anything about tennis, and he actually knew what in the hell he was talking about."

He asked, "Have you tried teaching your son or daughter tennis?"

Vernise used her napkin to dab away a tear that escaped down her cheek.

"It's kind of hard because of the arrangements I have with their father, and with my career. My son is into football. He's a defensive back. My daughter tried track, but she realized she was not that good at it. She's now a cheerleader."

Their conversation had reached a lull. Both of them seemed to wander off into their own world, contemplating and staring off at a distance. Garner was the first to break the inactivity. He cast his eyes intently upon Vernise, studying her facial features and mannerisms.

She was quick to catch on. "You really must like what you see, don't you?"

"And what if I say that I do?"

"Then you have good taste."

"That means you also have good taste."

Vernise noticed on the far wall it was about 9:25 p.m. She was impressed by how fast the time had passed. On most nights, she would be sitting on her bed with the television on in the background going over paperwork from the day. By eleven o'clock, the television would be watching her.

"Didn't you say you normally get back to the station around ten o'clock. You have thirty-five minutes."

Garner slowly extended his arms and legs and stretched. He then resumed sitting upright in the chair, folding his arms across his chest. He stared briefly at Vernise.

"I'm feeling the same way I did at the mall right now," he said, smiling at her.

"That could be anything." Vernise reared back in her chair, crossing her left leg over her right thigh. She ran her tongue across her top lip, angling her head.

"You're right, but I know exactly what I'm feeling right now."

Vernise began entertaining thoughts in French. Inwardly, she wanted to tell him the English translation: *"Garner, I would take off your clothes . . . Have you to lie down . . . I would start off by kissing your neck, your chest . . . your stomach. Then I would take your dick in my mouth, suck it for a while, and then I would suck and lick your balls until you beg me to stop."*

"Is it something that I could quote?"

"I don't know."

"I guess I better get back to the station, but I really don't want to go."

He stood up rather quickly, hoping that Vernise did not catch the bulge in his brown slacks. He mentioned, "I thought we made quite an attractive couple in the mall."

Vernise also stood up, admiring Garner's solid physique. His chest appeared larger beneath his white, long-sleeved business shirt lined down the middle with a light-colored silk tie. "I'm pretty sure we did. Didn't you hear me say that you have good taste in women?"

They both laughed at her inference. She led him to the living room. They stopped at the door. Garner wasted little time making his move, reaching out to Vernise and drawing her into his body. She made no resistance. She closed her eyes, allowing her senses to be swept away by his Truth by Calvin Klein cologne.

As Garner tilted his head downward and pressed his lips against hers, Vernise's pussy and clit reminded her once again what she missed. It didn't help when Garner slipped his tongue between her parted pink lips. She wrapped her arms around his neck, pressing her breasts harder into his chest. She felt his heart pounding through his shirt; hers was doing the same thing through her blouse. He slid his hands along her backside and into to her loose-fitting Capris. He squeezed her ass cheeks.

"Your place or mine?" he quizzed her.

"I want to say mine, but you won't be able to finish what you've started tonight."

"Damn!"

"Ditto."

Garner searched for a reason to keep the moment going; he had none. Vernise reached to her right for his jacket.

"Are you doing anything this weekend?" He inserted his right arm into his jacket sleeve, then the left.

She replied, "I don't know. I hadn't gotten that far into the week to consider."

"Well, I've been invited to a holiday get-together Saturday night at friend's home in Irmo. He's going to have a bunch of other people there, and I'd like if you would come with me."

"Can I get back with you on that? I just don't want to commit to something and I'm not able to keep it."

Garner kissed Vernise on her cheek. She opened the door partially for him. Before he walked out, he turned around for another handful of her ass and a deep, searching kiss. He felt the sudden heat wave emitting from her body.

She warned, "You better get going, or you might be going to back to work wearing just shreds."

"Maybe next time I'll let you do that."

"Yeah, maybe next time."

Vernise watched Garner walk to his car parked in the driveway. Just before he disappeared into it, he smiled and waved. She brought her thumb and pinky to her face.

When Garner left the station that night, he noticed a small, beige greeting card envelope placed under the driver's side windshield wiper.

The message simply read,

I was thinking of you and I miss you.

Chapter 20

Two days later

Garner planned to catch up on several items on his to-do list. He was a procrastinator and, like most men, he was a last-minute holiday shopper. He prided himself on being able to walk into any store and get exactly what he wanted with few exceptions.

The first item that he checked off was Norris and nephews De'Lonzo, Ne'quan, and Tre'vandre. Utilizing his media contacts, Garner purchased luxury suite tickets to three 2008 Richmond minor-league baseball home games of their choice at The Diamond. Out of courtesy, he also purchased a Macy's gift certificate for Shalinda, his brother's live-in and mother of his nephews. He felt she personified the "H" in hoochie with her ghetto mannerisms, weave extensions, and tight-fitting clothes that allowed for her stomach and ass to bulge everywhere.

The next item Garner planned to check off was shopping in the Village at Sandhill in northeast Columiba by roaming for gifts for Miriam, Carla, and Corliss. If that did not work, he would then trek along Two Notch Road, where many of the area's chain stores like Kohl's, Target, and Walmart were located. And if worst came to worst, he was willing to drive across town over to the Columbiana

Mall and its neighboring stores.

That phase of planning was scrapped once he encountered the bumper-to-bumper traffic filing into the Village at Sandhill. The only place Garner made any transaction was at a Bank of America farther down on Two Notch Road to purchase a Visa gift card for Carla and Corliss. For Miriam, he went back to his place and purchased online gift cards from Macy's, Dillard's, Speigel's, and Tony Roma's restaurant.

Feeling like he pulled off a major coup, Garner treated his car to a wash and waxing since it hadn't been done in nearly two months. He also dropped off several of his suits at the cleaners since he was headed for Atlanta to cover a bowl game. Then it was off to Bi-Lo grocery store for his final stop of the afternoon. He noticed after returning to his car there was a missed call on his cell phone from a familiar area code.

"Hi, Garner, could you give me a call at your earliest convenience?" Garner's eyes widened; he continued listening to the message.

"I have a couple of things that I would like to discuss with you . . . This is Sabryan. I'm doing a twelve-hour shift at the hospital so you can call me at this number . . . 713.526 . . . It's now 1:15 here in Houston."

Although he longed for reconciliation, Garner decided after his last conversation with Sabryan that she would have to be the one calling him. He figured that maybe she'd finally come to her senses.

"This is Nurse Caldwell—"

Garner thought he dialed the wrong number given to him. He hung up and replayed Sabryan's message before he tried again.

"This is Nurse Caldwell," she answered in her most professional voice. "May I help you?"

The voice was close to Sabryan's, but Garner was perplexed. He stammered, "I'm sorry, uh, I-I'm trying to contact Nurse Sabryan Fletcher. This is the number that she gave me to call—"

"This is Sabryan . . . Garner, is that you?"

All expression left Garner's countenance. He felt like he'd just coughed up his heart. He was agape and his eyes were bugged out. He was so stunned by Sabryan's greeting that his car veered right and bounced against the curb while driving along Wilson Road.

Shaken, Garner scrambled to down shift into second gear; he pulled his car into an Exxon station parking lot, turning off the engine.

"Garner?"

Sabryan salivated for this opportunity. Jerome Caldwell proposed to her during the summer, but she didn't accept until days after she last spoke with Garner. She never told Jerome that she still had feelings for Garner; those changed after Yurayna sent her the cellular phone picture of him and Kadrece in the Westheimer Hotel, and Garner failed to explain himself.

She intentionally waited until the weekend before the holiday to inform Garner of the news, knowing that it would be the equivalent of kicking him in the balls with a pointed pair of cowboy boots. And as she found an office chair to lounge in the nurse's station, she smirked with an arrogance that would have depicted a villainess.

Unless his hearing had deceived him, Garner never imagined the same Sabryan Leschelle Fletcher whom he last kissed goodbye during his visit to Houston, and the same Sabryan that had cursed him out earlier in the fall, would now be Sabryan Caldwell?

He was dumbfounded and slow to speak. "Sabryan, this isn't April Fool's day. This is December twenty-first.

"What's this Nurse Caldwell stuff?"

"I know what day it is."

Sabryan began sorting in her mind all the events that led to her marrying Jerome, who worked as director of media relations for the Houston professional basketball franchise. If there was ever a scenario where she knew two people simply did not get along, it was Garner and Jerome.

First, there was Garner, who often ranted stories to Sabryan about the running feud he had with Jerome, stemming from a series of confrontations prior to the 2004-2005 basketball season. Jerome threatened to limit Garner's access to the team—even up to revoking his station's media credentials—if he did not let up on his criticism of the franchise. Houston was coming off consecutive seasons of first-round playoff eliminations, and Garner had questioned whether the franchise really had the right coach.

His response to Jerome was that if he did that to KIAH and its staff he needed to do that to all the other stations and media outlets that covered the basketball team.

"Your media credential *is* a privilege," Jerome lectured to Garner, "and not some entitlement."

Garner retorted, "*Your* job is to act like it's a *privilege* to deal with us, and not like you're doing us some half-assed favor."

Then Garner made the matter personal. He challenged Jerome whether there was any blackness in him at all. He also accused Jerome, a darker complexioned man, of being indifferent to other black members of the media.

"You can never accuse me of kissing a white man's ass to get where I've gotten in life. Just remember, they'll still call you a nigger behind your back."

"At least they can tell I am a nigger," Jerome retorted, "and they not require a voice analyst to figure out that I am one!"

Garner responded by filing a complaint with the franchise's owner Ray Thomas Whitmire. Although he was not formally reprimanded, Jerome was ordered by the team's management to offer an apology to Garner and KIAH for his lack of professionalism.

The two hardly acknowledged each other after the matter. As word circulated that Garner was dismissed by KIAH in June 2005, Jerome was among those that openly celebrated his departure.

Less than a year later, Jerome and Sabryan met for the first time during the week of the All-Star game that was played in Houston. Jerome approached Sabryan by making light conversation and asking for her phone number. She initially rebuffed his attempts because she realized he was the same Jerome Caldwell whom Garner had often lambasted.

Sabryan glanced at her wedding and engagement ring, a one-carat combination diamond cluster, realizing how fast things unfolded since the summer. It seemed it was just a matter of days ago when she agreed on going out on her first date with Jerome.

Garner broke the long pause. "Sweet, uh, I mean Sabryan, uh, well, when did this happen?"

"Last month."

"No way!" Garner shook his head in disbelief.

"Well, it happened and I'm very happy with my decision."

"Whatever."

"Well, does it matter to you who I married?"

"Humph, not really."

"You know who he is, Garner."

The only person Garner recalled whose last name was Caldwell was the very person he suppressed guessing.

"You didn't marry him?"

Sabryan leaned back into her office chair and gloated over the whole matter.

"Yep, Mr. Jerome M. Caldwell!"

A burst of rage overcame Garner. He pounded his left hand upon the driver's side arm rest and then shifted the phone into his left hand, slamming his right hand upon the center console rest.

"You didn't marry that punk motherfucker?"

The phone clicked on him.

Fuming, Garner shut his eyes. His breathing was rushed, and his chest heaved. It took him several moments for his heartbeat and breathing to return to some semblance of normalcy. He opened his eyes, gathering in all the air that he could through is mouth before exhaling slowly.

"This is Nurse Caldwell—"

"I'm sorry for losing it; I was just stunned that you would marry somebody that I have very little respect for."

"It really doesn't matter who you respect or not. I won't let you talk about my husband any way you feel like," she said. "I didn't have to tell you a goddamned thing. But I thought you deserved that much of a courtesy since you were once a part of my life."

Garner felt the rush of anger returning. His eyebrows furrowed and his eyes became slits. "What courtesy? You planned on doing this!" He had never called Sabryan anything outside of her name, other than referring to her as "Sweet," but this was the first time that "bitch" was formed on his lips.

"You were never faithful to me while you were here in Houston. So I started dating others, figuring that you would be fucking other women where you are in South Carolina. I felt I just couldn't sit here in Houston wondering what you were going to do next.

"Jerome's the first man whom I've completely trusted; I've never had to worry about him doing things behind my back that he shouldn't."

In a narcissistic way, Sabryan felt this was more than an appropriate form of retaliation against Garner. It made up for the many tears and lost sleep she suffered once she became convinced by the bits of evidence funneled to her by her best friend and work colleague, Charmaine Nettoyer, who expressed her distrust and dislike for Garner from the first time she introduced him to her.

What Sabryan didn't know until her engagement party was that Charmaine and Jerome were classmates from Jack Pershing High School in Houston's Third Ward. And without her knowing it, Charmaine had always aspired to pair Sabryan with Jerome.

The scenario was further convoluted by Charmaine, who informed Jerome all along about some of Sabryan's concerns that she had about maintaining a long-distance relationship after Garner moved to South Carolina. Likewise, Jerome apprised Charmaine of the rumors that circulated about Garner's involvement with Idria Dalzell; he was never able to confirm the rumors that had traveled about Garner and Murlette Desormeaux, a news anchor at KIAH.

"Why would I have dated other women and I was the one spending my money every three weeks or so coming to Houston?" Garner said; it still took all of him not to call her what he really had in mind. "I could have easily used that money on other women rather than spending it to see you!"

"I didn't have anything to do with you and how you chose to spend your money, Garner. But it's not as if you ever carried yourself like you were seriously committed to me. A woman wants security in the man whom she shares her body with, and you never gave me that."

"Humph. Apparently, you have a warped definition of commitment and security. It was all right for me to travel to see you, but you always had an excuse why you could never come to see me.

"And you were always telling me how unpredictable your hours were at the hospital. Now I know why—"

Sabryan found a notepad and a pen. She started doodling tick-tac-toe boards and stars on it. After all, her mission was accomplished.

"You can't tell me that you were not fucking around. I knew it all along, but I just wanted to see if your lying ass would ever tell me the truth," she said. "My friends were always right. You were never somebody to be trusted."

"Now I get it. So you decide on involving yourself with a Clarence Thomas look-a-like based on the opinion of your friends?"

"My friends have been there for me when you weren't, so leave my friends out of this discussion!"

Garner yelled, "Fine! So now you're also telling me that last phone call was all an act?"

"It wasn't an act! I gave my heart, my soul, my love and you know what else, and you messed over me."

"Bullshit!"

"You did mess over me. Did you expect for me to just accept you fucking that woman in Shreveport and that whatever-that-was that lived on Jensen?"

Garner went on the offensive once again. "It's obvious that you had been involved with that dick sucking, ass kissing Caldwell who hates that he's black, and you were looking for a convenient excuse to push me out of the picture!"

"You pushed yourself out of the picture by the way you could never keep your dick inside your pants."

"Ah, if memory serves me, the last time I saw you my dick it was the first thing you wanted!"

Sabryan screamed, "So goddamned what!" She went on to remind Garner that she could never tolerate a man's unfaithfulness. She had promised herself as a teenager that she would never allow for her heart to be broken after she watched what her mother, Daunette Fletcher, endured with her father, Edwin.

"All that talk about how you loved me. It sounds like you were practicing your lines for him while you were with me," Garner said.

"That ain't all that I practiced with you!"

"I don't even want to think about that. And even if you were faking it all with me, it's all right. Jerome Caldwell's faked being a black man being as ugly and spineless as he is, and you've faked being some lady in my life. You two deserve each other.

"So fuck both of you!"

Sabryan huffed into the phone. "You still don't get it, Garner. You still don't. I just feel sorry for the next woman who makes the mistake of being involved with you!"

"Listen here, bitch . . ."

Another conversation with Sabryan ended in a familiar click and an automated voice reminding him if he would like to use the line he needed to hang up before dialing once again

After taking several moments to compose himself, he went outside to inspect his right-front wheel.

"Fuck!" he exclaimed, kicking the tire.

There was a significant gash across his factory wheel along with a white cement scrape across the tire where he had drifted into the curb.

Chapter 21

It was of little consolation to Garner that bumping against the curb did not flatten his tire. He blamed himself for most of the madness that transpired in Houston.

Such was life. It was just another damn boomerang that came back to smash out several panes from his glass house.

Garner was accepting that another man might some day have the moral right to fuck Sabryan. It was the thought of Jerome Caldwell being that man which pissed him off even more.

Punk motherfucker!

He tried making light of it by reminding himself that Sabryan will have a lot of explaining to people whenever she might have children with Caldwell.

Humph.

Garner slipped back into his car. He used the short distance back to his place to test whether his alignment was also affected.

There was some pulling to the right. Not only will it be a pricey trip to the Infiniti dealership to replace his custom eighteen-inch alloy rim, it also meant visiting a tire shop for a wheel alignment.

Damn!

Back at his apartment, Garner slung his keys against the wall and he kicked his refrigerator door for immediate release of his anger.

He attempted to dissipate the rest of it through the sounds of David Ruffin, Harold Melvin & The Blue Notes, and The Enchantments. He was sarcastic to resolve that his world would never be lost without Sabryan, nor would he ever miss her. Nor would he ever apologize for his lack of fidelity, nor would he allow himself ever to think that she was all he needed.

If anything, the rage and contempt that he felt for the Caldwells made him feel like he entered into a drunken stupor much like in the way he remembered Aaron. He spent the rest of the afternoon and early evening sleeping it off.

When he woke up just shy of seven o'clock, he wandered into the bathroom. A disconsolate countenance was what he first observed in the mirror. He looked closer and noticed there were strands of graying at the top of his thick, wavy mane.

After taking a shower, Garner resigned himself to considering that he had nothing to lose by attending Spencer's gig; it might also be a reasonable outlet. So he stepped into a pair of black denim slacks and put on a collarless gray pullover shirt. Before leaving, he clicked on the television for the weather. The forecast called for temperatures in the upper twenties, clear, with a chance of rain showers in the morning; the next day's high was in the upper forties.

He also waited for the projected forecast for the mid-Atlantic region, specifically the Richmond area. Then he grimaced, looking over to his right.

"Now who in the hell could that be calling me right now? Go away!"

The phone stopped ringing; it rang again. Although tempted to throw the phone against the wall, he grudgingly answered it.

"Hi Garner, I know I should have called you much sooner. I was out much of today trying to get some shopping done."

The female's voice was recognizable.

"I don't know how to say good evening in French, but I guess it's nice that you called," he said.

"It's *bonsoir, ça va?*" Vernise said. "How are you?"

There was a pause while Garner composed himself. He exhaled into the phone with a tenor of disgust in his voice. "It could be better today."

"What do you mean?"

"Just what I said; it could be better."

"I hope that's not going to be your mood when you come by and pick me up for this party that you told me about."

Garner held his breath and looked the other way. Still struggling with his emotions from earlier, he tried tempering his reaction again by convincing himself he wasn't the one who married Jerome Caldwell.

He managed a dry response. "Uh, I didn't know you were still interested. You hadn't called me about it."

"Don't you remember me telling you to call me?"

"I don't remember that."

Inhaling and exhaling through her nostrils, Vernise went on to recount to him that she gestured for him to call her just before he drove away from her place. "But that's all right. I'll be ready when you get here. How soon can you make it?"

"I, uh, guess I could be there in about thirty minutes. I'm coming from near Blythewood."

Vernise resisted from blurting out that she was well aware of where he lived when she accessed his information before her anonymous contact with him at the station. It was equally as tempting for her to offer a hint whether he recognized who placed the small envelope under his driver's side windshield wiper.

Beaming to herself, she thought it was a rather ingenious thing to have written the note with her right hand rather than her left hand. "You know, I almost literally wore bells for you when you were over here for dinner. Maybe next time I'll do that."

Now that perked up Garner. He was fond to recall the way things got steamy between them. "I'm sure you would have looked just as good wearing only bells. By the way, that meal and those crois- sants—I think you just might give my mother a run for her money!"

Vernise managed a demure chuckle for the comparison. She glanced over at the clock on her living room wall. She informed him that it would soon be 7:30, and they still had not gone anywhere.

Meanwhile, Garner closed his eyes recalling the wonderful feeling from grasping Vernise's ass cheeks. He wondered about what he had felt if she allowed him to reach down the front of her Capris that night.

"Now who is the one that's trying to start something she might not finish?"

"Don't worry about me. Just get here as soon as you can!"

"Your timing was very good; I'll see you in a little bit."

"Actually, I'm glad that I caught you. I'll tell you about it when you get here."

Vernise eagerly awaited Garner's arrival wearing a low-cut beige blouse that exposed more of her cleavage, a pair of white low-cut denim slacks, and black leather boots. She wore her hair long to the back where it stopped just short of her shoulder blades.

She made him feel even more welcomed in her place by approaching him in the doorway with a hug and a brief, searching encounter with his tongue. As she took a step back from initiating her goodwill towards him, Garner was reminded of all his previous reasons for being impressed by her obvious beauty, wit, and sensuality, although aided by a view of her cleavage.

"There's more of that where it came from." She smiled seductively at him. "I'll get my jacket."

He was left with savoring her fragrance that he inhaled much like her cooking. He was not sure whether to grab his heart, crotch, or forehead while he stared at her prancing over to the loveseat and retrieve a beige suede jacket.

"I'm ready, darling!" She gave him a light peck on his left cheek.

"I thought I heard a whole host of bells while I saw you walking over there for your jacket."

Vernise laughed off Garner's remark. "Oh, you were just looking at my ass." She gave it a playful slap. "It's nice, isn't it?"

"I'm sure you've had plenty of men agree with you."

"A few have—"

As they started their jaunt over to Irmo, Garner gave Vernise the disclaimer that this was his first time visiting the party's host place. He shared with her all that he knew was Spencer's home was listed on Kennerly Thorne Drive. He explained that he usually associated addresses with high schools or colleges in an area wherever he was headed.

A light chortle preceded Garner describing Spencer Watts the person as simply a crazy motherfucker who still had the best interests of black people in heart and mind.

"I don't know if it's true, but he'll tell you that he prayed for somebody like me to have come to Columbia. I think he'll also tell you he didn't expect for that person to have turned out like me."

"I don't understand—"

"Well, don't worry about that. But I'll give you a fair warning about this guy: After one glance at you, he'll probably follow you everywhere you go, checking you out from behind. He's just that kind of person."

"Oh, you mean he's a dirty old man?"

"Keep on . . ."

"So he's a crazy, old, dirty ladies' man. Am I getting closer?"

Garner nodded in agreement. "If you listen to him, he thinks he still can do what he used to do a half-century ago. I'll give him this much, he's actually taken good care of himself. That's at least what I've seen several women tell him."

She inquired, "And both of you are, for a lack of better words, friendly with each other?"

"I'm not sure if that's a good thing to say. My mother once told me that people might judge a man by whom he surrounds himself with, or by the people he considers his friends. I don't know if I want to be seen that way when it comes to Spencer Watts."

"Did you say Spencer Watts?"

"Yeah, he likes 'Doctor' to go in front of that among people he doesn't know."

Vernise waved off Garner. She gave him a brief lecture about her being in Columbia for the past several years. "I've never met Dr. Spencer Watts, but I know who he is."

"Are you saying Columbia is as small of a town like Tallahassee, where I went to college?"

"No, I'm not saying that. Spencer Watts has been in the news from time to time for his work in civil rights."

She didn't let Garner on that she was also familiar with Spencer's name because of the nature of her work. She went on to say, "Well, I'm sure we're going to have a good time over at Dr. Watts' place. I'm sure we'll see some interesting people. This sure will beat some of the Bureau's functions I've attended over the years."

Apparently, the FBI reference passed over his head. He was more preoccupied with putting in one of the CDs that he burned featuring the deep baritone and Caribbean lilt produced by the late Jon Lucien.

Although he never performed before any gathering of people, Garner felt he was more than capable of carrying a note without embarrassing himself.

Vernise was unfamiliar with Lucien's "Hello Like Before" but she also appeared to be quite comfortable with the playful teasing of the guitar that accentuated the tropical overtones of the song—and even Garner's voice. One of the places she always wanted to visit was her mother's native Martinique, and then travel farther south to Brazil during its famous Carnival celebration.

"I think you need to stop while you're ahead, *monsieur*. You might be starting something that's too early for you to try finishing."

"So you like the music?"

"How about the one who's singing?"

"He died earlier this year."

"Are you trying to kill the mood, silly? I'm talking about you!"

That brought a smile to Garner and a smooth stroke to his ego. "I just wanted to hear that from you."

The lyrics to the song also struck a chord with Vernise. When Garner glanced over to his right, he caught her looking out the window;

she appeared to have wandered into another realm.

Then she noticed him from the periphery. Before she could interrogate his intent, Garner had already down shifted, looking straight ahead. They just reached the I-20 and I-26 interchange to travel westbound towards Spartanburg.

"Who's this guy again on your CD?"

"Jon Lucien."

"What do you know about him? I'm the type of person that likes to know as much as I can about the music that I like; I like this guy's music, although I never heard of him until now."

"I thought you liked me?"

"Didn't I just say this guy's music? I wouldn't be sitting in this car with you unless I liked you, don't you think?"

"Oh, I was just making sure. I know singers, actors, and athletes always seem to have their way with women—"

"You didn't answer my question. What do you know about this Jon Lucien guy?" She pronounced his name hinting at her fluency in French.

Garner explained to her Lucien was from the Virgin Islands, and his music was commercially underappreciated. He also noted Lucien had appeared as a guest vocalist for several top artists like Nnenna Freelon and the late Grover Washington, Jr.

"If I'm not mistaken, he was married four times. So I think this song 'Hello Like Before' may have revealed a page from his life."

"Would you mind playing that song again? I felt something very strongly from it."

This time, Vernise listened to it with her eyes closed and her head arched back into the headrest. Garner did not sing along, allowing her to take it all in for herself. He was partly stunned when she reached over and grasped his hand tightly while it was on the gearshift knob.

Garner felt as if Vernise had transferred some kind of romantic energy to him—a connection that surpassed what he felt from earlier in the week. He wondered maybe there was a divine purpose behind their meeting each other.

She was somber to elaborate. "I think I can relate to what he was singing about. It's a difficult emotion to experience and express . . ."

Garner shrugged his shoulders. "I just liked the man's music and his style. Sorry about that."

"You don't have to apologize. I told you things go a little deeper with me." She grasped his hand tighter.

"I see."

Garner went ahead with accommodating Vernise's request by tracking back to the first song on his CD. There was once again the imagery of ocean waves crashing against the sand and Lucien's samba-like strokes on his acoustic guitar. He did not notice that Vernise had tears welling. She could barely recognize the businesses along I-26 that were so familiar. She tried looking up towards his roof.

He asked, "What makes this song so personal with you? You just heard it for the first time just a few minutes ago."

"Don't you know for many people there is also an emotional connection to music?" A slight sniffle accompanied her clearing her throat. She wiped away a tear that had streamed down her cheek.

Garner finally recognized Vernise was on the brink of crying once again in his company. She exhaled deeply.

"The lyrics tell me that he experienced a loss of relationship, but it seemed like they were able to move on with their lives. The irony is that they ran into each other perhaps years down the road—at least it seemed they were able to be civil with each other."

He grimaced and sighed. Vernise released her grasp of his hand, brushing her hair to the back. She adjusted herself in the passenger's seat so that she could have an unobstructed view of him.

He pondered silently about the lack of civility from his interaction with Sabryan earlier in the day. Especially since he recognized both of them were guilty of fucking around on each other.

She queried, "Have you ever been married? You look like that you have before."

"Not even close; it's funny you would mention that." He glanced to his right before setting his attention back on the freeway. "I kinda figured out that you've been married at least once."

"Twice." She settled back into her seat, looking straight ahead. Garner was more than stunned. He was close to stammering out a question; she filled in the blank for him.

"It's not something I talk a lot about. I got married [in 1987] without my parents knowing it shortly after I graduated from college. I was still hurt emotionally from my shoulder injury. I thought what I lacked in my life at the time was a man—you know, somebody to love me in a time that I needed it."

She gazed upward again. "But the guy I married, we both realized that [marriage] wasn't for us so we got an annulment. I'm glad I was able to keep that from my dad. He would have been heartbroken."

She went on to divulge to Garner that she had no idea where Cooley Brighton was these days. They've not been in contact since separating. Then she described the marriage to Pierre and Jenora's father.

"After I had started serving my commission in the Army, I was feeling lonely and sort of depressed, and that's when I met Thaman. You might call it a rebound situation. One thing led to another and I became Mrs. Thaman Aikens in 1988. I had two children for him, but then things happened over time and I'm here in South Carolina; he's in Louisville, Kentucky, with my children."

Vernise's reasons for marriage left Garner considering how fortunate he was for never getting that far with Sabryan. He attempted to relate with her. "My parents are divorced. It seems divorce is never a good thing."

"That's true. It's never a good thing, but it's a fact of life. I've learned some lessons along the way—things I'd probably would not do again if I had to do it all over again."

"Would one of them be not marrying your children's father?"

"Actually, no, I don't regret marrying Thaman. He's a decent man. But I learned when you marry somebody there's so much that you marry into. It could be their credit, health, past issues, and family. That's just to name a few."

"I never really thought about those things. Maybe it's because I've never had that deep of a relationship with somebody. Maybe some day I will be able to say that."

Once again, Garner reached for his gearshift lever to down shift while he angled his car for the Harbison Boulevard exit. He already had his GPS programmed for directions to Kennerly Thorne Drive. He mentioned to Vernise, according to his GPS, they were no more than five minutes away from Spencer's home.

Vernise brought to Garner's attention she was very much familiar with the area. "There are some very nice homes out here. Depending on where you go, there are half-million dollar homes that easily could sell for millions in other states. So I'm curious to see exactly where your *friend* actually lives."

Garner resumed conversing about her marriage to Thaman Aikens, whom she said worked as a systems analyst for the United Parcel Service's headquarters.

"How would you describe your relationship with your children's father now? Is the song we just listened to closer to that situation?"

Vernise appeared uncomfortable forming a response. Part of the difficulty from her day was the sting of Thaman refusing her offer to fly Pierre and Jenora to Columbia for the third straight holiday season.

She suspected Thaman' refusal was his way of retaliating against her for her act of retaliation against him, stemming from an incident in 2004. When the couple filed for divorce in 1998, just two years after she was hired as a federal investigator, Thaman sought custody of their children on grounds of adultery and Vernise was an unfit mother.

The impetus for his petition occurred when he walked in on Vernise lying on their bed with her eyes closed and her knees brought up to her chest while a former military friend of hers, Brittany Donaldson, was engrossed into licking and sucking her pussy.

Shocked and outraged, Thaman stormed back out of their home and arranged for Pierre and Jenora to be kept by his parents who lived in his native Lexington, Kentucky.

Thaman argued, "I will not be associated with a dyke for a mother, and I sure as hell will not let my children be directly raised by one, either!"

Vernise tried explaining to Thaman that she had experimented with lesbian sex while she played tennis in college. She told him she was introduced to it by a teammate of hers who was also her room-mate for their away tennis matches and tournaments.

One particular night, she recounted to him, the teammate asked of her if she did not mind having a conversation while they sat na-ked in bed. The conversation turned to sex.

"I told her that I had only been with boys, but then [Kari] asked me if I had ever been kissed by a girl—you know, really kissed by a girl. I told her no. She told me to close my eyes and relax and tell her how it felt," she explained. "I told her I didn't know, but I felt my nipples were becoming very hard and my clit started throbbing. Then she told me to lie back on her bed and hold my legs apart. I almost passed out as soon as she started licking and sucking on my pussy.

"It felt so good that I was fucking hooked. We dated each other until I blew out my shoulder. After I got hurt, I knew deep down within that I liked guys probably more than I liked women . . . My being with Brittany was really kind of an experiment to find out if I still liked being with women or not."

Thaman didn't believe Vernise. "When I get finished with your dyke ass, you'll be lucky to ever see our children."

His parents, Calvin and Zenobia, were a prominent black couple in Lexington. His father was the first black to serve on the city coun-cil, and he owned a string of Sonic restaurants throughout the state. His mother was a partner in a high-profiled law firm before she was elected as a circuit court judge.

Part of the pressure Thaman exerted on Vernise was if he did not get full custody of the children, and if she attempted to fight it, he threatened to use his parents' political connections that reached Washington, D.C., to ensure that she would be fired from her FBI job citing breaches of moral turpitude and falsifying a federal job application.

Vernise finally answered Garner, "My relationship with my chil-dren's father is what it is. I guess I was thinking about some of the losses I've experienced in life, and I've had to figure out a way to go on." Then she withdrew again. Garner just turned left onto Kennerly Thorne Drive off Broad River Road.

Sensing her discomfort, Garner tried relating to her another way. "Hey, I thought I had it bad today when an ex-girlfriend called to inform me that she married some guy that I absolutely despise and don't respect."

He leaned back into his seat, yawning. "I guess the worst thing that came out of it was that I bumped my car against the curb because I was so shocked by what she told me."

Vernise chided Garner that he had not experienced a significant loss in life if that was all that happened to him.

"Humph. I lost custody of my children because a spoiled man happened to have parents who had political and legal connections, and they managed to box me into a corner that I couldn't get out.

"My parents wanted to help me, but I didn't think it was worth them using every resource they had available to them. I just couldn't do that."

The mood inside the car was tense. She reminisced to herself the retaliation that she waged against Thaman.

When their divorce became final in the fall of 1999, she thought the best way to have better access to Pierre and Jenora was to make it as cordial and positive with Thaman. By 2003, Vernise and Thaman were going out on family outings with their children whenever she visited them in Louisville. She even spent nights at the home that he purchased for himself and the children and by the start of 2004, they even resumed having sex.

Vernise presumed since they were having sexual relations once again that he would consider allowing for joint custody. She broached the question to Thaman on four previous occasions that year; he would not commit either way on the topic. She asked him a final time on a humid summer night while they stayed at a five-star hotel in the Indianapolis area. She mentioned to him about her situation being stable in South Carolina, considering she worked her way up to her current position as supervisor.

Thaman was slow to respond. He hinted at Vernise maybe if she proved how much of a woman she was once again that he might consider it. Frustrated with his response, Vernise decided on executing her alternate plan. That meant when Thaman returned from the shower, expecting her to await him joining her in bed, she set out to ambush and subdue him.

Stunned and unable to react, Vernise had affixed a set of plastic handcuffs on Thaman, the kind that agents used as a back-up to the metal cuffs, while pressing her knee into his back.

He protested, "Why you're doing this to me?"

She placed her Glock pistol against his temple. "You've taken something away from me that really hurts. Since I can't have my children back, bastard, I'm going to make sure that you remember me for the rest of your goddamn life. Now tell your goddamn bourgeois family that I did this to you."

She then attempted shoving a six-inch dildo up his ass. "Tell them how you got fucked tonight!" Thaman was reduced to screaming and moaning from the excruciating pain and Vernise's rough treatment. "Oh, by the way, I've done some investigation on you. What's this about you seriously considering an encounter with a known gay man on your UPS job?

"Now, if you think you're man enough to tell everyone how much I liked a woman licking my pussy, you better be man enough to explain to everyone how you actually thought about sucking another man's dick. Or was it you wanting another man's dick up your ass? I just figured that I might help you out." She pushed the plastic dick farther inside his anal cavity.

"I'm not fucking gay, and I don't live on the down-low, bitch! You know what you're telling me is a lie!"

"I don't want to hear a fucking thing you have to say! You forgot about how you didn't want to listen to me when I tried explaining to you why I was with Brittany?"

Then she stood in front of Thaman and took her pistol off the safety lock. "I've thought about killing you ever since you walked in on me and Brittany. Actually, I thought you would have liked having a wife that was bi-curious so that it might add some spice to your marriage since you could never satisfy me with your dick. What could have been wrong with that?"

He answered, "What man wants a woman who thinks a woman can lick her pussy better than him?"

She pushed the gun back against his temple. "Well, why don't you find out in hell!" In a blur, she recounted to herself that she got dressed before she uncuffed Thaman. Then she threatened him that if he ever decided to use what she had done against him, she would make sure that he would be locked up for child abuse.

"You wouldn't do that to me?"

"Remember, I'm a special investigator. I've learned how to make connections, too. I could also have law enforcement knocking on the door of your parents' offices come Monday morning. Try me and find out!"

"Hey, are you all right?" Garner asked, startling Vernise.

"I'm fine. I was just thinking about something."

Vernise smiled to herself regarding her moment of payback. Meanwhile, he started down shifting when they came upon three large homes on plots of land to their left and there were four similarly large homes to their right on large plots of land.

There were cars parked on Spencer's lawn and driveway area, which could have been mistaken for a small parking lot.

"A lot of people are already here. I think we're going to have a good time tonight."

"Good, because I need one; I'm glad you were available when I called so late."

When Garner came around to let Vernise out the door, she thanked him for his courtesy and showed additional appreciation by kissing him fully on his lips. She pushed her tongue inside his mouth. She also reached down and tugged at his crotch; his dick immediately responded to the attention. She giggled at his reaction. "I guess we'll have to decide later on if it will be your place or mine."

Chapter 22

There was just enough of a chill in the air to convince Garner and Vernise they needed to break up what they were doing. The muffled sound of conversation and laughter was easily discernible from outside of Spencer's impressive, tri-story red brick exterior home.

Just before they reached the front steps, Garner leaned over and gave Vernise a light peck on the lips. "This is definitely not the place where you want to start something, babe," she joked with him.

He countered, "We could turn around and go somewhere else." He also gave her a playful pat on the ass.

Their conversation and footsteps set off a motion-and-sound yard light. Spencer's wife, Shirley, answered the door. She was a well-kept, brown complexioned assistant high school principal in her mid-sixties. She stood five-six and she still maintained a noticeably shapely figure. She had on a rose colored, three-quarter sleeve silk shirt tucked inside boot-cut designer jeans.

Garner had met Shirley on several occasions. Each time, he wondered why Spencer would choose to fuck around on Shirley. Then again, after more than a year of knowing the notorious Dr. Spencer F. Watts, he already knew the answer.

Shirley greeted Garner with a motherly hug. "Hey darling, come on in!" Then she extended her hand out to Vernise. "I'm Shirley Watts. Come on in out of this cold, child!"

"I'm very pleased to meet you, Mrs. Watts."

"The faculty and my students call me Mrs. Watts. Away from the school, I'm just Shirl or Shirley."

Shirley gestured for their jackets. "Garner, have you been here since we moved?"

"No, Ms. Shirley, I haven't."

Amid the noise and the flow of nearly one hundred people throughout their house, Shirley guided Garner and Vernise to their right and into the formal dining room area. There, a chandelier light above an oak wood dining room table that was capable of seating eight, and an oak wood china cabinet complemented the dining room's arrangements. There was a small gathering of people helping themselves to the array of libations, ranging from ginger ale and club soda all the way up to Bacardi, Courvoisier, and Jack Daniels No. 7.

Shirley guided them back into the vestibule area. To their right, where many were gathered, was the formal living room area. Garner recognized there were Persian rugs under wherever there was furniture to protect the hardwood flooring. At the far end of the living room was a stairwell and another doorway straight ahead, leading them into the great-room; that area seemed to be the most crowded. Garner immediately recognized the slapping of dominoes. That evoked memories of his days in Richmond, where neighbors' games were so spirited that he could hear their profanity-laced comments from the sidewalk.

Then she led them through another doorway and into the eating area where there were card tables set up for games of spades and bid-whiz. It lacked the hard-core bantering from the dominoes table, but there was no doubt the people were into their game. To their right was the kitchen area where Shirley mentioned to them the food was catered by Big E's Bar-B-Q off Monticello Road over near Columbia's Eau Claire section of town.

Shirley offered, "Help yourself to what you want. I stopped cooking fifteen years ago after my baby child [daughter Contessa] finished college—you should know that, Garner!"

Garner was reduced to mumbling under his breath that he did not know what she meant; he visited the Watts at their former residence in the Summit on Columbia's northeast side of town maybe twice. Before Shirley left, she apprised Garner that Spencer was more than likely in the lower-level family room with cue stick in one hand and a drink in the other. "Oh, by the way, I think Tamira's here tonight, Garner . . . I'm pretty sure that I've seen her."

Shirley spotted a small gathering of older women who had assembled around the large white sofa in the living room.

"Vernise, you're welcomed to join me. We're only going to talk about sorority stuff, anyway."

"Thanks for the invitation, Ms. Shirley. I might stop off in there later."

Garner was unable to conceal his emotions once he made eye contact with Vernise.

With raised eyebrows she inquired, "Is there anything you need to tell me about Tamira?"

Garner's lips tightened; he glanced down at the floor tiles. "She's somebody I met through Spencer Watts. We went out a couple of times, and that's about it . . . Humph. I haven't seen or talked to her in over two months."

Vernise nodded. She appeared satisfied with Garner's response. She eased next to him from behind while both observed the action at the card tables. She placed her arm around his trunk, brushing her breasts onto his back.

She started whispering into his ear, "Just one thing I need to tell you: you're with me now." Garner turned to his right. Their eyes met. Vernise initially appeared matter-of-fact, but then she lightened up her countenance into a bright and broad smile. He shifted his attention back to the card tables.

There was a change of opponents at the bid-whiz table. Garner turned towards Vernise almost whispering to her. "Do you play cards?"

"Of course I do."

"Or do you wanna play dominoes?"

She whispered back to him. "I play both, babe. I'm pretty much open to do anything except for animals, children, golden showers; you know, things like that, and certain forms of bondage and torture—unless I'm the one inflicting it."

Garner did a double take at Vernise's response. She smiled back at him.

"I'd love to play spades with you," Vernise said, raising her voice slightly to overcome the slight commotion at the table. Apparently, one team had made its blind eight and taken two extra books; they celebrated with high-fives and some trash talking. "I'd like to see just how well we could work together doing something."

While they observed the action, Garner recognized Spencer's very audible voice and hearty laugh as he emerged from the lower-level room. He discerned two other people were with him.

Spencer's mouth was at full speed bragging about his white neighbors in the adjacent lots of land and across the road from him were the ones that paid for his place. "It's a damn shame that so many black families have allowed their property to be stolen from them."

"I hear ya, my man," one of the two men sided with Spencer.

Garner looked over his left shoulder. He had not seen Spencer since going out with Tamira.

"Well look who's here!" Spencer's voice resonated; he pointed in Garner's direction. "Fellas, that's the person you wanna check out on TV if you wanna know what's going on in sports!"

Garner waited for Spencer to come over to where he and Vernise were standing. They shook hands and bumped right shoulders.

He nodded over to his right. "Spencer, I'd like for you to meet Vernise Aikens."

Spencer peered above his glasses. He partly mumbled to Garner they needed to talk real soon. Then he shifted his drink from his right hand into his left, extending his hand to Vernise.

"Dr. Spencer Watts. Good evening to you, my dear. And your name again was?"

"Vernise," she replied, smiling, and playing the lady-like role by softly grasping Spencer's hand. "I've heard a lot about you, Dr. Watts."

"Well, I hope it's all good."

He gestured his head towards Garner. "You know how those media folk are quick to give bad information." Predictably, Spencer angled his head upward so that he could get a better peak at Vernise's cleavage; she portrayed herself being oblivious to his subtle move. Then he focused his attention back on Garner. The other two men that accompanied him from the lower-level room had already ventured off into the great-room area.

"Uh, Ms. Vernise, do you mind if I steal Garner for a few moments? I've got a few people I'd like for him to meet. Better yet, why don't you come along? He can use all the help that he can get."

Spencer erupted into a hearty laugh while Garner dipped his head sheepishly. He knew it could have been worse. Before they followed Spencer, Garner had put his and Vernise's name on the waiting list for spades.

Vernise said, "You have a very impressive place, Dr. Watts."

"Why thank you. Almost everything on this property was paid for by white people. I sold about ten acres of land that I had around here and I made sure that they reserved me a lot so I could build this house."

He waved his hand freely, looking around in admiration. "The only thing I've paid for are the taxes and utilities."

Vernise was not fazed by Spencer's remark. She felt her parents' two-story place back in Chatsworth was proportionately as nice. It had three upstairs bedrooms, a guest room on the ground floor and a swimming pool in the backyard. She also had the homes of some of her old friends and high school classmates that lived in swankier areas of the Valley as a reference point.

Garner seemed more interested in Spencer's story. "How can a bunch of white people pay for your place?"

Because Garner was with Vernise, Spencer did not start with his usual light, bright, almost white motherfucker dig. Instead, he went along with the flow of the conversation explaining that he made sure he got a good price for the land that developers had inquired about for several years. He went on to say that he began considering offers after a private community of smaller homes were completed about a half-mile away on Kennerly Thorne Drive.

"You see, most of the developers in this area have stolen land that was once owned by blacks by giving them cash offers that were way below market value. Or, they jumped on their property if they missed paying their taxes. Then they turned around and made their money when they put homes on the land.

"If you come here in the daytime you'll see every one of the homes around me and across the street are worth at least $450,000 to $500,000. I figure if they're gonna make that kinda money I might as well hold out for the right deal and make sure that I still get a piece of the pie, dig?"

The first person Spencer had Garner to meet was Eric Lawson. He was president of Second Community Bank of Columbia, which was the city's other black owned and operated bank. Spencer's sale of ten acres netted him $750,000; he purchased a $100,000 certificate of deposit as a goodwill gesture to supporting black businesses.

"You know, young buck, in some ways segregation was good for the black man because the enemy was clearly defined," Spencer said. "We had no choice but to support each other, and the money was cycled within our community at least twenty times before it left. Now our money stays among us for maybe twenty minutes."

The next person Spencer introduced to Garner and Vernise was Thaddeus Greer, who was the president of the larger of Columbia's two historically black colleges. Greer served on the board of trustees to Second Community Bank. He also tried unsuccessfully luring Spencer out of retirement to become a professor emeritus at his school.

Another notable person introduced to Garner and Vernise was Sinatrius Highsmith, who ran the Highsmith Insurance Agency. It was arguably one of Columbia's largest independent full-service agencies.

Spencer pointed to Highsmith. "Now this is a brother you need to come to for your insurance the next time your policy comes up for renewal. I've known him for more than thirty years, going back to when he was working for da' man."

Vernise shook Highsmith's hand. "Do you happen to know Nilam Armstead? He's also an insurance agent."

"I vaguely know him. But I'm pretty sure that I run into him from time to time at the quarterly Underwriter's meetings. I'll let him know that you asked about him."

"Don't worry about that; I was just curious."

Highsmith reached into his jacket pocket and gave both Garner and Vernise one of his cards. "Call me if y'all ever need me for anything."

Spencer then led Garner and Vernise in the direction of a mature woman of a copper complexion and demure demeanor sitting in one of the folding chairs. A darker skinned man who appeared to be in his early sixties accompanied her to her left. Spencer mumbled into Garner's ear before they approached the couple. "Whatever you do, watch your goddamn mouth around this lady."

Garner looked back; Spencer nodded.

"Doctor Alvin Bickford, I know you're a sports fan. I'd like for you to meet Garner Davis, who is a sportscaster here in Columbia, and his friend Ms. Vernise, uh—"

"Aikens."

"And this is Ms. Raynee Bickford. I've known this fine couple probably twenty years."

Oh, shit, Garner internalized. *So this is the woman that this old crazy man talked about licking her asshole!*

Raynee was stunning in appearance. She was about the same height and build as Vernise, just fifteen years older. She wore her hair medium length. She had hazel colored eyes. Not surprisingly, a half dozen or so men tried stealing glances in Raynee's direction, as well as in Vernise's.

Meanwhile, Garner remained silent while he shook Alvin and Raynee Bickford's hands. Before Garner could strike up a conversation with Alvin Bickford on sports, Spencer ushered him and Vernise away.

Vernise tapped Garner on the shoulder, whispering into his ear that she was heading to the restroom.

Spencer peered over his glasses once more. "Young buck, you got yourself a woman. You don't need my goddamn help. So how did you meet her?"

While they were headed back toward the kitchen area, Garner gloated knowing that a woman who accompanied him incited Spencer's true dog nature. He jabbed his elbow into Spencer's forearm. "To be honest, I didn't really meet her. She called me out of the blue at the station."

Spencer immediately stopped walking. "Say what?" He downed the last of his rum and Coke.

Garner repeated himself. "She called me out of the blue at the station."

Spencer told Garner that he had been around the block enough times to make a virgin dizzy, but he'd never heard of a woman calling a single man out of the blue to introduce herself to him. He said, "The longer I live, the crazier the stories get." The smell from his beverage was still strong on his breath.

They resumed walking towards the kitchen. Garner's curiosity, however, was too much to resist.

"Say ol' man, why did you introduce me to Raynee?"

Spencer leaned closer to Garner. "I never would have introduced her to you had you come by yourself. Since you didn't, I couldn't let you out do the ol' man tonight. At least not in his own house."

He then looked over his shoulder, peering back into the great-room area. "Young buck, I better make sure Ms. Shirley isn't wondering if I'm trying to collect phone numbers."

The Watts' home had a half-bathroom near the stairwell between the great room and the living room areas. Vernise noticed a woman coming out of it that fit information that she accessed by using her license plate as a starting point. Her suspicion was confirmed two-fold when Ms. Shirley blurted out the woman's name.

Vernise angled herself in that direction, ensuring that she might run into her. All along, she made subtle observations of the other people in attendance mostly out of her nature as an investigator.

"Excuse me, I don't normally do this," Vernise said, approaching her. "Haven't we met before?"

The woman cleared her throat. "I don't think that we have."

"Oh, I'm sure that we have. I think you were a wise woman for following directions. It's obvious that you didn't forget my phone call advising you that I'm the lady that's now in Garner's life."

Although she remained as poised as she could, it dawned upon Tamira that the woman who stood slightly taller than her was the same person who called her house just a couple of days after she slept with Garner. In that conversation, she immediately dismissed Vernise as some fanatic.

"I've already decided that I would have anything to do with Garner. So you're just wasting your time," she remembered telling Vernise. *"And if you bother me again, I'll have the police investigate this phone call!"*

Vernise laughed with sarcasm. *"Go right ahead. I am the police! And I'll make sure that you are discredited from your doctor's degree program at the university. If you take me for a joke, I'll just visit a Mr. Jung-Kim Park who happens to be one of the more influential members on your committee . . ."*

Then she hung up.

The pursuit of a doctorate degree meant more to her than any piece of dick that might infiltrate her life. She noticed Vernise's bluish gray eyes became grayer in her presence.

"Well, I told you I had no further interest in him. I don't see the point in you approaching me," she said.

Vernise felt like she was in complete control. She savored watching Tamira's obvious discomfort. She countered, "I just wanted to say 'hi' to you, and thank you, as well, for finding other things to do with your time."

"Excuse me," Tamira said, walking in the opposite direction.

In a matter of thirty seconds, Vernise excited herself just as much as Garner had caused her pussy juices to flow outside of Spencer's home. Controlling as many variables as possible was one of the things she vowed to do different with the next man in her life. And if it meant her taking advantage of her investigative privileges, she would do just that.

Since they were second on the waiting list, Garner decided to venture back into the other part of the Watts' home looking for Vernise. They crossed paths in the living room area, smiling at each other.

He said, "I was heading over to the dining room. Would you like a drink from over there?"

"Oh, darling, you didn't have to worry about me. But since you asked, I'll just have a club soda with lime for now."

"Are you sure that's all that you want?"

Vernise returned a seductive look. She rolled her tongue along the inner half of her upper lip before responding. Then she cast her eyes towards his pants.

"What I want I can't have right now."

Garner smiled back at her, feeling also a slight protrusion in his slacks. "So are we close to deciding on your place or mine?"

"Very close!"

When he reached the formal dining room, Garner recognized Tamira from afar. She had accepted a drink made for her by a man distinguished by salt-and-pepper hair. He noticed she whispered something to the man before he headed to another part of Spencer's house.

Tamira happened to look to her right; they made eye contact with each other.

Damn!

"Hi Garner." She was unenthusiastic in her greeting. He paid little attention to her wearing a black evening skirt and a black and red blouse. Her hair was styled very similar to way she wore it the night they went out.

"You know, I tried several times calling you. I guess you decided that I wasn't worth the courtesy of calling back."

Tamira considered walking off without commenting, but the

counseling nature within her took over. "Do you remember when I mentioned to you that there are times you'll begin to wonder and want to know why one times one equals one?"

"I barely remember that, but what does that have to do with you not saying anything to me after we woke up the next morning?"

"I also told you that I made an exception. That was of my volition."

She took a small sip from her glass of white wine and departed with the same sophistication that once piqued his curiosity.

Humph.

Only this time it did not matter whether he was a nice guy or not.

Chapter 23

Vernise had already decided what she would do next once Garner returned. The crowd, in spite of him, was not exactly the kind she was accustomed to socializing with, but it did provide her some solace from the disappointment that Thaman Aikens caused her.

He handed her the glass and a napkin. "I figured I would let you decide how much lime you would want. Are *you* all right with that?"

She smiled. "I appreciate your thoughtfulness. Next time, remember two limes would suffice. Are *you* all right with that?"

Garner was in no mindset for making a big deal out of one lime, two limes, or no limes at all. He still basked in the compliment Spencer gave him about Vernise. He briefly entertained what his family's reaction might be if he ever brought Vernise home to Richmond.

Although it was premature, he supposed that Miriam would embrace Vernise simply because she was his choice of woman. He figured with Norris, if they got into a pissing match about women, he could easily insult him for his choice in Shalinda's hoochie and ghetto ass. As for Carla, he figured she would likely side with whatever was Miriam and Norris's reaction.

"Babe, you know what? I don't think I really want to play any cards or dominoes."

He checked the waiting list. "You know we're next—"

She returned him a mischievous look. Thinking in French, her clit was telling her that he could take her home and give her sensual tongue lashing for being such a bad little girl. She nuzzled closer to him. Garner's body tensed, hoping that she would not do anything too obvious. She then whispered into his ear, "I've got a pool table at home in my family room. Are you much of a trick-shot artist?"

He was cool to reply barely above a whisper. "It depends on the situation." He suggested they moved away from the other people near the card table. They stopped by the counter, talking just loud enough so they could hear each other.

"I'm ready to go, babe."

"Are you sure?"

Vernise nodded. Garner led her by the hand through the great room and living room areas. He noticed many of the attendees retrieved their coats or jackets from the closet in the vestibule area.

Being the self-professed California girl that she was, Vernise was emphatic about the upper-twenties temperature being beyond her range of comfort.

Garner could barely keep up with her as she hurried to his car. Once inside, he adjusted the temperature control up to eighty-five degrees.

"Spencer is a dog just like you described," she said, leaning back into her seat. "I think Shirley knows that he's run off a few times and, like most dogs, they always seem to find their way back home."

"That's Spencer Watts. He tells me that he's been married forty-four years, and I suspect he's fucked around all forty-four years. I'm pretty sure at some point Ms. Shirley has considered sending him to the dog pound once and for all."

Vernise unbuttoned her beige suede jacket. She glanced into the mirror visor, running her left hand through her hair.

"I doubt that. She's too well-kept of a woman just to sit there like nothing's going on and not have her own fun. She's just a lot more discreet about it. Didn't you notice that rock on her left hand?"

"No, I missed it." Garner had backed his car, maneuvered it out of the driveway and onto Kennerly Thorne Drive. He began accelerating through the gears.

"Babe, let me explain something real quick to you: I'm a woman, and a woman can be very perceptive. That rock says it was a peace offering between them. And didn't she say that she had a youngest child?"

"As far as I know, they have a son and a daughter," Garner answered.

Vernise continued with her character summary of the Wattses. "I would go as far as to say that one of those children isn't Spencer's. I've heard of a lot of stories like that. A woman does it and her husband might never find out. She will take it to her grave."

Garner managed a wry smile, shaking his head. He admitted to Vernise that he long suspected that Shirley might have romantic interests outside of her marriage. Perhaps, he added, their children and reputations may be the reasons why both of them have stayed together after all these years.

Besides, he further suggested that they came from an era where couples remained in marriages even if they weren't the most fruitful. "Who knows? Maybe they do love each other." He grimaced at the thought. "Humph. I couldn't say that was true for my parents."

"I know, in spite of how crazy my parents may seem to strangers, I'm convinced that they love each other," Vernise replied.

Garner now popped in another CD. Vernise immediately placed her left hand on his thigh, moving it up towards his groin as the music began. She closed her eyes, tilting her head back into the headrest.

"I thought 'Get Here' was sung only by Oleta Adams?" she blurted out to him.

Garner corrected her. "Brenda Russell wrote the song almost ten years before Oleta had anything to do with it." He turned left onto Broad River Road, heading back towards the I-20 interchange about five miles away.

Vernise began explaining to him why "Get Here" had special meaning to her. "I was concerned about being sent over to Kuwait or Iraq during the first conflict. The only reason why I wasn't deployed was because I became pregnant with my son, Pierre.

"I had a lot of friends that went over there. Fortunately, it wasn't as bad as it is this time."

Then she huffed with great annoyance in her voice. Unlike some colleagues from her unit at work, she made it no secret that she detested President George H. Bush for his failed domestic policies and President George W. Bush for his overall incompetence.

Garner noticed Vernise withdrew her hand from his lap. He kept quiet, allowing her to continue with her diatribe. He didn't want to blow it with her over politics since he was a staunch liberal and Democrat; he longed badly for 12:01 p.m. January 20, 2009.

She ranted, "It pisses me off that this Bush has lied to the people so badly. It's just my suspicion that this Bush stole the presidency from Al Gore, and he started a war to bolster an economy that was already slowing down. Humph. The best thing that could have happened for him was September 11th, because it gave him a reason to justify everything. Nobody has benefited except for those with their pro-war and pro-military mentalities. Everyone else—and world for that matter—has suffered badly for his dumb ass decisions."

Sensing the coast was clear, Garner offered his opinion: "When it comes to Iraq, thousands of people are dead based on a personal vendetta against some lunatic, who as we all found out was just crazier than the rest of them. They were just scared of him. In my opinion, it's a lost situation over there and billions are being wasted. I guess that means if there wasn't a war this country might be in a depression—although that's what people are already are saying—or very close to one."

"Babe, you won't get any argument from me. I worked in Intelligence in the Army, and the word some of my friends were telling me is when he invaded Iraq again, he thought it would end as fast as it did when his father invaded the place. But he failed to realize there were way too many other interests and distractions. If he had just concentrated on finding Osama bin Laden, he would have been caught long ago. I really believe that. There was enough information out there to catch him."

Vernise went on to tell Garner she and her father had differing opinions on the wars. "First of all, he's a major and I'm a first lieutenant, so he likes to pull rank on me. He says he's a soldier first. For that reason, he stops short of criticizing Bush. As you can tell, I don't hold back my tongue.

"But let's talk about something else, okay, babe?"

"Sure, I'd rather talk about how good you looked tonight. I really felt proud that you were with me."

"Really?"

Vernise had placed her hand back on Garner's groin. She roamed until she felt his dick through the material of his slacks.

"Keep looking straight ahead," she directed him. She leaned over the center console and ventured to unzip Garner's slacks, slipping his dick through its fly. She parted her lips and enveloped his long, thick shaft. Her head bobbed over his dick while she gave it gentle tugs along the base.

Garner felt only Vernise's lips, tongue, and the back of her throat. He placed his right hand on Vernise's head, offering subtle coaxing to continue.

She paused for air, looking up at him. "Do you like that, *mon ami?*" He moaned softly, inhaling very deep. She resumed tantalizing his shaft with her lips; he began pushing his pelvis upward to meet her sucking motions.

If Garner had any regrets, he wished he had owned an automatic transmission because they were interrupted by two stoplights along Broad River Road, and then when he yielded to oncoming traffic before he turned right onto I-20 westbound.

She asked, "What if I told you that I've been wanting to do this to you since I first saw you, would you believe it?"

"I'd probably believe you—"

"You shouldn't doubt me at all." She went back down on him; they were less than six miles away from the Augusta Highway exit.

Garner pushed his head back into his headrest while Vernise's lips provided the right amount of suction on the tip of his dick, causing him to feel that he just might bust his nut in any moment. Sensing the tension building up in him, Vernise ran her tongue up and down his shaft as though it had been her favorite Popsicle flavor. She stopped at the tip of his dick and tasted his pre-cum. She paused once again, but this time it was to unbutton her blouse so that she could pinch and pull on her right nipple.

I-20 exit fifty-eight could not come soon enough for Garner. He felt compelled to drive faster; he also knew the South Carolina Highway Patrol and the Lexington County police were very much attracted to luxury sports cars. Vernise's tongue went back to working a work that was beyond any comparison. She applied it wide and flat to him. Then she coated his dick with saliva so she could stroke his shaft.

"I bet you'll cum before we get to my place if I continue what I'm doing."

"I won't doubt you on that!"

Vernise ceased sucking him and reclined back in her seat. She unbuttoned the rest of her shirt and slipped her breasts from under her bra. Her pinkish nipples protruded like erasers. As he turned onto the Augusta Highway exit, he noticed Vernise sucking her breasts, alternating from the right and to the left and back, moaning to the sweet sensation that it sent throughout her body.

It was very apparent to Garner that Vernise was the kind of woman who knew how to enjoy her body and herself. He wished she would have worn a skirt so her pussy might have been accessible to rub or finger. Meanwhile, his dick leaked pre-cum once again. He yearned for her lips and tongue. He grasped her hand, guiding it to his lap.

"Why don't you wait until we get to my place," she said. "I've got something very deserving for him."

When they turned into Vernise's driveway, she lunged over the center console and kissed him on his cheek. Before he could react, she had stroked his dick through his slacks and kissed his earlobe, pushing her tongue inside his ear.

Garner sucked in some air before he turned towards Vernise. He aggressively filled her open mouth with his tongue, to which she eagerly enveloped and allowed to intertwine with hers. He also reached across for her exposed breasts.

Suddenly, she was the first to come up for air. She whispered something to him in French; he figured that by the way she reached for the door handle that she wanted them to head inside her house. She wasted little time finding her key and letting them inside.

After shutting the door behind him, they entered into a long embrace and indulged in another equally long, wet passionate kiss. She led Garner by his hand into the family room where she had an immaculately maintained tournament-size pool table. All the cue sticks were arranged according to weight in the holding rack. A recliner chair was situated in one corner and there were two barstools arranged against a wall opposite of the table.

She turned up the thermostat and excused herself. She returned with a bed sheet and a foam sleep pad that she placed on the nine-by-five table. Then she began spreading the sheet atop the foam pad.

"If you're as good as a trick-shot artist as you say you are, you'll understand the importance of your angles," she said.

A quick study in most games, Garner realized Vernise's reference to pool back at Spencer's place had nothing to do with a cue ball and a rack. She then placed her suede jacket and the rest of her clothes on one of the barstools. Her thirty-eight C breasts sagged slightly, but not enough to suggest that time and gravity had finally prevailed. Her hips were a curvaceous compliment to her bubble-shaped ass cheeks.

Garner also slipped out of his clothes and placed his on the other barstool. If his dick could have served as an approval rating, Vernise's would have gone off the charts.

She curled her finger. "Why don't we take a seat over in the recliner?" Behind them was a remote-controlled CD player on a shelf. She pressed the PLAY button and then nuzzled her body against his.

Almost in concert with the music—Teena Marie's "Portuguese Love" —Vernise solicited another kiss from Garner while she began hand stroking his dick. He moaned and inhaled deeply once again to her soft flesh gliding on his. With a slight nudging, Vernise instinctively drew face-to-face with Garner as their tongues slithered together.

Again, she came up for air; Garner then positioned her where he could now partake of her breasts. She immediately cradled his head into her bosom while he licked and nibbled her nipples.

"It's okay if you bite on them." She moaned in approval to his playful chomping down on her nipples. Garner then touched her inner thighs, and she allowed him to slip his hand between them and sample her wetness.

She whispered in French before translating it to him in English. "Isn't she sweet? She's hot and wet just for you."

Garner responded to Vernise by positioning her in the recliner so that he kissed and licked his way down to her Mohawk strip. She helped him along by pushing his head ever so slightly south. Her pussy raged with intense warmth and her clit pulsated. By the time he reached her navel, she held her legs apart to bridge the distance. He grabbed her ankles, lifting them above his head. There, he inhaled her scent and rubbed his face into her glistening pussy. He had every intention to savor her by any imaginary means.

She said, "*N'oubliez pas mon minet. Elle aime l'attention, aussi.*" But he had mistaken *aussi* to mean pussy; he knew he guessed right when she gasped to the sensation his tongue brought to her clit.

With his nose and mouth partially hid from her view, he peered beyond her mound to capture a glimpse of her reaction to his pussy-eating skills. Her eyes were closed, her mouth was agape, and she panted for air. She mumbled another phrase to him in French while she squeezed her breasts and pulled and pinched her nipples.

Just as he managed to come up for air, Vernise clutched the back of his head, ensuring that his face was pressed into her pussy. Her legs jerked slightly; he reacted to her by lifting her ankles above his head once again.

"Oh, shit, baby . . . Oh, shit, baby!" She arched her back and held it that way for several seconds before her body went limp. She panted silently while she caught her breath.

Vernise confirmed Garner's suspicion that she had this moment all planned after she went over to a mini refrigerator in the opposite corner and returned with a can of whip cream and a glass bowl of black cherries and grapes.

She said, "I don't recall you eating anything over at Dr. Watts' place. Are you still hungry?" She placed the two items on the railing. Then she climbed onto the table and remained on her knees—her ass cheeks having already naturally parted before him.

Instinctively, Garner clutched his dick and positioned himself behind Vernise so that he could slowly insert into her pussy. But Vernise envisioned other things for him to do. She handed him the whip cream and wiggled her ass, which was suspended about waist high to him.

She said, "Use your imagination, baby!"

Seconds later, she squealed and giggled to the sensation the whipped cream gave her as he squirted a small amount onto her asshole. Then he bit into a grape and placed half of it between her engorged lips so that it looked like a decoration atop a most delectable pastry.

Kneeling behind her, Garner quickly lapped the half of a grape out of her now flowing pussy, and he proceeded to give her clit the lashing that she desired from him. She also rocked back and forth to whenever his tongue prodded her pussy. Not wanting to let the whipped cream trail down her crack, Garner eagerly licked from her puckered entry. Now he definitely had something to contribute to the next conversation Spencer might broach on tossed salads, he thought.

Vernise, raring for Garner to push his tongue as far as it could probe up her entry, reached back and clutched his head so that it was pressed between her ass cheeks. She began rotating her hips and pushing her ass against his face just as she had once fantasized him doing.

Moments later, Vernise looked over her shoulder, giving Garner a perplexed reaction. Garner explained that he could not stand it any longer, and he wanted to enter her. She accommodated by lying on her back and holding her legs apart in anticipation.

"You're with me now, finally, baby," she said, smiling. "You'll never go without."

Garner closed his eyes in obvious ecstasy as he made the slow, sensual plunge inside Vernise. She placed her hands on his shoulders, and she clasped her legs around his waist, drawing him in further. As their bodies achieved a rhythm, she pushed her hips to meet his strokes.

She kissed him and smiled again. "I told you that I always knew you were black. It looks like my friends will never know what I know about you."

He replied, "Should you have ever doubted?"

"Obviously, I didn't, babe . . ."

The sensation inside Vernise was almost too much for Garner to withstand. Not wanting to be outdone, he attempted to display some of his own prowess.

"You've showed me how you can make shots in the side pocket. How about me banking something off that cushion of yours and into the corner pocket?" he said. "It doesn't matter what angle I have to work with."

Vernise got on her knees and held her ass cheeks apart for him. He knelt behind her and re-inserted his tongue into her asshole, provoking her to manipulate her clit while she muttered other things to him in French. He noticed Vernise's body tensed and she let out another gasp before her body relaxed.

While she remained in that position, he nuzzled against her, pushing his dick inside. He then grabbed her hips, unleashing a fury of thrusts that had her throwing her head back and yelling to each time he bottomed out.

"That's it, baby, beat this pussy up! You're with me now. You can have it any way you want it!"

Garner lasted for only a few strokes before he announced that he was ready to explode wherever she wanted.

"I want it in my mouth, baby," she said. He held back just long enough that Vernise could position herself for his offering. As they made eye contact, he noticed Vernise's eyes widened with each apparent gulping sound she made. She then proceeded to lick his shaft and balls, savoring the mixing of their fluids.

Minutes later, they helped each other off the pool table. She guided him by the hand to her master bedroom where they spent the rest of the night; they eventually fell asleep in each other's arms.

When Garner awoke around 7:30 a.m., he noticed his slacks and the shirt that he wore were ironed and placed on clothes hangers on the closet doorknob. His jacket was draped over the back of a chair, and his socks were laid across his shoes. He called out for Vernise, thinking that maybe she might be in another part of the house; no answer. His right hand brushed against something that felt like an envelope. He read:

> Babe, I had a fabulous time with you last night. But I'm sorry that I didn't tell you that I had an early flight out of Atlanta this morning so tthat I could visit my children in Louisville and then my family in California.
>
> Don't worry about the bed; I've straightened everything else in the family room. You can let yourself out of the house, and you can put the key under one of the flowerpots next to the porch. I will call you when I'm settled where I'll be.
>
> I should be back late this week. Just know that I'll miss you so much—Vernise."

Chapter 24

The ride back home was hollow. Garner drove in no hurry. He stayed in the far right lane on I-20 eastbound among all the slow-pokes and Sunday drivers.

Damn, Vernise's note seemed so impersonal. Even if she sincerely forgot to tell him, he felt he was nothing more than some live dick used in a one-night stand.

So what reason did he have to believe that she would miss him? What reason did he have to believe that she had a fabulous time with him? And what reason did he have to believe that she was always with him?

Humph.

Sighing and shaking his head, he did not think there was any. Those were just lines to soften the impact. He tried consoling himself by running his hand across his dick, which was still sensitive to touch. He could have used another thrilling ride from Vernise's hypnotiz-ing pussy and ass bouncing on him. He also caressed his balls with his finger while he maintained grasp of his dick. He recalled each ejaculation he experienced with Vernise felt like Niagara Falls rush-ing through his body. It reminded him why he was enamored with her in the first place.

Call it chemistry, although he felt like something else.

Silly me, he thought.

Some things in life just never seem to be fair. For once, he thought, being a nice guy may have gotten him laid, but t also left him wondering what went wrong once again with somebody.

He sighed heavily. "Let her have her damned fun in Louisville, or wherever in the hell she'll be in California. If she's really serious, let her call me whenever she said she would!"

Garner went on to reason to himself that maybe he should apply the lyric about a rose being just a rose to his own life. They bud. They bloom. They become a source of happiness for some and a source of food for certain species of animals. The petals fall off. Eventually, the flower dies. Thus, the rose is nothing more than a rose, and no more. He supposed at least that would be one way of making sense of her, but that would be a bit too simple. It had to be more complicated.

So he posed another question to himself: *Then what is reality?*

He contemplated why the holiday season was the worst time of the year for some people. He understood that depression could descend upon one's mind like a buzzard swooping down on a carcass. That made sense to him why the suicide rate increases at a time of the year when hearts should be merry and minds are consumed by peace and joy.

All of a sudden, Richmond did not seem as bad of a place to be for the holiday. It was a place where his heart could be encouraged by Miriam's fruitcakes and fruitcake cookies. It was a place where he could reflect on how far he had come since leaving there in August 1993 for Tallahassee and freshman orientation. There was no way he could complicate that reality.

He called Miriam later that afternoon, placing his request for two fruitcakes baked in rectangular muffin pans with as many cookies as she could possibly make with the rest of the batter. He also informed her that he would leave the morning of the twenty-fifth, and he expected to be there before noon.

Miriam warned, "Whatever you do, don't tell your brother and sister that you're coming."

"Why would I tell Norris and Carla? You know they're like peas in a pod. I guess that's why I hadn't spoken to them since the summer."

Miriam became wistful concerning her other two children. "They're just like their father Aaron at times . . ."

Throughout their childhood, Miriam steadfastly preached to her brood that it could not allow for jealousies, rifts, and chasms. She often said, "Norris, Garner, and Carla, you three needed to stick together no matter what, because when all hell breaks loose in life family is sometimes all what a person has to get through it."

Miriam was well aware of the closeness of Norris and Carla's relationship. Although they were five years apart, Norris and Carla were often partners in mischief, and Norris went to the extreme of sticking up for his youngest sibling if somebody ever attempted to pick on her. The only thing Norris would not do is take any punishment for his sister's misdeeds.

Garner's shaky relationship among his siblings was the one that troubled Miriam the most. One of her earliest and more indelible memories occurred while Garner was a toddler.

"Mommy, why my brother is white?" Norris innocently inquired.

Embarrassed, Miriam hugged and kissed Norris, hoping her outpouring of love might soothe his concerns. "Only God knows, baby, but your brother is not white."

Norris was not satisfied. He persisted, "If my brother is not white, then what is he?"

Miriam shook her head, sighing. She was not prepared to handle a situation like that among siblings.

"[He's] your brother, baby," she answered, "and he'll always be your brother. I love both of you just the same."

Norris still had a look of curiosity. "Are you sure, mommy?"

Miriam often dismissed the fights Norris and Garner had as children because she attributed it to boys being boys. But there was little she was able to accomplish overcoming the way Norris otherwise interacted with Garner.

The same could be said between Garner and Carla. She taught Norris and Garner that they had only one sister, and they needed to be there for her. It grieved her no matter what Garner did for Carla, it was never appreciated as much as what Norris would do for her.

"Your brother Garner loves you just as much as Norris loves you, and he would do anything for you," she once told Carla, who at the time was in the sixth grade. "See, he fixed your bicycle while Norris was out with his friends. Why don't you just try to be appreciative what both of your brothers do for you?"

"Mom, I know. But I can't explain it," Carla answered. "It just seems to mean more to me when Norris does something than when Garner does it for me. I just don't know why."

Carla then posed a question to Miriam that she never expected from her youngest.

"Mom, why is it you seem to love Garner more than you love Norris and me?"

With widened eyes and raised brows, Miriam stared at Carla for several seconds. She held her hand on her hip and wagged her right index finger in her face. "Carla Ruth Davis!" Then she paused again, stopping to laugh. She motioned for Carla to sit on her lap before kissing her on the forehead.

"I have never played any favorites between you and your brothers. I've always told y'all if I can't do for one of you I won't do for any of you."

Carla reacted in a huff. She immediately stood up, pointing defiantly. "Mom, I get tired of you comparing Norris and me to Garner. We're not like him, and he's not like us!"

Miriam's eyes squinted and she cocked her hand back ready to unload. "I'll slap those teeth out of your mouth if I ever hear you say something like that again, do you hear me!"

"Whatever. Who would believe you're my mother just like he's my brother?" She mumbled it just loud enough for Miriam to catch the gist of her comment.

Slap!

Miriam tagged Carla above her right ear lobe just as she attempted to stomp off. Carla crumbled to the floor clutching her ear, crying bitterly.

"As long as you're black, young lady, I'll kick your ass. Do you understand me?" Miriam yelled.

"Yes, mama—"

All three of you are my children! I don't treat any of you any differently. I don't ever want to hear you talk like that again!"

Garner mentioned to Miriam the only reason why Norris and Carla ever showed up at their mother's place in 2005, the last time he visited Richmond for the holidays, it was to antagonize him for being out of work.

"I know you don't like to hear me talk like this, but it was like they had a chance to show what true niggers they could be," he said. "That's why I was so determined to find work in 2006. I wasn't going to let them treat me like that again."

Miriam immediately chastised Garner. "I've told you about talking about Norris and Carla like that! They're still your brother and sister, no matter what."

"You know it's true," he protested. "No matter how much I've tried reaching out to them like you've wanted all of us to do for each other, they've not wanted to have anything to do with me."

There was a lengthy pause to their conversation. Very rarely Garner and Miriam ever had a difference of opinion. He volunteered to apologize. He went back to the reason why he called Miriam.

"So are you going to have those fruitcakes and cookies ready for me when I get there?"

Miriam chortled. "You just get your behind here!"

Chapter 25

For the day or so that he would be in Richmond, Garner convinced himself that he could endure any encounter with his siblings. Norris and Carla could act like absolute assholes if they wanted on Christmas Day, but Miriam was his sole reason for visiting.

Nearly an hour had passed since he crossed the North Carolina border when he noticed a **NUMBER WITHHELD** appearing on his caller ID. He grumbled at the thought somebody would dare to call him since he went almost two days without his home or cell phone ringing.

"Merry Christmas!"

It was Kadrece.

"Merry Christmas to you," Garner responded politely. More than three months had passed since he last spoken to Kadrece. Although he contemplated it on many occasions, he decided against contacting her since he thought she would be better served dealing with her emotional struggles without him. Kadrece's plea to forego sex with him in the Westheimer Hotel was a first in their casual-at-best relationship.

There were faint sounds of children in the background laughing and talking ecstatically to each other. Kadrece inquired, "And what did you get for Christmas?"

"I don't know," he answered. "I'll find out in a couple of hours."

"Now Garner Davis, if it ain't pussy for Christmas, which I know you'd accept on any day of the year, I know you've gotten something."

"I haven't received anything. I'm still driving north on I-95 to see my mother in Richmond. You do remember my mother?"

"Oh, yeah, I remember her. You've showed me several pictures of her. How is she?"

"She's doing fine; how about your family?"

"Everyone's here in Atlanta for the holiday. That's where I am right now."

Kadrece was the youngest among two boys and three girls for Hilton and Johnette Kendricks. All of her siblings attended historically black colleges in Atlanta, but she chose to break ranks and attend the historically black college in Tallahassee. But that was Kadrece being the free spirited and fiercely independent one of them all. That was one the qualities that Garner found most attractive in her.

He mentioned to her that he would be in Atlanta on the twenty-eighth to cover a college football bowl game in the Georgia Dome.

"Really? I'm staying here until the second. Then I'll drive back down to Tallahassee . . ."

As much as he missed Kadrece's conversation and sexual company, he held out in hope that Vernise's questionable move was an aberration. But he sensed in the way Kadrece's voice trailed there was more to the reason why she called him.

"How are things going for you at the law offices of Schaeffer, Bradley and Kendricks?"

She spoke with some resignation. "A bit slow these days for the way I like it; there's still plenty of action with Tallahassee being the capitol, but I'm starting to long for the big city. When I saw you in Houston, I began thinking whether I would want to start a practice here in Atlanta."

If she went to her siblings for help, Kadrece would not have any problem getting started in Atlanta. Her oldest brother, Wesley, was a legal counsel for DeKalb County, Georgia.

She also had an offer by M. Kevin Fauntleroy, who's married to her sister Kamryn, to work for him. An attorney by formal background, Kevin was a former legal counsel to the Atlanta professional basketball and baseball franchises when multi-billionaire Fred Hummer owned them. He branched off into becoming a sports and entertainment agent in 2001. He now has a thriving agency near Lennox Square representing thirty-one athletes and twelve entertainers. She passed up on the opportunity for concerns if things went wrong in her sister's marriage, she wouldn't be caught in the middle of it.

Garner said, "I've always believed you'll do well wherever you decide to set up your own practice." He could tell by her silence that his words were of no encouragement. "What is really on your mind?"

After a lengthy delay, Kadrece finally broke the silence. "Garner, how long have we known each other?"

"Humph, it's gotta be maybe a dozen years. I met you when I was going into my junior year in Tallahassee."

"You know, sex aside, we've sort of grown up together. Some times at a distance, but wouldn't you agree that it's odd we've never become serious?"

Garner tried making light of the moment. "There's never been an argument we've had that I've successfully beat you once you've gotten all your facts together. I think that's what makes you a brilliant attorney."

Kadrece reacted impatiently. "Just agree with me or not, Garner."

"All right, I agree."

"Thanks. You don't have to answer this question right now. But I want you to think about it. Next time we talk, I hope you'll have an answer."

"Okay . . ."

She repeated, "Have you ever thought about us having a serious relationship? I mean, the sex has been great whenever we've had it. No man has ever turned me on and satisfied me the way you have—"

"And no woman has ever done the same thing for me. I feel sort of dumb that I've not called you since Houston."

Like the attorney she was, she pressed for more with her follow-up. "Has it ever dawned upon you why?"

It was Garner's turn to pause and reflect. He recognized part of his problem was that he never saw Kadrece beyond a booty call or fuck buddy. He glanced at his clock, recognizing that they had talked for nearly an hour. He planned on calling Miriam once he crossed into Virginia.

As he contemplated Kadrece's question, his dick had its own opinion regarding her. "The best answer that I can come up with, I think we've always valued our friendship first over becoming lovers.

"I don't think we've wanted to lose that part of it. We've always been able to talk, and it's not mattered whom we've been involved with."

"Aunt Kadrece, we need you!" a child screamed in the background.

"I'll be there!"

"Sounds like your fans await you."

"I think you're right," she answered, sighing. "But think about it, okay Garner? Call me when you come to Atlanta. Maybe we can have dinner or something like that."

Garner's phone vibrated moments after hanging up. Of all people, Tamira sent him a text message while he was on the phone with Kadrece.

The message read,

> **Happy Holidays, I hope you get all that you asked for and hoped for.**

Humph.

He suspected Spencer already knew that Tamira had already met another man, or he was aware that she would bring someone else to his party. As he contemplated returning Tamira's message, he wondered why would she even remember him after she ignored every attempt he made following their one-nighter?

Things people will do.

Garner turned into Miriam's neighborhood on Chester Chase Drive in Chesterfield shortly before 11:30 a.m. It was an overcast day; the forecasted high was thirty-three degrees with a chance of snow in the late afternoon. Miriam's light green Toyota Highlander, the one she drove when she picked him up at Richmond's airport (RIC) in 2005, was in the driveway.

Stepping out of his car, the wind blew briskly as the few leaves on her winter-browned lawn were gathered up in a tight spiral before being whisked to another spot. He wasted little time scurrying to the front door, ringing the doorbell.

"Come on in!"

The glass weather door was unlocked and the chestnut stained front door was partially opened. Garner walked inside. "It's me, mom!"

"I know who it is!" Garner perceived that Miriam was in the kitchen to his left. It was beyond the dining room and formal living room. He walked farther into the house, tossing his bag on one of the two large, dark blue recliners situated in the regular living room. He took a seat on the matching king sofa.

He made sure Miriam could hear him while she was in the kitchen. "I hope you don't tell everyone who rings your doorbell the door's open."

Miriam appeared before him, smiling. "No I don't. I saw you from the kitchen as you turned into the driveway."

She wore a white and lavender walking suit with a matching jacket and shirt under it. She also wore a white wrap across the front section of her naturally auburn colored hair that she allowed for some graying streaks to coexist. The years had been far kinder to her since she moved into the new neighborhood back in 2001; she appeared to be less stressed out and burdened. Perhaps some of it had to do with her thriving court reporting firm that she founded in 2003. She had people making money for her, a dream that she often shared with Garner, rather than her making money for others.

Garner rushed to hug Miriam. They enjoyed a hearty laugh before she motioned for him to follow her into the kitchen.

She said, "Your fruitcakes have been ready since ten o'clock. I kept going back and forth to the living room wondering when you might show up. I stopped doing it around eleven. You shouldn't make your mother worry like that.''

"Mom, I called you about an hour ago after I crossed the Virginia border. So what do you mean worrying about me?"

"Shut up, little boy, I can worry about you any time and any way I want."

Garner blushed at Miriam's maternal-like comment. She told him there was a turkey in the oven with dressing, green beans, mashed potatoes, and rolls already prepared atop the range. He inquired, "You got up to do all that cooking this morning?"

"Of course not. I'm not about to wear myself out like I used to when you, Norris, and Carla were kids."

Why did she have to mention them?

He pressed his lips together, exhaling rather hard through his nostrils. Then he snapped his finger as though he forgot something. He excused himself, heading back out to the living room.

His voice faded with each step he took. "I guess they still don't know I'm here . . . Do you think I need to back my car into the driveway so they won't notice a car with a South Carolina license plate on it?"

Miriam reacted, "You're not going back out there like you are?" Garner had on just a pullover shirt and slacks.

"No, I'm not."

He returned to the kitchen with an envelope. He placed it on the counter. She then brought up her left hand to about face level showing off the Armani cream dial model watch he gave her during his visit in 2005.

"You know I tell almost anybody that's willing to listen to me that my little boy bought me this."

Garner sat down at the kitchen table. "For some reason, that doesn't surprise me."

"Your brother and sister and your nephews should be over here in a little bit. I told them not to come until I was ready to have them over since I was cooking today."

She poured herself a glass of apple juice while standing in front of the refrigerator. Then she joined him at the table. "So what's in the envelope? A trip to Hawaii, [or] the Virgin Islands?"

"How about a trip to Richmond—"

She gave him a suspicious look. "I know you didn't do that." It always gave Garner great pleasure to watch Miriam smile whenever he did something for her on special occasions. He explained to her that he took a more efficient route this year. Miriam's green eyes widened as she flipped through the gift certificates as she read off Macy's, Dillard's, Tony Roma's, and Speigel's.

She exclaimed, "These are some of my favorite places!" Then she motioned for him. "Come here . . ."

Garner wiped off Miriam's beige colored lipstick, blushing. "Mom, do you always have to do that?"

She waggled her right index finger at him. "I told you about that. You know you're never too old for me to whip you, kiss you, or hug you."

Garner reacted to his cell phone's buzzing with a perplexed expression. His ID indicated a call coming from the 502 area code. He ignored it the first time; it went off again. He excused himself from Miriam's presence, walking off to another part of the house.

"*Joyeux Noel, mon ami!*" Garner kept quiet. "Oh, I'm sorry, Merry Christmas, babe!"

Vernise was not the last person Garner expected to call him while he was in Richmond, but neither was she among the first. She went into an explanatory mode why she called from a hotel number to prove that she was in Louisville. Then she asked him to hang up so she could call him from her cell phone.

Seconds later, his phone buzzed with a number showing from the 803 area code. She said, "I didn't want to spoil the time I knew I'd be spending with you because of personal issues with my children's father. It's always an emotional thing for me whenever something involves them. I hope you understand."

Garner sat down on the edge of the bed in Miriam's guest room. "Maybe I do understand, and maybe I don't. All I will say is that I figured if you were worth your salt you would eventually call me."

"I'm sorry."

"Uh, you know what? Actually, I don't understand. How can you assume that I would?" He paused and glanced at the date on his cell phone. "Let's see, it just took you, uh, three days to do it."

"All right, Mr. Smart Aleck."

"No, it's being a good journalist. We're taught to be keen observers."

"Well, we're taught in law enforcement to always be aware of any changes or nuances in the areas you investigate. So what did you get me for Christmas? I forgot to give you your gift before I left."

"Oh, I thought you already gave it to me."

"No, I actually had a gift for you. Now what did you get for me?"

He spoke slowly to her. "What would you have said if I left a note next to you when woke up? Would you still be willing to talk to me on Christmas Day?"

Okay, I got the damned message!

Vernise tried keeping her cool knowing her timing wasn't the best three days ago. "What's so wrong with a note? I knew I'd be ripping and running through airports, and I wouldn't be able to call you. And I thought you would appreciate me telling you that much."

Garner got up and closed the door behind him for more privacy. He sat back down on the bed, reclining. "Appreciate what? Like, thanks for the dick. Hope to see you when I get back into town?"

"That's not what I meant."

"Funny. Lately, I've had women call me inconsiderate or don't say anything at all to me. I meet somebody I think I could really like, and I get one of those *'Oops, I've-got-a-plane-to-catch'* notes. You should have told me before hand."

Vernise reacted, "Garner, that's selfish! I mean, real selfish. First of all, do you think that I would bring just any man into my house?"

"I don't know. I know I don't bring just any woman into my place."

"Do you think I'd ask just any man to squirt whipped cream on the crack of my ass so he can lick out of it?"

"I don't know. Do you?"

"Ugh!"

Garner continued venting his disappointment at her. "Look, I know that's being facetious by questioning your sincerity. I just think that you might have asked me all these kinds of questions if I were the one that left you a note. Humph, I don't even know if you would have even given me a chance to explain."

Vernise, rubbing her temple, was on the brink of cursing at Garner. "All right, what do you want from me. A formal apology?"

"Mmmm, why not?"

She hissed at his insistence. "Garner, please accept my apology for not explaining myself, and leaving without kissing you goodbye. Now, I said it. Are you happy?"

"I'd be much happier if you were sucking my dick, or letting me slap those ass cheeks while you screamed out my name."

"Humph, you're such a freak. But I like it!"

He managed a smile. "I'm glad you do." He tugged at his pants, adjusting his erection. "Apology accepted."

"Babe, I've gotta get going. The kids' father agreed that I get to see them one last time for a couple of hours before he takes them to Lexington and visit his parents."

"You've mentioned your ex-husband a lot. I'm just curious, do you still have feelings for him?" Garner blurted; he had already figured that he should voice the rest of his concerns. And if she did not like it, too fucking bad.

"No!" She was emphatic and immediate with her response. "Those feelings are over and done with. Cremated and buried six feet under."

Now he felt he could transition to another subject—on his own terms.

"When are you coming back from California?"

"Saturday. I'm scheduled to fly into Atlanta that evening around eight."

"I'll be in Atlanta. Maybe I could pick you up at the airport?"

"I drove to Atlanta in my own car. Maybe I can come and visit you wherever you'll be. Can I call you once I'm in California?"

When Garner emerged from the guest room, he noticed Norris had showed up along with Shalinda and their three sons. Garner's bag was moved to the side of the recliner; Norris had taken a seat there.

"Yo, baby bro!"

Garner was surprised by Norris's presence, even more so by the pleasant tone in his voice. Norris stood five-ten; he was stocky much like Aaron, weighing two hundred and thirty pounds. All three of his sons were also of a similar build.

He peered over to his right and waved amicably at Shalinda, who had just run her hand through her extension weave. He then walked over to shake Norris's hand and give him a brotherly hug. Tre'Vandre, who was six and the youngest, ran over to hug Garner, grabbing at his waist. He darted back to his remote-controlled silver Ford F-150 pick-up truck.

"I got something for you, the fellas and Shalinda. It's over in my bag."

Ne'quan, who was eight, ran over to Garner. "What you have for me, Uncle Garner?" Garner reacted with widened eyes. "Well, can't you at least say hello, hug me or shake my hand?" Ne'quan ran back to playing with his Hot Wheels set; he started shooing away Tre'Vandre from the gift that Miriam had given him.

Garner searched his bag. He handed Norris envelopes with his name on one and Shalinda's on the other. After explaining to Norris he had arranged for luxury box tickets to three Richmond minor league baseball games of their choice, and there was a gift certificate for Shalinda, there was contriteness and gratitude in Norris's demeanor.

He spoke quietly to Garner. "That's all right, bro . . . That's really all right. Sorry I didn't get you anything. I would have if I knew you were coming. But your mother didn't tell me and your sister."

Norris then announced to his bunch the gift that Garner had given them. De'Lonzo came over and gave Garner a handshake and bumped his right shoulder against his. Tre'Vandre and Ne'quan also came running over, each giving him a hug.

De'Lonzo asked, "Uncle Garner, my dad says you've met Kobe, LeBron and Dwayne Wade. Is that true?" His voice showed signs of going through puberty; he was in the ninth grade.

Garner smiled, nodding his head. He then frowned at Norris, who hunched his shoulders and pointed at De'Lonzo.

"He came to me with an assignment about his family last year. I didn't have much to tell him about myself and his mother. I didn't think people would be impressed with what his aunt was doing at First Principal. So I told him about what you were doing. He didn't believe that you were a sports guy."

Garner looked in DeLonzo's direction, smiling. "If he told you about Kobe, LeBron, and D-Wade, then it's probably all true."

DeLonzo's eyes became like saucers. "You really did?"

Moments later, Corliss, a large boy for twelve, came into the living room from the kitchen and joined his cousins on the questioning. Carla was not far behind bringing a plate of food.

"Hold on guys, I need to give this to your aunt." He walked over and gave her a hug. He sensed that by the way she embraced him that she actually missed him. He suspected Carla's change of attitude might have had to do with whatever change that occurred in Norris.

She peeked inside the white envelope with her name on it. She held the gift Visa card with a surprised look. "Thanks, you really didn't have to do this."

Garner said, "I wanted to do this. There's one hundred and fifty on it. Get something for you and Corliss on it, okay?"

"Corliss, it looks like you'll be able to get that remote-controlled helicopter that you've been bothering me about all this month. Tell your uncle thanks.

"And as for me," she said, looking at Garner and then at Miriam, "I'll be going to one of the stores to get that make-up I've been looking at for a while now."

For the first time since they went on their own, Miriam had Garner, Carla, and Norris along with her grandchildren under her roof on Christmas Day.

Garner peered over at Miriam, who watched everything from the kitchen. Leaning against a doorsill, she had a grin wider than the one she had an hour earlier. She reminded him that his present was under the tree. He acknowledged it; however, he was more so preoccupied with telling his four nephews about his times interacting with some of professional basketball's biggest and brightest stars.

Chapter 26

Garner was back in his element once he crossed the DeKalb County line on I-20 eastbound. A major television market with four professional sports franchises, two Division I-A schools in Atlanta's downtown area, and another major Division I-A school in Athens less than ninety minutes away were just the right enticements.

He mused for a moment that a No. 2 anchor's job wouldn't be a bad one. There was something for being at a destination market in the business because if he never made the rise to ESPN, he wanted nothing less than a return to a top twenty-five market.

As it was in Houston, the lure of diverse pussy was another attraction Garner liked about a market as large as Atlanta: light skinned dark skinned, medium complexion, pecan tan, caramel colored, Hispanic, Ethiopian, Moroccan, Korean, and Chinese. They all made for a melting pot for his libido—maybe Atlanta was where he needed to have spent his free time?

He reserved a room at the downtown Peachtree, the designated media hotel. He would be within walking distance of the Chamber of Commerce where most of the media sessions were scheduled leading up to the bowl game. The Philips Arena and Georgia Dome were within sight and walking distance from the Chamber of Commerce. And once he navigated his way to the freeway, the Bengals'

practice venue in College Park was less than twenty minutes taking
I-85 southbound.

After checking in for his credentials at the Chamber, Garner maneuvered through the late-morning downtown traffic back to the
hotel. He already had an idea on the way he wanted to spend his first
night in town.

"Kadrece, where are you?"

"Oh, hey, Garner." She was her usual listless and yawning like an
old lion. "Why didn't you tell me you were in town?" Of all the people, Garner should have known Kadrece was not a morning person.
He found it amusing after all these years that she'd succeeded as an
attorney given all those early dockets and appointments.

"Well, I'm telling you now," he said. "I just got in town about an
hour ago. I've already gotten my credentials, and I'll be going out to
the Bengals' afternoon practice in a little bit. This is their last full-
contact session before they start winding down for Monday's game."

She yawned through her response. "You know how I am about
football; it's never been my sport. You know the band is the only
thing I'm concerned about at a football game."

Garner chuckled. "Well, these are mainstream schools; I know you
wouldn't be interested in this one."

"I know. So how was your trip to Richmond?"

"It was really nice, even better than I thought it would be. Are you
still here until the second?"

Kadrece excused herself to get in her final yawn. She stretched so
hard that she nearly caught a cramp in her hamstring.

"You're all right?"

"Oh, I'm okay; just stretching."

Christmas was three days ago. Garner still had not given any
thought to Kadrece's suggestion about them taking their relationship to a more serious level. When he returned to Columbia, he
spent all of the next day getting ready for his trip to Atlanta, picking
up clothes from the cleaners and setting up appointments for his car.
The following day, he went to the Infiniti dealership and replaced
the damaged alloy wheel, and later the car shop for the front-end
alignment.

Almost mischievously, the slight twitch by Garner's dick reminded him it had been nearly two years since they last fucked. In their
twelve years of knowing each other, this was the longest they'd gone
without being in intimate company.

"Kadrece, it was nice that you called me on Christmas Day. It had
me thinking about how much I've actually missed you."

"Do you really mean that?"

"Uh-huh."

"I've missed you, too. That's why I brought up about us becoming
serious. I'm tired of booty calls with men that I'm embarrassed to
say that I've slept with. I'm getting too old for that."

Garner found a seat among a cluster of plush couches in the lobby. He was conscious not to talk too loud for any eavesdroppers
getting an earful of their conversation.

"So you're really looking into settling down soon?" he inquired.

She closed her eyes and nodded. "Garner, I'm beginning to feel
strange whenever I come around my family. All of them are married
with kids. I'm the only one who hasn't even come close to doing
that."

He was slow to respond. He had never given any consideration of
her being the kind of woman he would ever ask to marry or become
the mother of his children. He glanced over his left shoulder.

"Garner, are your there?"

"Yeah, I, uh, really don't know what to say about that."

A woman with a light pecan tan complexion had just stood in line
at the front desk. Tugging a black Tommy Hilfiger luggage set, she
was dressed in a black maxi coat, wearing jeans, a lilac blouse and
black boots. A woman of darker complexion who was also tugging
a luggage set accompanied her.

"Uh, Kadrece, can I get back with you? I really need to get going
so I can put something together for the six o'clock broadcast."

Stuffing his phone in a jacket pocket, Garner sprang to his feet and
made sure that nobody stood in behind the two women. The one
with the lighter complexion showed the most impatience. She ran
her hand through her brown hair of medium length styled like former Olympic champion gymnast Dominique Dawes. She scanned

to her right, then her left. She shifted her laptop carrying case from her left shoulder to the right, as well as shifting the weight from her right foot to the left.

The hotel's desk attendant announced, "May I help the next person in line, please?"

"Looks like you're the one that needs help," she said; her friend giggled at her.

"Girl, leave that man alone. I don't think you'd appreciate somebody saying that about you."

She turned sharply and glared at her friend, replying just above a whisper and loud enough that Garner heard it. "Well, it ain't me. Just remember that." She reached into her pocket and flipped open her cell phone, checking her messages. She glanced up at the ceiling and exhaled loudly. She looked over her right shoulder. He nodded and smiled; she smiled back at him.

Garner was not sure whether her noticing him took off any edge; he figured this was as good of a chance to initiate contact. He was not concerned that he wore black slacks, tennis shoes, a light blue winter jacket and a beige Polo shirt.

He inquired, "Are you here for any of the sorority events this weekend?"

She was short of being taken aback by his question, placing her hand on her hip. "Now why would I be here for a sorority event?" Her voice was soft, but not as high pitched. She reminded him of Murlette Desormeaux with her directness.

He folded his arms, swaying slightly before steadying. "You just seemed to have that look of belonging to a sorority."

"Next in line please," the front desk attendant announced.

She shifted the large carrying case shoulder strap from her right back to the left. Before she could grasp her luggage handle, Garner had already pushed it forward for her, covering a distance of about five feet.

"Thank you."

"No problem."

She smiled before turning around to face the front desk.

He went on to say, "I remember where I went to school the sorors had a different look about them. If you're not one, I'm sure you've been asked if you've ever done any modeling—"

She turned slightly and faced Garner, folding her arms. "Well, they said I wasn't quite tall enough for it." Garner returned a surprised look. She said, "At five feet, six and a quarter inches, they preferred somebody that was at least five-seven."

He spaced left his thumb and forefinger to the approximate measurement. "You mean a less than an inch made that much of a difference?"

She nodded. "Apparently so. None of the major agencies in New York wanted me." She huffed again. "But I've gotten over it. I decided to get my degree. And I'm happy with my life doing what I'm doing."

"And what could that be?"

"I help design software for hospitals and health professionals. I got my degree in electrical engineering with an emphasis in computer science."

Another smart one, he reacted. She could probably run intellectual laps with someone like Tamira. *So that explains for her carrying a large laptop case.* "The computer must be a sign that your work is never finished. Are you here in Atlanta because of your job?"

She brushed her bang to the side. "It's not as bad as it appears. I finished all the hard stuff before I left. Now all I have to do is check for e-mails until I get back on Monday, the seventh.

"So what brings you to Atlanta?"

Garner told her that he was in town to cover the bowl game. She was coy not to show any interest. He managed a wry smile. "Well, if it helps any, if I ran a modeling agency, I would have offered you a contract. Now it's their loss."

"Why do you say that?" Her brown eyes never widened.

"I never would have met you if they had offered you a contract." He extended his hand out to her. "I'm Garner Davis. I work for a television station in Columbia, South Carolina. And you are?"

"Autumn," she replied, accepting his offer. "And this is my friend Patricia."

"Next please," the desk attendant announced.

"I guess that's me." She turned around and dragged her belongings to the front desk.

Meanwhile, another line opened. Garner, who was preoccupied with keeping visual contact with Autumn, did his best to kill time. He asked the desk attendant questions about things that he already knew.

"So you're saying all I need to do is attach this modem to my computer and then I pay for it by the day, using my credit card?"

"That's correct, sir."

When Garner noticed Autumn was preparing to leave with Patricia, he hurried to catch up with her just before she reached the elevators. "Excuse me, I hope we might see each other again soon." He reached into his jacket pocket for his wallet. He pulled out a business card, which had his office and cell phone numbers and an office e-mail address.

Autumn gave his card quick glance before stuffing it down a side pouch on her computer case. He extended his hand out to her again. "If I don't hear from you, it was still a pleasure meeting you, Autumn."

Garner felt an inexplicable connection when their hands made contact. He also discerned it in Autumn's eyes. Her smile became more of a grin when she released his hand.

"It was nice meeting you, too, uh . . . ."

She reached into the pouch, referring to his card. "Garner." When the elevator door opened, Patricia interrupted them, motioning for her to join. Her voice faded with each step toward the elevator. "I've got your card. I'll keep you in mind."

Chapter 27

After transmitting his Bengals report from Atlanta's NBC affiliate, Garner checked for messages on his cell phone. He deleted unfamiliar numbers from his call log. He did the same thing with his text messages until he came upon Tamira's from Christmas Day; he went against his better judgment and punched in her number.

The memories of her riding his dick and her allowing him to ejaculate inside her were too much to suppress.

"Hello, Lake residence—"

"Hi, this is Garner."

"Well, this is a pleasant surprise."

"How could this be a surprise? The surprise should be that you answered the phone."

"So how are you, Garner?"

"I'm fine, and you?"

Tamira was not surprised that Garner called her; she anticipated that he would have called her much sooner while Spencer's party may have been fresh on his mind. She cringed at any thought of Vernise. It was apparent to her that Vernise had no obvious attachment to Garner.

"I noticed you brought someone with you to Dr. Watts' party.

How long have you known her?"

"We actually met a couple of months ago. Why are you so interested? You had somebody with you."

"Yes, I did, Garner. I am a single woman."

"You are just that, and I'm a single man."

After all these years, Tamira felt proud that she managed to live a simple life, and it was her intent to keep it that way. Among her small circle of academic friends, she was proud of having very little gray hair beyond that which grew on her tuft of pubic hair.

She was more than glad to have met Stephen Raines, fifty-four, a widower, and with no apparent drama from his previous dealings with women. She also regarded his standing in the community as owner of the city's Ford dealership a plus.

"Garner, you happened to catch me just as I was heading out the door. Stephen and I were going to dinner. Is there any specific reason why you called?"

"I guess not."

"Well, I wish you the best. A handsome man like yourself probably has a several women vying for your attention. I really hope that you do take care of yourself."

"Why you're telling me to take care of myself?"

"I have to go, Garner."

Whatever!

Garner and Kadrece agreed to hang out at High Cotton in Stone Mountain, a popular nightspot in DeKalb County. It was known for playing old school and bump-n-grind music for its patrons rather than the kiddy hip-hop and rap genres. The High Cotton was also a place where couples could mix among singles, and it offered a full restaurant menu and a live band on the weekends.

Kadrece reminded Garner before they hung up to dress for the occasion—the men were required to wear a jacket. So Garner stopped by his hotel and changed into a white long-sleeved shirt, a charcoal pin-stripped suit and matching slacks, and his black leather shoes.

When he showed up at Kadrece's family home in Norcross, he expected to see her in dreads, wearing stylish slacks and a jacket, and evening boots. She answered the door wearing a slinky halter evening dress with plunging neckline, a deep V-shaped open back and thigh-high slit; she wore black three-inch pumps; her hair was short and wavy with side-swept bangs, and she had medium-size loop gold earrings. He was stunned by her transformation and his eyes were riveted on her cleavage.

"Come on inside, Garner. Just close the door behind you."

He still had not moved, though he made great effort to inhale her fragrance that trailed her. His eyes were now locked in on her ass, which bounced with each step. He let out a quick breath to calm himself.

She stopped to peer over her right shoulder. "You are coming in, aren't you?"

"Uh, yes, I am . . . I don't feel like fighting anybody tonight." He took a seat on the living room sofa.

"What do you mean by that?"

Kadrece knew she looked good for Garner, and it was the best she felt about herself in years. She hadn't lost any weight, but she hadn't gained any, either, on her size twelve frame. More importantly, she felt the dreads gave her a wild and exotic look, which translated into her attracting men that were only looking for a good fuck. She now had different expectations for herself.

"You know some fool's going to try it. He'll want to either give you his number or start some conversation with you, having no respect that you might be with somebody. That's usually how those things start."

"I've never known you to be the jealous type," she replied. "You usually handled stuff like that by ignoring them."

"You're right. But I might be jealous tonight."

"I'll go get my coat."

When Kadrece returned, Garner had already stood up and was in the process of undressing her with his eyes. He envisioned her breasts bobbling beneath her garment and her large, dark brown nipples enticing him to tantalize them with his tongue and lips. He held his arms out for her; they entered into a tight hug and sensual kiss, which triggered bodily responses by both of them.

Kadrece found the fortitude to ignore the acute throbbing of her clit and sensitivity of her nipples by separating first. She reminded Garner that she was in her parents' home. She giggled at their behavior. "It kinda feels strange telling you that. But I hope you understand."

"I do." He tugged at his crotch, making sure that his dick remained inside his boxers.

On their drive to Stone Mountain, Garner cut a quick glance at Kadrece. "When did you decide on this makeover?"

"I've been thinking about a sophisticated look for a while. I thought I might be able to see things from a different perspective, if I actually did something about it."

"I think it's more like you're offering a different perspective of yourself."

"I think you're right," she said. "By the way, one thing I'd like for us to do this time while we're out, okay—"

"What's that?"

"I'd like if our conversation just center around you and I, and not about anybody we've gone to bed with."

"That's fine with me. I've been thinking about what you've asked me, anyway."

Kadrece's eyes lit up. "You have?"

"Yeah. You know in some ways we're total opposites. But you know what they say about opposites." That was the extent of his thinking about them becoming serious.

"I do. But I've tried to look at things a little deeper." She pointed out when opposites attract it's usually because both people recognize their strengths are what complement the other person's weaknesses. She also felt they were borderline opposites. "I like to talk a lot. I know you can talk a lot, but it depends on what gets you going."

Damn, she has been thinking this thing through, he thought. Now the journalist in him reasoned he needed to survive this conversation. He had hoped a head fake or two would have kept him a step ahead of her.

"Okay, well, a couple of things I've always noticed is you're a strong-willed woman and you're excitable at times. I like that in you. I think I'm just as excitable, but I might be a little more laid back than you."

She nodded. "Good observation. You see it's things like that if two people come to appreciate each other that can make a relationship based on things other than sex."

And this the same Kadrece Renee Kendricks whose pussy craved for dick more than a man craved for pussy?

Garner glanced over his right shoulder. "I think I understand what you're saying. But I can't imagine you not placing a priority on sex. I think sex ranks up there with money in a relationship."

"Come on now," she huffed. "You ought to know me by now! I love sex like any other horny woman out there. But I've also reached a point in life where I have to make sounder decisions. I want a man who's going to be with me no matter what—a man who's going to be faithful to me and a man who will see there's more to me than this sweet chocolate pussy and ass that I'm sitting on."

He shook his head. "Now that's the Kadrece that I know. I just had to make sure that you were still there."

"Shut up!"

The High Cotton had a bright, yet soft ambience. Long, lavish bars lined both sides of the establishment where most of the single and presumably unattached men and women attempted making their fashion and social statements via flirtations and solicitations.

In the midst of the two bars was a relatively small dance floor. Few of the singles went out there on Friday nights; it was often occupied by the over thirty-five crowd that tried grooving to the tunes of the Isley Brothers and Jodeci, or by those bold enough to do line dancing. Beyond the dance floor were dining tables topped with fine linen and crystal candleholders.

Garner asked, "How many times have you come here?"

"I haven't come here since, uh, we said we were going to keep our conversation on each other."

"Oh, I see . . ."

Kadrece felt the intensity of some of those lurking male eyes setting their attention on her. She was flattered by it, and she might have played to it had she gone to High Cotton six months ago. She was conscious to stand close to Garner while she waited for the server, sending the obvious message to the female piranhas that were salivating for a similar opportunity with him.

The server seated Garner and Kadrece at a semi-circled booth. They had a view of the entire dance floor area, the live band, as well as the wannabe crowd that hung out at the bar.

Garner had only a complimentary chicken sandwich that was provided for the media at the Chamber, and that was back around midday. He had been on the road since 7:30 a.m.; it was now after 8 p.m.

"I sure hope the food is worth my while. If it weren't for the music, you'd hear my stomach."

Kadrece apprised Garner that High Cotton had a favorable reputation for its menu. She said, "When the server comes by, I would like a wine cooler to go with the steak and lobster platter."

"You've always been a woman of my heart when it comes to knowing exactly what you want."

"Well, if you know that, let's continue with our conversation from the car."

"Oh, yeah. That conversation . . ."

Kadrece rolled her eyes in the direction of the bar area. She referred to most of those people standing there were looking to fuck, and she was tired of existing with a similar mentality.

She said, "I look forward to the day when the man I'm with looks lovingly into my eyes and tells me how much he loves me while he's inside me. Is there anything wrong with wanting that after thirty-five, soon to be thirty-six years on this earth?"

Garner didn't think much of Kadrece's scenario. To him, it was like a page out of some romance novel when the heroine finally paired up with the hero and they were poised to exist happily ever after.

He yawned and committed his body to a mini-stretch before responding. "Can I just be honest with you?" She took a sip from her cooler, nodding.

"I have a lot of feelings for you, Kadrece, but I can't say that I've been thinking about settling down with any woman. I'm not saying I'm still trying to have my fun. I'm just saying it's not something that I've made it a priority."

It dawned on Kadrece that she didn't really know Garner like she thought she had known him. The depth of their conversation had been a function of the casual-at-best relationship they had developed. She felt it was just as much her fault as it was his for them never seeing each other beyond sexual terms. It pained her that they might be marching to different drumbeats.

She asked, "What did you expect from me tonight?"

He stared at her, exhaling through his nostrils. "To be honest, would it be wrong to say I was hoping if you were in the mood, maybe you would spend some time with me at the hotel?"

"Is that all?"

Garner sensed trouble was near. "What's gotten into you lately? You were like this in Houston after we were inside your hotel room. Then you gave me that line about being concerned about falling for me. Was that some excuse for saying 'no' to me?"

"I think I've changed and you haven't. That's what I think has happened."

He sat upright in his seat, leaning back against the booth's cushion. He then folded his arms.

"The next thing you'll be telling me is that you started going to church and you're taking that more serious."

"Actually, I have."

That explains it all, Garner thought. She had gotten a bit of religion, and now she started having a conscience for her actions.

"Well, don't try to evangelize me," he said. "What I do on my time with God is my business."

"Garner, this is not about me trying to convert you. Even if I went with you to your room tonight, and let's just say that we actually did something, I know in the morning I'd still have to answer the question 'Is this the way I really want to be living my life?'"

"No, it isn't. I guess what I should have told you in the beginning is that I've decided I won't have sex again until I'm married." She took another sip from her drink.

Garner's face became void of emotion, bordering pissed off. It was the second time that Kadrece showed a preference to avoid sex with him. Not even his experience with Tamira prepared him for this. He began mulling maybe there was some truth again about nice guys never getting laid.

The server came with their plates. Garner, who ordered a steak platter with baked potato and house salad with Thousand Island dressing, had little else to say.

"Garner, I've known you longer than any man I've ever been involved with. I just felt I could share this with you."

He continued eating, darting his eyes up on occasion. Disappointed, Kadrece took only a couple of bites from her steak and a taste from her lobster. Then she announced to him that she was going to the ladies' room. She made sure that she visited the one that was not in his line of sight. From there, she called her sister, Kanitra, who lived less than ten minutes away from High Cotton, to pick her up. She waited for her in the parking lot.

Garner finally recognized that Kadrece had been away longer than usual. He spotted one of the casually dressed managers and asked if he could send somebody in the ladies' room to check on Kadrece.

"What does she look like?"

"She's about this tall," he said, showing that Kadrece came chin high in height to him. "She was wearing a black dress with the back out. Dark complexion. Nice hair style. Very attractive."

The manager was quick to recall somebody that fitted Kadrece's description. "Oh, she left here about five minutes ago."

"Are you sure?"

"Positive," he said, nodding his head. "And you were right. She was definitely a very attractive lady."

Fuck!

Garner immediately grimaced about pissing away sixty-five dollars, including tip, on a meal that neither of them finished. From the parking lot, he tried contacting Kadrece on her cell phone.

"What happened? Why did you just leave me?" he ranted to her.

Kadrece maintained a calm voice. "Garner, I didn't feel like wasting your time. It may not have been the best way to end the evening; I preferred not to continue this game. If you want to conduct a meaningful conversation, you know where I am."

The phone clicked. Whether he agreed with her or not, she was always one for telling him what was on her mind.

Chapter 28

There was no use of implementing any damage control with Kadrece. She was not only a woman of academic, aesthetic and professional brilliance, she was a woman who was very much set in her ways. Garner knew it would take more than a simple apology to sway her opinion; a display of contrition was not what he had in mind.

For that reason, Garner was numb to this most recent one-eighty by a woman. He reasoned it was nothing more than payback.

Women!

Garner figured the best thing he could do since things were already awry was to seek refuge in his hotel room. At least if any trouble came his way it could only happen if he literally opened his door to it. He bore a contemplative look from the moment he stepped out of his car in the Peachtree's parking garage. But his countenance changed once he reached the elevators.

"Hi, we meet again!"

Garner smiled back at Autumn, who just exited the middle elevator car. "Yes, we do meet. Where's your friend?"

"You mean Pat? Oh, she's out with her family. She's from Atlanta, and I decided not to go with her."

Autumn had her hair combed straight, parted, and swept to one side. She wore dark blue Capris and a football jacket bearing the name and the orange and white colors of South Carolina's other major university located in Clemson. Garner immediately made the connection with her.

He said, "You didn't tell me you were here for the football game?"

"You never asked me."

Hmmm, that sounded familiar to him. "I guess I didn't."

She said, "See what happens when you judge a book by its cover? I never would have guessed you were a television reporter."

Damn!

He felt he had stepped on his tongue twice in less than three minutes with her. A bloody trail from his mouth was not the impression he wanted to make with her.

"Where are you heading?"

"To the bar." She told him about the Peachtree having a late happy hour on Friday nights from nine to eleven. "Now I don't have to worry about getting a cab or dealing with strangers in an unfamiliar setting."

"Well, can I join you?"

Going through her mental checklist, she looked Garner over as if he was livestock inspected by her father, Wallace Copeland. She admired the way his suit brought out a debonair look in him; his light-colored eyes were more than enticing and convincing.

She smiled at his gesture of holding up his right hand pledging that he would be on his best behavior. Her almond-shaped eyes then widened.

"I guess you could join me. Besides, if you prove to be a jerk, I can always get up and leave."

Damn, why did she have to say that!

Garner followed Autumn through the lobby. Since her jacket was rolled inward around her waist, it allowed him to pay particular attention to her hour-glass shape. He snapped out of gawking at her after a few steps; he didn't want to ensnare himself like he had with

Kadrece.

There were maybe two dozen patrons in the modestly lit lounge. Five were sitting at the bar. The rest were sitting at tables or in the plush chair groups. They agreed to sit at a table for two that was opposite of the bar.

Autumn seemed at ease amid the wood-trimmed furniture and specialty woodworks that made the lounge conducive for the corporate businesspersons who frequented four-star hotels. There was piano entertainment that both of them ignored.

He asked, "Do you come to Atlanta often?"

"Oh, I've been here a few times with my friends."

With arms folded, Garner leaned back in his chair, making a quick study of Autumn's features. She had thin lips that were adorned with mahogany colored gloss. She had high cheekbones with a small beauty mole on her left cheek just below her eye socket. She also had thinly shaped eyebrows.

He felt his cell phone buzzing inside his jacket; he ignored it.

"What are you drinking?"

She answered, "Mmmm, you know what? I haven't had a margarita in a while. I'd like one of those without the salt."

"I think I'll have one, too. I also like mine without the salt."

While they waited for their drinks, Garner tested Autumn's loyalty to her school by commenting about the rumors surrounding the Ragin Hogs' football program in Arkansas courting Bengals' coach Tripp Brody for their head coaching vacancy.

He went on to tell her that Brody, who made about $1.4 million in South Carolina, was said to have been offered a six-year contract worth $2 million a year in Arkansas. He also described to her that Brody reacted to him with a blank look when asked about it.

"The first thing he wanted to know was where I was from. I told him that I worked in Columbia. Then he stammered and stuttered his way through the rest of my questions."

Autumn appeared interested. She told him that she was a donor to her school's athletic program just like her father, who also attended the same school. "If he were to leave us, it's not like we'd be disappointed. We're getting tired of him telling us this is the year we'll compete for the conference championship and then we finish second or third. Then we're going to a bowl game like this."

"You said a lot of 'we' and 'us'; that usually comes from people who are big-time fans."

She was emphatic to respond. "I grew up a Bengals fan. For the longest, I didn't know there were other football teams. My dad took me to Bengals games in the Valley long before blacks started going there in numbers like we do now."

The server came by with their drinks. They toasted each other with a clicking of their margarita glasses. After placing his glass on a napkin, he directed their conversation back to the bowl game. Most of the predictions called for it to be close with the school from Alabama being a slight favorite.

He also felt his phone buzzing again; he ignored it a second time. He asked, "Do you think that's a fair prediction for the game?"

"Of course not; I hope the Bengals will come out on top."

"You really are a serious fan," he said, nodding. "I know never to say anything bad about them around you."

Autumn balled her right fist and shook it at him. "Yeah, or you'll have to deal with both me and my dad." Garner had now made another connection about her.

"Would I be wrong to assume you're a daddy's girl?"

She broke into a wide grin. "I'll answer it like this: My mom said when I was born, and they brought me home from the hospital, my dad placed me on his stomach and I went to sleep on him. Then when I was eight days old, he took me to church. Everyone said he carried me around like I was precious gold.

"Does that answer your question?"

Garner felt the least bit threatened by Autumn's references to her father. He actually thought it was different and refreshing. It forced him to remain on his best behavior, a challenge that he welcomed given his recent run with women.

"Do you mind if I ask you how old are you?"

"Twenty-five; I'll be twenty-six in April."

If for nothing else, he mused whether Autumn might be somebody whom he could proudly introduce to Miriam. "It sounds like you have a lot going on for you. I take it you were hired by your job coming out of college?"

"Yes, I was. My dad always stayed on me about having something for myself so I wouldn't have to depend on a man for anything."

Autumn recalled a list of questions her father suggested she should ask a man whenever she met one for the first time. Over the years, she adjusted it because his were simply too intimidating.

"Are you married?"

"No."

"Have you ever been married?"

"No."

"You asked how old I was; how old are you?"

"Thirty-two."

"Are you involved with somebody?"

Garner paused before responding. "No." Then he turned the question on her, asking with raised eyebrows. "Are you involved with somebody?"

She answered, "I'm the one asking the questions. But since you want to know, the answer is no. I've never been married, and I don't have any kids. By the way, do you have any?"

He shook his head. "If I'm not married, why would I have any kids?"

"Come on now, men are as bad as dogs. I don't need to elaborate."

Wallace Copeland also told Autumn to watch the man's eyes while he answered her questions. If they shifted and strayed, it was likely that he had been lying to her. He taught her to end the conversation and leave without any explanation.

"I hope you don't be offended by this, but if you have a car note where is it being financed?"

Garner returned a surprised look. Autumn's countenance became stoic. He hunched his shoulders, sighing. "Well, given that I'm paid to ask questions that people don't want asked, I'll answer this one only because you're asking it. For your information, my car's being financed through Infiniti Financial Services, a subsidiary of Nissan Motor Credit."

Wallace Copeland taught her that if a man had his car financed by a primary lender like IFS it was an indication that he could be taking care of his personal business in a responsible manner. She was to avoid those who had vehicles financed at institutions like Mercury Finance or TranSouth. He also told her if the man refused to volunteer the information she was to tread with extreme caution.

"It's obvious you try your best to be a careful lady."

"I do." He also wondered if that meant something else; it was too early to find out. "My dad told me you just never know who you're going to run into," she went on to say. "So you have to be alert."

Garner's cell phone buzzed again; he felt like this was worse than having a terrible itch. It was closing in on eleven o'clock. Autumn brought her hand up to her mouth, yawning. She took long sip from her drink, finishing it off.

"I know what that means."

"You do?"

He joked, "I must be boring you. Older people tend to do that around younger people."

"Actually, no, I've enjoyed talking to you, Garner. I'm glad we ran into each other."

"Has it's been a long day for you?"

"Very long day," she said. "We drove here from Myrtle Beach."

Garner related to Autumn that he also drove to Atlanta; he had been up since 6:30 a.m. and he left his place around 7:30. "I'm sort of used to this because we have long days like this during the football season."

"Well, I'm not used to them. I think I should have flown. But I have this thing about those small commuter planes. Prop or small jet, I feel like a sardine inside of them. My dad preferred that I got a job in Charlotte so then I'd be much closer to home."

"And where's home?"

Autumn told Garner home was Anderson, South Carolina, which was just down the road from her alma mater. She decided on moving to Myrtle Beach to prove to herself that she could make it on her own without her father meddling in her business.

She went on to say he still was very influential in the vehicle that she chose to buy, a Nissan Murano sport utility, as well as the apartment complex where she lived.

"He really means well, and I love him dearly. I don't know how I'd cope if he weren't around. But I think I've reached a point where I can make some decisions for myself."

"All I will say is that my mom is everything to me," he said. "She's never had a lot of say about the things I've done, but I know she's proud of me. As for my father, humph, he left us for good when I was ten."

"I wished my mom would have left us when I was ten; my dad wasn't one for divorce." She checked her watch once more. "Now I'm the one boring you."

She got up from the table, so did Garner.

"May I walk you to your room?" She gave him a suspicious look. He then countered, "Haven't I been on my best behavior so far?"

"I must say you have been a perfect gentleman."

Garner felt his phone buzzing; he ignored it once more.

Meanwhile, they walked side-by-side towards the elevator. While waiting, Autumn reached into her purse, wrote her cell and home number on her business card and handed it to him. She said, "Now you can keep me in mind." He tucked her card in his shirt pocket, smiling at her.

The elevator's bell went off. She entered ahead of him and she punched the "6," being quick to stand on one side of the elevator. He assumed a spot opposite of her.

He asked, "You're on the sixth floor?"

"Yes, I am."

Autumn's heart began beating faster. She was not sure whether the excitement was from her being in Garner's company, or because she would have loved to have gone to his room to find out just how smooth he was in bed. All along, she tried not making an issue out of him being so damned handsome. Patricia had already given her grief for striking a conversation with him, as well as her uncanny luck for attracting all the good-looking men.

When the elevator door opened, Garner allowed for Autumn to walk ahead. She stopped in front of room No. 628. She turned and extended her hand out to him. He grasped it, making a mental note of her soft skin and grip.

"I really had a nice time talking to you. It sure made up for a disappointing trip that I made over to DeKalb County earlier tonight."

She returned a coy look to him. "I won't ask what happened over there."

"Nothing happened. A friend of mine from Tallahassee, Florida, where I once worked, told me about the club. I realized I just didn't fit in there after spending twenty minutes. So I came back to the hotel."

"Oh, I see. Well, good night."

Garner pretended as if he were walking back towards the elevator. Then he waited several seconds before returning down the same corridor to his room. He didn't tell her he was just four doors away in room No. 620.

Chapter 29

Lying across the large bed, Garner mulled the definition of a gentleman. He reasoned that any man could chase and fuck. But what about a man who is gentle, kind, and considerate towards a woman? What about a man who regards a woman's emotions and sense of comfort when she's around him? What about a man who recognizes a woman's need for romance more than the wild romp?

He considered maybe there was a different meaning to nice guys not getting laid. Gentlemen didn't look to getting laid. They look to having a relationship with a woman whose results may include times of sexual intimacy. It sounded good, but was it realistic?

So, he rolled over to the edge of the bed and searched for the complimentary notepad and pen that was next to the phone. Then he turned on the desk lamp. He plopped into the upright chair and he began creating columns with headings of "man" and "gentleman". Then he drew horizontal lines to divide the questions that he asked himself. The names of Vernise and Tamira were also scribbled at the top of each sheet.

In every category, Garner recognized that he was nothing more than a mere man with both women. Not a single category had a checkmark under gentleman. He tossed the pen back onto the pad, sighing. He clasped his hands, leaned upon his elbows, and buried his chin into his hands.

Zzz-zzz-zzz!

He noticed his cell phone's display screen blinking. He didn't ignore it this time.

"You didn't return any of my calls."

"Sorry, I fell asleep."

Vernise's voice lacked her jovial tone. If Garner were a suspect of hers, he would have been Mirandized and handcuffed, and she would have exercised every legal trick she knew to deny him access to an attorney.

She queried, "Are you alone in Atlanta?"

"Is that your way of saying hello to me?"

"I don't know."

Garner guessed correctly that Vernise had tried reaching him while he was with Autumn. Considering her pattern of contacting him, he figured he could have waited until the morning to check his messages and return them.

He said, "Well, it would be nice if you did say hello to me; I do deserve that much respect—"

She huffed into the phone, struggling to speak in English than French. "You want respect? Don't you think answering the phone, checking your messages, and returning them would be a start?"

He interrupted her. "I said I was asleep. I left my phone in the car. I was just going through your messages when you called."

"Am I supposed to believe that?"

Do you think I'm going to tell you any different?

He closed his eyes, arching his neck. He inhaled deeply through his nose. "For your information, officer, I drove here to Atlanta today and put in a full day of work. I've been up since 6:30 this morning; I was tired."

There was a lengthy pause. Vernise tried working herself down from her rage. She went from considering telling him that no man ignored her to no man, especially one whom she shared her pussy and ass with, ever got away with playing her for the fool to settling on making a statement she felt would keep him honest.

She queried, "Is this your way of retaliating against me?"

Garner recognized a familiar tenor to her conversation. "Look, Vernise, let's not make something out of nothing, okay? Didn't I say I accepted your apology?"

She rolled her eyes. "Uh-huh . . ."

"If I accepted your apology, that issue was settled. Can we move on to something else, like exactly when do you think you'll be flying into Atlanta tomorrow?"

She finally calmed down. "I'm scheduled to fly in at 5:56 p.m. on Delta flight number 1196."

"Okay, I'm staying at the Peachtree Hotel downtown. It's down the street from the Four Seasons. Are you going to come here to see me, or do I need to meet you somewhere?"

"That's why I was calling you."

Garner chuckled. "So that explains for the sour talk. You're horny."

"If I told you, I'd have to kill you. Just make sure that you answer the phone when I call you tomorrow."

When they hung up twenty minutes later, and just for the hell of it, Garner went through his messages.

"California has been nice, but it's also rained a lot. I actually ran into a couple of old high school classmates . . . Give me a call. Let me know that you got my message.

"Bye, babe!"

Vernise's voice remained perky during the second message.

"I thought you would have called me by now. I'll be flying back to Atlanta tomorrow evening. I would like to hook up with you. Call me back."

The third message was a noticeable departure from the first two. She spoke with urgency.

"Garner, I'm worried about you. I hope you're all right. You are in Atlanta this weekend? I thought we settled our differences from last week. You said you apologized. Call me . . ."

She hung up the last time she tried contacting him. He felt no response had been the right decision. Maybe there was some truth to having a woman sweat it out. It gave him every reason to believe that he was in control.

The next day, Garner decided a peace offering of some kind would be preemptive against any of Vernise's scrutiny—a lesson that he learned after fucking up with Sabryan. He drove over to Lennox Square Mall where he visited The Body Loves Me health and beauty shop, buying her a Midnight Blossom fragrance gift basket. He also bought her a thinking of you card from the mall's bookstand.

Proud of his ingenious idea, he treated himself to a new pair of black reaction loafers from Kenneth Cole of New York before he returned to the hotel. There, he hung out in the lounge until Vernise called him around 6:30 p.m.

"I'm walking towards the baggage claim area as I speak, babe . . . Where are you?"

"I'll be waiting for you downstairs here at the Peachtree. Do you know where it is?"

"Garner, I've been to Atlanta several times. Besides, there is technology called GPS."

"A-hem, well excuse me!"

"I should be over there in thirty minutes. I'll call you when I turn off the freeway, okay?"

Vernise was easy to recognize. The afternoon temperatures were in the upper thirties, dropping to an overnight low in the mid-twenties. Most people entering the hotel were bundled up. She wore a light designer jacket, slacks of a thin material, and her purse was draped across her chest. Her hair was parted down the middle and combed straight, looking very much a California girl.

He noticed her drift to towards the lounge; he walked in her direction. "Looking for me?"

She smiled. "You look like somebody that I'm supposed to meet. How do I know that you're him?"

"Hmmm, you have an onion-shaped ass, and you have a birthmark on your inner left thigh."

She looked to her left then to her right, hoping nobody overheard what Garner just said. "You're quite observant, mister."

She drew near and hugged him; Garner also gave her a light peck on her cheek. She then handed him her car keys. "These belong to my silver Volvo S80. I'm parked on the first level in the garage. My bags are in the trunk. Just take out the carrying case, please."

"Why don't you come with me?"

She placed her right hand on her waist, looking defiantly at him. "Garner, I left where it was seventy-two degrees this morning. I land here, and I walked like a damned fool into that cold; you're asking me to walk again through that garage?"

"I get the message; you need to thaw out."

When Garner returned with her luggage, they headed for the elevators. The elevator car had barely closed behind him before they hugged and kissed. She pushed her tongue hard inside his mouth. He reached down and grabbed her ass, pulling her body against his.

Then she separated, licking her lips. "I can't wait to take a shower. I'm tired, hungry and horny, in no particular order."

He grinned at her. "I guess I survived, huh? Or is that until you get what you wanted?"

Vernise gave him a confused look. He reminded her about her threat to kill him if she divulged that she was horny. She kissed him lightly on his lips.

He mused, "Don't tell me your favorite animal is a black widow?"

"I'm too light to be a black widow."

The elevator stopped at the sixth floor. Garner went at a brisk gait down the hallway. Vernise joked, "Are you sure you aren't the one who's horny?" Garner looked back and smiled. Inwardly, he breathed a sigh of relief once he passed room No. 628. He made sure that he did not bungle inserting the card key.

Garner had already placed her gift fragrance basket on the long shelf dresser next to a pair of wine glasses. He had a bottle of Chardonnay chilling next to it.

Vernise entered the room ahead of him looking to her left. She reacted, "Babe, you shouldn't have!"

Garner nodded with satisfaction walking in behind her. "I've thought about doing this since yesterday."

"Well, I've been thinking about you all week. I'm so glad we're together right now."

He had barely put down her carrying case when Vernise turned and wrapped her arms around his neck. She pressed her breasts into his chest and her lips softly against his. As soon as his lips separated, she pushed her tongue between them. He sucked on her tongue, which gave way to their tongues slithering together.

Vernise, who sensed a flow of wetness between her thighs, grinned and gazed into his eyes with admiration. She reminded him how they were in each other's company almost to the hour just a week ago.

"I almost wish now that I hadn't gone to Kentucky and California. I could have been with you all week, and this moment wouldn't feel so awkward to me."

"It's only as awkward as you make it." He leaned forward and kissed her again. "Did you see your other gift?" She looked around; a card was lying on the pillow closest to the window. "I hope you weren't being sarcastic?"

"Oh no!" he answered. "When I placed it there, I was thinking about us lying in bed next to each other and you opening the card." He retrieved the card, handing it to her. Her eyes widened with anticipation.

She read,

> Vernise, please accept these items as a truce between us. I
> don't like to argue.

She gave him a seductive look. Then she curled her right index finger. "Babe, now that was some other crazed woman you spoke to on the phone last night. A real lady always shows her appreciation for what the man does for her."

Garner suggested that they just relax for a while. He turned on the radio from the television set and they listened to the local jazz station while they reclined on the bed. Leaning against him, they both mellowed to a glass of the Chardonnay while she filled him in on the California leg of her trip.

Tired of talking about her family and old friends, Vernise motioned for Garner to sit at the edge of the bed. She removed her jacket, shirt, and athletic bra. Next, she positioned herself directly in front of him. Then she removed her slacks, leaving only her black thong that barely covered her small strip of pubic hair. He ran his hands along her ass cheeks, cupping them at times.

Moaning and arching her neck, she draped her arms over his shoulders again. "I've had a long day. I left home around 9:30 [a.m.] California time to make it to the airport. I can sure use a shower. And you know what? I'm going to use some of the stuff you bought me in that basket."

He kissed and licked at her navel; she patted him on the shoulders, excusing herself for the bathroom. His dick sprung to attention at the sight of her pale cheeks jiggling and bouncing. Refusing to be left alone, he removed his slacks, Polo shirt and boxers and joined her in the bathroom. He announced, "I wanted to do this with you last week, but you were already gone."

She was more than receptive to his company. "I thought about you this way every time I showered this week." She tilted her head down, staring at him. "I also thought about that." Then she gave his dick a playful tug.

"That's nice to know." He mimicked her by tilting his head down, eyeing between her thighs. "And I've been thinking about that all this week."

After soaping each other down and taking turns rinsing under the cascading water, Vernise leaned against the shower tile with her legs apart, looking over her right shoulder. Smiling at him, she wiggled her ass and pushed it out to emphasize her point.

"I'm already turned on, babe. My pussy's been throbbing all day. You almost made me cum out there when you touched me."

Garner fulfilled Vernise's request by slowly guiding his dick between her eager pussy lips. Bracing herself against the tile with her right hand, Vernise choreographed rotating her hips to Garner's deliberate thrusts and her rubbing her clit with her left hand.

His ego and dick were being massaged the way he liked it. "Damn, you have a sexy ass!" He gave her a playful slap on her cheeks.

She replied, "And I know how to work it, too!"

As good as Vernise's pussy felt in the shower, Garner suggested that they took their action to the bed. Compared to the shower, there was a slight chill in the bed area despite the thermostat being set at seventy-eight degrees. But that made good for fun; they were quick to nestle together under the sheets.

Vernise maneuvered herself on top. She slowly kissed Garner from his shoulders, down across his nipples, to his navel and between his thighs, stopping to caress and stroke his dick. Then she enveloped his dick, making suction and slurping sounds.

Garner's hips rose and fell to the acute sensation. She ventured to make a long brush with her tongue along the underside of his dick. She paused and made eye contact with him while tasting his pre-cum with the tip of her tongue.

She said, "A woman could get spoiled having something like this at her disposal."

"Is that right?"

"I know it's right." She climbed atop him, guiding his dick inside her steamy pussy. She took little time achieving a rocking and grinding motion. He placed his hands on her waist; it was obvious who would be doing the work.

Eyes closed and her hands on his chest for balance, Vernise groaned to each stroke that reached her cervix—a sweet pain that she was more than willing to experience. She decided to quicken her imminent orgasm by riding him at a faster rate. Soon, Garner recognized that Vernise had stopped fucking. Her back and neck were arched. Gasping and panting, she mumbled something to him in French.

He smiled at her. "You do know that I know how to work this dick?"

She shuddered once more as her inner walls quaked and then relaxed. She shook her head, though still trying to catch her breath. "I haven't forgotten." She dismounted and cuddled next him. The jet lag and quick work of sex were catching up with her. But she was determined not to let Garner off that easy. "You've got some more work to do, babe."

Acting upon her cue, Garner suggested for Vernise to lie on her stomach. "Where's your fragrance basket?" he asked. She pointed behind him. He returned with the bottle of Midnight Blossom lotion. Squirting a small amount in his hands, he proceeded to massage it into her shoulders; she twitched at the strength of his hands before she yielded to his touch. He squirted another small amount of lotion into his hands and worked that into her back, starting from her shoulder blades down to her waist.

"Mmmm, baby, you sure know how to pamper a lady . . ."

Garner smirked. "Consider this a labor of pleasure."

With another squirt, he massaged it into her toned, left inner thigh down past her calf, stopping at her ankle. Another squirt was used to massage into her right ankle up past her calf and stopping at her inner thigh. He was careful not to brush against her pussy lips or ass.

Writhing and moaning, Vernise demanded that Garner enter her while she remained on her stomach.

"No, turnover—"

"Like this, babe?"

Vernise bent her legs and separated them, enticing Garner to mount her. It was even more tempting when he noticed her wetness gathering and glistening. Her nipples, firm and erect, also sought his attention. Knowing that he had her at his beckoning, he further tantalized her by massaging her arms, down to her fingertips. Then he lightly massaged her stomach.

She reached out for him to mount her, but he still had other ideas. He made it a sensual work of rubbing her right thigh down past her calf before stopping to massage her toes. She giggled at his ability to make them crack. He went through the same routine with her left side, starting from her thigh down to cracking her toes.

"God, babe, you're going to have me falling for you before I know it! You're going to have all my friends jealous of me."

He chortled. "I could care less about your friends; this isn't for any of them, anyway."

"I like that!"

Desirously, Garner lowered himself on Vernise and started kissing and nibbling her on her neck. She locked her arms under his, writhing against his body. "Mmmm, shit, man. What you're doing to me?" He responded by pressing his lips against hers. She groped for his dick, but he brushed her hand away.

"You don't like a little romance and affection?" he inquired.

"Why of course a lady likes all that, but you're torturing me!"

Vernise nudged Garner to go down on her. Slowly, he eased to her breasts; she gasped to the sensation of his lips.

"Remember, I don't mind a little biting and nibbling on them." She stroked his back in reaction to his tongue flickering against her nipples. Sensing no resistance, he sucked hard above her nipples and beneath her breasts.

He paused for eye contact with her. "Are you going to tell your friends?"

She inspected the passion marks he left on her breasts. "That's between you and me, babe."

"I like that!" he said, before venturing to lick and kiss her navel.

She placed her hands on his shoulders again, making slight nudges for him to continue his descent. She clasped her legs around his shoulders once his face reached her mound. She threw her head into the pillow once she felt the warmth from his breath against her slit.

He closed his eyes and made slow kissing and licking trails along her inner thighs. Finally, he tasted her pussy, ending a week's absence. She ran her hands through his hair, screaming out his name while he made repeated flicks upon her clit. She mumbled, *"Directement là, bébé. Léchez-moi directement là!"*

Then she spoke in English to him. "Babe, I can't take it . . . I can't take it . . . I'm cumming . . . shit!"

Panting, she motioned for Garner to mount her sixty-nine style with him being on top. She said, "Since you can do that to me, I can do it to you!"

With his balls dangling and his asshole immediately before her, she lunged forward and darted her tongue where he had longed for her to go, but had not yet suggested for it. He had long since embraced there was something unique about a black woman who is willing to lick a black man's asshole.

"Mmmm!"

She pushed her tongue farther.

"Damn!"

She ran her tongue along his puckered cavity. Then she slurped on his balls before going back to his crack. "I wished I'd brought some whipped cream. I love donuts with cream filling!"

Garner tried preoccupying himself by delving between her thighs and her sopping pussy. But the better feeling was with Vernise tongue fucking his asshole and her stroking his rock-hard dick, which oozed pre-cum into her hand. He looked back at her. "You know men damned near pray to have women like you . . ."

"Is that right?"

"Keep doing that . . . Damn, that feels so good!" He began rocking his hips and pushing his ass against her tongue like she had done to him the week before. Suddenly, he began inching away from Vernise, hoping she would recognize he wanted to fuck. "You're going to make me scream your name."

She teased him. "Where you're going? You can only give and not receive?"

"Okay, you got me there. Whew! A man can be spoiled by a lady like you."

"I'm glad you realized that. You're with me now, babe. You don't have to look any further."

With a final flick against his puckered hole, Vernise released her grip of his waist, allowing him to reposition himself atop her. They were quick to find a rhythm that made for beautiful sex. Their bodies worked in unison, drawing pleasure from each other.

Garner took the initiative by raising Vernise's legs up to his shoulders. Leaning against them, he hit places that she exclaimed had not been reached in years. Yet she was astute to his movements. She knew whenever a man began slowing his pace he tried delaying his ejaculation.

She stroked his lower back. "Don't you just love this sweet pussy, babe?"

He grunted. "Mmmm-hummm!"

She then clasped her legs around his waist. "Couldn't you just fuck it anytime, any place?"

He stroked her with more vigor, sweating from his brow. "Mm-mm-hummm!"

"I want you to do this for me, babe—"

"What?"

"I don't want you to pull out; I want it all for me."

She had no resistance from Garner. She coaxed him along by clutching his ass cheeks and then running her middle finger over his asshole. He was so engrossed in the moment that he positioned himself to make it even easier for her to insert her finger while he continued fucking.

Wiping the sweat from his brow, Garner proceeded to cup her ass and whispered into her ear that he was nearing ejaculation. She held her legs apart for him as he arched his back and grunted. She moaned with great contentment upon feeling his warm deposit against her sugar walls. He collapsed into her embrace after his dick's last spasm. He balanced himself upon his elbows, querying her: "Is that the kind of dick that you'd like anytime, any place?"

Vernise kissed him fully on his lips then pushed her tongue inside his mouth. She stopped for air. "That's the kind of dick a woman could go crazy over . . . maybe even kill somebody!"

When Garner finally withdrew, Vernise's pussy made a loud suction sound. They both giggled, realizing the extent of their arousal and attraction for each other.

The next morning, Garner explained to Vernise that he had a one o'clock press conference over at the Chamber. The head coach and two players from both schools would be in attendance, marking the final media opportunity before Monday's game. Vernise, who was more than content with the time she spent with him, mentioned that she needed to head back to Columbia in afternoon since she still had some paperwork to complete for in the morning.

She suggested, "Can we at least go out for breakfast?"

They agreed to drive over to a pancake house just off I-85 southbound in Fulton County. They returned to the hotel around 11:30 a.m.

While taking Vernise's luggage to the parking garage, Garner noticed Autumn walking towards the elevator. He smiled and nodded in her direction. "Good morning!"

She returned a smile and her eyes gleamed. "Good morning!"

As the elevator chimed, Vernise discerned some kind of connection between Garner and the younger woman who just walked past them. The door closed before she turned around for a second look.

Garner recognized Vernise had not kept up with him, but her voice made up for the distance in the immediate background.

"How do you know her?"

He waited for her to catch up. He turned to her once she drew even. "What makes you think that I know her?"

Vernise shifted her purse from her left shoulder to her right. She pointed at him, speaking loud enough only for him to hear. "I'm a very perceptive woman. I told you about that."

He shrugged his shoulders. "I've got nothing to hide. We were in the same line when we checked into the hotel on Friday. That's was all to it."

She raised her voice. "So that's why you couldn't call me back Friday night?" He tilted his head in the direction of the deep lounge chairs. She refused to move.

"I think you're blowing this out of proportion," he replied.

"The hell I'm blowing this out of proportion. You don't know who you're fucking with!"

Garner didn't say a word. He resumed walking towards the garage with her carrying case. She finally followed him; she was hardly satisfied with his response. When they reached her car, she pushed her left index finger into his chest.

"Don't play me for a goddamned fool, Garner." Her eyes were bugged and her lips became slits. "You maybe be with me, but don't ever cross me!"

"Who says I'm with you? You're the only one that's been saying it."

"Garner, I don't give my pussy and ass to just any man. I hope you understand that."

"The only thing I don't understand is you acting the way you have. First, it was the phone call. I told you I was asleep. Now you're acting crazy because I was being nice by speaking to somebody. Obviously, they don't do that in California. Should I have just looked the other way?"

Vernise snatched her carrying case from Garner and clicked her trunk and car door. "I'll deal with this later. I've got to get back to Columbia.""Columbia." He offered to give her twenty dollars for the parking. Without saying goodbye, she slammed her trunk and rushed inside her car.

She let down her window. "I don't need your fucking money!" Then she backed out of the parking stall in a hurry. He watched her speed off towards the parking attendant's booth.

On his way back inside the hotel, Garner began pondering his dealings with Vernise. He thought there was something about her that just didn't add up.

Meanwhile, he tried contacting Autumn. She was cautious to speak with him.

"I see you've had some other business here in Atlanta?"

"Autumn, it's not what you think. But I'd like to talk to you about it."

"Garner, I may be young. But my dad didn't raise me to be somebody's fool. Why don't I just call you."

Chapter 30

Garner made a left-hand turn onto Killian Road, accelerating through second and into third gear. It was approaching two in the afternoon and he was en route to the station. Just as he reached the intersection at Farrow Road, he noticed in his rearview mirror a set of blinking headlights and blue lights flashing from its windshield. He pulled over to the right lane, allowing the charcoal gray unmarked police cruiser to pass by. But the police car veered behind him.

Pissed at the inconvenience, Garner's Richmond instincts prompted him to slow down and stop; he knew he wasn't speeding. Nonetheless, he mentally rehearsed a few responses. He also prepared himself by having his driver's license, registration, and insurance information accessible.

When he peered into his driver's side mirror, he noticed the person walking towards his car wearing heavy black slacks, a gray Polo shirt and an embroidered badge emblem on the chest wasn't a Richland County officer. He shut his eyes and shook his head.

Moments later, Vernise peered into Garner's car, grinning. She removed her shades. Her hair was combed back with braids woven into the rest of her thick mane. "How's your love life, babe?"

Garner glared at her. Then he folded his arms, staring straight ahead. It all seemed ironic and amusing to Vernise that she would be on the outside looking inside the vehicle that could have driven her back to her place in Lexington County had things gone the way she preferred.

To the casual passer by, she made it appear like a routine traffic stop by standing just shy of the driver's door and placing her left hand over her pistol. She said, "Is this the way you say hello to women you've slept with?" Then she puckered her lips.

"I suppose this was some coincidence?" He pondered aloud how in the hell she figured out where he lived considering he had yet to invite her over to his place.

"Look, I can explain this. But the main thing is that I really wanted to apologize to you about blowing up the way I did in Atlanta. I thought we could—"

"Don't you think a simple phone call would have sufficed?" he interrupted her.

She persisted. "If you would just let me explain myself, I realized that I overreacted to you speaking to the lady walking into the elevator. I just happened to be out this way coming back from a lab when I noticed your car. I was so excited seeing you that I tried getting your attention the best way I knew."

"Bullshit! And you call pulling me over being the best you could do?"

Vernise's jocular countenance immediately soured. She was inclined to drawing her semi-automatic pistol at him, demanding that he stepped out of his car and put his hands on the hood. "If you don't accept my apology right here, I'll have your ass explaining to your employer why you were arrested today.

"Now you make the choice!"

He smirked and stared at Vernise while he mulled the possibilities. He resumed staring straight ahead. He also caught on to a line that she just rattled off to him. "Did you say you just happened to be out here coming from a lab?"

"Yes I did."

"Where in the hell is a lab out this way?"

"That's none of your business. See, I wasn't going to ask you again what business you had with that young woman walking into the elevator."

Fuck it, he thought. *This has gone too far.*

"Vernise," he said, "I think you need to just go your way; I'll go mine. It was real while it lasted."

Stunned, she straightened up and placed both hands on her hips. "What do you mean [it] being real while it lasted?"

"You know what I mean! In plain English, I don't want to see you any more. I don't even want to think about us having slept together. I just want to forget that I ever met you!" He shook his head in disgust. "I don't need it. I don't need the drama that obviously comes with you."

That was the last thing Vernise expected to hear from Garner. Her emotions shifted from rage, to tears welling, and back to rage. "I tried stopping you so that we could talk about us. I really like you, Garner. I've told a lot of my friends about you; they were telling me how happy they were that I actually met you. Now you're going to do this to me?"

"That's not my problem. I don't go around telling everyone my business."

She looked over her shoulder, making sure that nobody was suspicious about their interaction. Where they were on Killian and Farrow roads was an increasingly active intersection with more businesses and residential subdivisions being built in that area of northeast Columbia.

"Babe, do you remember I told you that was a crazy woman who was mad at you when you didn't return my calls? Do also remember I said a real lady appreciates what her man does for her? I'm that lady who appreciates what her man does for her. I'm willing to forget everything that resulted in an argument, if we can just work this out."

Garner recognized he had control of this interaction; however, he was suspicious of taking off because of the possibility of her lying that he committed some bogus offense.

He replied, "Who ever said I was your man? I'm not married to you. I'm a single man. I don't have to work out anything with you if I don't want to. That's my prerogative."

She hissed, balling her fists. "So that's the way it's going to be? I told you not to fuck with me!" Now she really felt like grabbing for the metal in her holster.

He cut another glance at her before staring straight ahead. "I'll just take that chance—don't fuck with me!"

Vernise made mockery of Garner through her laughter. She reminisced to herself what she had already done to Tamira and, for that matter, to Thaman Aikens in that Indianapolis hotel room nearly four years earlier.

She pointed at him. "Just remember that I warned you!" Then she stomped back to her cruiser. Inside, she huffed and wiped away a tear from her cheek. Then she left a small strip of burned rubber from where she was parked.

Garner waited until she drove a couple of blocks farther down on Killian Road before he put his car into gear. He decided not to take I-77; he turned around and went the long route driving eastbound on Clemson Road back over to the I-20 interchange. It took him about fifteen minutes out of the way for him to arrive at work, but it was worth the inconvenience.

After his encounter with Vernise, Garner was more than glad to be at the station sitting at his desk and compiling stories for the six o'clock broadcast. The biggest item he kept up with while away from Columbia was the fans' growing displeasure in Danny O'Meara, the Chanticleers' men's basketball coach. Next to football, men's basketball accounted for the second most lucrative revenue source, which was common for most major Division I-A athletic programs.

The Chanticleers entered their SEAC play in the midst of a three-game losing streak against lesser opponents. They were picked to finish among the bottom third out of the conference's twelve member schools. Since O'Meara replaced Ronnie Forney in 2002, the Chanticleers appeared in one NCAA tournament and advanced to the NIT semifinal game three times, winning it all during consecutive years in 2005 and 2006. They finished with a 14-16 record in 2007; that was not acceptable to a fan base that had higher expectations.

Garner was not as overly critical of O'Meara because of his previous success coaching at a private Baptist college in Winston-Salem, North Carolina. That program advanced to the NCAA tournament eight of the twelve years that O'Meara was over the program in the equally prestigious Pan-Atlantic Coast Conference (PACC).

In Garner's opinion, the difference O'Meara faced in South Carolina was the Chanticleers competed in a conference where there were seven or eight perennially strong schools ahead of them. So what could the fan base expect? Certainly, the Chanticleers could not be so delusional to think they would turn into a national power overnight?

Humph.

Garner knew he was definitely back to his usual routine when he began taking phone calls.

"Uh, hi, Mr. Davis, I'm still planning for our Super Bowl party. Could you be so kind to tell me what time is the kickoff?"

Goddamn!

He shook his head. "You do know the Super Bowl will be played the first Sunday in February?"

"Is it really? I thought it was the last Sunday in January."

Fuckin' stupid . . .

"Unless the NFL announces otherwise, I think you can count on it being the first Sunday in February. And with television, you can probably count on the kickoff being around 6:30 p.m."

"Thank you so much!"

Shit!

With the six o'clock broadcast behind him, Garner decided on unwinding at Gallardo's. Since he reported on the growing fan unrest with O'Meara, he called Shay Reasoner, a college basketball coaching contact in North Carolina.

"Garner, you know how it goes. It's only January. It's too early to speculate any names right now," Shay said. "Unless there's already a succession plan in place, you'll need to wait until after Selection Sunday [in early March] before you'll get a good idea who's hot and who's not."

"I know if there's anybody who's going to know, it's going to be you, Shay. But it's good to keep in contact with you. By the way, how was your Christmas and New Year's?"

"Great, Garner. How about yours?"

Garner shook his head, hoping to have avoided the topic. "I saw my family in Richmond, which was nice. And I had to cover a bowl game."

After hanging up with Shay, Garner figured he had nothing to loose by punching in the next number on his cell phone. He cleared his throat, saying, "You have my deepest sympathy from the bowl game; it's a shame your school lost in overtime."

"Who's this?"

"It's Garner Davis. Did I catch you at a bad time?"

"Oh, hi, I thought you were one of those Chanticleers fans trying to give me grief," Autumn said. "My dad told me today that he had to curse out a couple of them."

He chuckled. "If anything right now, I'm giving them grief about their men's basketball coach."

"Well, ours is doing great. It looks like we might finally get back to the NCAA tournament this year. We're ranked and we've got a good chance of having a winning record in conference play."

"I'm really impressed with how much of a Bengals fan that you are."

Autumn had just looked over her left shoulder, darting over into the left lane while traveling northbound on Highway 17 heading out of Myrtle Beach. "All right, Garner, flattery doesn't get you every-where with me. Uh, didn't I tell you that I'd call you?"

"You did. But I told you in Atlanta that I wanted to talk to you."

She warned Garner about her being subject to blurt out anything while driving during rush hour. "So pardon me, if my French is a bit offensive."

He closed his eyes and inhaled deeply. That was the last language he'd want to hear any reference. He allowed his chest to slowly de-flate. Suddenly, there was the sound of a horn honking in the back-ground. "Stupid asshole!" she then yelled.

Garner chortled. "You did give me a fair warning."

She breathed loudly into the phone. "My dad says I drive like my mom. She's from a big city, Baltimore. He drives really, really slow like he's on some back country road using a tractor. That might be the only thing that I didn't inherit from him."

He queried, "Can we talk another time? Maybe over lunch or dinner?"

"Garner, that's really nice of you. But how do I know you're not trying to be a playa with me?"

"I'm not."

"So tell me, who was that lady whom you were with? She was very attractive; she also looked older than you."

There was a slight pause. He made quick deliberation on what he would describe about Vernise.

"What is it you want to know about her?"

Her voice took on a serious tone. "I'm not going to ask my question again."

Garner felt good about having a clear conscience. "She was somebody whom I went out with on a couple occasions and we, um, you know, were also intimate. When you saw us, she was leaving for Columbia. She had flown into Atlanta the night before after visiting her family in California."

"Were you intimate with her in Atlanta?"

"We were, but that's over with. We agreed to go our separate ways."

Autumn was incredulous. That was about as amusing as some of her friends' drama with their men. "What do you expect from me after I saw you walking in the hotel lobby with another woman?

"Do you not realize that I saw her again later that afternoon?"

Garner was befuddled. "Did you say you saw her later that day?"

"I certainly did, and I'm not making anything up. Come to think of it . . I think she tried following me. But I was with a group of my friends. So I wasn't concerned."

He sighed. "Hey, nothing you say about that woman surprises me. All I'm asking of you is a chance to set the record straight. I can't do it all over the phone."

Autumn was near her apartment complex, which was roughly

twenty minutes from where she worked. It had a secured parking garage and a front-door entry system—amenities that her father was adamant that she considered when she moved into her place.

"Garner, can you call me back later tonight, like before eleven?"

"I can't. I'll be preparing for our broadcast at that time."

"Well, it sounds like to me you have to make a choice on what you think is more important: your reputation or your job."

"Can you at least agree on meeting me for lunch or dinner this weekend?"

"You have my card, and I have yours. I'm about to turn into my place."

Garner insisted, "Autumn, I'd rather find out right now if you're at least willing to meet with me. I wouldn't be calling you if I hadn't taken care of what I needed to take care of—"

She went into a brief lecture that she didn't rush into anything even when it came to men—another thing her father taught her.

Garner tried reversing logic with her. "I'm pretty sure your father's real proud of you. But I think you'd have a problem if all I talked about was my mother, whom I feel is just as great as your father. And you know what? She told me about girls who worshipped their fathers. She says I'd always be wasting my time. Nothing I'd do would ever be good enough for them. That's why girls like you are always alone."

It took all of her not to curse him out. She reacted, "Nobody talks about my dad like that. Do you understand? I told you that I didn't rush into anything. Now if you're willing to call me back later this evening, fine. If not, it's been real, okay?"

The phone clicked.

Chapter 31

Sighing, Garner glanced at the clock on his computer screen. He had thirty minutes before the eleven o'clock broadcast. Rather than calling Autumn, he flipped open his cell phone and text messaged her. He figured it symbolized his trying to meet her halfway.

He mentioned,

> I would consider it a privilege if we could meet for lunch or dinner on Saturday at a place of your choice in the Myrtle Beach area. Let me know if you're interested.

To his surprise, Autumn was prompt with a reply.

> Maybe.

He grumbled to himself about the merits of being a mere man or gentleman. The way he saw it, he was miserable either way. All it left him doing was fondling and stroking his dick while he was home alone. Maybe Kadrece was right after all. He needed to consider making a serious commitment to somebody, if not to himself.

Closing his eyes, Garner tried concentrating on his script for the broadcast. It happened to be a slow sports night. The real action would be on Sunday afternoon when the Chanticleers played host to their conference rival from Knoxville, Tennessee, who were ranked ninth in the latest media polls. He planned to cover that game and the coach's media session on Monday afternoon.

The buzzing on his hip holster startled him. He noticed the text message came from the 843 area code.

> Actually, I would like to meet you for dinner here in MB. Do you have a place in mind?

> I've never been to Myrtle Beach; I'll let you choose the place. How about 6 p.m.?

> Fine. I hope you know how to get here if you've never been here before.

> I have no problem getting there. I'll call you tomorrow; I'm about to go on air.

Garner felt good that he was able to make a strong delivery without struggling with being preoccupied by his personal business. Maybe it helped that he got the good news from Autumn before he went on air. Maybe it also helped that he had rid himself of Vernise. Maybe some of it had to do with him having set a goal of moving on to a larger market in 2008, and he convinced himself each time he appeared before a camera was his personal audition.

Driving back on I-77, he managed to get no farther than the Decker Boulevard exit when he noticed his car was driving like it had gone over a sea of potholes. He down shifted immediately and pulled over into the emergency lane.

Damn!

Surveying the problem, his right rear wheel went flat. The last thing Garner wanted to do was change a damned tire in the cold of winter while vehicles sped past him.

"Shit," he hissed as he drove off about fifteen minutes later, "if it isn't one thing, it's another!" He spent six hundred when he replaced the alloy wheel and had his front end aligned after fucking with Sabryan over the phone.

Zzzz-zzz-zzz . . . zzz!

He ignored the call from the 803 area code it since it was Vernise calling from her cell phone.

Seconds later, his phone buzzed again. He recognized it was Vernise now calling from her home number. He punched the REJECT option on his phone. Now he berated himself for being so damned stupid for even thinking that he had fully rid himself of this woman.

Annoyed, he contacted Verizon's customer service. He inquired, "Is there any way I can block a phone number similar to how we can block numbers using our home phones?"

"For security purposes, may I have the last four digits to your social security number?" the customer service representative replied.

Argh!!!

"Can't you people just answer a simple damned question without needing my name, my mother's maiden name, address, birth date, social and goddamn vehicle ID number?"

"I'm sorry, but I don't set the policy here at Verizon. And I cannot answer any specific questions you have unless you provide me with the information I've asked you."

Garner hung up rather than answering the questions. He reasoned if Vernise didn't want to go on with her life that was her damn problem. But he was determined not to let her ruin him from going on with his life. She'd just better not fuck with him like he warned her.

When he finally reached his condo's parking lot, Garner let out a roar of disgust. He shuffled inside his place, tossed his keys on the kitchen counter and played the messages on his phone.

"Garner, it's your mother in Richmond. You've been gone over a week. Have you already forgotten me? You know I worry about you, little boy. Call me this weekend."

He clicked on the television set, hoping to catch an ESPN *Sports Center* or any of the college basketball games from the west coast. He went over to the refrigerator and retrieved a bottle of Coors Light and Miriam's fruitcake in the rectangular muffin pan, cutting himself a hunk.

By the time his phone played the fifth message, he had already plopped on the sofa, reclining in it. *"Hi, babe. This is Vernise,"* she said, sniffling. *"I-I-I don't understand why you're doing this to me. We were so much into each other just a couple of days ago and now you're saying you don't want to see me anymore?"*

He buried his forehead into his palm.

"Do you think that I'm going to let you go that easily? You've got to be fooling yourself. All we had was some misunderstanding. I told you that we could work past this. Are you just that cold of a man? If you are, I can show you just how cold of a bitch I can be. You have a choice to make!"

Garner stared at his bottle of beer and placed it on the coffee table. He also lost his taste for Miriam's fruitcake, which virtually never happened. He inhaled deeply, going off into deliberation. He wondered maybe the bigger mistake was made when he cursed Tamira's effort to contact him while he was on the phone with Vernise.

Tamira was hardly any consolation. She was definitely more woman than Vernise had proven to be. He regretted that she had a change of mind after spending the night with him.

Overwhelmed by his predicament, Garner fell asleep on the sofa until he was awaken by the sunrays piercing through his living room blinds.

Garner made it his first order of business to creep down to Northeast Tire Wholesalers on Farrow Road so he would not be seen driving around on a space saver in a damn near $40,000 vehicle. After waiting for an hour and fifteen minutes, Randy, the front-desk clerk, summoned Garner to follow him out to the service area.

"Mr. Davis, I just want you to see the extent of the damage to your tire." He pointed out to Garner there were no signs of punctures in the tread. Because of the tire's low profile, and the fact he drove it nearly three miles on I-77, the tire wall built up a lot of heat, which caused tread separation. He told him it would cost him about three hundred and fifty dollars, including labor, to replace it.

"You're lucky the tire didn't just blow while you were at highway speed, or it might be a different story."

Garner was miffed. "I just drove to Richmond and back, and then to Atlanta and back. And don't you think you would have spotted it when I came here with my car last week for a front-end alignment?"

"Possibly, but you're talking about a lot of driving since then. That's more than a thousand miles. Anything can happen. My advice is you have to keep a closer watch with low-profile tires, or it can become very expensive."

Shaking his head, Garner grumbled about his run of bad luck with his car. "Yeah, tell me about it. I guess I was too damned dense trying to get home from work when it's cold rather than inspecting my tires at midnight. That really makes a lot of sense."

Randy motioned Garner to follow him back into the shop's showroom. "I'm sorry. But what do you want us to do? We've replaced the tire. We've answered your questions." He now looked back at Garner. "Hey, man, life happens—"

"That's the fucked up thing about it."

The sound of a cash register's *cha-ching* also played in Garner's mind.

Chapter 32

Garner and Autumn agreed to meet at Captain George's, a popular seafood buffed establishment in North Myrtle Beach, for dinner. He called her once he passed by the area's four-year university eastbound on Route 501.

She advised him once he noticed a Mitsubishi and Kia car dealership on his left, and then an outlet mall on his right, he would follow the signs leading to Highway 17 northbound. He would then drive two, no more than three miles. Along the way, he'd notice a mall and a NASCAR theme park before he reached the restaurant at the 29th Street North intersection.

"I hope you're good with directions," she said. "It shouldn't take you any more than fifteen to twenty minutes from where you are."

"Are you always this precise?"

"You have to be doing what I'm doing; we have to be right every time."

"Well, I hope that you are. If not, you'll never hear the end of it from me."

Autumn decided donning an aqua green short-sleeve blouse and purple slacks, and the same black leather maxi and black leather boots that she wore when they first met in Atlanta. She also maintained the same hairstyle with her bang swept to one side.

Her apartment complex was two miles away from Captain George's, so she took the liberty of arriving there about ten minutes before six. Out of habit, whenever she went out alone on first dates, she always contacted Patricia.

"Hey, girl, I hope you have my back. You know how my dad is about me letting somebody know where I'll be."

"Autumn Copeland, how old are you?"

"Twenty-five."

"Your dad isn't going to be around forever; what would you do then?"

"As long as Wallace R. Copeland has breath in his body, he'll always insist that I let somebody know where I'll be on a date."

"Girl, spare me the sympathy story. So you're actually going to see that fine ass man you met in the hotel?"

"Yeah, I said I would. He claims he wants to set the record straight with me about him being seen with that woman in Atlanta."

"Didn't you say the woman you saw him with made him look like a male escort rather than a TV reporter?"

"I did," she answered nonchalantly. "Let's just say he looked as guilty as one. I think she stuffed a couple of twenty dollar bills in his pocket before they left the elevator."

Patricia reacted, "I'd pay him a hundred and twenty and a little more." Then she turned even less serious. "Are you sure I don't need to follow you in my Ninja suit? I haven't had to use my razor-sharp stars and samurai sword in a while—"

Autumn saw where their dialogue was headed. "I'll tell you what. If I need you, I'll just buzz you on your cell, okay? I better go." She spotted Garner emerging out of his car wearing black denim slacks, pullover black shirt and a gray wool jacket. She also noticed him rushing inside the establishment.

She was unaware that he arranged for a half-dozen of long-stemmed red roses to be delivered. He planned to have them presented to her at their table. Then he stopped off in the bathroom to liven up his appearance after driving nearly three hours from Columbia. But applying water to his face didn't have the same effect as when he noticed her sitting alone at one of the bar tables.

When he joined Autumn at the bar, Garner said, "I feel very privileged to be in your presence this evening." She flinched upon hearing his voice, taking her attention away from the college basketball game that she'd been intently watching. Her beloved Bengals were in a close game against a conference rival from Raleigh, North Carolina; the Bengals were ahead by two points with less than two minutes remaining in regulation.

She quickly composed herself, smiling and thanking him for the compliment. "How was your drive? I saw you when you arrived in the parking lot. I thought I would give you a couple of minutes to yourself before I came in." She turned back to watch the game.

"You should have warned me about all those slow drivers being on the road. I thought I drove behind a caravan of tractors."

She pumped her fist when a Bengals player was fouled and went to the free-throw line with less than a minute left in the game. "You're lucky you didn't run into any police. They love drivers like you."

"I guess they didn't notice me; has the server come by here?"

"Not yet."

Garner decided to remain quiet until the game was over. The Bengals managed a 68-65 win over the Lobos, improving their overall record to 14-3.

"Yes!" she exclaimed. "It definitely looks like we're going to the NCAA tournament this year!"

He related to her that his alma mater made it to the NCAA tournament in 2007, the school's second of the decade. "Unfortunately, our coach was fired this past summer because a lady filed charges that he stalked her in public, dating back to 2005. I guess we didn't want the negative press; I would have had to cover that story if I were still working in Tallahassee."

"Well, that's nice—I mean that your school made it to the tournament."

She adjusted herself in her seat, making eye contact with him. She wasted little time getting into the nitty-gritty with him.

"So what's this talk about setting the record straight? I didn't know there was any misunderstanding."

Garner anticipated she would ask him that question; he just didn't know how soon. "I should offer you my thanks for the way you handled that scene in the hotel lobby."

"You're lucky I didn't slap you right there. I'm sure the woman whom you were with probably handled that for me." She ran her hand across her bang. "I actually felt you wasted your time calling me. It seems to me that you panicked for no reason."

He dismissed her comment, hunching his shoulders. "Stranger things have happened."

"Are you saying I had something to do with you wanting to set some record straight?"

"I'm not saying that."

The server stopped by their table. Autumn requested a strawberry daiquiri; he ordered a glass of Chardonnay.

"I probably shouldn't have said anything about setting the record straight. Actually, I'd rather not talk about her. She's history, in my book."

"I still don't understand why you're telling me you're through with her. I know the truth always have a way of rising to the top. But I'm giving you fair warning not to bring me into your drama."

When the server returned with their drinks, he suggested that they move to the dining room area. They were led to a booth with a view of the entire seafood bar and dining area. Autumn reacted with widened eyes when she noticed a slender gold box with a white bow for decoration.

She turned to him. "You think you're a smooth one, don't you?"

"Maybe. Diamonds are smooth. Velvet is smooth. And they say the right kind of bourbon is smooth."

She gushed at the sight of the red roses. She picked up one, inhaling its scent. "I must say you've earned a few goody points for these. I've never received roses on a dinner date. You know if I told my dad about this, he would want to know who you were."

Garner had hoped she wouldn't bring up her father. "You're always talking about your dad. Who is this guy?"

She placed the rose back into the box, positioning it next to her. Her face beamed with pride as she told him about Wallace Copeland, who made a tidy fortune after a string of successful business invest-ments. She also told him he currently served as a state congressman representing one of Anderson's five voting districts, and he recently turned down an invitation to serve at their alma mater's board of trustees.

"To me, my dad is everything. He's been my example in life. He made sure I had everything I ever wanted and needed." She paused, exhaling. "I could go on and on about my dad."

Inwardly, it took all of him not to show his annoyance. But the journalist in him realized a conversation about Autumn's father was the path towards further inroads.

"My high school and college baseball coaches were the men I held in the same regard."

She interrupted him, gesturing that the server was there to take their order. He chose to eat from the buffet bar while she ordered crab cakes, rice pilaf with linguini salad, and lobster tail.

She cut a glance over at the buffet bar. There were at least forty people mulling the selection that took up two large display settings. "You should see that place on Sundays."

"You're talking about the after-church crowd?"

She shook her head. "You're looking at a thirty- to forty-five min-ute wait in here. You picked a good day to come." She also noted Myrtle Beach's tourist season runs from spring break through Oc-tober. "On certain days, the wait can be even longer. I remember the first time I came here it was during Black Bike Week [in May]; I ended up going to another place."

"I've heard about Black Bike Week in Myrtle Beach." He gave thought to a mischievous occasion he shared with Kadrece back in 1999. "If it's anything like the Black College Reunion in Daytona Beach, I bet that's a wild time around here."

She shrugged her shoulders. "If you're into it, I guess it can be."

"Hmmm. Would I be wrong to guess if Black Bike Week isn't your fancy, maybe you come from a more conservative background?"

"Some say that I do, some say I don't—"

He inquired, "So how conservative are we talking?"

"Well, let's see . . . My dad's a registered Republican. He voted for

President [George W.] Bush because he thought he was the right man for our country at the time, and he still does believe that he his. He's against abortion and he's doesn't think affirmative action is the way to go to achieve any equality for blacks. He's also for faith-based initiatives."

Humph, fucking traitors!

It was as if a gulf formed between them. It took all of Garner not to react negatively to Autumn. He sucked in as much air as he could through his nostrils, allowing it to dissipate slowly.

"Let me guess. Do you also vote like your father?"

She took a sip from her daiquiri, sitting upright and haughty in her seat. "I do. Democrats think they can exploit blacks for their votes by making promises for welfare and handouts for jobs. That rhetoric doesn't work for me and my dad."

Garner tried hiding his disappointment that he had met Amy Holmes with straighter hair. He knew it was his fault for not asking more questions while he was in Atlanta. At least with Vernise they shared similar political and social opinions. He wondered whether he was the one who overreacted to Vernise rather than her overreacting to him.

How fucking warped could things have gotten?

At the rate Autumn was going, Garner felt her model-like features, intelligence, and pleasant personality were fast becoming lost and forgotten behind her social and political beliefs. He couldn't fathom a James Carville and Mary Matalin scenario evolving in his own life.

Reluctantly, he reminded himself that it was just a goddamn conversation, stupid, and those were just her opinions. He clasped his hands, resting his chin on them. "I bet you graduated at or near the top of your high school and college classes."

"How did you know that?"

"It's rather obvious in your conversation and demeanor."

About twenty-five minutes passed before the server returned with Autumn's plate. She also requested another strawberry daiquiri from the bar. Garner, who ordered a second glass of Chardonnay, immediately got up to visit the buffet bar, returning with a plate full of fresh fruit and vegetables.

"I hope that's not all you're eating?" Autumn inquired.

"This is just starters."

"Okay, I was just checking."

He gobbled down a couple of chunks of pineapples and cherry tomatoes before he paused to formulate another question.

She dabbed her napkin around her glossy lips, raising her eyebrows. "Is there something on my face?"

He shook his head. "Have you ever been in love with a man?"

That was not what she expected from him. She leaned back against the booth's cushion. "Why would you want to know?"

"I thought you would appreciate open, forthright questions rather than somebody just beating around the bush."

She folded her arms, titled her head slightly, and pondered the question. "I guess after my dad, I'm not sure. I've had a few boyfriends and a few male friends. But nobody's really been that special to me." She returned to dividing dainty portions of crab cakes with her fork.

"Is that because you're only twenty-five?"

She rolled her neck and placed her hand on her hips in reaction. "And I suppose you've been there and done it at age thirty-two?"

"I've been there, uh, well, maybe close to it." He excused himself for his second trip to the buffet bar. He returned with Alaskan crab legs and boiled shrimp. He sensed that by the way her eyes followed him until he sat down that she reloaded with an arsenal of comebacks.

She said, "You shouldn't start a discussion that you can't finish, mister."

He smirked at her. "I thought I'd give you something to think about while I was at the bar."

"You really think you're that smooth?"

"Did I really say that I was? I only meant in my on-air delivery. That's what pays my bills."

As long as Garner kept the conversation away from politics and certain social issues, Autumn was a bearable person, save for her habit of sucking her teeth after chewing. Hell, nobody's perfect. Not even black conservative Republicans.

After dinner, they agreed to take in a movie at the dollar show close to the Grand Strand. Autumn was insistent they saw *Rocky VI* because she grew up as a Sylvester Stallone fan.

At times during the movie, he contemplated generating some excitement for himself by placing his hand on Autumn's shoulder, or even resting his hand on her left thigh. But he also decided before hand this would be one of those dates that his dick would not influence his behavior.

When the movie ended, Autumn was willing to walk hand-in-hand with him back to his car. It was a strange experience for Garner that it took all this time before he made any physical contact with a woman. He considered that maybe this was what Kadrece desired from their date, but he wasn't willing to go along with it.

"Garner, I really appreciate you being a gentleman with me tonight," she told him as they settled in his car.

"You're welcome." He couldn't believe himself for having the discipline to go an entire date without bringing up the topic of sex.

Amazing what the mind could accomplish? he thought.

They drove back to Captain George's without much conversation. By now, three trips to the buffet bar, two trips for peach cobbler and two glasses of Chardonnay, and a Sylvester Stallone movie that he was uninterested in had gotten the best of him. He excused himself, yawning.

She offered, "You're welcomed to spend a night at my place."

He politely declined. "I'm prepared to get myself a room."

"I do have another room, so long as you realize that it doesn't mean you can sneak into my room—"

"That's really nice of you, but I'm pretty much set on a hotel for the night."

Autumn thanked Garner again for a nice evening. She gave him a hug and collected her box of roses before stepping out of his car. He waited until she had driven off before putting his car into gear.

Because it was early January, Garner had no problem finding a room at one of the hotels near Myrtle Beach's Strand at one o'clock in the morning. He settled for a second-floor room at the Best Holiday just off South King's Highway near the airport. After settling in, he figured he would leave for Columbia around 9:30 a.m., giving him more than enough time to make the Chanticleers' regionally televised basketball game at two o'clock in the McGinty Center.

He promised Autumn that he would call her once he was in his room; she didn't answer after two attempts. He figured that maybe she decided to go out with other friends since it was a Saturday night.

Minutes later, he answered the phone on the second ring. For a moment, he allowed mischief to corrupt his thinking that she reconsidered her cautious stance.

"Hi, babe, how are you tonight. Aren't you going to invite me into your room?"

Garner did a double-take. He could not believe whose voice was on the other line. Rage built up within him; his heart pounded faster. He balled his right fist, raising it to chest high. He also grimaced as though he experienced the agony of defeat.

"You didn't expect for me to let you go so easily?" Vernise stopped to laugh heartily into the phone. "I don't think you'll have to worry about your young little friend any more. I think she and I have a pretty good understanding just like that trick you fucked behind my back—"

"You bitch!"

She smirked into the phone. "That was both of your friends' reaction. I told them that you were with me, and I could be a cold bitch if they ever crossed me."

Garner was beyond stunned by Vernise's audacity of following him to Myrtle Beach. "You have no fucking life!"

"I would have one if you hadn't decide to break up without trying to work things out. Garner, you can't do the same thing over and over again to women and expect you're going to get off with it!"

"You're not going to make me miserable because your half-crazy ass is miserable!"

"But I can sure make life miserable for you like you've already done to me this week. I heard you had to get a new tire; it's a shame you were so damned careless not to put air in your tire—"

The phone clicked.

About twenty minutes later, Garner's cell phone buzzed. Vernise had already fucked with his mind, and perhaps more. He allowed it to go into voice mail; he was too pissed off to deal with it.

He woke up around 8:30 a.m., replaying his messages.

"Garner, this is Autumn . . . You may have told me the truth about you having nothing to do with your friend from Atlanta. But I also told you not bring me into your damned drama. My dad didn't raise me to be anybody's fool.

"I don't appreciate some old, half-white looking bitch calling my place at one in the morning, telling me that I better not fuck with her man, and then threatening to have me arrested for harassing her.

"Humph. If your friend thinks she's woman enough to fuck with me, I'll be the one having her ass arrested. And you can tell her that the next time you talk to her!"

Chapter 33

Ninety minutes into his drive back to Columbia, Garner put his cell phone on loudspeaker and replayed Autumn's message. The anger in her voice was unrelenting.

"If your friend thinks she's woman enough to fuck with me, I'll be the one having her ass arrested. And you can tell her that the next time you talk to her!"

He remembered during Autumn's rant that Vernise claimed he had fucked around on her. Tamira was the only one whom he had sexual contact with since meeting her. In times past, Garner would have shrugged off an accusation and any attempts at reprisal. Now he wondered just how far Vernise might go.

Following up on a curiosity, he made another phone call. It was picked up on the third ring.

"Hello, Lake residence—"

"Tamira, this is Garner."

"Why, this is a surprise. What earned me this privilege?"

"Maybe I should be telling you that. Were you heading out to church?"

She replied, "Matter of fact, I was." She donned an ivory jacket with olive green embroidered floral design, which augmented her black blouse and matching slacks.

"Well, at least you're going. I've not gone in a while."

"Why haven't you attended?"

Garner sighed. "A lot of reasons . . . But that's not why I'm calling you. I've had some drama to contend with lately. I want to know have you received any odd phone calls since we became acquainted?"

Tamira did not immediately respond. She was glad that Garner might have finally come to his senses about Vernise. But she was equally concerned for her own safety since Vernise made specific threats to her career and she made a mockery out of her warning that she would contact law enforcement.

The relaxed tone in her voice changed to evasive and hurried. "Garner, could we discuss this later today? I think right now it might serve me well to be punctual going to church at least once this year."

"Okay, would you be comfortable meeting me at that bookstore where we first met?"

"Call me later this afternoon. I'll have a better idea."

Garner crossed into Richland County traveling on I-20 westbound shortly after twelve o'clock. He made good time, considering he left Myrtle Beach around 9:45 a.m. He figured he had enough time to drop off his clothing at home while also picking up his press pass for the Chanticleers basketball contest.

Before heading back out, he checked his phone messages; Miriam had called him again.

"It's not like you to forget calling me after I call you. Are you all right? Call me, or do I need to drive down to Columbia?"

He knew procrastination was not suitable with Miriam Ruth Davis.

"You're home early today?"

"Yes, I know." He sensed relief in her voice. "I decided to attend the early service . . . I can tell you're calling from your cell phone. Where are you at?"

"I've got a basketball game to cover here in Columbia. It starts in less than an hour."

"Don't you think you need to be there like right now?"

The tone of his voice became agitated. "That's why I'm driving there."

"Watch your mouth, little boy . . ."

She apprised Garner about how overjoyed she was that her children got along so well on Christmas Day. "If it weren't for the fact that I'd given birth to all three of you, I wouldn't have known you were my children."

"Mom, I think you might have had something to do with that."

"Uh-uh. I think all three of you finally realized y'all need to stick together like I've always taught you."

She went on to update him about Norris and Shalinda were making wedding plans for later in the year. They were also planning to move out of their apartment and possibly into a house.

Garner reacted, "Now that would be news."

"Humph. It's either he marry her, or pay child support for all three of those boys. And you know how sorry she is. She just might even try for palimony. She hasn't worked a day since they've been together, and she ain't tried to find a job. All she does is sit around that place all day looking at every judge show, the latest talk show, and the Lifetime Channel. I wished Norris never gotten involved with her—I better talk about something else."

Miriam then apprised him about Carla's promotion to shift supervisor in First Principal's customer service department—a $5,000 a year raise also came with it. "You know I'm really glad for her," she said, "because I know what it's like to raise three by myself after your father left."

"What about The Brazelle Agency?" he inquired.

Miriam spoke with much excitement that she landed a contract with one the largest firms in Charlottesville, and she began interviewing candidates for two court reporter openings. "I'll probably be looking for more office space by the middle of the year. And I just might look towards expanding into northern Virginia by the end of the year."

She was determined to keep the conversation on him. "Now that's not the reason why I called you, little boy. I feel something's not going right with you. What is it?"

"Mom, everything's fine."

"Garner Michael Davis, I know what's going on with you even when nobody else knows what's going on with you."

"Mom, there's nothing up other than I've been thinking about moving on to a larger market. That trip to Atlanta really has me thinking. Columbia's been all right; I don't think it's a place I'd like to call a destination."

Miriam was not convinced. She pressed for more information. "I haven't heard you tell me anything about that girl you know from Houston. She used to call me from time to time. What happened to her?"

"She got married," he said, sighing heavily.

"Married?"

"Yeah, married to somebody I don't even want to talk about."

"I knew there was something up with you, little boy!" Miriam reacted. "You know I don't get into your personal business. I've always felt when all three of you finished high school y'all had to make certain decisions for yourselves."

"That you have, but I'm all right with it. There were some things that happened between us; there was more drama to it than I care to talk about."

Garner, who took Route 277 to the Bull Street extension into downtown, had already made a right-hand turn onto Gervais Street. "Mom, I'm almost near the McGinty Center. And this is supposed to be a big game today; it looks like there's some game day traffic ahead."

"You're not trying to run me off the phone? I told you, boy, I know you."

"Mom!" He was actually close to passing by the state capitol where Main Street intersected with Gervais. The next intersection was Assembly Street, where he would turn left, placing him three quick stoplights away from Greene Street and the McGinty Center.

"You better not," she replied sternly.

They both shared a light chuckle.

"Call me when you have time later this week, okay?"

"I will."

The Chanticleers' contest against the visiting Mounties was easy to cover. The Mounties routed them, 80-56, leading by as many as twenty-nine midway through the second half. The Chanticleers had no answer either on offense or defense for the nation's ninth-ranked team according to both major media polls. Chanticleers fans inside the McGinty Center booed and sang chants of "Fire Danny-O" during the closing minutes.

After the game, Garner pulled athletic director Bud Thacker to the side, asking him whether he remained supportive of O'Meara in spite of the program's obvious struggles. Thacker scolded Garner for sensationalizing the program's plight. He said, "I've already had to hire a new football coach because of you. Are you going for the daily double this year?"

Garner retorted, "I don't have anything to do with your basketball team's performance."

Inside the players' locker room, most of them shied away from answering questions about the fans' unrest after another lackluster performance. Those who commented remained vocal in their support for O'Meara.

When it was time for the coach's post-game session, Garner waited for the homer reporters who asked their usual lollipop questions about the team's loss, or if O'Meara had any early assessments about the team's next opponent.

Then he blurted, "Coach, does it bother you that fans were calling for your dismissal this afternoon?"

"I've been in this business long enough to know you're not going to please everyone," answered O'Meara, a sixty-something-year-old and veteran of twenty-five seasons of Division I head coaching experience. "Certainly, we have expectations and we played well short of them today. We just have to find the answers while we still have plenty of time in our schedule."

Garner rattled off a comeback question to O'Meara. "In your six years here, the best you've done is an 8-8 record in conference play, and that was four years ago in your third season. Overall, you've lost nearly twice as many conference games as you've won. Why are you confident you can find an answer to the team's inconsistent play?

Are you confident it will result in your team finally making it back to a postseason tournament?"

O'Meara's jaw was clenched. He adjusted his thin wire-framed glasses, taking a couple of extra seconds to form a response. Garner exulted within that he'd gotten under another interviewee's skin.

"All I will say is can we play in the postseason? Yes, we can. And I expect for us to play in the postseason. Will there be any more questions?"

The room was silent. Adverse tension was fast building up in the interview room. Garner looked around; he was bold to pose another question.

"What explains the team's inability to respond to the Mounties' run that opened the second half?"

O'Meara's head hung, and he rubbed the back of his neck, sighing. "I never dreamt we would come out of the locker room so flat. Are there any more questions?" He thanked those who showed up and walked off.

A reporter from Columbia's ABC affiliate came over and spoke incredulously to Garner.

"Man, you really laid it on him!"

He threw his head back, replying, "That's what I'm paid to do. Why didn't you ask the question?"

After the six o'clock broadcast, it was Garner's turn to deal with his own reality. Sitting with nothing to do in the parking lot, he mulled over driving home. But he didn't feel like going there. He thought about heading over to Gallardo's and hang out for a while; he felt he went there enough during the week.

Brooding, he considered contacting Vernise and cursing her out. He reasoned that would be exactly what she'd want him to do. And being a law enforcement officer, she would use it against him.

So, he checked his phone for messages. He still had not deleted Autumn's number from his call log. He felt he had nothing to lose by contacting her; his call went immediately into voice mail.

"Autumn, this is Garner. I thought about your message all day. I know I have a bigger issue on my hands with Vernise, and I plan to take care of it the best

way I can. If you get this message, call me."

He had another call to make; it was picked up on the third ring.

"Hi, Tamira, is this a better time for you?"

Tamira, panting into the phone, explained that she'd been working out on her step machine. "Are you free to come over to my place this evening?" She excused herself while she turned a liter bottle of water up to her mouth.

Garner still had the eleven o'clock broadcast to do. "If I do come over, I have no idea where I'll be driving."

"Don't worry. My place is very easy to find once you get off I-26." She detailed to him once he made a right turn after exiting at No. 139, he would drive about a half-mile to the blinking red light. That would be Highway 21. There, he would turn left and drive about four miles until he reached Sandstrom Avenue on his left. After turning left on Sandstrom, he would make a right at the first corner, looking for the second house on his right. He would notice her Solara parked in the driveway.

"It might appear that you're driving out in the sticks, but you're not. You're actually less than a mile away from Orangeburg proper."

Garner figured he had nearly four hours to kill, so what the fuck. "That sounds like somewhere I could be in about forty or forty-five minutes."

"That's correct. I'll see you then."

Garner made a sweeping right-hand turn into Tamira's neighborhood, which was unlighted and unpaved. All the homes on the block, however, appeared to be newly constructed. He slowed down and made another sweeping right-hand turn into her driveway, parking his car behind hers. After turning off the engine, he exhaled heavily and buried his face into his hands. It had already been a long weekend. He uncoiled himself out of his car and strode to her door.

Even in the darkness, Tamira's home was quite fashionable. The red brick exterior and white trimmings evoked memories of Spencer's place. Her home was built on a smaller plot of land and it was a single-story dwelling.

Tamira answered the doorbell after two rings. She greeted him with a towel draped around her shoulders wearing a large black sweatshirt and knee-length blue and black spandex workout bottoms. As he took a step inside her foyer, she advanced toward him with a hug and gave him a soft but sensual kiss. The warmth from her breath and nostrils and her breasts against his black suede leather jacket sent a subtle message down to his dick.

Shit, he was not sure whether to grab her ass or push his tongue inside her mouth, or both. Before he could react, she pulled back and made a pivot with her left foot. She then angled slowly over to a leather sofa to his right.

"I'm glad you came over, Garner. I've been thinking about you a lot lately."

Her living room was beige with white trimmings. She had a matching leather recliner. Across the room was a plywood entertainment center with a chestnut appearance; it was large enough to fit a forty-two inch flat screen television inside it. She also had a DVD and CD player and a set of speakers atop the console. On ends opposite of the entertainment center were blue antique chairs. Above them was a high ceiling and a ceiling fan.

"Can I get you something from the refrigerator?" She remained standing while he sat down.

"Oh, no thanks, I'm fine for right now." She joined him on the sofa. She sat with her right leg crossed over her left.

"Are you sure? Perhaps you would like some popcorn. I would offer you something else to eat, but I went out after church earlier today. That's why I'm in these workout clothes."

"To stay in shape?" he asked, looking her over without moving his eyes.

"More like to lose twelve pounds that I picked up in the past month. Since classes ended, it seems all I've done is catch up on eating. My resolution for this year is to lose fifteen and keep it that way."

Garner, still trying to process what just occurred, maintained a safe distance away from Tamira. Meanwhile, she offered a suggestive look while taking a sip from her tall glass of water. She smiled, patting the cushion next to her. "You can sit closer, if you like. I promise I won't bite."

He chortled back at her. "I'm okay where I am." He adjusted himself to a more comfortable position on her sofa. "Maybe I could use something to drink. You have any juice or soda?"

"How about Mountain Dew? I'm trying to wean myself away from it."

Tamira rose from the sofa. His eyes were trained on the outline of her narrow hips and her ass jiggling with each step; he tried adjusting his erection down his right pant leg. He shook his head. He reminisced about that lone masterful fuck she gave him over three months ago.

When she returned with his drink, she leaned over in front of him, giving him a view of her cleavage as she placed the plastic cup and coaster on the coffee table. She inquired, "Would you like anything else while I'm up?"

Garner did his best to keep a straight face, declining. He took a long sip. Then he buried his face into his hands, bellowing a loud yawn. As he made eye contact with Tamira, she noticed something different about him.

"Are you all right? You really looked troubled about something."

He nodded, sighing. "I am. Has Vernise ever called you? Last night, she called a woman I went out with in Myrtle Beach; I have no idea how she got her number. She also called me at the hotel room I where stayed at for the night. Not long ago, she pulled me over like some traffic cop not far from where I lived. The strange thing about it is that I've never invited her to my place. She's also done a couple of other questionable things to me."

Tamira placed her drink on the coffee table. She leaned into the back cushion. "Do you not realize you're dealing with an unstable woman?"

He hunched his shoulders. "At first she seemed stable. I really didn't experience anything unusual until we met up in Atlanta. Then it's been one thing after another."

She queried, "Do you remember when I told you to take care of yourself?"

"I do now."

"At first, I was really angry at you for allowing that woman to threaten me the way she did. But then I saw you at Dr. Watts' party; I realized you had no clue what was going on. You appeared like your nose was wide open behind her. She really had you going."

Garner's eyes widened and his thin eyebrows arched. "What do you mean allowing her to threaten you?"

"Not long after you and I had spent that night together, she threatened to discredit me in my doctoral studies. I told her that I'd be calling the police; she just laughed, telling me that she was the police . . . Then she approached me at Dr. Watts' party. She threatened me again. I've basically gone around looking over my shoulder since then wondering what else she might do."

"Not trying to defend her, but she is in law enforcement—a federal investigator. She also was an Army officer, attaining the rank of first lieutenant."

"There are kooks in the military just like there are kooks that are paid to protect civilians, Garner."

"I'm beginning to realize that."

"I hope you do. I really began feeling sorry for you when you called me today. That's why I invited you over; you looked like you need a friend more than another enemy."

"That's really nice of you. Spencer said you were good people."

"Thank you. I try to be."

Garner huffed and stared at the ceiling, wondering what he needed to do. Then he made eye contact again with Tamira. He showed remorse in his countenance.

"What's on your mind now, Garner?"

He peered to his right before looking straight ahead at the blank television screen. "I've lived all these years trying to be accepted by people, especially women. I've wandered in a lot of directions to find acceptance." He paused, admitting he's made a lot of mistakes during his adult life when it came to women and relationships.

"Ever since my freshman year in college, when the first girl ever saw me as attractive, I think I've also been guilty of trying to show how much of a man I could be after being told how less of a man that I was while growing up in Richmond."

Then he glanced again at Tamira. "I guess I've not been much of a man because of the way I've lived my life so far."

Tamira slid across the sofa, placing her arm across his back. She then traced a circle with her fingertips on the shoulder of his long-sleeved light blue business shirt. She leaned forward and kissed him on his cheek. She nestled against him; her body was more than soothing to him.

"It's not too late to show how much of a man you really are without the urgency to prove it solely in the bedroom. One way of doing that is making better a choice of the next woman you involve yourself with."

This time, he stared at Tamira, whose brown eyes seemed angelic. He noticed her hair was brushed to the back—nothing special to it.

"Then why—"

She interrupted him. "Did you forget that I told you that I made an exception with you?"

"You did."

She sat upright. She reached for her glass, taking a sip from it. "Garner, in most cases, a woman knows exactly whom she wants to share her body with and whom she wants to sleep with. Sometimes it's just for that one time. And if a man proves to be worth her while, she'll want more of him. Of course, there are others with odd and ulterior motives like the one who is currently a nuisance in your life."

He adjusted his position on the sofa, enabling her to lean back against him. She allowed him to drape his arms around her.

"She won't be a nuisance much longer. I'm going to figure out a way to deal with her once and for all."

"Garner, you're quite an intelligent man. You should know there are stalking laws against people like her."

"I'm not aware of any; I guess I've been guilty of trying to take the high road on this."

"It doesn't have to be that way."

Tamira turned over, resting her head in his lap. For a moment, Garner wished this visit would have been on a day he wasn't working. She made light strokes on his chest and stomach, gazing up at him.

"You know, Tamira, each time I've seen you I've seen a different aspect of you. Either you're just that multifaceted, or you've just allowed me to see just what you've wanted."

She smiled. "Let's just say I think you're beginning to understand why one times one equals one."

Suddenly, it dawned upon him something she previously told him. "Were you really serious about being a friend to me?"

"Yes, Garner. Nothing against your acumen in the bedroom, I just consider you more friend material than companion material."

"I guess I can respect that."

"Please do—"

Garner glanced at the time on her DVD recorder. It was 9:30 p.m, and time for him to be heading back to Columbia. Tamira locked her arm with his while she escorted him to the front door. Before she opened it, she turned to him, looking into his eyes.

A part of her wanted to give in to her attraction and weakness for him. She arched her neck, endeavoring to press her lips against his. Maybe it was just for old time's sake. Maybe it wasn't. Garner, who was more at ease, dipped his head to accommodate. He gave her a tight embrace; their tongues slid and intertwined.

Sensing the throbbing her between thighs, and her nipples becoming sensitive to movement, she withdrew from him. A willing spirit yet a weak flesh was tormenting enough.

She unlocked the door for him. "Goodnight, Garner. I really appreciated your company."

"Goodnight, Tamira."

He took a step before he turned around, gesturing to her with his right hand. "What happened to your male friend who accompanied you at Spencer's party?"

She waved him off. "Oh, Stephen's in Raleigh attending a regional auto dealer's convention."

He returned a slightly confused reaction. "Okay . . ."

She smiled at him; she also gave him a longing stare. "I'll see you again soon. Do take care of yourself." Keeping the foyer light on, she watched Garner get into his car and drive off.

Chapter 34

The Chanticleers held their weekly press conference starting at one o'clock inside the McGinty Center's basketball media room. The format was slightly different on this particular Friday. Garner and the rest of the media contingent were first afforded opportunities with any of the players during a twenty-minute time block. After a five-minute break, O'Meara would be available for forty minutes.

Usually, it was divided into three, twenty-minute blocks. Selected players were available for the first one. After a ten-minute break, O'Meara would speak with reporters during the second block. After another ten-minute break, players and assistant coaches, as needed, would be available during the final twenty minutes.

When it was O'Meara's turn, he approached the lectern with his wife, Bonnie, flanked to his right and with Thacker to his left. He opened his session by making a surprise announcement that he would be retiring at the end of the season. There was no successor in place, as had been the fashionable trend with other established basketball programs in Stillwater, Oklahoma; Syracuse, New York; and Tucson, Arizona.

O'Meara appeared to be at peace with his decision; he showed no emotion while reading his prepared statement. "I'm facing the realities about my life and my coaching career: I'm nearing the end to both. I can see it, and it's rather clear to me."

Garner, who stood among a bank of television cameras in back, was quick to scribble down notes. He also noted to himself that it was odd the Chanticleers' sports information staff orchestrated it to ensure the players were already out of the way.

Meanwhile, O'Meara maintained fan unrest and media criticism was not his reason for stepping aside. He made sure to seek out Garner. "There will be some of you who will thump your chest and say, 'We got him! We made him mad enough where he finally decided to hang it up.' I will tell you unequivocally that was far from the truth."

O'Meara went on to speak for five more minutes before he opened the session for questions. Garner was the first at blurting out his.

"Coach, if you say you're retiring because it had nothing to do with fans or the media, was you decision then based on the fact you could not achieve the same success as you did at your previous coaching stop?"

In his professor-like mannerism, O'Meara folded his arms and cocked his head back, smiling. "Garner, I knew you'd ask me that question—"

The room erupted in laughter.

Garner held his hands outward, hoping to induce O'Meara into elaborating.

O'Meara said, "Can you not accept that you sometimes wake up one morning and realize that it's time to move on to another phase in your life?"

"Coach, I'm not there yet," Garner retorted. "That's why I'm asking you."

Garner later sought comment from Thacker, who declined. Nor would Thacker discuss anything pertaining to a coaching search. He said, "This is Danny's day today. I'm sure there will be plenty of opportunities down the road for you to hotly pursue me."

After the media session, Garner hurried back to the station. O'Meara's announcement was easily the lead item for the six o'clock broadcast. His cell phone went off just as he clicked opened his car door.

"Are you in some hurry, babe?" Vernise greeted him.

With teeth gritted together and him growling, Garner shut his eyes tight. "What do you want with me?"

"You know what I've wanted since you've tried kicking me out of your life—"

"Look, I've got a busy day ahead of me." The annoyance in his voice was forceful.

She was spying on him through a set of long-range binoculars while she spoke to him with her cell phone on loudspeaker. "I can see that you're busy. You do look nice today wearing your dark blue jacket and matching slacks. Did you also get a haircut this week?"

Garner instinctively scanned the area. There was a smattering of vehicles still at the McGinty Center's parking area. There was another parking lot across the street, but there were easily hundreds of vehicles over there.

"I know you're following me; I don't have any time for this bullshit."

Vernise persisted. "Babe, wait, please!"

"Make it fast."

"Babe, do you know it's going to be cold tonight? If you need warmth, I'll always provide it for you, giving you all the love and attention you deserve. And if some other woman ever gives you a hard time, I'm more than capable of turning up the heat on any of those bitches . . ."

He reacted, "Fuck this!"

Then he hung up.

Back at his desk, Garner mulled Tamira's inference that Vernise was a stalker. Before editing his opening report on the Chanticleers and O'Meara, he took time out to browse the Internet for any information on the subject.

He discovered stalking was grouped with harassment according to South Carolina's state statute. Harassment was defined as a pattern of intrusion into an individual's personal life that would cause a person in his position to suffer mental distress. Stalking was defined as a pattern of conduct that would cause a targeted person to fear for death for himself, or herself, or a family member; other definitions included assault, bodily injury, criminal sexual contact, kidnapping, or damage to property against the targeted person or a family member. Pattern was defined as two or more acts within a ninety-day period.

The state's statue also categorized harassment and stalking as misdemeanors. The first conviction for harassment was punishable by a fine of no more than $200, thirty days in jail, or both; stalking was punishable by a fine of no more than $1,000, a year in jail, or both.

He realized based on those definitions Vernise had done only enough to annoy him. And even if Tamira or Autumn tried filing a complaint, he was rueful for them that Vernise's antics had not met the state's definition.

Equipped with that tidbit of information, Garner figured he would take his chances. He was determined not to let Vernise get the best of him.

Exhaling heavily, Garner was glad to be home after the eleven o'clock broadcast. Vernise was right. It would have been nice to have female company especially on a Friday night since it was butt-freezing cold like Richmond. WCAE weatherman Joe Bledsoe said the cold front coming through was fast moving, and temperatures would dip to the mid-teens. Tamira also came to mind, yet he wanted to be respectful of her request that they remain as friends. He fantasized the warmth emitted from her soft, toned sexy body as they lay under the bedcovers would provide a sensual prelude to slipping off to sleep after having satisfied each other.

He went into his other bedroom that served as his study area. Pressing the ON/OFF button on his computer, he took solace in knowing the only way trouble could come inside was if he opened his door to it. He placed his jacket over the back of his office chair. He also removed his slacks and shirt, replacing them with a Colt

45's baseball jersey and some Nike green sweat bottoms. Then he stepped into the bathroom, taking a piss.

"Damn, I shouldn't have held it as long as I did!" He nearly passed out by the relief.

Afterward, he darted into the kitchen for a late-night snack. He returned to his computer screen, browsing for more information on the subject of female stalkers.

He discovered according to a 1998 National Institute of Justice survey most stalking victims were followed and spied on from outside their home or work place more than eighty percent of the time. The victim received unwanted phone calls about sixty percent of the time. They also received unwanted letters or items about thirty percent of the time, or pets were threatened to be killed or killed nine percent of the time.

Other sources he compiled from the Internet noted women comprised only twelve to thirteen percent of all stalkers, but they were just as dangerous as male stalkers. The average age of a female stalker in one study was about thirty-eight. Female stalkers were more likely to be discreet; they were more likely to use electronic means of communication like phone calls and other forms like text messages, as opposed to men who were more likely to physically follow their intended victim.

Garner was so engrossed in his search that he was startled by the knocking on his door. He checked his computer clock; it was 12:35 a.m. He ignored it initially, but the knocking persisted.

Grudgingly, he answered the door, thinking it was somebody who mistaken his place for a neighbor's. That happened during the summer when a man profusely apologized after failing to realize his female friend lived in No. 31; Garner lived in No. 33.

Vernise's eyes gleamed as the porch light shined on her. "Hi, babe, I saw you on tonight's newscast and I could sense something was bothering you. Your eyes had really said it all. So I put on my coat and came over here to check on you."

Garner cursed himself for failing to check through his peephole. "You know, there are privacy and stalking laws out there."

She stood before him with her arms folded and huddled to stay warm. A section of her hair was parted and swept to the side. The rest of it was combed to the back and arranged in a bun.

She queried, "Babe, what's wrong? You don't like your lady checking in on her man? You don't like having a lady who's willing to serve and protect you?"

He pointed at her. "You need to get the fuck away from here!"

Vernise didn't flinch. She leaned against the doorsill. "You're acting like you're so damn uptight." She smirked at him. "So what's wrong? No pussy lately? I know for a fact you haven't had any—"

Then she opened her coat, revealing her naked body partially veiled by her red fishnet body stocking. She had on red leather pumps. Her bright pink nipples were at attention through the netting; she felt her wetness seeping past her slit.

Garner stared blankly at her shapely figure; his dick and balls had a different opinion than his mind.

"Babe, can't you tell I've not had any dick to satisfy me? I've been masturbating all week, see—"

She angled her thighs outward and inserted her left middle finger. She stroked herself a couple of times before withdrawing. She extended her hand towards him and ran her finger over his upper lip, glazing his late-night stubble and titillating his olfactory senses. Then she inserted her finger back inside her pussy and sampled some of it for herself.

"We could be satisfying each other's needs right now if you would just give me another chance." Then she cupped her breasts, moaning. "Aren't you going to let me in?"

"I'm calling the police right now!"

She immediately closed her coat, placing her hands on her hips and rolling her neck. "Go right ahead, what do you have on me? Nothing! That I stopped by to check on you? Besides, you've never once said you didn't want me to come over here or call you ever again!"

She then sneered at him, processing her thoughts in both French and English. "The law states this pattern has to be established at least twice over a ninety-day period, although recent cases have shown three being the threshold, before the definition of stalking is met. Now fuck with me and see what will happen to you. I'll have your ass arrested for harassing me. It will be your word, coming from a clueless television reporter's, against a law enforcement veteran and former military officer!"

Furious, Garner slammed the door in her face. As she walked away, she mumbled, "The last man who rejected me regretted his decision!"

Garner planned to wash and wax his car as he usually did on Saturdays when he didn't have games to cover. As he opened his privacy fence, he stood agape and bug-eyed.

What the fuck?

He sprinted towards his car. He ran his hand across the windshield and rear glass trying to convince himself there was no black spray paint on them. "Not again!" He stomped his foot on the asphalt, and he ran inside to fetch a straight razor. He cursed, "Shit, I can't believe she did it to me again!" He returned to make a furious attempt at scraping the paint. He realized after several minutes that he would be wasting his time.

"That bitch!"

He kicked his left front tire and sprinted back inside, contacting the police. It took nearly two hours before a Richland County officer responded. Officer E.L. Collier, a white male in his late twenties sporting a paramilitary appearance, told Garner he could file a report that he'd need for insurance purposes.

Garner inquired, "Officer, I had a former lady friend come over here last night harassing me and she left pissed off after I slammed the door in her face. I strongly suspect she was the one who did it. Isn't there anything you can do about that?"

Collier asked if Garner had any witnesses. He also said, "Unless you have somebody to come forward with any information, this might be seen as only a random act of violence. I'm sorry to tell you it happens all the time."

"Look, can you at least take her name, address and phone number?"

"Mr. Davis, I can. But—"

He wanted to vent his anger on an inanimate object. "But what? You feel like you're overburdened with catching real criminals rather than some crazy woman trying to harass and stalk me?"

"I didn't say that."

"Your actions are saying it!" He went on to complain it would probably cost him his insurance deductible before the windows were replaced. Worst case, he would need to rent himself a car while work was performed on it.

"Sir, I don't know about that. You'll need to check with your insurance company," Collier replied. "Look, here's my card. What I would suggest to you is keep a record of things you know this lady has done to you. And if there is something you know can be directly attributed to her, call me."

Things just couldn't get any worse. Or could they? When Garner contacted Top Notch Glass, they quoted him it would cost seven hundred for the windshield and rear glass to be replaced. Since he had a five-hundred dollar deductible, he reasoned he was better off paying for it out of his pocket.

He was informed by Top Notch Glass to expect a call on Monday morning between ten and noon alerting when someone would come to his place. That was fine with him since he didn't leave for the station until shortly before two in the afternoon.

"Mr. Davis, I'm sorry about this. We just happened to have somebody with a 2007 Infiniti G35 Coupe just like yours had both his windshield and rear glass smashed out; you happened to be number four on our list today," said Wesley, the glass installer informed Garner around 11:15 a.m.

"Okay—"

"It means we're going to have to reschedule our coming out to replace your glass. The earliest we can do it is Thursday. That's how long it will take for your glass to come in from our supplier."

A wave of rage began swirling up within him. "You're telling me I just happened to be the odd man out today?"

"Uh, Mr. Davis, that's a bit cruel to describe it. But we have no control over what happens out there."

He gritted his teeth, doing all he could not to erupt in a profanity-laced tirade. He slammed his open hand against the kitchen counter. "It's obvious you people under charged me, and you're trying to save face by easing your way out of it!" Thoughts of Vernise entered his mind. If she were standing there in front of him, he grimaced at the thought of what he would consider doing to her.

Wesley remained patient with Garner. "Mr. Davis, our prices are among the most competitive throughout South Carolina. It just so happens there's been a backlog from the supplier and everyone's hurting because of it. Even the dealerships around this region are facing a backlog; it's not like they keep spare inventory like that."

"I don't believe you!" He slammed the phone.

Out of curiosity, he called three other places in the Columbia area. It turned out Top Notch Glass was telling him the truth. Not only that, all the other places quoted prices fifty to eighty-five dollars higher. One even charged thirty-five for coming out to do the work.

Tempered by his additional misfortune, Garner called back Top Notch Glass. He ended up speaking with Wesley again, and apologized for his outburst.

"Mr. Davis, we don't have a problem with you. It happens all the time. A customer feels he or she can find something better—sometimes it does happen. Other times, they're too prideful to admit they're wrong and they'll just pay more for the same service. Then there are people like you who suck up their pride and call us back. We're just appreciative of your business."

On Wednesday of that week, Garner received a text message from Vernise.

You know I have contacts with the county sheriff departments in this area. Somebody told me you filed a vandalism report. Something like your windows were painted black? What a shame, babe. If you weren't so damn stubborn, do you think these things would happen to you?

Chapter 35

Two weeks later

The familiar deep bass voice resonated into Garner's earpiece. "Where the hell you've been?" It startled him because he tried being more cautious with phone calls that he took at the station since Vernise succeeded at fucking with his mind through her stalking him. Although he had no control over what came in, Garner decided if a female's call had nothing to do with sports or something work related he would summarily end the conversation.

"You're lucky that I know you, ol' man."

"Shiiiit, you're lucky that I'm in a good mood or I'd curse your light, bright, almost white mothafuckin' ass out!"

Spencer did not allow Garner any chance to reply. "Damn, you show up at my home with somebody just as light and bright as you, and you sneaked out without even saying goodbye to the host!"

He corrected Spencer. "I did say goodbye. That is, to the hostess."

"Don't worry, man, I ain't mad at you for hiding from everyone if you've been hanging out with, uh, what was her name?"

"It doesn't matter any more."

"Just what are you talking about?"

Garner spoke in a downcast tone. "Just what I said, it doesn't matter any more."

"Look here, young buck. I'm heading out to Camden right now. Maybe we can hook up, say, next week?"

Garner paused, checking his desk calendar. "How about Wednesday at the usual place?"

"Where's that?"

"You know, Ruby Tuesday near Fort Jackson just off I-77."

"Over there? Yeah, that'll work." He stopped to chuckle. "I think I'll be coming back from Camden even on that day, if all things work out for me."

Garner shook his head; he knew what that probably meant. Making matters more sensational, if what Vernise apprised him to be true, there was a good chance that Ms. Shirley could be out doing the same thing behind Spencer's back.

Shit, he thought it probably served Spencer's ass right knowing that he had the audacity to invite somebody he'd been fucking for at least twenty years to their place.

"Let's plan for one o'clock, okay?"

"Sounds like a plan to me."

"Later ol' man."

"Later, Negro."

It was unseasonably warm the Wednesday that Garner and Spencer met in the Ruby Tuesday parking lot. The afternoon high was seventy-five degrees with a light breeze. A week earlier, it barely reached the mid-forties. Spencer emerged from his gold Mercedes with a slick grin on his face, sporting a beige blazer and slacks and a matching Stetson.

Garner, who wore a light green business shirt and black slacks, shook his head in bewilderment. He suspected that Spencer had just gotten his thrill for the day.

Or was that for the week? Or month?

They shook hands. "What you say, young buck?" They also

bumped shoulders.

"I don't know, ol' man."

"When you turn seventy-two like me, you'll always have plenty to say."

Garner braced himself for another onslaught of bullshit about Spencer being able to fuck without the help of any of those damn colored pills, or he'd be bragging about giving another younger woman a lesson on how experience is a valuable commodity in the bedroom.

Spencer looked jokingly at Garner. "So, you decided to hang out with your own people today, huh?"

Garner returned a slightly contorted look. "What do you mean?"

"I'm talkin' 'bout you hanging out with some black folk. You know we all gotta come together next week and help a brother out?"

For all that Garner knew, Spencer was talking in some strange code to him. Spencer then elaborated, "I'm talkin' about voting for Barack Obama, fool!"

"Oh, him," Garner reacted. "I can't say I've been keeping up with the presidential primaries lately."

"Say what? Man, this might be the chance of a lifetime to partake in a process that could culminate with Dr. King's dream being realized!"

They started walking towards the restaurant. Their strides matched each other. Garner reached out to open the door for Spencer.

"Thank you. You still have respect for your elders. That's good."

Garner smirked; Spencer ignored him, returning to his initial thought. "See, young buck, you might not have been around when all the shit was really going on back in the day. But Dr. King spoke of the day when people would be judged by the content of their character and not the color of their skin.

"That means if Barack Obama is elected president, it will be solely on what he has to offer this country, and race won't have a goddamn thing to do with it. Nobody's talking about it right now, but keep listening."

This was one time Garner recognized sincerity in Spencer's voice, and it had him captivated. Spencer scanned the dining area and foyer.

The lunch rush crowd was beginning to dissipate. He flagged one of the servers. "Uh, young lady, where is your manager . . . Joleesa?"

The server replied, "She's no longer here."

"What do you mean she's no longer here?"

She shook her head and hunched her shoulders. "One day she was here; the next day we're told we have a new manager."

"Damn," Spencer reacted. "That means I've got to get to know another manager around here, especially if it's a woman."

The server walked off. Seconds later, unlike previous times they've met at Ruby Tuesday, a white man in his mid-twenties was their host and led them into the dining area. They chose a booth near the window. Spencer was eager to return to the conversation piece that was his passion—marked by the intensity in his eyes.

"So who you gonna be supporting?" he inquired.

"I don't know yet."

"I hope you're not talking about going out this weekend and showing your support among them?" Spencer made reference to the Republicans holding their primary that weekend. Garner thought about Autumn and her father. He mused to himself they would be at some hopeful's rally talking about how great of a job the current President Bush was doing and how the country needed more conservative judges.

Humph.

He hissed at the thought. "You don't have to worry about me, ol' man. I despise a Republican agenda."

"Well, that's nice to know. This country did damned good under Bill Clinton. Say what you want, but we were much better off with him than we've been with this damn clown. He's fucked up worse than his ol' man."

When the server stopped by for their order, Garner asked for a ginger ale since he would be heading into the station; Spencer ordered just a salad bar and a Diet Coke.

"What up with you? You're trying to eat healthy because one of those younger women you're fucking around with is sapping out all your energy?"

He waved off Garner. "Nah, got nothin' to do with that. Doctor says I need to watch my cholesterol. Says it's slightly above normal. Don't need to be fallin' out with a heart attack or stroke."

Garner chortled. "I can't believe what I'm hearing. Is the Spencer Watts, otherwise known as the playa from the first half of the twentieth century, finally recognizing his mortality?"

Spencer brought his glasses down to the tip of his nose, peering over at Garner. "Listen here, goddamn it, how many times do I have to tell you? Don't start any shit and there won't be any shit. You dig, you light, bright, almost white motherfucker?"

Garner leaned against the back cushion, folding his arms. "Yeah, I dig, old black ass motherfucker."

"Well, since you started it, if my memory serves me correct, you said you and that young lady you showed up at my party with are no longer an item. I know y'all fucked at least once. What happened?"

Huffing initially, and then sucking down half his glass of ginger ale, Garner inhaled deeply, before allowing for his chest to slowly deflate as he expended his breath. He brought his left hand up to his mouth, contemplating what he should even tell Spencer.

Meanwhile, the server returned to the table with Spencer's salad. He queried, "Uh, young lady, would you be so kind to tell me if this is tossed salad or the house salad?" He peered beyond his glasses once again.

Garner hoped that part of Spencer's routine might cease no sooner than it began. Then he folded his arms, being the curious observer that he was.

She replied, "Sir, it's house."

"Just checking."

Garner waited for the server to leave. He whispered, "Uh, ol' man, will you stop trying to find out if some damn server is going to tell you if she likes her asshole licked?" He let out a small belch.

"Listen, I'll ask the questions that I want to ask. And you ask the questions that your ass is paid to ask." Spencer then shuffled the lettuce and crouton bits around while shaking pepper onto the large plate. He also added the honey mustard dressing that came with it. He pointed his knife in Garner's direction. "Now, tell me what happened to you and that young lady?"

Garner stared briefly at the ceiling before he made eye contact with Spencer. "There's nothing really to talk about. She turned out to be more trouble than I bargained for."

Spencer nodded while making loud munching sounds. He now pointed his fork in Garner's direction. "You know what, young buck? If you live long enough, it's gonna happen."

"I guess so. I just wished it didn't happen to me."

"Ms. Shirley said she met your, uh, *former friend* at the party. And she thought you might have been in a little bit over your head."

Garner felt he could use some constructive feedback on his choice of women. He leaned forward against upon his right forearm on the table.

Spencer continued, "I didn't even ask Shirley or tell her. She just came to me and said your young friend, Garner, might be biting off more than he can handle."

Since Vernise's last intrusion, Garner had taken several occasions to contemplate the kind of woman he really wanted in his life. What he came up with was somebody who had Murlette's professionalism, Kadrece's freak nature, Tamira's intelligence and sophistication, Sabryan's tight and sexy body and, hell, even Vernise's housekeeping and cooking ability.

Was there a woman out there who possessed all those traits and capabilities?

"Can I ask you a question, ol' man?"

He nodded. "Proceed—"

"If you had to do it all over again, and knowing what you know, what would be your ideal woman?"

That was a smooth stroke to Spencer's ego. Seizing the opportunity, he adjusted himself in his seat. He took a sip of his Diet Coke, clearing his throat. He adjusted his lenses on the bridge of his nose.

"I'll tell you what, young buck; I've been with many women. I still wouldn't change my decision to have asked Shirley Rosemary Bryant Watts to marry me."

"I see. How did you know she was the right one?"

Spencer glanced out of the window to his left. "After all these years, I knew she was the one because no matter what, she's always stayed in my corner." He then leaned forward upon both elbows with a solemn countenance. "Whoever you finally end up with, and if you ever have that privilege, make sure you know she's somebody who wants something out of life just as much as you do."

Garner felt like he had heard enough. Vernise was too depressing of a subject. And he was too damned embarrassed to even divulge any of the shit he suspected she'd done to him. He glanced at his watch; it was closing in on two o'clock.

"Say ol' man, I need to be pulling out of here. We're supposed to have a long staff meeting today and I still have to put something together for the six o'clock broadcast."

"All right, young buck, call me. You still didn't tell me who you gonna be supporting next week."

"I'll let you know after the primaries."

When Garner showed up at the station, there were two brown manila envelopes that he discerned whose contents were press releases. There was also a smaller white manila envelope. He presumed it was a release with paper folded inside of it. Usually, those packages came from the local or second-rate sports organizations. These days, almost nobody sent paper. If it's not blasted by e-mail, it's sent on CD or there's an Internet site to access what's needed.

He opened the smallest one first, but a pregnancy test stick showing a blue line dropped into his lap. Inside the envelope was a small, folded note.

> *Garner, I figure you might want to talk about this. Call me at your convenience . . . Vernise.*

His heart nearly sunk into his stomach, pounding harder than a kettle drum. He began feeling light-headed. The last thing he expected from Vernise was some damn note and a pregnancy test stick.

He figured, yeah, she asked him to ejaculate inside her but she probably had taken care of those matters long ago after having her second child. But then he berated himself for being so fucking stupid. *You'll never learn, huh, dumb ass!* He quickly placed it back in the envelope and stuffed it in his jacket pocket. He was beyond stunned. He was stupefied. He rushed out of the station to hide it in his car. There, he tried collecting his thoughts as he sat behind his steering wheel.

When he finally went back inside the station, he slumped into his office chair. He could not fathom being linked to Vernise perhaps forever through a child coupled by her drama. He glanced at his desk calendar. Thinking back to December, it had been just over two months since the first time they ever fucked. So it was realistic, he thought.

"Yo, Garner; ready for the meeting?" Pete DiCarlo yelled at Garner, snapping him back into some semblance of reality. "You know [Chuck] Redfearn's going to talk for about an hour today. Hope you're ready!"

Garner nodded slowly. It was more like him responding to the referee after an uppercut floored him, and he barely got up once the count reached seven.

"Yeah, I think so. We don't have much going on today. I guess I can at least stay awake."

Garner didn't recover too swiftly. He stumbled through the six o'clock broadcast. He mispronounced the names of two local athletes and he didn't keep pace with the Teleprompter. He tried laughing it off, but it was one of his most embarrassing efforts as a paid professional.

Six-thirty couldn't come fast enough. Without speaking to anyone after the show, he walked solemnly out of the station. He tried contacting Vernise at her home and cell numbers while driving back home in no particular hurry.

Fuck!

She was not available. He berated himself again for being so damned stupid keeping his nose wide open for her just as Tamira described of him.

With those kinds of women, he thought, *you never leave your dick inside them!*

Once inside his place, he angled for his bedroom to call the first person who came to mind.

"Hello?"

Garner's heart pounded faster. He cleared his throat. "It's me," he greeted Miriam, speaking barely above a whisper.

"Little boy, what's wrong with you?"

"Woman says she's pregnant . . ."

"Say what?"

He said it louder and with more clarity. "The woman I broke up with now says she's pregnant."

Miriam tried making sense of the whole matter. She'd gone through this with Norris and Carla; she never expected she would ever go through this with Garner before he got married.

"Little boy, are you sure?"

He nodded before responding. "She sent me the pregnancy test that she used."

"She did what?"

"She sent me the pregnancy test stick she used."

"Wait a minute, something doesn't sound right here. Why would she be sending you a pregnancy test stick? I knew something was wrong with you the last time we talked. You thought you could get over on me, didn't you little boy?"

"There you go again, calling me little boy!"

"How many times I have to tell you that I'll call you that any time I want?"

"All right, all right. I called you because I got this letter today from Vernise. I've never had a woman ever do this to me, or even claim that she was pregnant."

Miriam placed her left hand on her lower back region, pacing. "So her name is Vernise. What all do you know about her?"

Garner went on to describe that he met Vernise nearly four months ago. She was as a federal law enforcement officer, and she was divorced with two children.

"Hold it. You said she was divorced with two children?"

"Uh-huh . . ."

"How long had she been divorced? How old are her children?"

"She said she's been working in Columbia for like ten years; both of her children are in high school."

"How old is she?"

He spoke barely above a whisper once again. "Forty-two . . ." There was a lengthy silence before Miriam responded.

"Boy, I don't even want to hear it! So now you gonna tell me about age being just another number?"

It was precisely what Garner thought about telling Miriam. He gave quick thought to his interacting with Tamira, whom he knew was forty-five. Hell, the words she spoke while riding his dick in his bed also came to his remembrance.

"Mom, I've already tried calling her. She hasn't called me back."

"When was the last time y'all spoke?"

"It was a few weeks ago. But that's only part of the problem. She's been stalking me and doing crazy things like letting the air out my tire; she's spray painted my car windows; she's followed other women I've gone out with and threatened them; she's even pulled me over like she was going to give me a ticket."

Miriam, whose pacing had reached the master bedroom, decided to take a seat back at the kitchen table.

"Garner Michael Davis, I've raised you better than that," she said. "I didn't raise you to be fooling around with some nut like her. She ain't got it all upstairs!"

"I'm finding that out, mom . . ."

She huffed loudly into the phone. "Garner, you know what? It sounds like she's trying to get over on you. Can you tell me what this pregnancy test stick looks like?"

"Hold on—"

When Garner returned, he described the pregnancy test stick being white and blue with the letters "EPT" on it. It also showed a solid blue bar.

Miriam interrupted him again. "Little boy, that's an old test stick. It's probably the one she used when her youngest child was born. I know that was the type Carla used when she found out she was pregnant with Corliss. Don't you know what the new ones look like?"

"No. It's not something I've tried keeping up with."

"This is not the time to be some smart ass! Like I said, that's an old one. What you need to do is force her to tell you she isn't pregnant. Then it's up to you how you'll handle it."

Garner felt some sense of relief. He actually became embolden by what Miriam described to him. He thanked her for helping him process what had actually happened.

"That's what mothers are here for—"

"Well, I'm glad you're still here. I plan on talking to her and finding out when she'll start going to the doctor. When she does, I plan on telling her I want to go with her." He nodded emphatically. "Yeah, that's exactly what I'm going to do!" He also began entertaining other ideas that he needed to do in order to plan an effective counterattack on Vernise.

"All right, boy," she said, with a tone of encouragement in her voice. "You're dealing with a stone nut. I know you haven't even told me half of it. You better be careful because if something happens to you, so help me . . ."

"I'll let you know what happens."

Chapter 36

It pissed Vernise off greatly that she had no choice in the security detail for the Republican presidential candidates who campaigned in South Carolina. Of all the five who visited the state, the regional director assigned her to former Arkansas Governor Mike Huckabee, who portrayed himself as the truest conservative both fiscally and socially.

After pulling twelve-hour shifts from Wednesday through Saturday, she was more than glad they had packed up and left early Sunday morning to the next stop on the campaign trail. She was more so relieved to complete all her paperwork by that afternoon.

When she returned home in Lexington County, all she wanted to do was have a Calgon moment to herself. She tossed her purse onto the living room sofa. She placed her holster on the closet door in her bedroom. And she shed her navy blue pant suit down to her bra and thong, stopping off in the bathroom to fill the bath water.

Then she played her messages. Garner's was the second of three. She smirked with sarcasm that he replied to her letter. *"Vernise,"* he said, sighing heavily. She savored that he seemed utterly depressed and discombobulated. *"I don't know what you mean with this. But I'm returning your message. Call me at your earliest convenience . . ."*

She returned to the bathroom and stopped her bath water. Back in her bedroom, she pressed the '4' on her phone and replayed Garner's message. She mimicked his behest that she called him at her "earliest convenience." Then she plopped on her bed, unhooking her bra and sliding her thong down to her ankles. She replayed the message a final time, mouthing his saying *"call me at your earliest convenience."*

Humph.

Only after I take care of this!

Leaning back against the headboard, she proceeded to make fast circular motions on her clit. With her eyes closed tight, she also pinched and pulled hard at her nipples. Several days of stress and pent-up sexual energy needed to be released. She slid into a supine position, bent her legs and teased herself with light strokes, recalling to herself how Garner once licked and sucked her pussy in the same bed. She then cupped her breast and pinched her nipples again.

She arched her back and tensed. She groaned, "Oh, shit . . . oh, shit!" Her inner walls released its tension, making it easy for her wetness to flow down her inner thighs.

Savoring her moment of relief, Vernise got up and strode into the bathroom, washing her hands and toweling off her pussy. Refreshed, she returned to the bedroom. Then she chortled. "Now I'll call you at my earliest convenience." The phone answered on the third ring.

"Babe, it's me. You know how it is on my job. I know you called me, but I couldn't return your messages until this afternoon. I hope you understand."

"What's this thing about you being pregnant?"

She answered, "Well, you do know where babies come from? It just so happens I was fertile when we did it. Don't you remember how beautiful of a time we had?"

Reclining on her side, she stroked her pubic region, which she made a mental note it needed trimming. "I missed my cycle a few weeks ago; I've been like clockwork since Jenora was born. I've even felt a little tenderness in my breasts. You have the test stick that I used. Is that enough?"

"I'm not going to stay on here long," he said. "I just want to let you know I'll do whatever I need to do to be supportive of you.

Since you said we needed to talk, would you be willing to meet me for lunch this week?"

"Can't do it this week, babe."

"Don't play me for a fool. Can we meet this week?"

Feeling like she was in total control of this situation, Vernise withheld from retaliating. "Babe, I really have a lot of work to do this week. I'll be free next week, and I plan to visit the doctor. I know I have to be on top of things, considering I am over forty."

Garner had heard enough. "Look, I'll give you the benefit of the doubt this time. I'll call you next weekend. Just let me know what day is your appointment."

It was late the following Sunday night before he contacted Vernise. He was in a good mood, and he hoped she would not siphon away that feeling.

"Babe, it's you! I missed your voice all week. How have you been?" she said, answering the phone on the second ring.

He went along with Vernise's line. "I'm fine so long as you're fine."

"Well I'm glad to hear that. I didn't forget. I set up an appointment to see the doctor on Tuesday at one o'clock. Can you make it?"

"Did you say Tuesday?"

"I sure did. Or do I have to say it in French? *Ce sera à Mardi.*"

He huffed into the phone. "I get it. I can make it. Would you like to meet for lunch?"

"That will be fine. The doctor's office is over at Northwest Baptist's office building just off the I-26 exit [No. 101]. It's across the freeway from the Columbiana Mall. You remember where that's located?"

He tried down playing its significance. "Could you refresh my memory?"

"Shit, Garner, stop insulting my intelligence!"

He felt rage quickly building up within him. He knew it was time to end the conversation. "I'll find the place."

"Fine, meet me at the food court at, oh, between 12:15 and 12:30. Then we can drive over to the doctor's office together, if you like."

There was hardly any excitement or giddiness as Garner showed up at the Columbiana Mall. He spotted her from a distance standing near the food court entrance while she gazed out towards the parking lot. She was dressed in a black pantsuit and white blouse; her purse strap hung diagonally across her chest rather than over her shoulder. He noticed her hair was cut shorter. It was layered all over and tapered. It was quite attractive on her.

Humph.

Maybe if circumstances were different. But things were what they were. He wished that he didn't have to put himself through this. He berated himself again for if only he'd kept his dick inside his pants. Better yet, for if only he could have picked up on Vernise's unusual behavior.

He found a parking spot closer to the Dillard's side of the mall area. That was a good one to two hundred yards away from where Vernise stood. As he walked back, she noticed him once he crossed the driveway. She waved at him, smiling.

"You look so good I can eat you for lunch," she said, adding a cat-like growl as he approached her.

He offered no immediate response. He reminded himself only a weak mind could give into her game. He knew that throughout history pussy had been the fall for so many men.

"Garner, please don't cop any attitudes with me, okay?"

"I won't."

He opened the door for her; he didn't smile back at her as she did when she walked past him. Inside, she angled left toward the Cajun chicken stand. She looked back at him. "You don't mind if we go here?"

He shook his head.

"Well, I'm going to order a meat plus two; what are you going to have. I'll pay this time."

"I'm not really hungry. I've got a lot on my mind today."

"What's wrong? You're already nervous?"

He shrugged his shoulders. "This is the first time I've ever been through this."

"How old are you again?"

"Thirty-two."

"You'll get over it. It's all in how you want to approach this. It can be an enjoyable experience. That's what I'm determined to make of this."

Vernise went ahead with ordering Bourbon chicken with side orders of potatoes and jambalaya. She also requested a medium iced tea. Then she turned to Garner. "Are you sure you're all right with watching me eat?"

He nodded.

"Okay, suit yourself—"

The food court was unusually busy. Maybe it had to do with another wave of warm weather. With temperatures in the low seventies, it attracted an increased number of older people doing their power walking through the mall. Another common sight was the many patrons who glanced impatiently at their watches while standing in line, hoping to get something before their lunch breaks ended. Over near the merry-go-round, there were grandparents and young mothers with their little ones—Garner was annoyed by the merry-go-round's music.

Meanwhile, Vernise tried making additional small talk with him. "I haven't had a chance to check you out on TV lately."

"Is that right?

"Yeah, I can't tell you what's been going on. But I think this latest assignment will end this weekend. I had to really beg and plead my boss into having the rest of the afternoon off today."

He adjusted himself in his seat, leaning back in it.

"Are you sure you don't want any of this?" she queried him, holding out morsels of the tangy and popular Bourbon chicken and jambalaya on her fork. Then she gave him a seductive look. "Or would you rather have something else?"

He shook his head; his eyebrows furrowed. "You just won't stop, will you?"

She folded the plastic container; she ate only half of the mound of food that was served. She stood up, glancing at her watch.

"It's about 12:45; the appointment is at one. Would you at least take me there?"

"That's why I'm here."

Vernise asked, "Did you recall seeing Lowe's when you got off the freeway coming over here?"

"Yeah."

She instructed Garner to take Harbison Boulevard over the freeway and make a left-hand turn at the Lowe's intersection. "You can't miss it. You'll run right into the Northwest Palmetto Baptist parking lot."

Garner recognized this was a similar route to Spencer's party. He found it ironic his next trip in the area would involve him finding out what Vernise would be advised to do, if anything, over the next several months.

She pointed out the white, multi-story exterior building to his left. Across the street from there was a Cracker Barrel restaurant and an Extended Suites hotel adjacent to each other. After finding a parking space close to its entrance, Garner glared at her.

"What's with the attitude change?" she inquired.

"I can't believe that I'm caught up in something like this."

She leaned against the passenger door, resting her chin against her hand. "You need to think about what you're going to do for our child, and not about yourself."

Garner stared straight ahead. His lips became smaller slits; he shook his head once more. He tried composing himself by exhaling through his nose. "Well, let's get on with this."

"Thank you, that's more like it."

Vernise took the lead walking inside while Garner lagged a couple of steps behind. She was also first to enter the elevator. Once the door closed, she tried nestling herself against him. She went as far as giving him a small peck on his cheek, but Garner did not respond with any affection.

"Babe, I bet you and I have created a beautiful child."

"Humph."

Inside the doctor's fourth-floor office, Garner took a seat next to the bookstand. Vernise went ahead with checking in.

"May I help you?" the receptionist inquired.

"Yes, I'm Vernise Aikens. I have a one o'clock appointment to see Doctor Nashua."

"Okay, do you have your insurance card with you?"

"I sure do."

"Is this your first time here?"

"No, I'm a regular patient of Doctor Nashua's."

"Let me check . . ."

Vernise glanced over her shoulder hoping to make eye contact with Garner. He appeared to be engrossed in a *Sports Illustrated.* Typical male, she smirked.

The receptionist resumed the intake process with her. "Ms. Aikens, you've not been here in a while. What I need you to do is fill out this form so we can update our records. You last visited Doctor Nashua when we were over on Harbison."

More than a year had transpired since her last doctor's visit. "Has it been that long?"

Garner shifted his eyes at Vernise when she joined sitting next to him. There was no interaction between them during the time that passed before she was summoned to the back by one of the nursing assistants.

"You're welcome to join her, sir," the lady clad in green said.

Vernise noticed the nursing assistant who introduced herself as Sharon giving more visual attention to Garner as they walked past her.

Leading them to one of the waiting rooms, Sharon, who was compact and chunky in build, looked back at them. "So we've got both mom and dad here today?"

Vernise smiled, but her eyes conveyed a different response. "Yes we do . . ."

Sharon handed Vernise a specimen cup as she walked past her. "Honey, if you don't mind would you go ahead with getting a urine sample out the way." She pointed to their right. "The bathroom is over there."

Vernise glared at the nursing assistant as she walked off to the bathroom. The nursing assistant rolled her eyes and took off towards the front desk. "I'll be back in a little bit for your sample."

Several minutes passed before Garner became suspicious. He thought it shouldn't take someone that long to produce a urine sample. So walked over to the light green colored door and knocked on it.

"Are you all right?"

She yelled through the door. "I'm okay. My body just seems not wanting to cooperate. I'd rather be masturbating."

He grabbed the doorknob; he didn't realize the door was open. He stuck his head inside. He did a double take to Vernise's reacting to him in shock. Apparently still fully dressed, she tried stuffing an empty pyrex into her purse. There were two specimens of urine sitting on the sink.

She yelled, "What in the hell do you think you're doing?"

"No, what in the hell do you think you're doing!" He slammed the door and stormed out of the office. Vernise reacted by hastily flushing the fake urine samples and she took off in pursuit of him. She waited until they were in the hallway before she tried calling for his attention.

"Garner!"

"Don't talk to me!" He didn't look back at her.

"I can explain, babe. Please stop!"

The stairwell door slammed behind him. She heard him yell "fuck you" while his steps echoed throughout the hollow enclosure. She headed for the stairwell. She yelled back at him; he was already a half-flight ahead of her.

"I said stop, goddamn it!"

"Go to hell, bitch!"

She stopped on a flat area between floors; she drew her gun from her shoulder-strap holster, standing in a three-point pistol firing position. "I said stop, or I'll shoot your ass right here!"

Leaning against the railing with his arms folded, Garner looked up into the barrel of her Glock pistol aimed at him. "Then go ahead, shoot me!" She caught up to him, stopping a step above him. Her breathing was slightly heavy. She said, "If you try walking away from me right now it's really going to be your word against mine. I'll just tell anyone and everyone you made aggressive move towards me that, given the situation, I determined was life threatening."

He glanced to the left, identifying to himself where he stood in relation to a door. "Well, you're going to need a better explanation than that."

From her vantage point, she pressed the gun against his temple; it evoked fond memories of the fear she tried to inflict on Thaman Aikens. "Do you really think so? Right now, it appears to me that I have the advantage."

A police officer's gun drawn at Garner—even at point-blank range—didn't scare him one bit. He'd experienced being at the wrong place at the wrong time more than his share of unwanted occasions as a teenager in Richmond. He calmly reached inside his vest pocket and flipped his cell phone. He checked for reception bars on his display screen.

He countered, "No, I think I have the advantage."

She pushed the barrel harder against his temple. "It doesn't matter what you say. Now put down the damn phone, or I'll shoot your ass right here!"

"Fuck you, go ahead!" He resumed his descent.

"Babe, don't do it!"

He had already traversed another flight before he looked up again. "So you're going to shoot me because I knew all along you weren't pregnant? Go ahead; you're crazy enough to do it!" He made sure that he yelled loud enough hoping somebody might hear them. After all, it was the early afternoon and people were coming back from lunch or still going to lunch.

Not wanting to create any further unwanted attention, Vernise backed off and returned to the fourth floor. She breathed a sigh of relief that nobody had peered off into the stairwell, or had bumped into her as she emerged from it.

Chapter 37

Two weeks later

Appearing before Judge Judson Shumpert, who presided in Lexington County, Garner had his day in court petitioning for the state's Order of Protection against Vernise, who did not respond to her subpoena.

Shumpert peered over his reading glasses periodically while he queried for Garner's facts. His argument for a restraining order was based on their confrontation at Northwest Palmetto Baptist, her vandalizing his car with spray paint, and her following him on his dinner date with Autumn in Myrtle Beach.

After five minutes of dialogue, Shumpert reached his decision.

"Mr. Davis, I find it quite sensational this defendant whom you describe works as a federal agent and is a former military officer would go to such extremes of maintaining communication and contact with you; however, in light of the fact she was properly served and is not here to present her case, the Court finds in favor of the plaintiff. You will be granted an Order of Protection of no more than ninety days from the day the defendant has the Order served. At which time, you may re-apply for an extension of this Order, if it warrants."

Garner left the courthouse exulting in his personal moment of victory. He was confident the entire time that Judge Shumpert would side with him. He was eager to share the good news with Tamira, whom he apprised a week before about his court date. She provided an affidavit of her encounters with Vernise.

Since he did not have Tamira's number at the school, he left her a message on her cell phone.

"Tamira, I've taken the first legal step ridding myself of Vernise. The judge granted me a three-month restraining order in which she can't have any contact with me of any kind . . . letter, fax, e-mail, text message or in person. Call me at your earliest convenience."

Then he contacted Miriam at her office. She answered her direct line on the second ring.

"Mom, I got a restraining order against Vernise. Hopefully, she'll have enough sense to stay away."

"Do you remember, Garner, I had to do something like that to your father, Aaron? That was the only way I felt I would be able to get my life back together and provide some kind of life for you, your brother, and sister."

Garner had been able to suppress and compartmentalize his memory of Aaron's departure to the extent that he faintly remembered that fateful humid August evening more than twenty years earlier. After downing a couple of beers, Aaron was up to his usual no good by picking an argument with Miriam. She pleaded with him not to fight her, but once he started into his verbal abuse, which was usually a prelude to some form of physical terror, Miriam made like she went to the bathroom but then she went next door to borrow the neighbor's phone. When she returned twenty minutes later, Aaron was at the door with his fists balled, his nostrils flaring like an angry bull.

She walked past him with a resolute countenance. "I'm warning you, Aaron, you mess with me today it will be your last."

"Look here, you redbone bitch, if you don't fix me dinner and do what I say, it might be your last goddamn day!"

Garner was in his bedroom while all the arguing went on. The next thing he knew, Aaron had stopped, he'd gone outside and was met by police in the front yard. Norris and Carla were already peeking through the living room window; Garner soon joined Miriam, who stood in the doorway.

"Is there a problem here, officer?" Aaron inquired, with a tall can of Schlitz Malt Liquor in his right hand.

"Are you Aaron Davis?"

"That's me."

"Mr. Davis, would you please put down that beer can, put your hands behind your head, turn around and face the house."

"What you're talking about?"

The plain-clothes officer was more forceful speaking to him; his partner drew his gun. "Mr. Davis, I said put down the beer can, put your hands behind your head, turn around and face your house . . . Now!"

He was reluctant to comply, and he questioned aloud why he was being subjected by their directives. Within ten minutes, Aaron was whisked away by the police. He was later ordered to stay away from Miriam, Garner, and his siblings until Miriam's petition for divorce was finalized.

Garner spoke wistfully to Miriam. "Mom, I never thought I would have to do something like that . . ."

In the background at Miriam's office, there were phones ringing and another female's voice answering questions. Miriam excused herself to handle an immediate issue. She returned to their conversation several seconds later. She said, "You never know what you'll ever have to do in life. Little boy, I've always prayed hard for your safety. I'm just glad you're in one piece and able to tell me what you've done."

He described to Miriam that he was convinced he needed to do something legally after she threatened him with a gun at Northwest Palmetto Baptist. "That was after I caught her trying to give a fake urine sample."

"She really tried to hook you, didn't she?"

"Mom, to be honest, I've been a fool [in] this entire situation. A friend of mine said I had my nose wide open behind her. She was right."

"I hope you've learned something out of all this. I've got to get going. We have a deposition being taken here in the office and I need to get ready. By the way, when you're coming up here to see your mother again?"

That was the last question he wanted posed to him. "Soon, mom, soon."

"Take care of yourself, little boy!"

Vernise was awaken and startled by her doorbell ringing and a strong knocking on her door.

"Ms. Vernise Aikens?" Lexington County sheriff's deputy T. N. Denton inquired. He was clad in a dark brown long-sleeved uniform with three gold service stripes on his right forearm and three gold chevrons on his shoulders, and beige pants.

"I'm Vernise Aikens."

"You are being served an Order of Protection. Please read it carefully."

"What are you talking about? Don't you know that I'm a federal law enforcement officer?"

Denton reacted without any emotion; he was a twelve-year veteran having served scores of them. "I don't get into who's who, Ms. Aikens; but if you have a problem with it, consult your attorney." Then he walked off.

The interaction with Denton snapped Vernise out of any early-morning stupor. After she groped for the handle to close her door, she glanced at the document in total derision, cursing Garner's entire existence in French then in English.

"Why that fucking bastard. Who in the hell he thinks he is? I'll have his ass arrested for shit he didn't know he could be arrested for. I'll fix his ass. I know exactly what I'll do!"

Later that afternoon, Vernise used some of her contacts in the Richland County court system in Columbia to expedite having a restraining order also executed on him. She also gave special instructions for how it would be served. This was her way of making it a *de facto* mutual restraining order, which would deflect any possible scrutiny occurring on her job.

Richland County deputy sheriff C.R. Timmons was assigned to stop by WCAE after the six o'clock broadcast seeking out Garner, whose mood had been jubilant all day. Timmons, who wore a black short sleeve shirt and matching black pants, was allowed to come inside and wait for Garner as he came off the set.

"Mr. Garner Davis?" he inquired as Garner almost walked past him.

"Yes, officer."

"This Order of Protection is being served to you. Please read it carefully."

Garner returned a confused look. Worst of all, this was being done in the presence of colleagues and peers at his job. He was overcome by embarrassment; he hid his face into his hand, shaking his head.

He eventually made eye contact once again with Timmons. "I should have known this wasn't over."

Timmons pointed at the document in Garner's hand. "If there is something in this Order you do not understand I strongly recommend that you seek an attorney who can explain it." Then he walked off the set, heading for the station's front lobby.

Thoroughly indignant of Vernise's counterattack, Garner stormed out of the station while others talked amongst themselves and pointed at him.

Out in the parking lot, Garner sat in his car brooding and trying to come down from his rage. He opened the restraining order to decipher through its jargon. He noticed that Vernise was granted six months with similar restrictions imposed on him.

"Humph, fuck it," he surmised to himself. "At least for three months we'll be on equal terms."

Chapter 38

Vernise still would not let go of Garner. She continued blaming him for betraying her. She felt all he had to do was apologize for his misdeed with Autumn, and things would have been fine. She felt he would have never encountered this other side of her.

Although she performed her duties as a federal agent supervisor to her usual perfection, she became withdrawn and depressed. She made less interaction with her circle of friends, and she was embarrassed to tell them such an enviable catch had gone awry.

Her way of coping with the loss was ingesting samples of antidepressant medication and continue following Garner around Columbia. Over the next several weeks, she picked Mondays, Wednesdays and Fridays to sit across the street from WCAE in her black 2000 Camaro, spying on wherever he went after the six o'clock and eleven o'clock broadcasts. She even mused to herself that she was so inconspicuous that maybe she should consider becoming a private investigator in a few years.

To her dismay, she observed him simply going to work and home. It nearly convinced her it was about time to go on with her life. Maybe she'd proven her point, she thought, by stalking and harassing him. What she did not know was Garner finally decided on adhering to one of Miriam's axioms that there would be times when a person might be better off alone rather than seeking the company of others.

Acting upon a whim, she decided she would follow him once more, this time on the last Saturday in February. After spotting his car from outside the complex on Killian Road, she waited for him to leave his place. Her hunch and patience prevailed. She did not find it odd that he sped off to I-77 where he headed southbound, nor when he drove all the way to I-26 eastbound.

Garner broke his recent run of social inactivity by accepting Tamira's invitation late Friday evening to attend a Black History Month program hosted jointly by both of Orangeburg's historically black colleges. This year's event was held on Tamira's campus where she served as one of its organizers.

"I just want to warn you that Dr. Watts will be the keynote speaker," Tamira said. "I'm sure he probably called you about it at least once this week."

"You know he did," Garner answered while he drove along I-26 eastbound. "I thought I would have to have a restraining order served on him."

"Now, Garner, you wouldn't do that to a seventy-two-year-old man. Or would you?"

"I don't know."

They shared a good laugh on the mischievous thought. Tamira reminded Garner that she had a VIP ticket waiting for him outside the school's convocation hall.

He then inquired, "What are you doing after this?"

"I'm not sure what I'll be doing. This has consumed as much time as my studies and teaching workload."

"Well, if you're up to it, maybe we can stop by the bookstore for another best-of-three in backgammon." He mused to himself perhaps it might lead to a return engagement between her thighs based on the mixed signals she sent him when he visited her nearly two months ago.

"That might be the kind of social outlet I'll need today after dealing with all these personalities."

For Vernise's sake, the drive over to Orangeburg was a much easier than the one she followed him to Myrtle Beach. Once Garner exited I-26 at No. 145, it was a direct trip on Highway 601 southbound into town. She seemed less suspicious of his activity when she noticed him making a left-hand turn onto a street between both schools.

She drove two stoplights past the school before turning around. She was well aware of the size of both campuses after serving on a security detail the previous year when the Democrats held their initial presidential debate in Orangeburg, kicking off the 2008 campaign.

It took her less than five minutes to spot Garner's G35 Coupe among the parked cars while a steady flow of people headed towards the school's convocation hall facing Highway 601.

Approaching a female door attendant reminiscent of Sharon from the doctor's office, she figured Garner would be easy to identify. "Have you seen a light-skinned man with gray eyes, dark hair?"

The lady's eyes widened. "I remember seeing somebody like him just walking in here. I think he's a guest of Tamira Lake's. Would you like somebody to locate him for you?"

It took all of Vernise not to become crestfallen in front of the woman. "Oh, no, that won't be necessary. Uh, I'll just catch up with him after the program. I better go back out to my car and get my ticket. I left it on the dashboard."

After wiping away a torrent of tears, Vernise sat in her car with her eyes affixed on Garner's car. So many thoughts ran through her mind, none of which was good, but not once did she question her sanity for following him.

More than two hours passed before the first signs of the crowd began dispersing from the event. It was another half-hour before Vernise spotted Garner walking Tamira over to her car. They appeared to be more than comfortable in each other's company.

Fuck the restraining order, Vernise fumed.

"Bastard!" she then yelled, although she didn't let down her window so they could hear. "And I told that bitch to stay away from him!"

Thoughts from living in Southern California and drive-by shootings invaded her rationale. She also gave thought to simply cutting off their path, get out her car and confront them. But that would be a violation of the restraining order. She knew it would be hard to defend against it especially if there were any witnesses.

"Calm down, girl, before you do something you might regret," she told herself. "He's not worth it. She's not worth it. They're not really worth it . . ."

The curiosity, however, was too great to resist.

Garner agreed to follow Tamira over to the city's lone shopping mall at the intersection of North Road and Broughton Street. Vernise observed Garner scurrying to join Tamira after she emerged from her car. They walked across the parking lot over the bookstore with his right arm draped across her shoulder while she was nestled up to him.

Glancing down at Tamira, he recounted Spencer's remarks on Black History Month. "I think he really touched the fabric of a few people's soul by drawing a comparison of 1968 and 2008 to the current political landscape."

Tamira placed her arm around Garner's waist. "You've never heard Dr. Watts speak before a crowd?"

"That was my first time. He's like two different people in front of an audience."

"That's Dr. Watts for you. He really knows how to captivate people."

"Last month, he was on me about voting in the primaries. He mentioned to me about Barack Obama's candidacy could very well evoke memories to Dr. King's dream that people be judged by the content of their character. It looks like he might be the party's candidate if he can pull off wins next week in the Texas and Ohio primaries."

"You're right." She gazed up at him almost half-apologetically. "Would you forgive me if I voted for Hillary [Clinton] last month?"

"Did you really?"

She chortled. "Of course not!"

"Could you imagine telling Spencer that you voted for somebody other than Obama?"

"I'd rather not."

Inside Regal Books, Garner searched for a seat near the café stand, but the area was crowded. The only available seats were over by the storefront window facing the parking lot; it was in the same vicinity where they played the last time.

"I remember the last time you had espresso roast caffeinated and one of those banana-nut muffins."

"You have an excellent recollection, Garner. I like that about a man."

"Speaking of men, what happened to Stephen?"

Tamira showed no emotion telling Garner that Stephen claimed he still was not capable of dating despite it being three years since he became a widower. "Personally, I think he was more concerned about his dealership making money; I'm not sure if he ever really took an interest in me."

He recognized that she left open a window of opportunity. "I think he's missing out on a gem of a lady in you."

"Why thank you. I've also shared the same opinion."

"Are you ready for your espresso and muffin?"

"I think I am. I'll set up the board."

Garner noticed his cell phone buzzing while he stood in line; it showed a private number message on his caller ID. He dismissed it as maybe somebody making a wrong phone call. When he returned to the table, Tamira sat back in her seat with her left leg crossed over her right thigh admiring Garner's handsome features.

As much as she tried resisting, she could not. She asked, "Can I share something with you?" She broke off a corner from her muffin, bringing it up to her mouth with a napkin under it. "What if I told you I've always had a weakness for you?"

"Hmmm . . ."

"And what if I told you, despite wanting to be friends only, that I'm still sexually attracted to you?"

Garner's raised his eyebrows on that comment; that was not the only thing that had endeavored to rise on him. "So where is this conversation leading?"

She smiled. "It only goes as far as I allow it." Then she took a sip from her beverage. "You still have not answered my question, Mr. Davis."

"I'll tell you what. I'll answer your question if you beat me two out of three."

"Very well, make sure you answer in complete sentences. I despise fragments and hackneyed jargon."

In the first game, Garner was the first to advance all his checkers into his home quadrant. He required only forty-one moves and took a twelve-point advantage entering the second game.

"Now you know that's three in a row I've beaten you."

Meanwhile, Vernise tipped inside the bookstore for a closer view of Garner and Tamira, eying them from the fiction book section in the lower level.

In the second game, Tamira started with a double six and she put two of Garner's checkers to the rail. The dice fell very much in her favor and she routed him with a convincing ninety-four point victory.

"Well, Garner, it appears your moment of truth has come. Have you prepared what you will divulge to me?"

He leaned back in his seat, folding his arms. "Why should I? I have other things in mind in celebration of my pending victory over you, Ms. Lake—"

"And what do you have in mind?" she reacted.

"It'll be a function of your volition."

"Are we now making sarcasm out of other people's words?"

"No, more like when one begins to understand why one times one equals one."

Vernise felt she'd seen enough. She sneaked out of the bookstore in a hurry. Her car was among a cluster of vehicles in the far southeast quadrant of the parking lot. From her vantage point, she had an unobstructed view of them playing while staring from a slight downhill grade.

Now it was time to get Garner's attention; there was an 803 area code number appearing on his caller ID. He excused himself from Tamira.

"I'd better check on this."

Vernise was terse with him; the anxiety in her voice was unmistakable. "You need to come outside. Now!"

He thought it was some prank call. "Who's this?"

"I told you once, you need to bring your ass outside. Now!" Nighttime was fast descending on Orangeburg.

Garner recognized it was Vernise on the other line. He remained calm while browsing the bookstore. "You do know you're already in violation of the restraining order?"

She retorted, "I can say you're harassing me; it works both ways. So if you're smart, you'd come outside right now."

"I'll just take that chance." Then he hung up on her.

Seething, Vernise contemplated returning inside and make a scene. Impulsively, though, she climbed inside her car and revved her engine. She drove around the parking lot trying to cool off. As she completed her counterclockwise circuit past the bookstore, she glanced to her left and noticed Garner and Tamira still were talking and playing backgammon.

She yelled, "No way!"

As she began her third circuit in the lot, she changed her path once she reached the end to the southeast quadrant, turning back down the first parking aisle facing the bookstore. She stopped about halfway down the slope; she was just yards away from where she parked her car after they first arrived. Then she mumbled, "He's not worth it. She's not worth it. They're not worth it!"

She drifted down the parking aisle, making a right-hand turn for another counterclockwise circuit.

"Fuck them!" she scoffed.

As she reached the top of the uphill grade in that southeast quadrant, she made a hairpin turn back into same parking aisle. This time, she intended to make a sharp left-hand turn at the end of the aisle. As she raced her engine in PARK, she flung the gearshift into DRIVE and accelerated so forcefully that her head flung back into her sport bucket seat. She kept both hands on the steering wheel.

Just as Vernise reached the end of the aisle, she noticed a small beige Toyota Corolla creeping just beyond a bush and into her path. Rather than taking off the Toyota's front end, she flinched and turned right, stomping on her brake pedal as hard as she could. Her car entered into a skid; the left rear flared out as it crashed into the building's exterior support column.

Inside the bookstore, Garner and Tamira had just finished setting up the backgammon board.

"Garner!" Tamira reacted, before she dove behind her chair in the opposite direction of the car's intended path.

He instinctively dove away from the window, hoping the car would miss him.

BOOM!

It all happened so fast. The driver's side door was first to make impact before the rest of the Camaro spun around. Pieces from it flew everywhere. The force from impact knocked Vernise into the passenger's seat. All the car's windows were knocked out. The car's frame was dented inward several inches on the driver's side. Amid all the confusion, most of the bookstore's patrons screamed, cried, and yelled as they fled.

"Somebody call 9-1-1!"

"Somebody call the fire department!"

"Somebody check on the driver!"

The driver of the Toyota drove off once he realized his car remained intact from the crash that just occurred in front of him. Other cars in the parking lot merely avoided the scene.

Garner, who quickly recovered from diving onto the floor, and the bookstore's manager were the only ones willing to walk outside and inspect the crash site. He noticed a female's crumpled and motionless body; he could not get a good view of her face. He was reluctant to move her for fear of additional injury. There was a pool of blood in the passenger's seat.

He yelled over to the assistant manager. "Did somebody call 9-1-1?"

"I'll go back inside to check on that!"

"Miss, can you hear me?"

There was no response.

Garner tried prying open the passenger door; it was jammed by the collision's impact. So, he sprinted back over to the driver's side, making sure the ignition switch was on OFF. Then he went back over to the passenger side.

"Miss, can you hear me? I'm checking your pulse!"

There was still no response, nor was there a discernible pulse. By now, Garner had an eerie feeling that this might have been Vernise because the rings on her third and fourth fingers on her left hand appeared familiar.

He ran back inside to find Tamira. She stood next to some bookshelves sobbing and trembling. He whispered, "Tamira, I think that's Vernise over there."

Struggling to regain composure, she buried her head into his chest. "Garner, are you sure?"

He tried consoling her. "I noticed the rings on her hand; her hairstyle is familiar. I also think she's dead. She has no pulse. And if she does have a pulse, she's lost a lot of blood; I have no way of prying open the door." He started back towards the entrance.

Tamira protested, "Garner, don't go back out there!"

He looked over his right shoulder. "Wouldn't you help a person even if you didn't like him?"

"I don't know . . ."

Nearly twenty-five minutes passed before the first emergency unit showed up at the scene. A paramedic, having donned in his purple protective gloves, peered inside the car and checked for a pulse along

Vernise's neck. He moved without any urgency. Garner was stunned to have witnessed an individual's life slip away in his presence. He explained to the paramedic that he also didn't get a pulse when he initially surveyed the damage.

Minutes later, a fire safety unit appeared. Then a South Carolina Highway Patrol officer stopped; he began blocking off the area. After surveying the car, a firefighter returned with a Jaws of Life tool to pry open the passenger's side door. Vernise's lifeless body tilted over to the right and dangled outside the car. A white sheet was draped over her.

Vernise Colette Aikens, forty-two, was pronounced dead at the scene.

The paramedic walked back over to where Garner stood in front of the bookstore. He said, "Judging from the facial and skeletal injuries, I doubt she survived the impact against this column structure. She probably and immediately went into the next life—"

Garner went back inside the bookstore. Tamira sat at another table at a much safer distance away from the storefront window. Still shaken and emotional, she questioned Garner why would Vernise wanted to have killed both of them.

It dawned upon him that Vernise missed them by no more than thirty feet from where they sat. He shrugged his shoulders. "I guess for the same reason why she pulled that gun on me at the doctor's office when she claimed she was pregnant and she was not . . ."

Eyes reddened by tears, Tamira's countenance changed from distraught to angry. She pounded her fist into his chest. "Garner, this would not have happened if I had not agreed to play backgammon with you!"

He grabbed her wrists after her third blow. He tightened his grip. "What do you mean? For all I know, if it didn't happen here, it might have happened somewhere else. How can you blame me for something that I had no control over?"

"Yes you did! You didn't have to sleep with her. You didn't have to do anything with her. I hate you, Garner Davis! I hate you!" Tamira broke into sobs again. There was nothing Garner could say or do that made it right with her.

Suggested Reading Group Guide Questions

1. Have you ever met somebody anonymously? Did the meeting amount to anything significant? Would you do it again?

2. Would you have suspected Vernise would turn into a stalker? What was your overall impression of her?

3. Have you ever had somebody stalk you? How did you handle the stalker?

4. Do you feel Garner was a victim? Or did he bring it on himself?

5. Was this book helpful in any way shedding light to stalking?

6. What was your overall impression of Garner? Do you think Garner's personal life circumstances contributed to his wandering for women's affections and companionship?

7. Was Spencer Watts a positive influence at all for Garner? Was Miriam a positive influence at all for Garner?

8. What was your overall impression of Tamira? Do you believe she had honorable intentions with Garner?

9. Do you believe Garner had honorable intentions at all with Tamira?

10. What is your opinion on male-female relationships when there is a significant difference in age?

11. Could Autumn Copeland have been a better choice of woman for Garner? Did he learn any lessons about his choice of women in *Warped Intentions*

12. Which of the sex scenes was most erotic?

13. Were the characters believable? Was there a character who reminded you of somebody you already know?

14. What is your feeling about the ending to *Warped Intentions*?

Just when you thought that Garner learned his lesson with Vernise . . .

PREVIEW CHAPTER

Presumption of Paternity

If there was ever somebody who could catch Garner Davis at the most opportune of moments it was Miriam Davis. He had long since accepted that she was just being herself. If he had any protests about her calling him, she'd remind him that she was the one who put him into this world, and she had the license to take him out of this world, no matter how tall and old he got.

This time, she caught Garner just as he passed exit No. 37 on I-20 eastbound. He was returning home from attending Divine Grace Fellowship in Pelion, a two-stoplight rural community in Lexington County just twenty minutes west of Columbia, South Carolina.

"Just what are you doing at 1:30 in the afternoon?" she inquired.

"You know I should come down there to South Carolina and whip you for not calling me."

Garner rolled his eyes. He knew she had a legitimate argument. He was supposed to have apprised her of what came from Vernise Aikens' fake pregnancy ploy and other warped intentions. It was now late June, more than four months after that episode and her death, which occurred when she crashed into the side of a bookstore building trying to kill him and Tamira Lake.

"Don't tell me you've been busy at the station."

"I won't," answered Garner, the sports director at NBC affiliate WCAE Channel 6 in Columbia.

"So how have you been, little boy?"

"I've been getting along. I started going to church lately. I think I've found a place that I like."

"That's good. If there's one thing that I do regret with you, Norris, and Carla, is I did not make church a priority in your lives. But I did the best that I could."

"I know you did," Garner interrupted her. "And I have no complaints about that."

Garner figured that he would tell Miriam about Vernise only if she asked. Otherwise, he would not volunteer anything. Not wanting the conversation to linger, he was quick to inquire about his eldest sibling, Norris, whose wedding to Shalinda was scheduled in October.

"I hadn't talked to him in a couple of weeks, but it looks like he's still dead serious about marrying her," Miriam answered.

"I guess that means I might have to take some time off and come up there."

"Probably," she said, sighing. "But you know what my feelings are about Shalinda. If it weren't for those three boys that they have between them, I'd have nothing to say good about her." She went on to volunteer to him that his sister, Carla, and his nephew, Corliss, had moved to a new apartment complex, and that meant Corliss would likely be starting the eighth grade at a new school. "I'll give you her new address whenever she gives it to me."

Miriam's voice was somber, and she was not her usual jovial with Garner.

"Are you all right?" he asked.

"I'm fine," she answered, sighing again.

"So what's up; how's the court reporting business?"

"We're doing fine in spite of this economy. We might have to hold back on expanding into northern Virginia until after the election, but other than that I can't complain. We're still paying the bills and meeting payroll, and I'm able to pocket a little bit along the way."

Miriam's tone still had not changed. There was silence that lasted for several seconds.

"Mom, are you sure you're all right?" Garner asked.

Miriam took in a deep breath before responding. "I'm sure I know how they got in contact with me, but Aaron's sister, Faye, called me this morning to say that he had a brain aneurysm last night."

Garner had not given any thought concerning Aaron in years. "What are you talking about?"

"I'm saying that Aaron was found dead in some woman's place in, of all places, here in Richmond. Faye said the woman ran out of her place naked and screaming that he'd died on top of her."

"No, you got to be kidding me?" Garner instinctively pulled off the freeway, exiting at No. 61; he continued the phone call from the newly constructed Wyndham Hotel's parking lot.

"I wish that I was," Miriam said. "I just got off the phone with Faye; we talked for about an hour, and you're the first one I've called."

He excused himself. He parked his Infiniti G35 Coupe and turned off the engine. "I barely remember Aunt Faye. Didn't she have a couple of kids?"

"A couple of kids?" Miriam reacted. "How about six of them." She also reminded Garner there were two uncles and another aunt on Aaron's side of his family tree, and among them there that had to be at least ten first cousins and countless other second and third cousins.

This was the first time there had been any interaction between Aaron's family and Miriam since she served him a restraining order August 1985, when Garner was ten. Aaron was escorted away by Richmond's police department, and Miriam's divorce became final a year after that incident. Aaron never bothered to contact his children, and over the years Garner and his siblings all vowed amongst themselves never to have anything to do with Aaron or his relatives.

Miriam told Garner that Aaron found a new job at a major trucking company in Baltimore, Maryland, and he commuted regularly between there and Richmond. There was word that Aaron had fathered a daughter who should be at least high school age; Miriam said she was not aware whether the child's mother was the same woman whom Aaron died during sex.

"Are you thinking about going to his funeral?" Garner asked.

"I don't know. I mean, I was married to him for fourteen years out of my life. I might have been the only woman who ever stood up to him."

Garner admitted to Miriam that he might have felt even more emotional had it happened to ol' Spencer Watts' crazy ass.

"I know you're going to tell Norris and Carla about all of this, but do you think we all should go to the funeral?" he asked Miriam.

"Well, Faye's telling me that Aaron's funeral will be on Thursday here in Richmond. But I have something else to tell you." That was followed by a lengthy pause.

"What is it?"

"I've always been honest with you all your life, and I admit that sometimes I protected you a little more than your brother and sister," she said, biting her bottom lip. "The truth is that he was not your father."

Garner straightened up in his seat. "Did I hear you right? You're saying that Aaron Davis was not my father?"

"That's what I said, little boy."

"I don't understand."

The derisive things that Aaron once said to Garner invaded his mind along with the things he remembered Miriam saying in an attempt to soothe the sting of those comments. Then he considered the obvious differences between himself and his siblings who were dark skinned as opposed to his fair skin complexion and light colored eyes much like Miriam. Now it made sense to him.

"Then who is my father?"

Miriam hesitated. "The day I gave birth to you it was both a time of joy and sorrow. Joy that I had you. Sorrow because I could never share that day with the person whom I know would be proud of you."

Garner became impatient. "Just give me a straight answer."

Tears began welling in Miriam's eyes. She excused herself for a moment, returning with some tissues.

"Okay," she said, composing herself. "Your real father was a hell of a man. He was smart, well spoken, and focused. He was tall and light skinned. You remind me a lot of him. I met him when things weren't going well with Aaron. Obviously, we had an affair. But it was not the typical affair. We really were in love with each other, and I was going to take both you and Norris and leave Aaron. Then I got pregnant with Carla, and our plans changed. I don't regret anything. But I guess I am sorry for myself that I never had a chance to start a new life much sooner."

"You said *was* while you described this man. So what was, or is, his name?"

"His name was Garrett Chaney. He was a military officer, a lieutenant colonel."

"Why do you keep saying was?"

"This is tough, little boy," she answered; it was obvious that she started choking back tears. "You father died of a rare muscle disease while you were in high school. Remember when you were in tenth grade, I told you I had to leave town for a week, and I had your aunt Leah to watch over y'all?"

"Barely."

"He called me and we talked about a lot of things. The hardest thing was visiting him in that hospital room. I don't know how I got over it, knowing that it would be the last time I'd ever get to see him. I guess because I had you, I was able to make it without having to be committed to some mental ward."

"What did he have to say?"

Miriam's face beamed with pride. "A lot of our last conversation was about you. He would have been so proud of you—I know that I am."

"Whoa, it's a good thing that I got off the freeway when I did,"

Garner reacted. "This is a lot to handle."

"If there's anyone who could handle this kind of news it's you, Garner." Miriam said. "That was why I never petitioned for child support from Aaron because I did not think it was fair that he should pay for another man's child; he'd already paid enough by helping to provide a place to stay and put food on the table while we were together."

Numbness began creeping in. He struggled to say the right words to his mother. "You still didn't answer my question; should I go to his funeral?"

Miriam pursed her lips. "I don't know, Garner. I just don't know. Personally, I'm not sure if I want to go because my heart was never with that man even before Carla was born. I've never said this, but Carla is the result of him forcing himself on me one night when I begged him not to . . . I guess you understand why."

Garner nodded. "That you wanted to make a clean break, if you could."

"Yes, something like that."

Both Garner and Miriam tried speaking at the same time.

"I'm sorry if I've disappointed you. I'm sorry if it appears that I've lied to you after all these years," she said. "But I promised myself that I would never tell you anything about it unless Aaron died before me. And if I had died before him that was something I was willing to take to my grave."

Other Books from MavLit Publishing

Presumption of Paternity
By S.B. Redd
978-0-9831152-8-1
$14.95

Temptation.com
By S.B. Redd
978-1-9377051-4-5
$14.95

Love, Song & Dance
By Jevon L. Mack
978-0-9831152-0-5
$14.95

The Shades of Passion
By S.B. Redd
978-1-9377051-5-2
$14.95

Thoughts of Life:
360 E. May St. B.H., Michigan
Birdman '313'
978-1-9377051-6-9
$14.95

www.maverick-books.com